The BOOK of BRIARS

THE BOOK OF BRIARS

C.J. BERNSTEIN

Ackerly Green Publishing
333 S State Street Suite V-60
Lake Oswego, OR 90734

www.ackerlygreen.com

Orders by U.S. trade bookstores and wholesalers. Please contact Lightning Source: www.lightningsource.com

Cover Design: Micaela Alcaino

Publisher: Ackerly Green Publishing, LLC
ISBN: Digital - 978-1-7357912-3-4
ISBN: Paperback - 978-1-7357912-5-8
ISBN: Hardcover - 978-17357912-4-1
1. Fantasy - Contemporary 2. Fiction - Alternate History

For the Mountaineers

Preface

BY C.J. BERNSTEIN

The Book of Briars is part of a series called *The Briar Archive*, which contains both traditional novels like this and adaptations of the immersive experiences I create online, where readers interact with characters and shape the canonical narrative.

Though *The Book of Briars* isn't the first in *The Briar Archive*, I wrote it as a second entry point for the story.

The novels *The Monarch Papers: Flora & Fauna* and *The Monarch Papers: Cosmos & Time* occur before the events of *The Book of Briars*, and though they introduce and establish the world of this book, it's not critical to read them beforehand.

But if you find yourself curious about the lore, history, and characters of the "Briarverse" as you read *The Book of Briars*, there is a natural place in the story where you can stop and read *The Monarch Papers Vols. 1 & 2* before continuing on.

You'll know it when you read it.

Either way, thank you for joining me on this adventure, however you choose to experience it.

PART I

Chapter One

No one remembered the books but her. That was the first
sentence in The Book of Briars.

Ilya bristled when she first read that line because
she knew the "her" mentioned in the passage was not *her* and felt
the line had been a nasty, underhanded swipe from the writer at
Ilya's own failing memory. It was cruel. But waiting for new pages,
waiting to know what would happen next, had been even crueler.
The writer had not written in nearly two months—a still, late,
sweltering summer without a single click of a typewriter key from
the fourth floor. And Ilya desperately needed to know what
happened next. But the room in the tower of the old, dark house
was quiet. The typewriter keys remained untapped. So Ilya
wandered the dark and waited for more of the book—a book
through which the writer had promised the truth, the truth she
could no longer remember. Ilya resented the "her" from the story.
The "her" who hated the very same memory that Ilya was so
desperate to recall. Ilya waited for the writer to finish, season after
season, longing for the appropriate autumn, the one that began the
book. The autumn that would begin everything.

The whole of Ilya's existence was in service to the writer. Tending the home fires, washing the cracked dishes, mopping the creaking floors, caring for the caretaker, and caring for herself. It might have all seemed like self-preservation, but instead was solely in service to the writer, and the books. *Not* books. *Singular, wasn't it?* Book.

Ilya could see the first leaves begin their fade to fire from the kitchen window. The thick air of summer was still holding on, but autumn's fingers had begun to wind around the sticky ebbs of heat, tugging the late season to other ends of the world. Ilya's withered hands made quick work of the dirty dishes, rinsing them and drying them with a rag. She took up the last plate and stopped to look at the half-dissolved pattern painted on its chipped surface—purple vines spiraling toward a rose at the center. *Who used this plate?*

She couldn't remember. Was it her? The caretaker? Memories were getting harder and harder to hold on to. It wasn't just her age that was slowly eating away at her once-sharp and now failing mind. Memories had always been hard to keep here in this place. Ilya opened a cabinet door with thin, tapered fingers that were stained at the tips, like a cluster of gray-white fountain pens smudged with ink. The cupboards had buckled over the years, some had started pulling away from the wall, leaning out and over, as if they were falling asleep. She put the dishes away and noticed summer light bleeding in through the rotting plaster at the back of the cabinets. The shreds of cobweb tucked inside billowed in the air like dress hems. *That's where the memories went. Through the cracks, into the gray outside.* She watched the gossamer threads flutter for a while. A small cup sat dust-covered in the back of the cabinet. Porcelain, with a ring of ducklings circling it, eternally following their mother duck as she in turn followed them. *Had there once been children here?* Perhaps belonging to the writer? Hadn't she cared for them, then sent them out over the water as they, one by one, grew too big to stay? *Yes, there had been children.*

But now the house was quiet. Once grand, it was now a

decomposing Victorian monster filled with dim corners and shiny-dark floors that peeled off to winding halls and countless, cluttered, unused rooms. Rooms with floors that moaned without footsteps, where morning fog entered freely and settled into the moth-plucked sofas and cracked plaster. It all felt dark, wet, and exposed. If the house hadn't been completely forgotten by the outside world it would've long been condemned and destroyed. The back wall of the kitchen was almost completely gone and what remained was crumbling brick peeking out of plaster like broken bone, covered over with hastily hammered-up fence pickets. Vines crept through the slats, coming to see what inside was like. *What happened to that wall?*

Ilya's fountain pen fingers scribbled along the edges of the broken wall like she was worrying a scar. Someone had scrawled a message near the broken edge.

1998—a storm passed over the house.

That's right. Screaming wind and stinging rain, but also dust and debris. She had written the message herself. A storm had feasted on the house, and the house, being far removed, and Ilya, being old even twenty years ago if she was right about how much time had passed, had resigned that this was how she and the house and the writer would live. There was no choice really. One would have an idea or a plan to do something about it, to repair it, and this place would take those thoughts of plans, like it did with the past, and scatter them in the underbrush, or in the black water beyond the trees.

Upstairs, a typewriter key clicked. Another. Every key struck with labored choice. Ilya scurried to the sitting room and listened. A shiver ran through her thin frame, a smile in her eyes, disconnected from her grim lips. She decided a fire was in order. *A fire to celebrate new pages and the end of summer.* She fed the mouth of a deep and crooked hearth, expertly setting a flame. Ilya could feel the autumn chill coming before anyone else. Autumn carried cold, and the ghosts of memories lost.

Her large, round eyes reflected the growing firelight. When she blinked back the heat, the lids crept slowly over the wet orbs, dreading the journey ahead of them. Her skin was thin, a glazed window hinting at the interior, blue veins and bones and thin ribbons of muscle. A beached creature from the deep sea. Translucent, alien, weak-looking. But there was hidden, unused strength in her long, lean body. The lone contrast to her pale skin were the faded numbers etched into her forearm. Marks of a war long gone, but not entirely forgotten. She'd been fortified in the depths that eventually bore her here, to this house, and she was strong. *How did we get here? The caretaker, the writer, and me?*

This was a question she asked herself every day. Ilya slid into an armchair by the fire, fountain pen fingers intertwined in her lap, and there she waited while the writer worked.

⚜

The light of early evening peeked through the windows, casting stretched-out shadows of bare tree limbs, like a trick in a carnival haunted house. The writer was spent, having churned out several new pages in a fever of productivity. Ilya shut the tower room door behind her as quietly as she could, the stack of fresh pages in hand. She shuffled down the four flights of stairs, devouring the new work with her orb eyes, finishing them by the light of the fire she'd built. When she was done, she held them to her chest. Tears rimmed the edges of her lids as she rocked the pages in her arms. *This autumn.* The story, while still unfinished, had been uncurled just enough in the new passages that Ilya finally knew what she had to do. Where this all was leading. Like kindling, the pages had set a fire in her old, cold body.

She shuffled the typed pages into a neat stack and took them to the dining room, adding them to stacks of other pages on the long, warped table, each chapter pinned under a gray stone. The pages she had collected season after season. She took a moment, staring down at the rows of stacks, the paper edges rippled from age and humidity, fluttering in the ever-present draft. She looked down at the book that was slowly being conjured over the course of years, as if she were peering over the edge of a cliff—*The Book of Briars* being born.

This autumn. Today is the day she would clean the plate, light the fire, and walk to the boat. Just like the first chapter always said. She took a breath, then began moving stones aside, collecting stacks of pages until she held a chunk of the book in her hands. Just the right chapters to begin, to set events in motion.

In the study, Ilya sat at a small desk and copied an address from a notebook to an envelope, then she slathered the corner with old stamps. She slid the pages into the large envelope, along with other smaller envelopes, then moved to the front hall, where she shrugged on a patched canvas coat. She yanked the jammed front door open and marched out against the cool evening.

The old gray house stood at the end of a small, densely treed island, which itself sat at the heart of a forgotten, rock-shored lake. The island's shape was irregular. Deep, black inlets and thick, fingerlike jetties. Paths that once crisscrossed the island had long been consumed by plant life and mostly vanished. But Ilya moved along them by instinct, muscle memory, pushing through the deep vegetation to the other side of the island. The sky was dim and frosted. Autumn. She moved quickly from the ornate, rotting house, peeking back to see the pair of leaded windows that had been thrown open on the fourth-floor tower until the foliage of the island hid them again.

Ilya ducked under a branch, swiping aside a silver necklace that hung from it. The trees, bushes, and overgrown paths on the island were littered with old, worn artifacts. Scarves and watches, rings and keys, pens and bottles, and mirrors and books. The deep green foliage encrusted with gold, silver, and colors both deep and long-faded. Most of the objects were brushed aside and piled up at the edges of the paths, or into the underbrush, but there were newly arrived trinkets that Ilya kicked aside as she moved to the other end of the island with purpose. She disregarded the objects as nuisance, not as treasure. It was as if they had washed onto the island from places unknown, like sea glass.

She approached a man at a clearing in the center of the island, on his knees, picking the last berries from the throng of tangled, thorn-ridden bushes that stood between them. "The caretaker," Ilya called him. She couldn't remember his name. Names didn't matter here. They were the first to go, names, carried over the black water, into the fog. The berries were delicate, and their skins split between the man's thick, rending fingertips, staining them purple-black. Like Ilya's. But his fingers were blunt and gnarled like the rest of him. He stood, wiping his hands on his dark canvas pants. He was broadly built, and tall, even though his body was warped as if he were always standing in a narrow doorway only he could see. To the unfamiliar he may have seemed disabled, broken. Like an old oak that had succumbed to weather or disease. But Ilya knew better. She feared the caretaker because she knew his power. She didn't remember how she knew, but a kernel of fear in the back of her mind rattled as she looked up at him. Somewhere she imagined that his dense crookedness was caused by rigid, angry ropes of muscle that had been held clenched for so long that the pressure had turned them to stone.

He watched her over the thorn bushes with icy, impatient eyes, awaiting instruction. Ilya nodded to him, raised the envelope from under her coat. He wiped his hands on his pants and lumbered around the crop of bushes, following behind her as she continued across the island, like her towering, crooked shadow. He too had waited for the day in early autumn that the book foretold. He knew what he'd have to do when it *was* time. Where he'd have to go.

The bird. Ilya looked up and noticed the fat crow sitting in a tree off a ways, hopping from branch to branch, following the pair to the edge of the island, its black-bead eyes trained on her. Its broken beak clacking as it barked at them in strangely human tones. The caretaker picked up a stone from the path and chucked it at the bird, barely missing it. *Just like the pages told her he would, on the right day.*

The lush greenery and looming trees ended at the gravel and rock-strewn shore that surrounded the island. Ilya and the caretaker arrived at a small green boat which had been lashed tight around a tree trunk with rope. She could see the far shore across the black lake, ensconced in fog. The caretaker waded into the water, then slammed one booted foot into the boat. Ilya pulled the envelope out of her coat and left it on the boat's bench, weighing it down with a stone. She stepped back onto the shore as the caretaker crouched his crooked frame down into the boat and, taking up the oars, began to row away from the island. She watched him lurch across the black water, his eyes on her, through the fog, until he, the boat, and the chunk of manuscript, had vanished.

This was the beginning. How it all would start. The Book of Briars told her so.

She glanced down, and under the water, beyond the reflection of the gray sky and the shadows of gnarled branches, Ilya saw the edge of an old wooden sign, half submerged in silt. Its ornately carved border barely visible. *What was it that the sign said?*

She saw the fat crow watching her from a branch in the water's mirror. It squawked a throaty squawk at her, took off, circled once, then disappeared into the fog where the caretaker had vanished.

Ilya pulled her coat tighter around her neck and made her way back through the dense woods, to the old gray house. A shiver of autumn wind spun across the lake, through the trees, carrying with it what smelled like spice and dew. *Memories she almost knew.* Ilya half remembered something she'd forgotten. Only for a moment, before the memory left her and lost itself somewhere on the island like an old trinket. The ghost of a memory. The sign in the water, how it used to hang from a post at a dock. A dock that had buckled in the long-ago storm. She remembered the sign's forest green letters and gold-foil border. And for a moment she remembered the words—WELCOME TO NEITHERNOR.

Chapter Two

No one remembered the books but her. *Alistair's eyes drifted open. *No one remembered the books but her.* The phrase had become something like a blink. A yawn, involuntary. It was the first thought she had every morning since she was ten and she had long come to accept that she had no control over it. Instead, she thought it, she acknowledged it, and she let it slip back into the dark place it came from.

She would've loved nothing more than to forget the damned books like everyone else had managed to do. She'd spent years trying everything in her power *not* to remember them but trying to forget something was like saying don't blink, don't breathe. It just made you more aware of the thing you wanted to forget. She didn't *really* remember the books anyway, only pieces. The feelings they triggered in her as a child. The imprint of a vivid passage of text, the sound of a strange name. She'd gotten good at not thinking about the little bits of the books, not letting them bubble to the surface. Skillfully not remembering them was how she survived to early-ish adulthood. She used to remember more, but over the years many of those memories had sunk into the deep where everything else had gone. In a rarely frequented corner of her mind she called them *the briar books*. Not because she wanted to, but because naming them kept them separate from the rest of her life. Because Alistair's *entire life* was books. So, there were *books*. And then there were *the briar books*, and the latter, for the most part, had been locked behind a door in a remote part of her for fifteen years.

She rolled onto her back, still toasty under the worn, heavy quilt she'd bought from a street vendor on Houston Street the first year she moved to New York at seventeen. The quilt had been a hard refusal to the little voice telling her to go back home. Although she'd only crossed the Manhattan Bridge from Queens, she refused to go back. Even when she thought she'd freeze to death in that old drafty hostel in the Village. She'd had to grope for the quilt last night. Fall had arrived, finally. Her room's lone, long window glowed faint with cool, near-morning light. Her room was directly over the kitchen of a family-owned Chinese restaurant in the far-east dregs of the Village. It was a studio, if you defined a studio as a large storage room with a hot plate and a toilet in the shower. Alistair felt that, all in all, she had her priorities properly straightened out: less-than-ideal living conditions in exchange for all you could eat egg rolls. Her bed was a frameless mattress in the middle of the tight space. A sink and the aforementioned toilet/shower hybrid anchored one corner of the room where mismatched shower curtains hung from pipes in case she had guests and needed what Danny Chen, whose grandparents owned the restaurant, thought amounted to privacy. But Alistair didn't have guests. Or furniture, aside from a thrown-out dresser she'd dragged through the restaurant's kitchen one late, and drunken, summer night a few years back. Instead, she had books—piled three, sometimes four, rows deep, against every available stretch of wall, and scattered in half-read heaps across the old floor. She was surrounded by them, nested in them. She could squint in the early light and imagine she was lying on the floor of an old bookshop's back room. Cocooned. A short stack of books acted as a coffee-ringed nightstand, a tall stack covered the vent that chugged out cold air regardless of the weather, other stacks held piles of clothes, unopened mail, and her beloved, dinged-to-hell-and-back leather messenger bag. This was Alistair's cave of paper wonders, her stronghold. And if a fire ever broke out downstairs, she'd be dead in five minutes flat.

She cast an arm out from under the quilt and hooked her cell phone off the floor, bringing the shattered screen close to her bleary brown eyes. She hadn't charged it last night and it was almost dead. A notification from her aunt Kath. She clicked the shattered screen off and let it drop to the floor without checking the text. *No one remembered the books but her.* Alistair rolled over, rifling under the covers until she produced the book she'd been reading when she fell asleep. A vellum-paged collection of eighteenth-century romance. She flipped back and forth through the brittle pages, trying to find where she'd left off, trying to drive out the involuntary thought by losing herself in a real book.

She was a voracious reader. She loved books, just not *those* books. Those books were fixed on strings to a time she'd tried to cut clean away. And when the books resurfaced, really surfaced, so did that dark part of her life. Like an anchor bringing up rotting jetsam. The handful of times she'd talked about them, or rather the circumstances surrounding them, she'd handled it matter-of-factly, coldly, to try and dull the loss, the wide and groaning pain they dredged up. Alistair was more often than not matter-of-fact, in fact. It helped keep things clean, distant. Instead of revealing the truth about what happened to her, she drifted through life and relationships, play acting a young woman's life like she was on wires in a play, never touching down, until she couldn't bear another day as the girl everyone needed her to be to feel better about what she really was: shattered pieces of a thing that everyone thought could be wished whole again.

But books, otherwise, were her life; the irony was not lost on her. Her one true love. For Alistair, books were addiction and escape, and also an income source, both passion and trade. Books were how Alistair survived. The volumes in her room had no value beyond their ideas, because she moved valuable books, from estate sales and auctions, to greedy collectors and wealthy investors. They didn't care about the books, their stories, their authors. Their histories. To them, books were totems of wealth and status. It was gross, mostly, but it kept a Sichuan-scented roof over Alistair's head. The books that built her cave though were for her: for reading, for keeping, and for keeping out everything else. She wasn't a collector. She was a hunter.

Alistair's stomach growled. She hadn't eaten dinner. She looked over at a hook on the wall, holding six or seven layers of shirts, sweaters, and jackets. And under it all, her prized camel-colored coat. It was finally cool enough to break it out, and that was motivation enough to finally slink out from under the covers. She brushed regrettable, overlong bangs out of her face and got up. She grabbed a hair tie from her dresser and wrapped the rest of her dark, wayward hair into a knot at the back of her head, then threw on heavy sweatpants. She decided to leave on the long john top she slept in and shoved her socked feet into heavy black boots. Then she pulled everything off the hook until she revealed her coat. With its collar tall enough to pop up against the howling East River wind, belt that cinched at her waist and always made her look somewhat put-together, and best of all, a secret interior pocket that was wide enough for a paperback. She was in her Lower Manhattan armor.

It was now dawn. She eased around the books and took the stairs down into the bowels of the dark restaurant, her boots slipping on the freshly-mopped kitchen tile as she passed through. She deftly disconnected the fire alarm on the restaurant's back door and stepped outside. A grimy back stoop wound through a narrow alley and beyond. Cool air blew over her, a little tainted by the city, but refreshing. She wrapped the coat around her and looped the belt once at her belly. She liked the streets at this time of morning— dark and nearly dead. No one wandering close enough to burst her personal bubble.

Alistair ducked into her favorite bodega and grabbed chocolate milk, a pack of generic Oreos, and sour-cream-and-onion chips. She petted the napping bodega cat and approached Sergio, who was asleep at the register, head on the counter. Their relationship had always solely consisted of knowing, familial head nods that Alistair attributed to them both being working class, or brown-skinned, or both. She tossed everything onto the counter. He didn't startle, but instead lifted up like a day-old balloon left over from a party and started punching numbers into the register. He knew the price of everything.

"How's it goin'?" he asked, barely opening his mouth.

"Same as yesterday. You?" Alistair replied.

Sergio shrugged. "Yeah, yeah. Same."

She swiped her card in the taped-together reader and waited. Declined. He wordlessly reset the transaction, let her swipe again. Declined. She sighed, thought. Alistair was beyond feigning disbelief or confusion at the fact that her card didn't work. She was incapable of being embarrassed, always had been. Embarrassment required a certain level of self-consciousness that Alistair lacked, and was usually triggered by feelings of being exposed, which Alistair didn't allow. Instead, she turned to the door, grabbed a warm newspaper off the stack, and tossed it onto the counter. Digging into her jacket pocket, she pulled out a meager fan of single bills, "How much for just the milk and the paper?"

"I know you're good for it. Hit me up when you get paid," Sergio answered, before putting his head back down on the counter. From the crook of his arm he mumbled, "Take the cookies too."

Living in Manhattan as a self-employed high school dropout meant you were always just shy of poverty. But Alistair had a plan. She always had a plan. Maybe not a five-year-style plan, one that might ensure some kind of reliable future, God no, but one that would get her through the day, a week, maybe a season if she stayed stingy (and hungry) enough. Alistair had no future. She had the next day. The next meal. The next book to devour in record time. The next story to sell. The past couldn't catch up to you if you never made the mistake of plotting out a path it could follow to your future. She sat in a cold, dusty corner park as the sun crept over the east river about three long blocks that way, guzzled chocolate milk, tore into the paper, and flipped straight to the obituaries.

When Alistair left high school, and her aunt and uncle's house, and Ozone Park, Queens, she'd first made an early living as a hired gun for a grizzled, unapproachable rare books dealer. She'd heard his name a few times, heard from shop owners that she and Ed were circling all the same shops and sites, heard they had a lot in common. They finally met at a literal fire sale in Chelsea, and it turns out he had also been hearing about her. He offered her a job sourcing books for him and handling his bookkeeping. She was barely qualified to deal with the administration and high-level trading he entrusted her with, but no one else was willing to put up with Ed Cumberland so he kept her around. Books were the only thing she cared about so she figured she'd try to make a living out of her sole love. She went to auction and lot sales for Ed, cultivating both the knowledge and gut instinct it took to tell what kind of books were worth snatching up and which ones weren't. And then Ed would pay her next to nothing and he'd make a slim margin off the resale. She'd done that for four years, living in the old hostel, before she decided she could do it on her own. And without his modicum of scruples or moral integrity to impede her, she could make a lot more than he was making by not only bypassing the middleman, but also the bigger dealers who always had first dibs and first choice. By the time all the A-list dealers and scroungers showed up, next to nothing was left. So, Alistair ventured out on her own and developed a new business model. It was a simple but successful plan: wait for the New York and tristate surrounding elite to die off and then pick their bones before anyone else got a chance to. How? Well, it was shady. And slightly morbid. But it was legal in the strictest sense, and while it only afforded Alistair a paycheck or three a year, they were big enough to keep her one tier above the garbage-eating rats. This wasn't exactly a retirement plan, but she was twenty-six, working for herself, and living under her own steam in Manhattan. How many assholes from Ozone Park High could say that?

She circled an interesting obit. It was upstate, two hours and change north by train. No matter what, she always kept the cost of a round-trip rail ticket in her savings account. She could make it up there by early afternoon. Weasel her way in. Fingers crossed they had the goods. Call a couple collectors before dinner, secure a deposit or two, have cash before breakfast tomorrow. She killed the chocolate milk and tossed the carton in the garbage.

Chapter Three

C rystal Ridge Hardware had inhabited the same creaky upstate house for nearly eighty years. No one remembered who'd built the place or who'd lived there previously. It had, at some point, been intended to be a house and not a hardware store. People by and large felt comfortable looking for pool toys in what was obviously a kitchen and bags of mulch in a downstairs powder room.

"Mister Kriminger . . ."

Ben was heading for the back of the store when he heard the cringe-inducing title echoing behind him. "Mister Kriminger . . ."

Ben turned and found Stevie, the store manager, rushing up behind him.

"Stevie, buddy, you're my boss . . ." Ben huffed with a forced smile. "You have to stop calling me that."

Stevie brushed bangs away from his spot-dotted face. "It's just how I was raised."

"To respect your elders." Ben answered with a wince.

Stevie slumped, unsure how to answer.

"It's cool. Just . . . Ben. If you can. Ben is good. I was about to clock out—"

"I know," Stevie interrupted. "But I have to watch the front counter, and, um . . . well . . ."

"You need me to do something?"

Stevie nodded.

"Which would be . . ." Ben said, trying to coax it out of him.

"Oh, well, all the trees, you know, outside? 'Cause fall's coming, the leaves are starting to blow through the front door when people open it . . ."

"You want me to sweep up the shop?" Ben asked.

"I can do that. But someone needs to be in the shop, and someone needs to, well, you should probably . . . you know, rake the leaves that are outside, so they don't blow in?"

Ben smiled.

"Hey, look at you. That was good. You totally delegated."

"Yeah?" Stevie asked, smiling, exposing braces.

"Oh yeah, boss mode. I'll grab the rake."

Ben noticed he could see his breath as he gathered the first fall leaves. He scraped the rake teeth against the sidewalk. The sound gave him a sick satisfaction. He gave a glance up Main Street—on one side was a nameless cafe, and a notary. Across the street was an old department store that had been gutted and was now a bingo parlor. The rest of the storefronts were dark or papered over. Every once in a while, an old truck would trundle up the hill, and even if the single light on the street turned red, they'd roll right through. When Ben was sure Stevie wasn't watching, he shoved the dead leaves down the storm drain instead of raking them into garbage bags. It was past 3 PM. And 3 PM was quitting time.

In the back of the store, Ben stowed the rake in what used to be a pantry, punched his card into the forty-year-old time clock, and slid it back into its slot on the dusty, wood-planked wall that used to be part of a back parlor. He'd been working there for three weeks and was getting paid less than his twenty-two-year-old supervisor, nearly a decade Ben's junior. When he wasn't being sort of asked by his child-boss to rake leaves or mop the basement or clear cobwebs out of the screw bins in the attic, Ben spent the rest of his days guiding potbellied men with bloodshot eyes up and down the three floors of the narrow house, hunting down random fasteners, pipe fittings, and brads in varying lengths.

Earlier in the day, he'd used his thirty-minute lunch break to load his pickup with pressure-treated two-by-fours and rolls of aluminum sheeting. A tree had come down in a summer storm while he was still in New York City, before he'd moved everything to the cabin fifteen minutes outside of Crystal Ridge. The fallen tree had smashed through part of the cabin's back wall and window and crushed one of the corners of the old cedar-shingled roof. Ben had woken up from a third cold night determined to finish fixing the wall and start on the roof. He spent just enough (with his employee discount) to keep a buffer of a couple hundred dollars in his bank account.

Before heading back to the cabin, Ben pulled into a lot behind Main Street and parked. He slid his old laptop out of his rucksack and booted it up, siphoning internet from the nearby cafe. Three technicians later and he still hadn't gotten the phone working in his cabin, and there was zero cell signal out there. He sunk down, wedging the laptop between the steering wheel and the slight bow of his stomach. He'd also let his beard go wild in the weeks since he'd been out of the city, and it itched like a mother. This morning he'd decided he wasn't going to scratch it once today. Mind over matter. Control over something. Although he was already imagining how he was going to scratch his whole damned face off come midnight. He clicked the truck's heat on. Nothing but a low groan and a handful of clattering metal sounds bellowed out of the vents. He sighed.

This is the kind of moment he'd been experiencing more and more over the past three months. A how-the-hell-did-I-get-here moment. Earning minimum wage at almost thirty, stealing internet in a nowhere Northeast shithole, cajoling a barely working truck to keep going, and doing anything to not have to go back to the three-room cabin that was once supposed to be his "writer's retreat" and was now his "home."

How the hell did I get here? Less than two months ago he'd been living in the glorious, grit-clogged heart of New York City, and this week he almost couldn't afford a pancake breakfast from the twelve-seat restaurant he was stealing Wi-Fi from. He waited as his inbox attempted to yank his email from all the way across the internet, hitting refresh over and over, hoping someone from the outside world would wonder what had happened to him, until his battery petered out. Then he'd have no choice but to go back to the drafty cabin, lined with the dozen boxes that loomed like cardboard totems, full of his life as it used to be before he screwed everything up.

His email pinged—one message and a ton of spam. His book agent. *What are you working on? Can't wait to read new pages. Remember, you're one idea away from being back on top!* Ben closed his laptop and tossed it in the passenger seat. He scratched the air in front of his beard instead of his actual beard, started the truck, and banged on the dash to try and get the heat to kick in. It didn't.

He steered his truck along the dirt road that led to the cabin. At the top of the steep drive, the little house rolled into view. Ben's heart sank every time he saw it now. It was a crooked box with a shallow pitch roof that was home to a thriving moss colony. He'd bought it at the height of his brief but warm success. A not quite best-selling novel, and an advance for his second, he'd thrown every dime into buying this place. He'd planned to spend weekends here in the warm months, writing, taking breaks to repair the plumbing and electrical, ripping out the old insulation. Maybe going solar. He'd also imagined Corilee pulling weeds in the yard, their dog, Volley, rushing down the drive to meet his truck, none of which ever came to be. After everything that happened with the first novel, the subsequent novel rightfully never materialized. Ben ate through his savings, lost Cor (breakup, he didn't misplace her) and all he had left was this place. Practically uninhabitable. But he couldn't go back home—*actual* home. North Carolina. Out of the question. Not *even* a question.

The upside to the cabin being a near-collapsing, element-exposed shack in early autumn was his beer stayed pretty cold. Ben spent the last few hours of the afternoon finishing the wall frame and replacing rain-soaked insulation. He had no idea how to build a house, but he knew how to fix broken things—the one benefit of his upbringing. Nothing was ever repaired on his father's farm, only patched over.

The sun was falling and Ben, now seventy-five percent smashed on no-name beer, had just made it up to the roof. The memory of scaling the tin-clad barn roof in the far-off of his childhood came rushing back to him: the back of his exposed neck sizzling, holding a sack of roofing nails for his dad, scared of falling, scared of dropping the sack, sweating. Smelling the beer his dad was coated in. No talking, no stopping. Just that sledgehammer hand reaching out, waiting for the next nail. That moment between the asking and the giving always seemed like an hour. How many childhood memories were framed in the feeling of "When will my parent explode next?" And "What will I have done to trigger the bomb?" Ben stared at the smashed roof, into the dark interior of the cabin. He swigged away the memory, wondering whether he should be scaling the roof in his state. Eh, who cared? Literally, no one. That was, of course, an exaggeration. Stevie would have to rake the leaves himself.

Ben finished the patch job on the roof, enough to keep the rain out, and sat back, looking out over the deep, tree-rimmed valley behind the cabin. Not a single house in sight. Lonely, but exquisite, a swath of red and orange was weaving through the green across the hills beyond, cutting through like a river. He'd never seen this place in fall. He and Cor had wanted to, but then things got so bad day trips to look at foliage hadn't really seemed appropriate. It was getting really cold up on the roof. Ben tried to finagle his beer bottle, a bag of nails, and a hammer, but lost the hammer, watched it ding his new aluminum patchwork, and slide off the far side of the roof.

Back down the ladder, he tromped across the flat-packed dirt yard, around the house, to the small front porch, where he found a dusty rubber-banded thicket of mail that had fallen off, into the bushes. His address forwarding had finally kicked in. He couldn't afford a PO box yet, and nothing worth getting ever came in the mail anymore, but it was the perfect excuse to quit.

He scooped up the bundle and ducked inside the cabin.

Ben flipped the wall switch, igniting the lone ceiling fixture. The glass shade was permanently skewed to one side. He thought it looked less like someone installed it and more like it had been hanged for its crimes against good taste. A fireplace anchored the wall opposite the barely-call-it-a-kitchen. Ben lit a fire last week when the weather finally turned cold, and smoke poured from between the chimney bricks, nearly choking him to death while he sat on the toilet. He'd been forced to finally splurge on a space heater with his employee discount, which now sat in the middle of the room on its own like a monolith, tethered to the wall by a frayed extension cord he found in the cellar. It was both art installation and fire hazard. A musty recliner sat across from the heater. Ben tossed his knit cap on the floor, mussed his wild thatch of dark hair, and plopped into the recliner. He kicked his boots off, clicked the heater on with his socked toe, and snapped the rubber bands off his mail.

Crap. Crap. Crap. Flyers for takeout places he no longer lived near, ads for New York neighborhood representatives that no longer represented him, old bills he had no means to pay. Wonderful. An envelope from his agent. Ben knew what this was. He almost ripped the envelope to pieces, unopened, but instead tore it open, checking the amount of the royalty check inside. Nearly $400. He pulled out the check, gave it one more look, then leaned over and slid one of its edges through the front grate of the heater, jamming it into the orange coils. It burst into flame, turning to ash in seconds. Ben sat back and took a deep breath, the rest of the mail in his lap. Anchoring the back of the stack was a long envelope, crumpled and coated with soil. Ben flipped it over and over, no return address. He slid his finger under the envelope's flap and tore it open, pulling the pages out.

He leaned forward, his tensing fingers crinkling the edges. Bubbly and buzzed from beer, he read the first page, about a young woman named Alistair, who lived in a little hole like him, but instead of a crumbling cabin, she lived in a room made of books.

Chapter Four

"I thought Alistair was a boy's name," the lanky train conductor mumbled with a smug underbite smile as he checked Alistair's state ID and scanned the digital ticket on her phone. Alistair pointed at the chunky headphones she was wearing. She wasn't listening to music, but he didn't need to know that. This was a regrettably necessary tactic for a young woman living on her own in the city. *Be prepared for everything you hear, act like you didn't hear anything.* The train lurched and started moving, into a dark sub-Manhattan tunnel, on its way upstate. Alistair slouched down, favored coat across her lap. She pulled her hoodie over her head, planted her feet on the back of the seat in front of her, and cracked the spine of an old paperback of Ursula Le Guin short stories, using the obituary for Eleanor Pry as a bookmark.

Eleanor Pry had finally passed away, surrounded by her four grown children, who'd moved to moneyed map points in adulthood and now were forced to return upon her death. She would be dearly missed, et cetera. The bereaved had managed to set aside their bottomless grief long enough to put every stitch of Eleanor's belongings up for grabs in an estate sale so they could bequeath the house itself to the state of New York, in exchange for a probable healthy tax credit, endowment, or whatever rich people did. That's how things like this went. Alistair didn't know the Prys but knew that where there were enormous estates and enormous estate sales —and bequeathing of houses to states—there were also books. Good books. Rare books. She knew some of the best hunting grounds were grand old houses being sold brick by brick by the bereaved. Estate sales were potential gold mines for rare finds, but the world of book collectors was a caste system, and Alistair was barely hanging on at the bottom. By the time an auction in the tristate area started, everything worth having had already been snatched up by well-dressed grave robbers. Then they'd sell it all to private collectors who'd hide the treasures behind locks and glass for another generation, or put especially good finds up at auction. Alistair saw herself as the Robin Hood of books. Get a *very* good deal from the insanely rich, then sell to the slightly poorer but still well-off, with a quick personal read, sometimes a page-by-page scan. There would be a bit of profit for her somewhere in between. But to get first dibs, she had to bend a couple rules. Laws really. Like breaking and entering. Well, entering at least. Alistair was on her way to the estate, but the *estate sale* wasn't for another four days.

It was a two-hour ride upstate, then a long slog of a walk to the gates of the Pry property because she couldn't afford a cab. The house sat on a hill above the Hudson River, naturally. A stunning old block of a house, built with grey stone, lined with ivy and verdigris gutters and elegant, tasteful patina. It looked more like a stately museum than a house, and would possibly become one soon enough. On the roof were three small glass domes, one in the middle, one on each end. The property was walled-in by a mile of hundred-year-old privet and heavy iron gates, which now hung open, no one left living to be locked inside. Alistair threw her messenger bag over her shoulder, sweating from the walk, even though it was colder up in the Hudson Valley, and headed up the crunchy gravel driveway, catching a glimpse of a sailboat bobbing beyond the privet, out on the river.

She cased the exterior: one car out front. Someone was home. An early aughts CRV. Definitely not one of the Pry's vehicles. She walked up the winding topiary-lined path, took a deep breath, and rang the doorbell. After a few moments she saw someone approach through the windows that flanked the story-tall door. A housekeeper. Excellent. The door was pulled inward with a low croak.

"Yes, hi, can I help you?" the brusk housekeeper asked, wiping sweat from her brow.

Alistair smiled, "Good morning. I'm an associate with Watson-Jones, the estate auction facilitators? I have an appointment this morning to start putting things in order, photos for the auction site, blah blah blah, can I pop in? I just need an hour, maybe two."

The housekeeper squinted, confused, "I don't work here, normally. I'm from an agency. You're here to what?"

"We're selling everything." Alistair motioned to the house and everything in it. "Mrs. Pry. Dead. And we're— selling *everything*."

The housekeeper tilted her head, hesitating, "I'll have to call—"

"Yeah, that's fine, if you think you need to," Alistair checked her watch, which hadn't told the correct time in two years, feigning mild urgency, then looked back with a smile. "I'll only be an hour, hour and a half, tops? And I'll stay out of your way."

The housekeeper considered for a beat, then shrugged and let her in.

The house was vast, but warm. Richly oiled wood-paneled walls, tastefully colored upholsteries, and carefully chosen furniture, all well within the style and time period of the house. Alistair didn't know furniture or art or tapestries, but this looked like the good stuff. The housekeeper stood behind her as Alistair took it all in, scanning the place to figure out where to start. It seemed like the housekeeper wasn't going anywhere so Alistair pulled her phone out of her pocket and faked a call.

"I'm sorry, excuse me," Alistair whispered to the housekeeper.

She scurried down the nearest hallway. Once out of sight, she ducked around a corner and wandered into the belly of the house. She had a nose for this sort of thing. She could follow the living mustiness of books the way a hungry cartoon character could be dragged away by the scent of a juicy steak. Books were vital— literally today, because she was starving, but figuratively too. For her, books were beautiful lies told to a girl who had no use for the truth. The walls Alistair put up between her and the world were leather bound.

To be clear, Alistair had no intention of stealing the late Mrs. Pry's books. She wasn't a thief, though she *might* have absconded with a book or two in the early days of starting out on her own. But no, she'd just do some *subtle relocations*, so when the sale started properly in four days, and the house was besieged with sharp, shrewd Manhattan collectors, Alistair could calmly make her way to a remote attic, or basement, or housekeeper's quarters, and what do you know? Someone left a box of precious first editions labeled CLEANING SUPPLIES in the back of this closet. How fortuitous.

She set out to find it. The library. Every old-money mansion worth its salt had one. She'd seen every kind of collection. Endless halls, or stories tall, lined to the ceiling with spines. Even underground rooms like wine cellars. All heaven for someone like her. After a few wandering turns, she found the house's heart, its stash. At first, she was disappointed. It was a single long room with a modest collection packed on shelves that had been built into the low walls. A study, really. Maybe you'd call it a den. But library? Alistair wandered in with a huff. It was humble on first glance, until she stepped in further and saw that an arched doorway had been carved into one of the bookcase-lined walls, and through the arch was another room with books, and beyond that, another. Room after room of subsequent libraries, each with an arched doorway leading deeper and deeper into clothbound rapture. Alistair wandered in through the arches. She had the feeling of being on a forest trail, with the books and arches and wood ceiling serving as bowing branches, creating what seemed like a never-ending canopied path. In each room were more built-in bookcases, long tables with stacks of books, and old leather books laid open, perfectly positioned to seem as if someone had just been called away from intense study. She retraced her steps, positively giddy, closed the initial door behind her, and went to work.

An hour and a few *Beauty and the Beast* library ladder rides later, she had pulled two foot-high stack of books. She was a little disappointed, frankly. She suspected a lot of these books were bought by the foot, just to beautifully fill the space. But she had found some worthy contenders tucked in the corners. A few rarities, and first prints of *One Flew Over the Cuckoo's Nest, To The Lighthouse, The Power and The Glory*, a full Narnian chronicle, and a handful of well-spined first-print Lovecrafts. Not too bad. This stack of leather, glue, and cream-toned paper, once scanned and sold, would support her for the next three months, four if she skipped breakfast every now and then. Her stomach growled at the thought.

She assembled a flattened shipping box she'd hidden in her messenger bag, along with a spool of packing tape, and started stowing the books. She taped the box closed and emerged from the library, looking for a quiet place to stash it. She heard the housekeeper vacuuming nearby on the main floor, so she hefted the box of books up the obscenely wide carpeted stairs, to search the second floor for a place to hide them.

The upstairs was deathly quiet. A stillness pervaded, almost as if the top half of the house were frozen in time. The endless carpet runner muffled Alistair's footsteps, adding to the eerily muted atmosphere. It was sunny, but even the light was strange, surreal. The windows let in waves of river-reflected light, which rippled on the hall's coffered ceiling, like spirits pooling in the air. She wound through endless wood-paneled halls, the wood periodically broken up by oversized paintings of old people and older European landscapes. Far from the stairs, she found a short side hall with a powder room that was bigger than her apartment. She squeezed the box into an under-sink cabinet.

She turned and headed back along the creepy-quiet hall to get her bag and coat, and give the library a last once-over, but stopped short at the edge of a longer hallway. The doors along the hall each had a brass letter nailed to it. *S, Z, E,* and at the end of the hall, on an open door, an *A*. Children's first initials, Alistair assumed.

The room beyond the open door was warm and bright and drenched in pastel lavender, pink, and cream. She could see the edge of thick pale carpet and delicately laced bedding, and beyond the bedding, a bookcase with bright spines. A child's room. *It couldn't hurt to check out the books.*

Alistair pressed down the hall and nudged the open door wider. The room was sprawling, S, Z, and E could have easily shared the space with A, but where there was money, pointless, useless space was never far away. It was the kind of room that out-of-touch parents put together the moment they heard they were having a girl, because, of course, girls love pink. The room was neat, clean, and free of dust, but the overall style was from two or three decades prior. "A" was long gone.

Alistair padded across the thick carpet and around the plush four-poster bed to the bookcase, running her finger along the books. Nothing of note, or monetary interest. Not a cracked spine among them. "A" obviously hadn't been much of a reader. Once again, the books were for show. Alistair wondered what her own room had been like as a child. Not her room with Aunt Kath and Uncle Gus. *That* room she remembered. *That* room was largely still intact, back in Ozone Park. No, she wondered about the room before. The one her parents had made up when they heard they were having a girl. Was it pink and frilly and gender normative? Had she been a reader even then, with all her baby book spines cracked to hell? Her memories took a hard stop around ten-years-old and there was no one left to tell her the kind of bedding she slept under.

No one remembered the books but her. A current of electricity ran up Alistair's spine. That was unexpected. That thought usually only came to her in the vulnerable twilit fog of waking up and falling asleep. She must've been diving too deep into the dark of her memories. She rolled her shoulders and shook her head, willing the thought away. She muttered, "The only thing that's real is whatever I can feel," as she rounded the bed, heading out of the room, when she noticed a closet door on the far end of the pale room, only slightly open. It stopped her cold, her brow furrowing. She couldn't explain why, but she felt a compulsion to open that door, as if her gut were telling her *that's where the goods are.* She needed to see inside.

She turned back to the bedroom door, listened for anyone in the upstairs hall. She probably wouldn't be able to hear footsteps on the carpet until it was too late, but she could just say she got lost looking for a bathroom. She turned back to the closet and walked over, taking a moment, then pulling the door open wide. It was deep, and unlike the rest of the room, was mostly swallowed by dark. She felt the inside wall for a light switch and found a nubbly button that she pressed, illuminating the closet.

No one remembered the books but her. It was empty. Nothing but two bare rods stretching from one end to the other, and an empty row of shelves at the end.

Another explosion of prickly fingers lanced up her spine and she whipped around, sure someone would be standing in the bedroom doorway, wondering what she was doing up there, but she was alone. She turned back and took a step into the closet, then another. It was so quiet, the small room seemed to eat the sound of her breathing, as if she wasn't there at all. It was so disconcerting, she snapped her fingers, making a single, echoless *snap.*

Alistair's gut instinct was glitching. There was nothing there. *What the hell was she doing?* She turned to walk out, reaching for the light switch, but something near the floor caught her eye before she killed the light. Something below the last shelf on the far wall. A toy. Blue, plastic, not more than two inches tall.

No one remembered the books but her. Alistair stared at the half-seen thing, almost in a daze. Something was wrong. Her head had turned foggy and muddled, and she wanted to go, but instead she walked deeper into the closet and knelt down. She realized her heart was now racing. A wave of anxiety, or fear, had washed over her, but by the time she realized why, that she was strangely and inexplicably afraid to see the toy, she had already reached down to grab it.

She watched as her fingers unwound around the toy, as if she had no control over them. She was holding a small plastic figurine on a pedestal. Like a playing piece in a board game. It was all blue, a little girl, her dress permanently whipping in an unseen wind. She was carrying a bow and quiver, an arrow nocked and ready to fire.

Alistair whispered a word to herself, barely audible, *"Iris."* Like a light snapping on, a deep, wet wave of dizziness shot through her. She physically folded inward for a moment, as if shielding herself, then she scrambled to her feet, rushing for the bedroom door, bouncing off furniture as she tried to get out.

Alistair. A strange voice called to her from the room. She shook her head, trying to will the feeling away, but another wave of nausea rose up and the room began to feel like a boat in rough water, growing longer, twisting slightly in one direction, then the other. She had to get out of here. She plowed into the hallway, taking turn after turn, faster and faster, but now the hall seemed unfamiliar. She couldn't remember which way she'd come from. She grabbed at walls to keep upright. Every step she took pushed her deeper into the rocking sickness. She stopped to catch her breath and heard a noise behind her that blast-chilled the blood in her pounding heart. A *clicking clack*, like nails on hardwood. Something pacing behind her. Something with claws. Alabaster claws. *No one remembered the books but her.* She thought she had escaped, but she was down in the dark now. She'd found an anchor, and it was pulling up the black.

Don't turn around. She kept walking, knowing she was going the wrong way. And ahead, around the next turn, was the sound of the thing with claws. She stopped cold, spun around, and found herself staring down at an impossible sight. A small, amber-colored fox was sitting at the other end of the long hall, wearing thin, round glasses. It watched her with a slight tilt of its narrow head. It took two steps toward her. Even against the padded carpet: *clickety-clack.*

Anyone else would struggle to try and reconcile the mind-boggling sight. A fox. In a house. A fox, with glasses. A nearsighted fairy-tale fox. But Alistair had seen this creature before. She had seen things that no one else could see. A byproduct of the traumatic secret childhood that she thought had been finally swallowed up by adulthood. She'd been taught coping mechanisms by her therapist, but hadn't had to use them in years. She knew this wasn't real. But there it was. The bespectacled fox. The strings of the past had bound her again and yanked her deep into the abyss.

She ran. Into another unfamiliar hallway, looking for the stairs, but he was there, closer now, waiting. The fox at every turn, and Alistair dodging it, rushing into another part of the house, desperate. It wasn't the fox itself that scared her. It was that the fox was a harbinger. *It was what she saw before the other thing arrived.*

This had happened before. A handful of times since she was a kid, but not in years. She was muttering now, louder and louder, trying to remember a kind of mantra she'd been taught as a child. "My name is Alistair . . . My name is Alistair Mead. I am—twenty-six years old. The only thing that's real is whatever I can feel. Nothing more, nothing much . . . If I fear something's real, all I have to do is touch. Because—real things feel like something, and fake things feel like air. I can touch the thing that worries me and know it isn't there."

She passed a tall grandfather clock in the hall and could hear the ticking begin to slow until it seemed like the ticks were eons apart.

The view from the windows turned dark. Instead of a sun-dappled river beyond, she saw a dark forest, a slow-falling snow covering the trees' evergreen branches, weighing them until they surrendered, bowing under the weight, creating a vaulted wintry ceiling. And she saw glimmering eyes in the dark tree line. Watching her. Following her. The windows between her and the forest were shattered now, the snow floating in. Only feet away from the thing that was stalking her. She was losing her mind again, right here, right now.

Alistair a voice called over her shoulder.

The *clickety-clack* was closer, no matter how fast she ran. *Nothing more, nothing much. Nothing more, nothing much.* She looked back, her body pulling her forward as she searched behind her for the fox. And at every turn, he was there.

Tears streaming, unable to catch her breath, she felt the floor all at once disappear below her feet, and realized she'd finally found the stairs.

The house spun upside down as she fell. Alistair thought the thud of her head hitting the first-floor hardwood sounded like a book slamming shut.

Chapter Five

I t had been almost a week since Ben found the bundle of mail by the front porch. In that time, he'd traveled back and forth to the hardware store for three shifts, had a breakfast at a truck stop that he was sure had given him mild food poisoning, finished patching the roof a day *after* a nasty storm, insulated the new back wall a day after a severe cold snap, and lay awake every night, trying not to think about the Alistair book pages. Everything that went wrong back in New York City had started with someone sending him stories in the mail. Fevered, obsessed, nonsensical stories that, looking back, had been the literary equivalent of the tide pulling miles out from shore just before a tsunami. It didn't feel like disaster at first, and then—

He chalked up the pages arriving to an errant envelope from months prior finally shaking loose in some outer-borough fulfillment center, somehow making it to Manhattan, triggering the address forwarding request, and finally making it to Crystal Ridge. No one but Cor knew where he was, and no one, not even Ben, knew where Cor had ended up. They both were safe.

So, he "forgot" about the pages, and tossed them, with only two chapters read, on a pile of junk in the cabin that he was going to leave at the garbage dump the next time he went into town.

Ben spent his two days off by clearing out the clay cellar under the house and the shed by the driveway. A mess of gardening tools, broken furniture, and boxes full of mold-covered things belonging to previous owners. Even though Ben had no inclination to put pen to paper, the story-searching, investigative machine in the back of Ben's brain always chugged to life in times like this. The workbench in the shed may have belonged to a rough-handed husband and father. Father, because he'd found mildewed dressage trophies in the basement. Husband, because he'd pulled out an old hand mixer jammed in the back of a kitchen drawer. Rough-handed, because Ben had a box of work gloves he'd found in and around the shed that had all been torn or worn clean through. Probably had a name like Will, or Sam. Sam loved woodworking, but it was now a hobby. He'd given it up for a better-paying job, hell, given up everything. His wife, Julie or Juliette, no, Gabrielle— and daughter . . . Fran—were living in a two-room house, so they could funnel every free dime into Fran's crazy dream of riding horses. Maybe she had Olympic hopes? Bigger stakes. Sam built the house himself. This cramped but cozy family home, or maybe it was a downsize when their big dreams collapsed, when Fran was paralyzed in a tragic horseback accident. Or was thrown, and then died. The ribbons and trophies damned to the darkness of the basement like every dream they used to represent. Too many memories, too much pain. The cabin was just a starter home while Sam planned the house of their dreams up the hill, but ended up selling off chunk after chunk of land as they spiraled into debt and grief until nothing was left but three rooms crumbling around them. And then Gabrielle walked away, on her own, or with the young hardware store manager who was trapped in a fine but loveless marriage, leaving the man to rot away here, alone, nothing left of himself to give up. The American Dream-cum-nightmare. The slanted light hanging in the middle of the lonely room a vivid mirror of the old man's ultimate fate. So maybe Ben was in a darker place than he realized.

He was hauling a stack of Gabrielle's framed needlepoints out of the cellar to the garbage when he heard a car door slam. Ben leaned around the side of the house—and there she was. Corilee, just standing there, in the driveway, with the light that followed her, making her look crisp and warm and . . . glowy. She'd rented a small, sensible car. Before she saw him, he noticed the back seat was full of boxes and some of his old clothes. Jackets, heavy coats. Things he'd left behind. She hated driving. She would've hated going through the process of renting that car. He knew she'd thought long and hard about her clothes, about the boots she was wearing. Those dark, suede boots that went almost up to her knee, with her jeans tucked into them. He knew she chose them because he liked them, but not too much. He knew she wouldn't want to do anything to miscommunicate her intentions because she was kind and empathetic. She made sure there'd be no question *why* she was there. She had her hair up because it felt responsible, appropriate. She was doing everything possible to seem comfortable, and kind, because she had a big, soft heart, and because she always over-considered everything. All of these observations and reflections ran through Ben's mind in about three-quarters of a second. He was hyper-processing everything he knew about her, a checklist of sorts, like he was proving to himself that at one point he and Cor were together. It wasn't make-believe. And even though he knew her and knew she had done everything possible to make this seem like a casual, friendly visit, he couldn't help but think in the back of his mind that there was no way she would've gone through all this trouble if there wasn't still some flicker of something inside her. A tiny flame that mirrored the one he'd been trying to shield from guttering for the past year. She finally saw him.

"The place looks great, Ben," she called out.

Ben. Not Benny, which is what she used to call him. Ben.

"What are you doing up here?" he asked.

She approached with a warm, open smile and arms to match. As she came in for a hug, he caught a glimpse, just a sliver, of the thick pink scar running from her hand to her forearm. He felt guilty, seeing it. Guilty for looking for it. They hugged like friends. Tight squeeze, quick pat, and release. Their eyes locked in, and for a second neither knew what the hell to say. She finally broke the tension.

"My new place is smaller and when I was packing I found a bunch of your stuff, like your winter gear. I thought you might want it before it gets too cold."

Ben could think of a thousand things to say in response, about her apartment, about her move, about packing, their dog, about her, about him, about them. About why he didn't answer her previous calls or texts. But somewhere between his head and his mouth, all of it turned to soup and he was afraid to say anything for fear it would come out *How move is dog head, apartment, together, miss you?* Cor squeezed his shoulder and moved past him, walking toward the cabin. She was nervous too. She needed something external to fixate on. It was so weird. He'd been in relationships before, and yes Cor was special, and his feelings for her ran deep, but this kind of thing never changed. It was universal, where this person you shared absolutely everything with, was suddenly a stranger, and you both knew you were thinking the same things, but knew you weren't allowed to say them anymore. The universe had rescinded permission. What did she want him to do? Follow her? Rush to get everything out of the car so she could get the hell out of there? The woman he knew better than he knew himself was standing in front of him and he couldn't make out her most basic wants or intentions. Their relationship was a phantom limb, something once so intrinsic, now nothing more than neurons misfiring.

He had to admit, he kind of wanted her to get the hell out. He wanted this to not be like this. They had said their goodbyes in the city. They'd spent half the day on the couch together, hugging Volley, the rescue mutt, and crying. That had been the goodbye. So what was this? Confusing. Annoying. Embarrassing. He turned to see that she had just rounded the edge of the cabin and saw the horrible patch job on the back wall. His eyes scanned the property, trying to see what she was seeing, how bad it was, or maybe how it wasn't so bad . . . and then his eyes met hers again. She was looking at him. He felt so vulnerable. This, he couldn't fix. She caught him so completely off guard, and although there'd be no way to hide the fact that he had hit rock bottom up here in Crystal Ridge, if he'd known she was actually coming, he would've had time to pretend better. Fortify his lie. Shave. Shower. But here he was, covered in grime, stripped metaphorically naked in front of the woman he still loved very, very much.

"You don't have to stay here," she eked out with a barely audible whisper. She was choked up. Seeing all this hurt her.

"No, no, no . . . I swear to God, Cor, if you came up here just to feel sorry for me . . ."

"I came to see you, and bring you your—stuff, but then I see your house is missing a wall and yeah, I'm sorry, now there's pity. You're missing a wall, Benny—"

He couldn't help but smile. Benny. The way her voice sort of cracked on *wall*, the weird, unexpected tension suddenly bled out between them. They were just them for a minute.

"This is so weird," he said.

"SO weird," she replied, wiping tears from her eyes.

"Can we . . . just walk?" Ben implored.

They ended up hiking the perimeter of the property together, talking. Four acres is a pretty quick walk, even on uneven and forested terrain, so they did it a couple of times, Ben pretending there was something he forgot to show her, the raspberries he found, the view of the valley, the sliver of lake you could just make out across the network of low hills in the southwest corner of the property, holes in the ground that might be rabbit warrens. He thought of mentioning the chapters, but had convinced himself they were nothing, and knew it would bring up bad memories. He didn't want to put either of them through that. All of that was done.

He wasn't sure if she wanted to be there, wanted to see it all, or was just placating him, but she didn't protest, and as the hours went on, and the sun started to fall, he realized how hard it was going to be to watch her drive away. It was one thing to leave the city, and the memory of everything that had happened, not just between them, but *to* them. Driving north out of the city that day had been somewhat hopeful. Ben—despite everything, and all of this with Cor—was an optimist. Leaving the city, he had convinced himself it was the right thing to do, they couldn't go back to the way things were before . . . And this was his chance to reboot. And then a summer passed, and not a damn thing had changed. Well, not exactly, it had gotten a lot worse. And now, the thought of watching her get into that stupid little rental car, and pull out, overcautiously, down the dirt driveway, then vanish in the tree line, felt like his soul was being plucked out of his chest. He kept walking her around the property, waiting for her to say the fateful phrase . . . "I've been thinking . . ."

He'd gone through every scenario and knew there was no going back to what they had, but hell, Cor was threefold smarter than he was. Maybe she had come up with something.

"Can I ask you something?" she muttered.

Ben swallowed hard, like she'd caught him thinking what he was just thinking.

"Anything. What's up?" he replied, over-casual.

"How are you doing—money-wise?"

That hitch in between the first and second half of her question had Ben's heart racing one second and then sinking into his gut the next.

"Oh. I'm—I'm good. Yeah. Everything's fine."

"'Cause the last time I tried calling your cell was disconnected?"

Oof. Ben nodded, hoping a lie would come to him before his head stopped moving. It did. "There's no signal up here. It felt like a waste. We're working on getting a landline from town to the cabin. Should be any day now."

"Okay, that's good. Have you been writing?" she asked as they ended their second loop around the cabin.

"A little," he lied with a smile. He was *not* going to tell her that his only source of income was a part-time job sorting screws under the supervision of a college freshman.

He couldn't tell her the truth because it would bring up everything else. Ben had slowly come to realize—on all those lonely nights in the cabin over the past few months—why he couldn't write, when before, writing was all he could do. Writing had done this to them. The book he wrote. And everything the book brought into their lives. What he'd brought into *Cor's* life. In truth, he'd had a hundred new ideas. A complete change of scenery and upheaval of his life had a way of inspiring him. Part of him had wanted desperately to sit down and start spewing words onto the screen. Sam and Gabrielle and Frannie . . . But to write again, in a way, was to tell himself he would never have her back. That the words in him were worth all the pain.

He noticed she was getting antsy in ways only he would notice. She probably wanted to get on the road before it was night. They stood side by side, overlooking the valley behind the cabin. Ben felt her fingers reach out for his, slowly sliding together, until they were holding fast. She squeezed his sweaty palm, he could feel the scar that extended into her hand, and then they both slipped away. Like they couldn't let the universe see.

"Okay, I'd better go before it gets too dark," she said.

She turned and kissed him on the lips. Maybe out of some old, ingrained habit. It was quick, with no subtext. Not because she was cold, but because she didn't want to hurt him anymore. She, who'd been hurt the worst.

"You finally grew your beard out. It looks nice," she said with a forced smile before walking ahead of him, and away.

Back in the driveway, he pulled the boxes out of the car, but left one of his shirts in the back seat. He wasn't sure why. It would probably get left in the rental when she returned it. He just didn't want to erase himself completely from her life. He watched her overcautiously pull down the dirt driveway, blinker on a half mile before the main road, and disappear in the tree line. Then he closed himself inside his almost-four-walled cabin and cried until he got a nosebleed.

It was night. Ben had been lying in the bathroom doorway, staring at the cracked plaster ceiling with toilet paper plugged into one nostril for two hours. The floor was freezing, the cabin was freezing, and the heater had stopped working the night before. He had to get up. His nosebleed finally dry, he washed up, checked his face in the small medicine cabinet mirror, nodded reassurance to himself, then walked out and tripped over a box Cor had brought, falling face-first back onto the floor.

He got up, kicked the box across the room, and howled. That was it. Enough. He grabbed duct tape out of his toolbox, stretched strips of it across the crumbling brickwork above the fireplace to keep the smoke out of the cabin, and with a bit of effort, started a fire.

Then he started feeding the blaze with the boxes Cor brought. Unopened, he shoved them in one by one for hours, watching them burst into flame and turn to ash before adding the next. There were a couple times he'd catch a glimpse of something inside, something he wanted to reach in and save, a book, a hat, a cigar box full of photos, but he resisted. It was over. It all had to go. He had to let it all go.

By midnight the fire was finally fading to cinders. Ben sat in front of it, knees to his chest, arms around his legs. Chilly and drunk on a bottle of scotch he'd salvaged from the flames. Days alone in the cabin were bad enough, but nights were unbearable. Crushingly lonely and seemingly eternal—not to mention terrifying. Every errant snap of a branch outside was a ravenous yeti or gang of anarchistic marauders bent on claiming this hellish place for their own. But the quiet in between the terror-making noises was the real killer. Nothing but Ben's thoughts. The past. The book. Cor.

No. Not letting it all in again. Ben looked over and saw the dozen or so boxes he'd originally brought with him when he moved up from the city. The stuff he'd packed himself. He wanted to burn it all. He got up and stumbled over to the cardboard totems. He grabbed a heavy one, and as he picked it up, loose pages trapped between it and another box scattered across the floor. The book pages he'd been mailed. *No one remembered the books but her.*

He dropped the box, gathered up the pages, and walked them to the fading fire. He wanted to burn them, but the writer in him needed them in order first. He shuffled the pages until they were in sequence—*Alistair told the doctors a metric ton of lies* was the first line in the next chapter. Ben had to admit, they weren't like the mad ramblings he'd received from the crazies who'd taken his book to heart. It was a comprehensible story. About a lonely young woman who was lost and hiding from the world just like Ben. Sure, she'd had some kind of strange, waking nightmare in an old upstate mansion, but who hadn't? Maybe his agent had sent them. Maybe it was an advance reader's copy of another client's work. Maybe they were from some tertiary cousin from North Carolina trying to break into the novel-writing business. Ben tossed leftover scrap wood from the roof on the fire instead of the pages and slumped into the cold leather recliner. He wasn't alone. There was Alistair Mead. The girl who remembered books that no one else could, and who had just woken up in a hospital room.

Chapter Six

Alistair told the doctors a metric ton of lies. *I skipped breakfast. I was dehydrated. Nothing like this has ever happened to me before.* If she'd told them the truth, the whole truth, she wouldn't be five minutes from walking out of the hospital. She'd be under mental wellness observation. The truth was this had happened to her before, but it hadn't happened in years. Not like this. She'd had dark weeks, but not a full-on escape from reality like had happened in the Pry mansion. That, she hadn't suffered through in over a decade. Since then, she'd harbored a little light inside herself, a light that had been kindled by the hope that maybe it wasn't going to happen again. So, while she lied about breakfast, dehydration, and this never happening, the little light died because it hurt to know how badly she'd wanted all those lies to be true.

Groggy, feeling like she'd overslept and had her bell severely rung, Alistair slowly dressed behind a thin curtain. The question asked by curious police and hospital staff—*why* she was in the Pry mansion to begin with—was waved away with an "I got the date for the estate sale wrong; I wasn't feeling well earlier but brushed it off."

Unable to locate her socks, she shoved the grippy hospital-issued slippers into her boots.

Alistair had had to ask where she was. She was in a room of her own, so this obviously wasn't some overbooked, understaffed city hospital. Turns out she was only twenty minutes from the estate. She'd spent most of the night there, half-in, half-out of consciousness, sleeping through a CT scan and IV drips. Now she was dressed and ready to go with a mild concussion, an otherwise clean bill of health, and absolutely no idea how she was going to get back home, but her secret was still intact.

Not the secret about what she was really doing at the estate, but her real secret: The noted distinction of being a former missing person. Alistair was nine when she had disappeared. Disappeared in the sense that she ran away, or someone took her. She wasn't sure how she vanished, to be honest. When she came back, she found that her parents, who she only vaguely recalled as "strong, dark hands" and "laugh like wind chimes," had not survived a nasty car accident while she was gone. And her memories of her missing year had not returned with her. Nothing at all. Nothing but dread darkness, aching cold, and the vague flicker of a series of books. Books, that, at ten, she recounted stories from to police, social workers, therapists, and her aunt and uncle.

As each person who heard the story shook their heads and refused their existence, the memories faded, and Alistair "got better," which is to say she got better at hiding and compartmentalizing whatever was left back there in that year and getting on with her life.

So bits and bobs of her truth were out there, but she only ever told the whole truth, about the fox, and the forest, and all the rest, to one person—her childhood therapist. And only because she didn't know better not to. She was ten. She was in shock. Which was understandable, given the circumstances. A drowsy truck driver had almost obliterated a cold little girl walking in winter on a lightless road, a year, almost to the day, from when she disappeared. Then she came home, with no recollection of who took her, where she'd gone, or why she was back. And although her aunt and uncle had taken her in, and although her therapist had listened to what little she remembered, *the books, snow, the dark, the fox*, the actual and whole truth was somewhere, locked inside her, or maybe somewhere else. Stolen away. A part of her torn out and kept, while the rest of her had been dumped in the snow. She wasn't whole, and eventually she realized she never would be.

In time she had adjusted. She'd adapted. Children aren't fragile like people think; they're soft, yes, but that enables them to sway. They can mold themselves around tragedy, warp themselves under uncertainty, grow callous around places of pain. Children can bend. It's adults who break. Alistair could go on with her life, not in spite of not knowing what had happened to her, but maybe *because* of not knowing.

When she was finished dressing, a waiting nurse led her down the white, winding halls of the run-down hospital and through a set of double doors where she shuffled into the hospital's small waiting room. Aside from an infomercial bleating from the wall-bolted TV, it was quiet. The little waiting room was empty, and no one was behind the front desk.

"Alistair," someone grumbled from behind her.

She spun and found her old boss, Ed Cumberland, waiting by the window that overlooked the parking lot. Her former, and only, boss —bags under his already baggy eyes.

"What the hell are you doing here?" she asked, surprised, the sea of empty chairs between them.

He shrugged. "I'm your emergency contact for some godforsaken reason," he answered.

Confusion bled away to an old memory.

"When I broke my toe."

He nodded and smiled. "Right."

She'd just moved to the city. Not wanting the hospital staff to call her aunt, she'd listed Ed as her person to call, back when they'd hunted books together. They'd gotten along as well as they possibly could. Alistair, on occasion, had the demeanor of a grizzled, short-fused, middle-aged hermit, and Ed *was* a grizzled, short-fused, middle-aged hermit. He'd lost a little more hair since she saw him last, but his high-and-tight buzz cut hid it pretty well. His build and posture were byproducts of the habits drilled into him in the Marines, and every time she saw him it made her stand up a little straighter by proxy.

"So? You all right?" he asked, his voice always sounded like he'd just been shouting. Rough. Tired.

She nodded and hoisted her bag onto her shoulder. "Yeah."

That was the equivalent of the two of them hugging.

She appreciated it. The easy distance. She felt raw, unfolded. She didn't like either of those feelings.

"Let's get out of here," he said.

They took a cab, a train, a subway, and a half-mile walk together. Two-and-a-half hours of appreciated silence, aside from the chatty cabbie in Poughkeepsie, who they'd both ignored. *What a waste*, Alistair thought. Fourteen hours, thousands of dollars in eventual hospital bills, and not a single book to show for it.

Ed wanted to walk her all the way back home from the subway stop, but she declined. As she turned to head down Third Avenue, he finally piped up.

"Hey, did you hear about that local dealer who found the pristine Peter Rabbit in a storage unit last year?"

Alistair shook her head.

"The one with a note to a little girl inside from Potter herself? First print signed by the author. That's an eighty-thousand deal, easy."

"Easy."

"But the dealer ended up tracking down the little girl's granddaughter instead and giving *her* the book. No charge. Probably changed that woman's life."

"I hadn't heard that," Alistair said.

"No? That's one benevolent dealer, huh? Dumb as a stump, but . . ."

Alistair couldn't help but smile. "Grade A idiot, that one. Night, Ed," she called back, about to walk away.

"It doesn't have to be an emergency, you know?" he said. "If you ever need anything . . . even just somebody to talk at . . . it doesn't have to be an emergency."

Off her silent reaction, he shook his head.

"Just keep it in mind. Whatever's going on. If you need leads, cash . . . you can't eat kindness," he said with a wink.

Words reached the brim of her mouth like a cup about to overflow. But she choked them back, scared sharing even a drop would drag it back up out of the dark, when all she wanted to do was let it sink down again. She appreciated that he knew what she was and wasn't capable of sharing. It was a comfort, despite her reticence.

"All right, get home, get some sleep." They shared a nod and then Alistair headed off into the cold night.

She had to wake up Danny Chen to get into her apartment. He was a generally nice guy, a couple years younger than her, in college for something or other that Alistair didn't remember. Also, Danny Chen hated Alistair Mead. Her agreement with Danny's grandparents had been that she could eat there for free, but she had to be home before the restaurant closed at 11 PM. It was 4:37 AM. So, because of this, and moments like it, Danny Chen hated Alistair Mead. He let her in, but before he could say anything she showed him the hospital ID bracelet on her wrist. He let her off with some mild grumbling this time.

She crossed the darkened restaurant, passed the bathrooms, went through the darker kitchen to the stairs that led to her room above. She flopped onto the mattress and undressed horizontally. She felt utterly wiped, despite having slept through most of the past twelve hours, yet she didn't want to close her eyes. She knew what was waiting there if she did.

When she was a kid, after episodes like the one she'd just had, dipping into the dark, she'd sleep for days. But he was still there, the fox, wandering the book-lined halls in her head. She couldn't help but let her eyelids slide down. And there he was. The bespectacled fox. Watching her, waiting for her.

⚜

Alistair shivered and sat up. She fumbled through the pile of clothes on the floor, grabbed her jacket and tore through the pockets, then her bag. The figure was gone. Of course it was. Part of her hallucination, her descent into the dark. Lit by the yellow light from the alley outside her only window, Alistair wrapped her arms around her bent legs, chin on her knees. An image floated in her mind. The girl. She remembered it had sparked a memory in her mind like steel on the flint of her childhood. A name. A name that completely escaped her now. *Nobody remembered the books but her.*

Alistair stared at the pockmarked concrete ceiling above her bed until the sun started to break over the East River. She was hungry, tired. Icy ribbons of panic occasionally billowed through her, like curtains of snow. She needed to get up, move. She showered, changed, and crept through the dark, cold kitchen, hoping to avoid waking Danny Chen again. She took the A train headed for Ozone Park, Queens.

She was her aunt and uncle's only child. After everything happened, they took her in. They did the best they could, gave her their last name, worked hard to make sure prying journalists and other opportunists never discovered where she'd gone, and most importantly, never made her talk about what happened, what she did or didn't remember. It was probably unhealthy to pretend none of it ever happened. But they did. And for Alistair, that's all she wanted. Then, and now.

Ozone Park was the perfect name for this stretch of Queens, an acrid mix of lively Catholic immigrants, desperate poverty, pungent car washes, clusters of TV satellites sprouting on roofs like electronic mushrooms, and miles of packed-tight row houses with stamp-sized patches of green space. It all soaked you in an acidic tang that lingered even years after leaving it behind. Alistair's aunt and uncle, Kath and Gus respectively, were the proud owners of one such row house, crammed between two identical row houses, one owned by the Liebermans, the other by an extended Armenian family. The only thing that made Kath and Gus prouder than owning their little patch of Queens was how they never complained about kids running through their yard or all the outdoor birthday parties. It made them feel like fine upstanding white liberals, all the not-complaining. They weren't "woke" in the strictest sense, but they'd never had a bad thing to say about anyone else, and they'd always pushed back at people who'd asked stupid questions about Alistair being multiracial, them being white-out white, and what had really happened to her real parents. When Alistair was older and started asking them about her ancestry, or her background, or her hair, they'd print out articles or borrow books from the library and leave them on her bed to find when she got home from school. Magazines about black hair, poetry collections about being brown, and children's books about how we're all beautiful, special, one-of-a-kind miracles. Their efforts felt well-intentioned, kind of embarrassing, and not at all useful.

They *never* talked about Alistair's parents. Alistair knew her mom grew up with Kath in New Jersey and she knew her father's father was from Antigua, her father's mother was from Japan, and her parents met at Aunt Kath's bachelorette party in Atlantic City. That was it. They were so determined to do the right thing and not say the wrong thing that they basically didn't say anything at all.

Alistair still had a key. She let herself in.

"Kath?" Alistair called out. *Aunt Kath* had been slowly phased out over the years since Alistair moved to the city. Kath was her aunt, her mother's sister, but it still felt like a formal holdover from a different time.

"Honey?" Kath peeked in from the kitchen pass-through, and screamed, her hands in the air like she was being arrested. "Gus is gonna be so mad he missed you!" Alistair was relieved to have missed her uncle. One concerned, huggy family member was enough. "He's on that bike tour in Vegas. Did I tell you about that?"

Kath wrapped her arms around Alistair. She was a little sweaty, stuffed into a tube of Lycra, proudly displaying every middle-aged curve. "I just finished a ride myself, sorry. You hungry?"

Alistair shook her head. "I got back late from an auction. I was on the train already . . . I hope it's okay."

"How long have I been harassing you to come out? Are you okay? You sick? You look flushed," Kath said, rubbing Alistair's cheek. Alistair had to grin and bear it.

"Tired. I might crash upstairs if that's okay," Alistair said.

"Awwwwww, of course. I'm happy anytime you're not sleeping above those mean old . . ." Kathy stopped herself. "I gotta shower and run, but I'll take a long lunch and pick you up?" Then she nodded, like Alistair had said yes. "Great!"

Kath was retired, officially, but still worked part-time doing bookkeeping for a small family-run grocery store down the block. She had too much energy to sit at home.

Alistair's old room was still her old room but now also had a half dozen bicycles hanging from the ceiling like mechanical slaughterhouse meat. Something her aunt and uncle had "taken up" in their middle years. More power to them. She dumped her bag on the bed and went right for the closet. It was packed to the door with plastic tubs full of everything from Alistair's childhood, post-return. She tore through the bins, tons of crap that she would've gotten rid of years ago. It seemed like Gus and Kath couldn't in good conscience throw out anything of hers. Like she'd lost enough already.

She found a handmade paper box in a back bin. The box was made from dozens and dozens of book pages, doubled and tripled, folded just so, until they formed a rigid structure. She'd made it herself as a young girl. Alistair sat on the end of the bed with it, her hand on the lid. After a reverent moment, she opened it. The pages held inside were covered with fantasy drawings, far-off magical lands . . . things and places inspired by the books she'd read as a child. Near the bottom of the box, every other page or so had a question, or assignment written at the top: *Write about the snow* or *Tell me about the books.* Prompts posed by the therapist Alistair saw when she came back. Dr. Bolden—a slight, sophisticated, gentle woman with deliberately oversized glasses. Another prompt: *Tell me about the fox.* The hallucinations of the dark, the cold, the fox—they'd been less hallucination back then and more ever-present, plaguing thought, which had haunted her first years back from the dark place.

Alistair had a vague recollection of how she felt being with Dr. Bolden. Warm, trusting, almost safe. Bolden had told Alistair about *her* family, her daughter specifically, who would make drawings for Alistair every once in a while. They talked a lot about the time she was gone, not the time before. Not her parents, or whatever friends she'd had, or teachers, or toys, or pets. She could barely remember that time anyway, by the time she was seeing Bolden. By fourteen, she was basically *Alistair AD.* Alistair after disappearance. And everyone was happy to leave her be when it came to what she'd lost, what she'd left behind.

Would it be weird for an adult to start seeing their childhood therapist again? Sounded perfectly New York to her. Alistair needed to know why she'd had this episode after all this time. Why now? In the paper box was a drawing she'd made of the bespectacled fox, on the doctor's old stationery, which included her office address and number.

Alistair's ancient, half-shattered cell phone wasn't much for making or receiving calls when it wasn't on Wi-Fi, so she waited until she heard Aunt Kath leave for the morning, then used the landline to dial the number. After a few rings, she was forwarded to voicemail. A gruff baritone woman spoke, her tone belying her scripted greeting.

"You've reached the offices of Sixth Avenue Psychiatric and partners. We are either on another line, or you're calling outside office hours. Please leave your name, number, reason for calling, and referring doctor, and we'll return your call when able. Thank you."

After the beep Alistair replied, "Hi, I was a patient of Doctor Bolden's when I was a kid. Deborah Bolden. I was hoping to get in contact with her. If you could have her call me back when she gets a chance." She gave her aunt and uncle's number. "My name's Alistair Mead."

How long had it been? Over ten years. Though Bolden was affiliated with a Manhattan practice, her office had been in Ozone Park, less than a mile from their house, and Alistair saw Dr. Bolden every week, twice a week, until she was about to start high school, until the fox had finally disappeared.

Alistair flopped onto her childhood bed and within minutes she was falling asleep, still not recovered from the house on the Hudson. She hated Ozone Park, but she had to admit that she felt a little safer under her aunt and uncle's roof, in her old bedroom, so she drifted away, watching the origami animals suspended above her bed. Made by a young Alistair out of book pages. They swayed in the dry breeze of the central heat.

৩৵৩

A dull thump-thump-thumping woke Alistair. Orange sky bled through the bedroom windows. It was either dusk or the following dawn. She could hear Kath downstairs in the kitchen, cooking. Kath must've found her in bed when she came home for lunch and left her sleeping. Another thump-thump-thump, on the wall behind the headboard. Alistair was still groggy, a little confused, but she quickly caught on, a smile on her face. She sat up and knocked back. Morse code.

How did you know
Smell fried chicken. Only when you here

Alistair's smile broadened. She replied—

Why are you home
Laundry. Meet me

Alistair found Zev Lieberman leaning on the fence in the front yard. He was much scruffier than she remembered. She'd seen him one or twice since she moved into the city, but she always expected to find the short, chubby boy with big glasses she remembered from childhood. Instead, Zev looked exactly how you'd expect someone to look who was getting their master's at Columbia and who was planning, if Alistair remembered right, to someday be a literature professor. Rumpled button-down tucked into jeans, sort of cool, sort of sensible oxfords, a sports jacket, and hair that had just had fingers quickly dragged through it.

His chubby cheeks were long gone, and although not tall, he had grown out of a good bit of his young awkwardness.

"What in God's name are you doing out here?" he asked loudly, over the din of street traffic.

"Don't let your mom hear you taking the lord's name in vain."

Zev's father was Jewish, but his mother was Catholic. He'd gone to a Catholic school and studied Hebrew after, and had been both confirmed and bar mitzvahed. His mother was a warm beast of woman, aggressive and aggressively affectionate. Zev's father had always seemed a little distant, but kind, and more than a little sad. Alistair remembered a story Zev told her about his parents' wedding and why his dad was such a mope. Zev's dad had been an icon of cultural Judaism, loved everything about being a Jew, and had fought tooth and nail to have a traditional Jewish wedding. The only thing he'd loved nearly as much as being a Jew was long-distance running. When he smashed the glass at the end of the ceremony he'd fought so hard for, a piece of glass cut through the sole of his shoe, severing something, and ending his two loves all at once. He felt betrayed and lost and eventually let his son slide more and more into Catholicism, only putting up a final fight to have Zev confirmed as a man at thirteen. Or that's how his father told it. But Zev seemed to have emerged from the dissonance of his upbringing fairly unscathed.

"How've you been?" he asked as she approached, leaning beside him against the fence. She could feel his warmth and noticed a bead of sweat on his forehead even though it was sixty degrees outside.

"Solid. You?"

"Same."

"Well that was some catch-up," she said

"I have a few days off. I can't get away without a visit when they know I'm not in class. Mom would guilt Dad, Dad would guilt me. You?"

"Just visiting," Alistair replied.

"Just popping by the OP for the fun of it. Sounds *totally* like you."

That familiar energy returning. They had a "pick-up-where-we-left-off" friendship. It was close, intimate.

"You still working for that book guy?"

Alistair shook her head. "On my own now. It's easier."

"Sure," he replied. It was just a word, but it felt like a jab. *Sure, it's easier to be alone for someone like you.*

A quiet moment. He wiped away the bead of sweat. He seemed nervous.

Aunt Kath poked her head out of the front door.

"Zev! Dinner's ready if you two are hungry!"

Zev and Alistair turned to each other, Zev finally shrugging, said, "I'm always hungry."

Zen and Alistair gorged themselves on chicken, mashed potatoes, and a green bean casserole that had pretty much appeared out of thin air. Aunt Kath sat across from them, glowing, both because of how much they were eating and because of the bottle of rosé she'd already killed.

"How's school?" she said a little too loudly.

Alistair and Zev looked at each other before realizing what she meant.

"Me! Oh, good!" Zev answered, covering his half-full mouth with his hand. He quickly finished the bite and continued, "I got my master's in Philosophy last year and now I'm pursuing my PhD. I plan on teaching."

Kath smiled and shook her head. Bemused. "Wow," she replied in a long, buzzed drawl.

Zev looked to Alistair and tried to hide a smile.

"Teaching what?" Kath asked.

"Comparative Literature, basically." Zev answered.

"Is that because of—um—" Kath pointed at Alistair. Alistair's name seemed to escape her.

"Me?" Alistair asked, incredulous.

Aunt Kath nodded without taking her eyes off Zev. "I don't remember you being such a reader when you were a little boy. I thought maybe you picked that up because of—"

"Alistair?" Zev asked. "Um . . . no. I read. I like . . . books."

Alistair bowed her head, laughing through a too-big bite of potatoes.

"Now you're both making fun of me!"

"We're not!" Alistair answered with a laugh. "One question . . . what's my name again?"

Kath's smile faded, stung. She stood. "I have a pie if you little monsters are interested. Blueberry." She got up and disappeared into the kitchen.

"She's smashed," Alistair whispered, nodding in Kath's direction.

"I'm gonna explode," Zev answered.

"Oh, you're staying for pie now."

"Did you ever find those books?" Zev asked.

Alistair was confused by the question at first, then realized . . .

Right. She'd told him about the books. Parts of them. As a kid. It wasn't just Bolden who knew about *the briar books* before they mostly faded away. Lehman and Zev.

"No," she replied as the home phone rang with a loud rattle.

Kath picked up the call in the kitchen. A moment later: "Hon? It's for you!"

Bolden.

Alistair hurried into the kitchen. Kath shrugged her shoulders, not knowing who was on the other end. Alistair took the receiver.

"Hello?"

"Alistair Mead?" said the woman's voice on the phone.

"Yes?"

"Deborah Bolden hasn't worked for this practice in years, ma'am."

Alistair pushed. "Do you know if she's still practicing in the city?"

The assistant replied, "She is no longer with *this practice.*"

Alistair didn't like the woman's tone. "And you have zero forwarding information?"

"She disappeared nearly a decade ago, ma'am. I don't know *what* she's been up to."

"Disappeared?" Alistair asked, the word sinking into her stomach.

"I mean . . . She left. We never heard from her again with forwarding information or anything else. That's all I know. You wanna know anything else, you're gonna have to google her."

Alistair sleepwalked through blueberry pie, good nights, goodbyes, and the train ride back to Manhattan. She searched for Bolden online and just like the woman on the phone had said, she'd vanished a decade ago. No record of her working anywhere, living anywhere. No record at all. *Disappeared.*

Alistair made it back before Danny Chen locked the front door and shuffled past the kitchen crew. She took the stairs to her room and on the top step sat a box. Small, and made from book pages. Just like the ones she used to make.

She knelt down, picked it up, and opened it.

Inside, was the little blue girl with the bow and arrow from the house on the Hudson. It might as well have been a severed head, given the rush of fear and revulsion that exploded in Alistair's gut. Not a vision. Not a waking nightmare. Real, and in her hands. And there was a message written inside the lid of the box.

Follow me.

Chapter Seven

ollow me.

F   Ben had waited for the dark blue of impending sunrise to finally, thankfully, start peeking over the hills behind his property before he burst from the front door of the cabin. He was carrying one of the totemic boxes of his old life in his arms, with his ruck sack piled on top. He was bundled up, but shaking, his face ashen. He hurried across the dark yard, to his pickup, quickly hitting the lock button on the door once he was inside. He gunned the cold engine, launching the truck backward down the driveway with an aching growl.

It was quiet in town. Like someone turned off the world for the night. He didn't like it. Not now. Not after these pages. He wanted people, light. He pulled into the parking lot behind the closed cafe and parked. He fired up his chilly laptop, connected to the cafe's Wi-Fi, and searched for "Alistair Mead missing" and several variations. Nothing. She wasn't real, according to the internet, at least. Whoever was sending him the pages took the time to make this all up. It couldn't be Frank. He knew that. Frank was dead, so it couldn't be Frank sending him pages again. Ben kept repeating that reassurance in his head, but the words never made it to his shaking hands. It wasn't Frank. Ben knew better than anyone that it couldn't be Frank—the man who had destroyed his old life. *But it had to be about the book*, Ben thought. The book he wrote. Someone was coming back to torment him all over again.

Ben closed the laptop and stashed it on the dashboard. He pulled the collar of his coat up around his neck, burrowing in. He glanced over at the box in the passenger seat, which had the word *Research* scrawled across its side in blue marker. *Book Research*. Ben's debut—and only—novel, *All the Stories Left Behind*, was a series of fictionalized, often fantastical, musings about what might have happened to *actual* missing people. Joining supernatural circuses, seeking mythological objects, stealing away to magical otherworlds . . . Some people loved it. Some people thought Ben was cashing in on the pain of the real people left behind, hurting the nonfictional who had already lost so much, even though he'd gone to great lengths, both literary and legal, to hide who he was really writing about. It had ended up being mildly, and unintentionally, controversial.

Ben had always had a vivid, rambling, possibility-conjuring imagination. It was an asset and a curse. Imagining all the ways things could be also allowed him to imagine all the ways things could go *wrong*. His imagination frequently left him overwhelmed at best, and terrified at worst. But the micro-controversy of his imaginings had kept the book aloft in the cultural eye. Bloggers and half-wit social media "journalists" had gone digging, harassing those "left behind" all over again, probing for answers, trying to find new life in old mysteries, wanting to hear what they thought of Ben's book, hoping they'd break down on their middling podcasts and vlogs—it was a disaster. But then the packages started arriving, first in the mail of his publisher, and then to his home address after an assistant mistakenly gave it out, gruesome crime scene photos, heart-wrenching testimonies of last-known whereabouts, and crazed inverted stories about all the horrible things that could've happened to the people in his book.

Then someone from a midsize paper reviewed the book and wrote a companion piece about its surrounding controversy. And while the review was by all accounts positive and sent his book semi-skyrocketing sales-wise, Ben fixated on one passage from the review, a line he'd read so many times he'd memorized it—*While Kriminger is a keen talent and reveals wells of still-untapped promise as an emerging contemporary voice, one wonders if his sacrifice of truth for fantasy will follow him in future works. Nay, haunt him. After all, what is a writer without some responsibility to the truth?*

If you wanted to cut to the core of Benjamin Kriminger, that phrase, *his sacrifice of truth for fantasy* was the easiest way in. If you wanted to tear open every old wound from his childhood and send him to drink in a corner as an adult, well done. Ben's father was a man who believed in nothing if not that a rigid, unrelenting spine of truth should be the thing holding up every man because fantasy and make-believe and pretending the world wasn't the way it was, was weak, soft, disgusting. The word *queer* was batted around more than a few times to describe anyone prone to flights of fancy, including Ben. His father's hostile pursuit of unflinching, cold, hard truth included drunken threats of violence countered with days of aggressive, neglectful silence. His father believed children, boys in particular, were soft, unfinished, needing to be toughened up and calloused over to live in the world, to know truth and embrace it. He believed you could scream the truth into your kid until that's all there was inside, because that's what had been done to him. And all fantasy, all naive wonder and recklessness lay where he left it, in tears on the floor.

After the positive but devastating review, the weird, threatening packages escalated, spurred by Ben's increasing success, in spite of his personal crisis. He was a broken rocket, spiraling skyward as he burst into pieces. The book eventually faded from view and favor, like most books do. The packages stopped, and Ben was left wondering what the hell had happened.

Cor kept him sane even as her life was sucked into the

whirlwind. They stuck together through all of it, until Frank finally broke the back on Ben's old life. Frank was a neurologist from Maryland. A family man, well-off, happy, seemingly sane. But Frank had become obsessed with two things: the strange conspiracy theory known online as the "Mandela Effect"—that there was an alternate history of the world only a few remembered—and Ben's book. And in Frank's mind, they were intertwined. He believed, per rambling notes and thousands of blog posts, and eventually late-night phone calls and shouting into Ben and Cor's apartment window, that the people who vanished in Ben's book had really slipped through to the alternate history. Frank believed Ben either knew the truth and was signaling others who also believed in his insane cause, or later—when Ben had a restraining order placed on Frank—that Ben was trying to cover up the truth, was part of some secret cult, and wanted to make everyone think Frank was crazy. But everyone already thought Frank was crazy. He'd been fired from the hospital he'd worked at for three decades, his wife left him, his adult children abandoned him. In the end, he had nothing but Ben and the book.

And then Ben came home one night and found Cor alone with Frank in their apartment. Frank had a hunting knife in his lap and Cor's right arm was burbling blood, barely wrapped in a smelly T-shirt Ben had left on the couch when he'd bolted out of the apartment to catch a movie just hours before. Ben would later learn that Cor had come home alone and found Frank in the apartment, and when she tried to run, he'd impaled her hand against the living room wall. She fought him in the midst of the pain, and when he pulled the knife out to threaten her with it, he ended up running the blade halfway up her arm. When Ben arrived, Frank demanded the truth, or he'd hurt Cor even more. Kill her. Because she, and all of this, was just a lie. Only those who saw the truth were real. And Frank believed Ben was going to show him the truth about the world.

Ben gripped the cold steering wheel of his pickup and clenched his eyes shut against the memory. His brain wouldn't let him follow that thread to its conclusion, where everything else that happened that night waited. Instead, Ben remembered the initial wave of pain he'd felt upon opening the door, how guilty he'd felt for leaving, even though no one could've anticipated this, and how shocked he felt at the sight of Cor's blood. All over the sofa they'd spent months choosing, on the floor he'd been meaning to wax. Sprayed across the coffee table, covering the book she'd been half reading next to him while he binge-watched something on his laptop the night before.

Thinking about it again, now, re-created the same flood of confusion, anger, and fear. Why would someone do this? *Who was sending the Alistair pages, and why?* Well, Ben knew why, or at least thought he knew. And the contents of the box across the bench seat from him would answer him definitively.

Ben wished he'd burned this box first.

He steadied himself, then reached over, opening the box like he was carefully prying open a bear trap. Reams and reams of loose-leaf paper, battered notebooks, and half-filled hardcover journals that every writer collects on birthdays and Christmas. Somewhere in those notes was information about Dr. Bolden, the therapist who, according to the pages, had cared for Alistair as a young girl. He scoured the pages, scattering them across the cabin of his truck. Finally, he found what he was looking for scribbled at the bottom of the page of contact information: a list of therapists volunteering for a nonprofit that helped children who'd experienced trauma to readjust to life. At the bottom he found *Dr. Deborah Bolden* and a phone number. And next to the name were two words that sent fresh glacial rivers down his spine: *The Six.*

The Santa Colette Six.

Alistair's story was like The Six, and Doctor Bolden was a thread tying them together. Ben had first heard of Bolden because she'd crossed the country to treat the Santa Colette Six, a group of teenagers who, in the early 2000s, had disappeared from their sleepy little town in Northern California, returning a year later with no discernible memories of what had happened to them.

It was all coming together in Ben's mind. Someone was taunting him, teasing him. Alistair's fictional story was a parallel of The Six, but what made it all the more terrifying was the fact that, despite all of his research into The Six and trying to track them down—the majority had taken on assumed names and all but disappeared from society—in the end, Ben had decided to not include them in the book. It was obvious that they desperately wanted to leave that part of their lives behind, and because of the specifics, and number of them, there'd be no way to hide who he was writing about. So whoever sent these chapters was proving they knew more about the book he had written, and what he'd left unwritten, than anyone else in the public.

What was the point and where was it leading? Why? Why now? Ben's cold comfort was that the pages had been mailed to his and Cor's old address. The writer didn't know where Ben was, and they couldn't know where Cor was. The thought of her alone there in the city, unaware of all this starting again, made him ill. He knew at some point he'd have to tell her, but right now he imagined her warm and safe in bed, with Volley sleeping under the covers at her feet. She was safe in that moment and he couldn't possibly shatter her life all over again, not unless he had to, not until he knew more.

He wanted to kick the box out of the cab, and all the paper with it. He wanted to go back to the cabin and hide. But the cabin felt unsafe now. He didn't want to admit he was scared, but he was. He was opening the hardware store in a few hours, so he tucked his hands under his arms and curled up on the bench seat of the pickup. Nowhere felt like home. Nowhere felt safe. He closed his eyes, beating himself up for feeling, even for a flicker, that anything would ever be right again.

Ben had never been more grateful to be a part-time stock boy at Crystal Ridge Hardware. He opened the store, clocked in, made a pot of coffee for him and Stevie, and busied himself, stocking and sweeping and pretending everything was okay. But he couldn't keep it up. He kept eyeing the phone on the wall behind the counter in the old living room. He wasn't sure why, but he wanted to call Dr. Bolden. He wanted to ask—well he wasn't sure what he wanted to ask. He wanted to know if she'd been harassed. If she'd been in contact with The Six. If someone was sending her strange things in the mail. Stories about make-believe young women who'd been in her care. The writer of the pages wanted him to do something. Shit himself with fear, sure, but the fine details, mentioning Bolden, hinting at The Six, there had to be something there. Something else. And yes, he could wrap his shift, eat at the diner, go back to the cabin, and rinse and repeat, but that didn't mean this was going to stop. Ignoring Franks didn't make Franks go away. And if Ben didn't care, if Ben wasn't going to do anything about it, then why had he folded up the page with Bolden's number on it and put it in his back pocket?

Follow me.

It was near closing time. Stevie took a customer upstairs to plumbing, and Ben finally walked behind the counter and picked up the receiver. After a brief hesitation, he dialed Bolden's number.

A woman picked up.

"Sixth Avenue Psychiatric. How can I direct your call?" she asked.

Ben couldn't answer. It was the same tone of voice he'd imagined the woman on the other end of Alistair's conversation having.

"Hello?" the woman answered in the silence.

"Hi—Hi, I'm looking for Doctor Bolden. Deborah Bolden."

It was quiet on the other end.

"Doctor Bolden doesn't work with this practice anymore," the woman answered.

The synergy between the pages and the voice on the other end of the line was making Ben nauseated.

"Do you know where she's working now?" Ben stammered.

"No, I don't. She hasn't worked here in a decade, sir." the woman hissed. "Is there something going on I don't know about?"

"What do you mean?" he asked.

"You're the second person to call asking me the exact same thing."

"What? Why were *they* looking for Doctor Bolden?"

"I have no idea. She said she was her patient."

Ben's legs felt weak and wobbly. He put a hand on the counter.

"The person who called—what was her name?"

"That's confidential. I can't—"

"You said *was* her patient. She's not anymore. Please. What was her name?"

Quiet on the other end.

Ben couldn't believe the words leaving his mouth.

"Was it Alistair Mead?"

"I'm sorry, what is this about?"

"Was that her name?"

"It was."

Ben's knees buckled. He felt like the floor was falling out from under him, like he was on an old carnival ride that had just begun its first drop and he was wholly unprepared for how fast and dangerous it felt. Ben wanted to hang up, wanted to pretend he never called.

"Sir?"

The voice on the phone was muted, muffled, like his brain had decided to block it out.

"Hello? Sir?"

"Do you remember when you spoke with her?" he asked.

Quiet on the other end, and then—

"I would hope so. She just hung up."

PART II

Chapter Eight

Ilya stumbled through the woods with a bright and beaming smile on her face, and a single phrase running over and over in her mind: *The great silver bells have finally rung.* Today was Ilya's birthday. Her father had asked her if she would like to stay home that morning, given that so much had changed in the city over the past few months. He couldn't give her a party or sweets, but he offered to let her stay in bed and read, which she loved to do more than almost anything. But Ilya insisted on going. She wasn't sure how much longer she would have with her friends and she wanted to see them and spend as much time as she could with them before they were gone. She hadn't planned on mentioning that it was her birthday, but when Anya, the young woman who'd taken on the job of teaching the class after Mr. Dask was called away, learned Ilya was turning nine, she'd asked what Ilya would like to do if she could do anything. And Ilya, as always, wanted to play games in the forest with her friends.

Her favorite game was a combination of games that she and her six dearest friends had invented. It was a mixture of hide-and-seek and telephone that they called "Find and Tell," in which one person would search out their hiding friends with a phrase in their mind, and when they found someone, they would whisper that phrase in their ear and that child would go to find the next child, over and over, until all the children were found, and the phrase had been curiously, and often hilariously, changed beyond recognition. Everyone knew Peter purposely changed the phrase, and although that would normally irritate Ilya, it wouldn't today. Even freshly nine years old, Ilya had learned a difficult lesson in her short time of being alive—a lesson that children that age should never have to learn. She learned to hold precious everything in the moment, because it could all be taken away.

Ilya's older brother, Izaak, had helped her in learning that lesson. He knew it all too well. Although Ilya still had a handful of friends from her classroom, Izaak had lost everyone his age that he cared about. Now he was waiting for his letter—a letter that would order him to board the train that went to places only whispered about and rumored. Off to join some military organization that was working to make way for what everyone had begun to call "the transports." Ilya felt much older than her years, having seen the way her family's friends and neighbors had been treated in the city streets, how it all changed seemingly overnight. In little ways at first, like ordering her and her family, and all of her neighbors, to only ride on the last car of the local tram. The cars with broken benches, the ones that most needed repair. But everyone adjusted to the orders. So, they had to ride in the last car. They could still travel around town. They could visit the parks, and the grocer, and the theater. And then one morning the last broken cars of the tram were all gone, and they were no longer allowed to ride at all.

So, they adjusted. They walked.

Ilya didn't mind. She liked walking with her mother and father, her brother always walking ahead, his long legs covering more distance than even her father could. They walked and stopped to speak with friends who lived in other parts of town. Ilya overheard them talk about places they were no longer allowed. "Like walls were closing in," they said. Her father had squeezed her hand, knowing she was listening. He gave her a wink and shook his head a little. She knew it all was true, but he was telling her that it would be okay. They could take away their shops, their permission to wander the parks, but they couldn't take away their walks.

And then one morning the stars were delivered.

The stars her family and all the families like hers had to wear. To mark them. The stars gave unspoken permission for others to first whisper in their direction, then yell, then spit. Then block their way and turn them around, then force them back into their homes. Izaak refused to wear the star in the beginning. He was caught in the marketplace and beaten by boys that he used to play handball with. Word traveled of beatings and worse, people who didn't wear their stars would just never come home. So, Ilya's family wore the stars.

And that's how they took away their walks.

Ilya knew all of these changes happened over months, almost a year, but time seemed to move so quickly these days that, as far as she knew, it was as if it happened overnight. Mother and Father tried to stay cheery, but Ilya was sad, and also angry. At dinner two nights earlier, Father had asked about class, and Ilya started telling the story about an old woman, their neighbor, who'd fallen in the streets, and Ilya had seen people step on her, kick her aside. Like garbage. Izaak, his eye still a little swollen and bruised, interrupted her to tell them a story about how he and his last friend were trying to rescue a cat from an abandoned building—a scrawny little thing, that they wanted to feed and rescue. But Ilya knew it was a lie, because all of Izaak's friends had been transported away, knew he was lying to cheer up Mother and Father. Ilya ate her meager dinner in silence, then hid away in her dark, cold room, reading by candlelight, flipping the pages furiously, swearing she'd never talk to Izaak again. When you're nearly nine, two days feels like never again.

The forest was quiet. Ilya's pace slowed, she listened to the rustling green leaves above her, trying to hear the giggles of her classmates, the snapping of branches under little leather-soled feet, but it was quiet. Her thoughts had overtaken the phrase that Angelica had whispered to her, something about bells. What color had they been? Ilya stopped in place, unsure where to turn next. Suddenly she felt far from the city, lost. No sight nor sound of her friends, or Anya. Where had she wandered? A shudder ran through her. Fear. Just a drop of it, speeding through her body, into her feet. Urging her to run, or call out. She refused. Yes, she may have wandered too far into the woods, but she could find her way back.

The woods where she stood felt warm and wet. The fallen leaves under her feet had begun to rot and turn back to soil, leaving a dampening blanket everywhere she turned. Ilya took a deep breath to calm herself, and a current of warm air sprang up from somewhere deeper in the woods, billowing her dress hem and cooling the sweat on her forehead. It smelled like . . . Ilya couldn't place it. Familiar, but far away. Like a mostly forgotten memory. Ilya decided to walk against the gust. If she didn't stumble upon a friend or the edge of town within two hundred steps, she agreed to herself that she would call for help. She began to hum, the gust of wind tickling her neck. She calmed herself by talking quietly, working out a poem about her day in the woods that she would recite to her father. Her father always said that having a plan for tomorrow, even a small one, always made the bad things feel less bad.

"If you're walking in the wood one day and feel a wind from far away. . ." Ilya repeated the sentence a few times, pleased with herself. "Which carries scent of spice and dew, or memories . . ."

Ilya felt the odd sensation of the wind beginning to turn, first at her back, then moving to her left side, slowly around her. And then she noticed something out of the corner of her eye. She turned and found a worn path, lined by thin trees that bowed at the top, creating a tall and narrow tunnel, dappled by sun and the occasional falling leaf. Was that where she'd come from? Was that the pass back into town? The wind billowed from deeper down the path, cooling her. The scent on the air was stronger—a spice of some kind, like cinnamon or clove. Like the smell that used to escape the bakery near their apartment, before it was boarded up. The trees lining the path were unfamiliar to her, their thin trunks wrapped in pale yellow bark, and so tightly clustered together that they almost looked like walls. Ilya took a step toward the path, but then she remembered her friends, and the game. This wasn't the path home; this felt for some reason like a path that led farther away. As she thought that, it seemed as if the path began to retreat. The spot where the path began seemed so clear and immediate just moments before. Now it looked distant and indistinct. The line of trees was a bit more crooked than she first had thought and maybe just a trick of her eyes as she stepped a little to one side. The thin trees that looked like the walls of a wooded hall just a moment prior now faded into the surrounding forest, the sunbeams dispersed, the wind faded. The path fell away into nothing but woods. It was never there.

Ilya started as her friend Peter grabbed her shoulder, his chubby cheeks wet with sweat and flushed red.

"Can you see it?" Peter asked.

"The path?" Ilya replied.

"The partridge, there," Peter answered, pointing to the nearby underbrush.

"That's a root, Peter," Ilya sniped, not really upset with Peter, as much as she was upset with herself. Forgetting her fear now that she knew she wasn't alone, she was strangely upset that she'd somehow lost track of the path.

"I'm going back," Peter whispered. "What's the phrase?"

Ilya thought, trying to will the words back into her wandering mind. She figured it didn't really matter, because Peter would change it, make it something wholly juvenile and silly.

"A knothole that goes on for days," Ilya whispered into his ear, feeling the heat radiating off of his round head. And just like that, he was off, leaving Ilya alone in the woods again, where the path had been. The path that she had wondered, only moments before Peter found her, if only she could see.

She began to follow in the general direction Peter had taken, kicking the blanket of brown-black leaves, turning back every now and then to look where she thought she'd seen the path. She walked for a while, until she could see the steeple of a church in the far-off distance, breaking through the tops of the trees and knew she was close to town.

"If you're walking in the wood one day and feel a wind from far away, that carries scent of spice and dew, of memories you almost knew, then look around . . . for in your gaze . . . a knothole that goes on for days." Ilya smiled to herself at her nonsensical poem. But her smile faded as she felt the hem of her dress begin to rustle. The warm wind from her poem returned. She felt it slowly travel all around her until it finally settled behind her right arm. It felt like warm sun on a late winter day. She turned her head, just a little, and in the corner of her eye, the path was waiting for her again.

Ilya remembered nothing that happened after that. Only the cold wet leaves against her cheek, and a root sticking out from the ground against her back. And cold. And a feeling of hopelessness. Had she fallen? Her feet ached like she had walked for miles, but the pain in her side was relieved all at once as she was lifted off the ground into someone's arms. It was her father. Ilya opened her eyes and saw the panic in his; it was very dark now. Ilya could only remember that Peter had run off, she had followed, and she had glimpsed the path again, but never found it. Now, it was very late at night, and her father was afraid.

Her father carried her out of the woods whispering that everything was all right, and that she wasn't in trouble. She heard more footsteps behind them. She looked back and saw her mother, also in the woods, her best shoes soaked and muddy. She was weeping. Ilya whispered, "I'm so sorry, Mother." But her mother just looked away, hiding her face with a handkerchief.

"Where is Izaak?" Ilya asked with an aching whisper.

"He got his letter. He's been called to Terezín," Father explained.
Ilya's heart fell. She hadn't talked to him in two days.

"I will talk to him, tell him it will all be all right."

Ilya heard her mother choke back tears.

Her father whispered, through tears of his own, "My dearest, he's already gone."

Chapter Nine

Cor answered the door with a smile and an inquisitive tilt of her head.

"What took you so long?" she asked.

Ben didn't want to tell her it was because he looped around the block three times to make sure no one was following him. He knew in his heart he had to be overreacting, at least to some degree, but he wasn't willing to take any chances with Cor. As a matter of fact, that's why he'd come back to the city.

"You're gonna laugh, but I got lost," he lied.

Ben had missed his thirtieth birthday because of everything that happened. Cor had emailed a few days prior, hoping he'd come down for a quiet thirty-first as friends. Ben agreed, but also knew he'd have to tell her about the chapters first. He wanted to tell her before they walked to dinner because, well, he wasn't sure how she was going to react. Dinner might be canceled.

The speedy tip-tap of dog claws came sounding down the hallway and Volley the super mutt charged straight for Ben, nearly knocking him off his feet. Volley already had his unfortunate name when Ben rescued him. But now Ben liked the name. Cor and Ben had joked about it after the breakup—that Volley would bounce back and forth between their places and keep them together. Not *together* together, but friends. Who had history, connections, and a drooling dog that was too big for 95 percent of New York City apartments.

Cor closed the door behind Ben. She'd wasted no time getting her new apartment set up. It was smaller than their old place. He knew Cor could afford something bigger. She was the trusted manager for a wealthy restauranteur's multiple properties, but a small, simple apartment was exactly what she wanted, and probably needed. No extra rooms, no dark corners, and just enough space for her and her pup. Ben noticed two shiny-new dead bolts drilled into the front door. Another byproduct of the last couple years.

Volley quickly settled down. He was a fat red log, after all, and mainly wanted to sleep near, or on, one of his owners, preferably Cor. Ben and Cor plopped down on the couch, and Volley scrambled up between them, curled into a ball, and was asleep in two minutes flat. Volley was the reason they got together in the first place. They'd gone on two or three pretty great dates, neither interested in nailing it down quite yet, but then they'd gone for a walk, and Volley stopped to smell something, and Ben didn't notice immediately. In his effort to not step on the dumb dog, Ben overstepped, twisted, went face-first off of the curb and broke his leg and foot. His apartment at the time was a fourth-floor walk-up, and Cor . . . well, Cor had an elevator. Although Ben protested, Cor insisted he stay in her guest room, at least for a few days, until he was used to the leg brace and crutches. It was so out of the ordinary and weird, or it should've been, but their flickering chemistry began to grow from that moment on. He couldn't deny her care, she was able to dote on someone, and all the lies they put on the dating app, about wanting to explore the world, the city, every restaurant, pursue hobbies, etc., were all wiped away. They really just wanted to hang out on the couch, eat really awesome take-out, read, watch TV, make out, and more. Aside from the broken bones, it was perfect.

"What's going on?" Cor asked, nudging his shoulder, Volley snoring between them on the couch.

Ben wasn't hiding it well. He wanted to get it out of the way, before the guilt over how kind she was being killed him. Ben took a deep breath, sighed, and finally said it: "I've been getting letters again."

He knew that she knew what he meant immediately.

"Okay." She took a silent moment to process. "Are they bad?"

He knew that she knew they were. Or else he wouldn't be telling her about them. But she was in about as much denial as he had been up until a few days ago.

"They're not gruesome like some of the other ones. But . . . they're not good. They're referencing stuff that I researched . . . but didn't put in the book."

"The Santa Colette kids."

Ben nodded. Cor had this thing—it wasn't even a thing; it was just her. She would remember little things you mentioned, things you liked, things you didn't, dreams you had, your favorite cereal when you were eight, and when she casually mentioned them later, it wasn't to prove how well she knew you, to engender favor, it was because she just liked you and thought about you. It made Ben sick to his stomach now. He wished they were strangers and he wasn't hurting her all over again.

"How?" she asked.

Ben shrugged. "I have no idea. They could've gotten something from the publisher, or maybe my notes—"

"How would—" she asked before realizing she already knew the answer, "You think there might've been another break-in, at the old place? One we didn't know about?"

Ben didn't have to answer.

"Jesus Christ." She exhaled and stood, alarming Volley. "How long? How long has this been going on?"

"Not long."

She didn't need to know the details, the seemingly prophetic content, the call to the psychiatry office. It was already too much without the apparently supernatural that Ben hadn't figured out yet. Cor went to the other side of the room and grabbed a cardigan from a wall hook beside the front door, shrugging it on. He didn't know if she was leaving or just trying to comfort herself. He'd understand either way.

"So, when I came up to the cabin, you already knew."

"I thought it was a mistake at first. They started off normal, or kind of normal. I wasn't sure what they were, if they were from my editor, or—"

"Don't keep lying to me, please."

"I didn't want to scare you. That's the truth. I didn't want you to be scared again. I called Detective Strathern, but the letters were forwarded from the old address, so she didn't think it was anything new. She told me to call if . . . they had our current address. I mean, addresses."

Cor walked to the other end of the living room, her back to him. She ran her fingers through her hair.

"I haven't stopped being scared. Have you?"

Ben looked out the window. He had always been the one to reassure her, tell her everything was going to be okay, even if it wasn't. That he wasn't worried, even if he was. It might not have been the right thing to do, but he did it. But now . . . what good was it?

"I thought about leaving the city. Just quitting and starting over. I should have."

She was starting to freak out.

"It's gonna be okay." He couldn't help it. Habit.

"Is it?" she asked, turning to him, dark clouds in her expression. "How can it be okay when it seems like it's *never* going to end? You never should've written that book."

Ben grimaced, trying to keep his temper in check, he knew how she felt, how fragile her sense of safety was right now. She had encouraged him to write the book. He knew it. She knew it.

"There's no way either one of us could have known what would happen. This is an insane situation. I mean, don't mistakes usually feel like mistakes? Like, you know you're gonna do a crazy thing and you do it anyway hoping it will work out. *This* wasn't that. This was . . . just a book. Just a bunch of stupid stories I made up."

They soaked in the silence. Volley was nervous and tried to lick Ben's face. He gently pushed the dog away as something occurred to him.

"What do you mean 'stop lying' to you?" Ben asked. Cor wouldn't look at him.

"What does that mean?"

She finally answered, pacing, "I keep telling myself that book is what broke us up, but you keep secrets, and you keeping lying so you can keep them."

"What are you talking about? You know everything—"

She finally turned and looked him in the eye.

"Yeah? I don't know about your childhood. Your dad. Why you left."

"He was a dick. He was a dick, and I left as soon as I could." That was the truth, but she was also right. Not that he had some specific secret he was keeping from her about his childhood, but that he wanted to hide all of it, the shame, and the doubts and fears he carried with him still because of his father.

"I don't know what happened with Frank."

Ben felt dizzy. He knew it would be bad, but not this bad.

"I told you already."

"Not everything. Not about that night. I know when you lie, Ben. When you say you're writing again. When you say you're okay. When you say you have money. I just don't know why you're lying about that night, and your lies keep pushing me further and further away from you. I was there. It happened to me too."

She might have found a new apartment, but she was still back there, in Chelsea, in the old place, that night. Still cowering in the bathroom. Still bleeding.

He couldn't tell her how he felt the night it all came to a head—the violence that had flooded through him. The dark, sick feeling demanding he take action. After seeing what that man had done to Cor, Ben had wanted to crush his head, smash his teeth out of his thin mouth. He'd harassed them for months and now he'd hurt her, and Ben couldn't put all that blood back in. He wanted to destroy this man. In that moment, Ben was his father. Blind and possessed by violence. He'd never felt more lost, more out of control, or more powerful.

◈

Ben stumbled out of Cor's building like he'd barely survived a bombing. He stood on the corner and let people bump and brush against him for a couple minutes. His parked truck was racking up half-hour charges, but there was no way he could drive back upstate right now. He sucked in a chestful of city air, clogged with exhaust and food and life and the atoms of himself he had left behind. He let it out in a white puff of fog. He didn't know what to do, where to go. He just started walking. All he wanted to do was tend to her, hold her, fix it, but he was the thing bringing her pain. There was nothing he could do, so he walked. He was fifteen blocks away from her apartment, fifteen blocks closer to nowhere, when something dawned on him.

The train dumped him off in the Lower East Side. Alistair Mead. There was absolutely no guarantee that she was a real human being. Whoever called the clinic could've said they were anybody, and the fact that they called just before Ben called *could've* been some one-in-a-million coincidence. Even the most astounding of coincidences was easier to swallow than prophetic, literary time travel.

There was nothing concrete in the pages about *where* exactly Alistair lived. He'd now read the two chapters several times, but there *were* clues to follow—to verify or disprove. Sergio at the bodega near the Chinese restaurant. Danny Chen, grandson of the owners of the Chinese restaurant, although the Lower East Side was just east of Chinatown and *Chen* was a common surname. Kath and Gus Mead didn't appear in any online searches, but that wasn't entirely surprising. They were older, retired, and as the pages mentioned, careful of protecting Alistair. There *was* one concrete clue, however. *"She sat in a cold, dusty corner park as the sun crept over the East River about three long blocks that way."* The park where Alistair found the Pry obituary.

The Lower East Side was barely fifteen blocks long, which meant that a quick map search would narrow down the possible "corner parks" to two contenders: Dora Cohen Memorial Park and the Captain Jacob Joseph Playground. This is how he would spend his thirty-first birthday, distracting himself from the fight with Cor, from the inevitability of having to return to that cold, dark cabin, from a life still crumbling, two years after the explosion.

It was dark now. Dora Cohen Memorial Park was nothing more than a concrete pad in a fenced-off construction zone, and Ben had dressed for dinner, not fighting against the bracing fall wind coming off the East River. It didn't matter; the playground was only four blocks away and it kept him from having to go back to Crystal Ridge. He passed Seward Park, which was *technically* a corner park, but only because it ran the length of the block. It didn't feel like Alistair's park, although there *was* a library anchoring one end. Captain Joseph's Playground definitely fit the bill. It was closed after dusk, but Ben could imagine Alistair there, in her favorite coat, swigging chocolate milk, and combing through the morning paper.

At this point, he could wander the surrounding neighborhood, and the dozen Chinese restaurants, pop into every deli and ask for Sergio, but the wind had been taken out of his sails. He sat on a bench across from the park. Was this what the writer wanted him to do or was this just a bunch of random nonsense that he had managed to organize into the illusion of truth? Part of him hoped someone would be there in the park, waiting for him. Just to know. He couldn't handle any more uncertainty. Even if it was another lunatic. Or fictional Alistair Mead: brown skin, brown eyes, wayward hair, and regrettable bangs. Standing there waiting like . . . wonder. Distraction. Fantasy. But also truth. She was a sphinx, but she also knew the answer to the riddle. And so there he was, freezing, sitting outside a Lower East Side playground, waiting for the impossible, dark-fantasy Daisy Buchanan to show.

Like a schmuck.

He wanted to go back to Cor. Tell her everything. Ask to stay. He knew they were done, but he couldn't go back home. That cabin was supposed to be theirs. Sometimes the only thing that put him to sleep at night was imagining getting to fall asleep there with her. The broken roof and the broken fireplace were all funny and manageable, and adding to a life's worth of memories, if only she were in bed with him at night. Her back against him, or his against her. He wasn't opposed to being little spoon. But there, in the whirlpool of failure, disappointment, trash-binned dreams, and screwed relationships was Alistair Mead.

Ben sat on the bench for a while, and then he took the train back to his truck. He waited outside Cor's apartment until the living room light turned off, then he headed back to hell.

What was the point of all this? Why send three non-sequential chapters? And then why stop? What was he supposed to do with this information? Did it even matter anymore? It was clear that whoever sent them didn't know where they lived now.

Ben was wiped mentally and physically by the end of the drive back upstate. He began to pull up the long driveway, back to the cabin, then slammed his foot onto the brake pedal, the back of his pickup fishtailing before coming to a stop. The headlights lit up the front of his run-down little cabin, and the white envelope leaning against the front door. Ben put the truck in park and stepped out, the hairs on his neck tingling, like someone was standing behind him. He walked up to the porch, the headlights casting a long, grotesque shadow puppet version of him on the front wall of the cabin. He knelt and picked up the envelope. It was letter-sized, small. He slid his finger under the flap and tore it open. Inside, *Chapter Ten*. He'd received chapters two, four, six, and now ten. What had happened to the rest of the chapters? What events were happening in all the other pages, the dark corners that Ben didn't know about? Why these and not the others? He suddenly felt like a thousand pairs of glittering, hungry eyes were out in the dark woods, watching him, waiting to see how he'd react to what was inside. Relishing his fear.

But it wasn't what was inside that sent jags of electric chill through his body. It was the envelope. There was no postage, no postmark, no address.

It just said: *For Ben*.

Chapter Ten

old fall rain hammered the city, purging what little warmth was left from summer.

It had been almost two weeks since the house on the Hudson, the hospital, and Ozone Park, but Alistair was still raw and foggy. Her hands still occasionally shook, residual rattling from her episode, and her brain was clouded and opaque, like a thought cataract. She remembered Aunt Kath being prone to occasional migraines, and Kath had always said the worst was the migraine itself, but what followed could be almost as bad—days and days of foggy, zombified confusion from having your brain explode. Alistair could relate. She'd almost forgotten over the years how these episodes always took it out of her, but it had been so long, she'd underestimated their power. Forgotten their cost.

The last time she'd lost herself completely was when she was twelve, in a library bike shed in Queens. Although there had been blips of darkness since her treatment with Bolden ended, flickers of the past resurfacing, she had been able to rely on her coping methods, her mantra, and her leather-bound walls to armor her in adulthood. She didn't want to be in the world right now. She wanted to be alone in her room. She wanted to patch her cracked walls with old pages, and hide herself from *the briar books*. But she couldn't, because sitting on her window ledge was the paper box, and inside, the little blue girl with the bow and arrow.

She couldn't bring herself to open it again for fear of triggering another descent into darkness. Over the past few days, she'd even imagined that what she saw inside, the girl and the message, had been another lingering, residual effect. But the box was there. The box hadn't disappeared, and neither, Alistair feared, had its contents.

Who had left it at her door? How had they found it and brought it here? Ed? Maybe they'd given it to him when he picked her up? No. He wouldn't have left it on her doorstep with a cryptic message. Maybe she'd dropped it when she came home, and Danny Chen found it? Left it for her because he didn't want to have to talk to her? But what about the message? What about the box? And if the figure *was* real, and was still inside the box . . . how had she found it in the first place? How had she been drawn to it in that empty closet in a far corner of that sprawling house?

Two days prior, Alistair slid a stack of books against the box so she couldn't see it from her bed and hoped object permanence would just cease to function at some point. It was all too much to manage, and Alistair felt that the longer she dwelled on the questions, the deeper she sank into the dark place she was trying to climb out from. Hell, the most likely culprit was *her*. She was in an absolute daze when she first came home. She might have found the toy in her bag or coat, made the box herself when she was lost in all those memories . . .

No one remembered the books but her. True, but now she had proof they existed. That's why she couldn't bring herself to get rid of the box. She knew the books were real, and always had been, despite no one else remembering. But her memory of them had faded over time, like most childhood memories do. There were highlights, blips of memory, and then long stretches of nothing. All the moments that weren't tended and occasionally replayed got lost as she grew older. They were smoothed over, and only the knotholes of revisited moments remained.

A knothole that goes on for days.

The strange phrase flickered in Alistair's mind, something bubbling up from the dark. She couldn't stay in her room and brood over the box; it was too dangerous. Alistair mumbled her mantra as she dressed and forced herself out of her room and into the world. Namely, to her favorite branch of the New York Public Library, Seward Park, which was bright, light, and as long as she avoided the children's section on the second floor, felt generally safe. She still needed income, and her phone was becoming less and less reliable since she, and it, fell upstate, so she needed alternative internet access to find her next gig. The small roll of cash Aunt Kath had "accidentally" left by Alistair's bag would take care of maybe three days' worth of subway rides (and the replenishment of her emergency train fund), but she had to use the library's public computers to check the paper and her email, and hope there was a job or a tip waiting.

There was an email from Ed, checking in on her. "Let me know you're okay." In one week, she'd had more contact with her old boss than in the past two years. Hell, they didn't talk this much when she *worked for him*. Also, an email from Zev, who'd gotten her address from Kath, the meddler. Just one line. "It was inexplicably great to see you." It made Alistair smile, despite herself. It *was* great to see him.

An obituary led her out into the rain and uptown to a wealthy hoarder's condo in the east 80s. Alistair performed her usual schtick to get in early, packing away a set of books that would keep her alive for the next month. She was in and out in an hour. Reluctant to go back home, she stopped at a Parisian-themed cafe on Third

Avenue, all art nouveau framed mirrors, cracked white floor tiles, and rickety little bistro chairs. She warmed her still-shaking hands on a chipped cup of coffee and told the server she was meeting someone who had been held up in the rain and wondered if they could bring bread and butter while she waited, hoping it wouldn't end up on her bill.

It was inexplicably great to see you.

Zev's email kept popping up in her mind, a welcome reprieve. For a moment, back in Ozone Park, Alistair had looked over at Zev. Kath was boiling water for instant decaf coffee after dessert, and Alistair watched Zev, a lock of his hair slipping onto his forehead as he looked down to scoop up the last piece of pie. He brushed the hair back again. She imagined, for a moment, putting her hand on his hand, having him look at her. *And then what?* Telling him what happened at the house on the Hudson? Telling him about her hallucinations? The thought snapped her back to reality as Kath walked in with two weak and watery cups of coffee. Alistair knew she was just feeling vulnerable, fractured. She wanted someone to see what she was feeling, what she was fearing. Understand her. But there was a part of Alistair that no one could understand. Or more, a part that no one could understand was missing. The harbinger fox, the blackouts, whatever. But below all that was a hole left behind, like someone had dug out a soft bit in a piece of fruit. Part of her was somewhere else. Maybe still waiting wherever she'd gone. Whatever had happened, it wasn't as simple as repressed memory. She'd gone through that therapy with Bolden. As far as anyone knew, there was nothing there to remember. Maybe whatever had happened to her while she was gone was just plainly so heinous she would never remember. Maybe she'd been abused or tortured. Maybe someone beat the memory out of her. Maybe. But Alistair didn't really believe that. The truth was, all that was left down there, below the fox and the black, was the feeling. How it felt to be cored out. Hollow. And the loss, the *need* for whatever had been taken away. She didn't know what she lost, but every atom of her body, in the rare moments she allowed it, ached for what was missing. The missing thing that would make her whole. Alistair would sometimes lie in bed while waiting to drift off to sleep and imagine life as a different version of herself. Alice. Or maybe *Alis*. A girl who could touch and feel and connect, who never had her core ripped out, or had, but somehow learned to fill the black hole with light.

Having overstayed her welcome in the cafe, Alistair was now waiting out the chilly downpour under the sidewalk awning, the popped collar of her coat pulled up around her neck, when her phone rang. She must have still been connected to the Wi-Fi inside. An unlisted number. *Zev?* She answered.

"Hello?"

"Alistair?"

It was an older woman's voice.

Alistair's first assumption was that someone from the hoarder's condo had seen through her lie.

"Yeah, who is this?"

"Did you find the gift I left you?"

"I'm sorry?"

It was quiet on the other end, and then—

"The gift. The little blue girl in the box. Proof that you were right all along."

Alistair felt her knees go weak. She had to brace herself to keep from crumpling.

"Who is this?"

"You used to buy dime novels from the bookstore down the street from my office while you waited for our sessions. You'd tear out the pages and make animals and people, flowers, and boxes. Little paper boxes made of books."

Alistair huddled in the corner under the awning, straining to hear. "Doctor Bolden?"

"We made the boxes part of your treatment, remember, and you made that one for me because I was so taken with them. I kept it all this time. It was special to me—"

Alistair was overwhelmed by the sound of Bolden's calm, caring voice, her lip trembling, breath stuttering as she tried to keep from crying on the street corner.

"You must have so many questions. How did I know you were looking for me? How did I find the figurine? But most pressing, what is really happening to you, and why are you seeing the fox again."

"How? How do you—"

"I can explain all of it, Alistair, when we meet. Treating you, and the others like you, led me to the edge of a path, and when I finally conjured up the courage to walk it, I found the truth waiting at the end. The truth about you, the books, everything. I know why your episodes have returned. I know what your visions mean. I think I know what you lost down there in the dark, but if I tell you myself, now, you'll never believe me. And it could do more harm than good. You have to see it yourself, like anyone else who wakes up to a truth, step by step. Just like our sessions. One step at a time."

Alistair stood there silent, listening to the strange paradox of Bolden's calming voice, saying the strangest, most incomprehensible things.

"I don't understand."

"Not yet, no. But you will. The path I walked is waiting for you. And I'm here at the end. All you have to do now is follow me."

"I don't know what the hell you're talking about."

Alistair wanted to hang up but couldn't bring herself to disconnect. She didn't know what Bolden was saying, and frankly the therapist sounded insane, but Alistair felt like she'd somehow accidentally connected to the ghost of a loved one and if she hung up, she would lose her forever.

"You're not alone, Alis. I'm here. I've always been here. And there are others just like you, who remember."

Alistair turned her back to the storm, to the oblivious pedestrians rushing past her in the rain.

"What are you *talking about?*" she pleaded, desperate for a clear answer.

"I'm talking about the night that changed everything. November 11th, 2004. That's where it all started. The night you came back. The night you *all* came back."

Chapter Eleven

Ben was fifteen when he first heard about them. Wyatt Haim was the youngest of the Six. He'd been fifteen, just like Ben, when he and the other five vanished from the quiet northern California inlet town. Janie Grant. Billy Holtzman. Veronica and Marjory Morrow. Aaron and Wyatt Haim. The Santa Colette Six.

They'd all missed school on that day back in 2003. They weren't known to run in the same circles, so no one noticed until Janie didn't show up for her father's birthday dinner. Some said they'd purposely hid the fact that they were friends. It was fall, and Santa Colette was known for its mist-laden cliffs and deep-black coastal waters. After searching the surrounding woods, that's where the search continued: the beaches, the water, and the nearby counties, for fear that hellish riptides had carried the kids away. Then the state police searched the Mexico border, then the FBI the Canadian border, then ship manifests and state parks.

Aaron and Wyatt's dad became a suspect at one point. A mechanic whose painkiller addiction and bad temper had crushed his family and his middling career as a stock car racer, he'd always been a pariah, and the town was eager to pin it on him. But he had an alibi.

Marjory and Veronica. Twins. They'd been transplanted to the sleepy town when their mother took over as superintendent of the school district. The older and entrenched (read: white) Santa Colettians would say they shunned the family because their mother had laid off a half-dozen teachers her first year on the job, and not at all for the color of their skin.

Janie. The paragon perfect teenager whose parents had dutifully hidden her ongoing mental health "complications," complications that were all dredged up and exposed while they were missing. Her parents divorced within months of her disappearance, each blaming the other.

Billy Holtzman. An unremarkable loner whose mother had cleaned every house in Santa Colette at one point or another. He was the only one of the Six who had chosen to stay and stand in the spotlight of their story after they came back. He became a loud, loquacious "impact guru" who toured the world bellowing platitudes on bouncing back from failure, pain, and a past he perpetually teased revealing. He packed stadiums of people and made millions of dollars without ever really saying anything of substance, and *nothing* about himself.

November 11, 2004. A few weeks after Ben's sixteenth birthday. His dad bought him a case of beer, which they'd responsibly split, and then blew the empty cans off of fence posts with a 16-gauge shotgun his grandfather had left Ben in his will. Ben, drunk for the first time, saw it on the news that night, the Six returned. They were spotted on the road, late at night, heading into Santa Colette. They were wearing pants and shirts they'd stolen from someone's clothesline. Aaron was carrying Marjory. She was unconscious.

Weeks of questioning and pleas for privacy. They wouldn't say what happened to them, where they'd gone, or how they got back. People jokingly called it "the Six pact" believing they'd sworn amongst themselves to never tell the truth. Some papers thought it was a cult, or maybe occult, or a failed human trafficking attempt. Although she was never in public after their return, Marjory was the only one who ever told the police that she didn't know what happened. The rest were silent as the grave.

Within weeks, their story had been eclipsed by new headlines covering financial crises and recalled lettuce, but Ben couldn't let it go. He stayed up nights researching them and other similar disappearances, which then led him to other, even stranger stories and conspiracies like the incident at Dyatlov Pass, the Mary Celeste, the Picnic at Hanging Rock, Lucy Lightfoot, the Man from Taured. The Six had cracked the world open for sixteen-year-old Ben, and although fantasy and make-believe were all but banned from his upbringing, Ben had found a key hidden in their story, a key that had unlocked a door, and beyond was a strange and mind-altering world. The Six were why Ben became a writer, if he was being honest. They were why he wrote the kinds of things he wrote. Why he ultimately left North Carolina and never looked back. The door couldn't be locked again.

So when it came time to write *All the Stories Left Behind*, the Six were the first on the list of stories he wanted to reimagine. It also gave him an excuse to try and track them down. But no one knew where five of the Six were. Billy, now Bill, had millions of social media followers but was completely unavailable for comment and every interview he'd ever done was obviously preplanned and scripted. He refused to talk about what had happened to them, where they'd gone, or the circumstances surrounding how they came back. Thanks to what some believed was California's Witness Relocation and Assistance Program, the other five had disappeared off the face of the map for the second time.

Doctor Deborah Bolden had been tasked to treat them in their first months back. Ben had found her name in his research but knew client confidentiality would prevent her from sharing anything. Still, he called. She never responded. Early on, Ben learned he was less interested in arming his fantasy with enough information to make it feel real than he was in ultimately uncovering the truth about the Six. He didn't want to expose them. He just *needed* to know. There was a hole in the world that he couldn't explain, and he needed to fill it. The mystery consumed him. Then he received a call in the middle of the night; the voice on the other end was altered, eerie. The man on the phone told Ben that he wasn't the only one looking for the truth, and then the caller told him something he claimed would help Ben on his path to enlightenment. It was a way to find one of the hidden five.

The call freaked Ben out. How could someone have known what he was doing, what he was researching? He was nobody. And what they'd told him . . . it scared him. He abandoned his search. Looking back, Ben realized it was probably the first time he'd ever heard from Frank. Before Frank became convinced that it was *Ben* who knew the truth about the secret history of the world. That call was the first secret he ever kept from Cor. A decision that would eventually spiral into rivers of blood and the loss of everything that mattered to him.

Alistair's phone call with Bolden had all the strange and cryptic trappings of Ben's first call with Frank. A beckoning to look a little deeper down the rabbit hole, so that whatever was waiting at the bottom, in the dark, could get hold.

Several quiet days and nights followed Ben finding Chapter Ten hand-delivered to his cabin. A sobering nod that whoever was writing them knew exactly where he was. But since that night, no more pages, no strange phone calls, just shipments of lumber and a leaky roof. But in that time, Ben slowly began to lose it. Barely eating, barely sleeping, scared of every sound. He called in sick to work three times but couldn't bear to be alone in the cabin either. He drove around the county through the night until his low gas light blinked on, then he'd walk the black roads around the cabin, lost. He felt like a ghost, barely inhabiting the world of the real. All he had was time to mull it all over: Alistair, the Six, Frank, and the past five years, and to slip deeper into darkness. It was like these four random chapters were meant to put him on the path to the Six again. Like they were renewing the calling he'd first felt when he was sixteen, now re-created in print. But *why?*

Exhausted, Ben walked back to the cabin and collapsed in the recliner. He woke up face-down at half past one in the morning, covered in sweat. He'd been dreaming about Volley barking endlessly at the door of his old apartment, barking at someone on the other side.

Ben rolled over and rubbed his bleary eyes. No Volley, no Chelsea apartment, just the cabin and the cold and the pages. But the barking had been real. Or rather, something that sounded like barking, just outside. It wasn't constant, more of a rhythmic burst of sound every thirty seconds or so. Now that Ben was coming to, he realized he had no idea what was actually making the noise. He sat up listening for a minute or two, then scrambled out of the recliner, blankets wrapped around him, and shuffled to the front window. Moonlight bathed the ground around the cabin and the woods beyond. Whatever was making the noise was close but hidden beyond the tree line.

He slid back into the recliner and put his pillow over his head. The noise didn't let up. Sometimes more frequent, sometimes less. There were a few times when it was quiet just long enough for Ben to start drifting off, and then the noise again. It wasn't a bark. Ben tried to suss out what animal could possibly be making the strange noise, which was more multisyllabic than a dog's bark. It sounded more like something out there was trying to say something. Maybe *sorry* or *borrow*. Ben got up a few times, banged on the cabin wall, yelled out the front door, trying anything to scare the thing away so he could sleep, but it always returned.

Ben felt like he was being tortured. He finally jumped out of the recliner at 4 AM, grabbed a flashlight and the walking stick he kept leaning by the front door, and marched out into the cold in nothing but unlaced boots and underwear, ready to kill the damned thing that was trying to drive him over the edge. He stalked the edge of the woods, listening. *Borrow. Sorry.* Ben charged into the woods, giant puffs of white breath clouding his own vision as he searched for the beast. He could hear it coming from higher up, in a tree. *Sorry. Borrow.* His flashlight beam lanced through the turned leaves, across the upper branches of the maples. He finally found it: a big fat crow, sitting about ten feet up a young oak. *Borrow.* Ben slammed the walking stick against the trunk.

"Hey!" he yelled, panting, trying to scare it off.

Sorry.

"You're *gonna* be sorry if you don't get the hell out of here!"

Borrow.

Ben could see the crow's breath and its black bead eyes looking down at him from the branch. There was something wrong with its thick, glossy beak, like a crack or break in it.

Sorry.

Ben yelled a few more times, then tried to scare the bird by throwing the walking stick, javelin style, up into the tree. It barely reached the bottom branches before he had to scramble away to keep it from hitting him on the way back down.

Sorry.

"God damn it, WHAT DO YOU WANT?!"

Borrow.

Ben screamed, crouching, digging through the leaves on the ground, looking for something easier to throw. He found a rock. And just as he reached back to throw it, the bird bellowed again, and Ben thought he heard something else.

"What? What did you—say?" Ben asked, realizing the bird had succeeded in driving him mad.

The bird bellowed again, and this time it was as clear and crisp as the night air stinging Ben's body. The crow leapt from the branch and took flight.

"Wait!"

Ben watched its black feathers glowing in the silver moonlight until it vanished in the far-off trees, echoing one last call.

Follow.

৩%৩

Ben watched the sun come up from his porch, wrapped in a flimsy blanket, nearly frozen through from sitting outside all night.

Follow me.

He wanted to be out of Crystal Ridge, out of New York State. The family farm was sitting derelict and gone to seed back in North Carolina. He could just go back. There was no one left to care or judge him. He could start over. Or sell the land and disappear with the money. Buy a boat in Nags Head and drift away. Alone just like his narrative proxy, Alistair Mead. Hell, even Alistair had people in her life to lean on. Her aunt and uncle. Ed. Zev.

A realization flashed across Ben's mind.

Zev Lieberman.

Zev wasn't hiding. Zev wasn't a former missing person trying to avoid prying eyes. If Zev was real, Ben could find him, ask him about Alistair. And if he didn't exist, then maybe *none* of this was real. It was just someone tormenting him again, haunting him. But *that* he could manage, that the *police* could manage. Zev was the key that could lock the door again.

Ben knew Zev was working on his PhD at Columbia from the chapter in Ozone Park. He knew he was planning on becoming a comparative literature professor. The English department at Columbia was the place to start. The plan lit a fire in Ben. He felt rebooted. He showered, dressed for work, made his apologies for leaving Stevie in the lurch, and on his lunch break he went to the cafe and found the number for the Department of English and Comparative Literature on the Columbia University website. He searched Zev's name online, but there were actually quite a few Zev Liebermans in New York. Unfortunately, none fit the bill exactly, unless Zev was a precocious ten-year-old with his own social media accounts or one of three rabbis on Long Island.

105

Back at the store, Ben waited for Stevie to start unpacking inventory upstairs, then used the store phone to call the college and left a message asking to be put in touch with Zev Lieberman. He went back to work, sweeping, dusting, leading customers up and down the store stairs, all the while listening for the phone. He felt like he'd been reunited with his body. He was back on the physical plane. But when no one had called back by 4 PM, closing time, Ben left another message, this time lying, saying Zev had reached out to him and he was returning his call and that it was a time-sensitive matter. He left the back door unlocked, and once Stevie was gone for the night, he slipped back in just in case someone called.

The phone rang just before 8 PM. Ben had fallen asleep behind the front counter. He bolted off the floor, startled by the loud mechanical ring of the old phone. It might not be Zev, he thought to himself, although his pulse didn't get the memo. It might be a professor or admin calling to say there's no such person. It might be a bill collector. Ben took a deep breath and answered.

"Hello?"

"Hello? Is this Ben?" It was a young man's voice on the other end of the line, deeper than he'd imagined for Zev, but still within the realm of possibility.

"Yeah, that's me . . ." Ben didn't know what else to say. He wasn't good at this stuff. Not like Alistair.

"I got a message that you called me?" the voice on the other end said.

"Yes, that's—yes. I'm sorry, who is this?"

Quiet on the other end. Ben could hear his heartbeat in his ears as his whole head flushed with blood.

"This is Zev Lieberman. The office admin said this was time-sensitive?"

Zev Lieberman.

He was real.

"Hello?" Zev asked.

"Hi. Yeah. I—I was calling because . . ."

How in God's name had he not thought of a reason for his call?

He honestly didn't believe he was going to be real.

"I'm a recruiter," Ben finally answered.

It was the first thing that came to mind. He had no idea where he was going with this.

"A job recruiter?"

"That's right, yeah . . . I recruit. For jobs."

"Hmmm, you might have the wrong guy," Zev answered. "I'm still in school and working on campus right now. What is this for?"

"Well, it's for—a job where—"

Ben's mind had gone completely blank.

"Sir?" Zev said.

"It's for—" *Alistair.* "It's actually for—" *Say it.* "A friend of yours."

"I'm sorry, I don't understand."

Ben felt faint.

"It's . . ." *Got it.* ". . . a reference call. For a friend of yours. They listed you. As a reference. For a job."

"Alistair?" Zev asked, clarifying.

"Yes. Alistair Mead."

Quiet on the other end.

"Do you know an Alistair Mead?" Ben asked.

More unbearable quiet.

"I do."

Ben sank against the counter. His mind spinning. It still didn't mean that any of this was true, his logical brain was screaming. It just meant there were two people someone had used in their story to torment him.

"What position is this for?"

"Uh . . . book—book—bookseller."

Ben smacked his own head in frustration. "A position as a bookseller."

"Oh, that's great. Well, she'd be amazing. She's been working in book sales since she was barely twenty. What would you like to know?"

Does Alistair remember an imaginary books series? Did Alistair disappear when she was a little girl, only to reappear on the same day the Six did?

"Does Alistair—work well with others?"

"Ummm, I'd say yes. I think she's comfortable working with minimal supervision, but is also a great team player, so I think she would be a great fit in any environment."

Ben actually smiled. If what he knew about Alistair was true, Zev was lying through his teeth about her ability to "play well with others." He was helping her get the job. The one that didn't exist.

"She's always laser-focused on the goal at hand, and really knows her stuff when it comes to literature. She'd put a lot of my professors to shame."

"That's great," Ben answered.

"What else would you like to know?"

Does Alistair hallucinate about nearsighted animals?

"I see here that she is originally from—Queens, is that correct?"

"That's right. We were in school together there."

"But she lives in Manhattan now?"

"I believe so, yeah." Zev answered, something akin to concern, or maybe doubt in his voice. Ben was losing him. If he ever really had him on the hook at all. Ben had to go for it.

"Alistair mentioned uhm—on her application, a book series she loved as a child. A series she's been looking for. Do you know about those books?"

Zev didn't answer.

"I ask just to—get a better sense of . . ."

"I'm sorry, what exactly *are* you asking?"

"Um—she called them . . . *the briar books*, I believe? We're just curious about—her love of books."

The quiet on the other end of the line was excruciating.

"Who is this?" Zev asked.

Ben opened his mouth to speak, and not a damned word came out.

He'd gone too far. Panicked, Ben hung up.

He didn't say it, but if Alistair had never mentioned the books to Zev, never connected them to her missing time, Zev might have dismissed the weird question, but Zev was— worried for Alistair in that moment. They were both real. And against all reason, it seemed Alistair did remember books no one else did.

Fiction had become reality and Ben was going to vomit.

❧

"Mister Ben?"

Ben's eyes flew open to find Stevie tapping on his driver's side window. He'd brought a sleeping bag and slept in his truck.

"Mister Ben, are you okay?"

That's as far as they'd gotten with the name situation. No more "Mister Kriminger," but now he sounded like a Sunday school teacher.

Ben rolled down the window. It must have been around mid-morning.

"Hey, Stevie, what's up?" Ben asked.

"Are you okay?"

"Yeah, just, I wasn't feeling great, so I crashed in my truck."

"I saw you when I got in this morning. I wanted to let you sleep, but there's a call for you? At the store."

"For me?" Ben asked.

No one knew he was working there, not even Cor.

"You're not really supposed to have personal calls while you're on the clock, but since you didn't come in at all, I guess it's okay cause you're technically not on the clock," Stevie said with a half grimace, half smile.

Ben wanted to congratulate him on asserting himself, even passive-aggressively, but he was too overwhelmed with anxiety about the caller. "It must be some kind of emergency."

They hurried back to the store together. Once inside, Stevie

109

walked away, giving Ben privacy. Ben picked up the receiver, his heart thumping.

"This is Ben."

"Hey, buddy, how are you. It's Conor."

His editor. Conor had been assigned to Ben on *All The Stories Left Behind* . . . by the publisher.

"Hey, how did you . . . get this number?"

"*You* gave it to me."

Ben couldn't remember under what circumstances that would have ever happened.

"This is good, Ben. This is very good."

"It is?" Ben asked.

"So let me pitch it back to you to make sure I get it."

"Get—"

"Ben Kriminger's life was turned upside down by his own work of fiction, and now, years later, he's seeking the truth behind the lies, and the six people who hold the key to a decades-old mystery. How's that sound?"

Ben's mind was blank. What the hell was Conor talking about? Had Conor talked to Cor?

"I'm sorry, I'm lost," Ben finally managed.

"The pages, buddy! They're great! I'm telling you, I think it's a slam dunk concept-wise. Everybody here believes in you, and I told you from the start that you never should have cut the Six from the first book. I could forward these upstairs and have a green light for you by the end of the week. I just want to make sure I'm pitching it right."

"You got a chapter."

"Just part of one." Conor covered his end of the line and yelled to his assistant, "Jess, is this all that came in the packet?!" and then got back on the line. "Are you all right? Can you hear me okay?"

"What chapter is it? What number?"

"Uhh... Fourteen."

What had happened between chapters ten and fourteen?

"Read it to me."

"What?" Conor asked.

"The pages."

"I just have what you sent me, and a number to call you."

"Yeah, read them back to me. It's a writer thing. I'm . . . having second thoughts and I just want to hear what you see in them."

Quiet on the other end.

"We gotta get you back in the city. You're going nuts up there. All right, hang on . . ."

The bell on the front door of the store rang as a family walked in. Ben ducked behind the counter with the phone, hiding, waiting.

Conor began reciting, *"Ben had drawn a dotted line across the country, each dot representing some iteration of a ratty, dank, and dust-ridden motel. His pickup started billowing chugs of smoke if he spent more than ten minutes above sixty miles an hour, so it had taken Ben just under four days to get to Phoenix. He'd had countless hours of dry blinding white and endless black to think, his deepest wonderings surfacing on those long, post-midnight stretches between barren farmland and shuttered roadside gas stations. Where there was nothing beyond the emptiness that your headlights showed you. His mind primarily bounced between two powerful poles. Alistair and the Six. It was easy to think of them as existing only on page. The lot of every writer, worrying yourself dead over invisible people who don't know you exist. But these people were real. And they were the key to everything. The truth was waiting for him in the darkness just beyond his view. So Ben drove on, through the dark, knowing he had what maybe no one had. A secret he kept with him always. A way to find the Six."*

Time stopped. Ben felt frozen. *He* was the subject of the missing chapters. Chapters that claimed he was going to inch back down the rabbit hole on his own, across the country. It wasn't about Alistair or Bolden. It was him. Ben reached into his back pocket and pulled out his wallet. Buried behind discount cards and his driver's license was a folded-up piece of newsprint that had long turned gray.

"It's great," Conor finished. "Is it true? You found one of them?"

Ben unfolded the cutout. He hadn't looked at it in years. It was part of an ad for a car dealership in Southern California. It had a name and a bio for one of its dealers, a man named Jeremy Newhouse. Ben had crossed the name out some years back and written in pencil *Aaron*. Frank had set him on the path to finding Aaron Haim with one phone call all those years ago, before he'd ever written the book, but he didn't pursue it. And now it was all coming back. There was no escaping it.

The truth was waiting for him in the darkness just beyond his view.

"Ben, buddy, I'm so glad you're getting back in the saddle. Just let me know what you need."

Ben folded the newsprint and slipped it back into his wallet. He took a breath, sighed, and finally said, "I'm gonna need an advance."

Chapter Twelve

Alistair shambled back home in the rain. Soaked through in minutes, she barely noticed, her mind preoccupied with absorbing, dissecting, and trying to make sense of what Bolden had told her. There were others. Others who not only remembered the books, but who had come back home the same day she did.

Hours later, she was kicking herself for not interrupting, for not asking the hundred questions pinballing in her brain now. How did Bolden know what happened to her? What exactly had Bolden learned over the past decade? Why couldn't she just tell her?

Finally, back in her cave, Alistair left her dripping coat to soak the floor by her front door. She walked to the window, staring at the box on the windowsill, willing her ice-cold hands to pick it up, afraid that she would open it and slip into the dark forever. At the same time, she was afraid that she wouldn't pick it up, and the life she'd barely stitched together would come undone regardless, and she'd still never be whole again.

Follow me. Bolden's words haunted her.

Alistair watched her hands reach out for the box as if she were remotely operating a human-shaped machine from a thousand miles away. Her fingers were too numb to feel the paper it was made from. If she didn't open it, none of it was real. If she did, and it was, there was no going back. What if she was out of her mind? What if she opened the box, saw the little figure, but no one else could?

She had to check. But she didn't want to be alone. She needed help. Someone she could trust, someone who was real. Someone who didn't know anything about any of this, who could tell her she wasn't insane. Or confirm she was. She stole six beers from the downstairs kitchen fridge and waited until the first light of morning to head uptown.

❦

She wandered the dim college campus for half an hour before she finally found the building the dozing security guard had nudged her toward, and snuck inside—Columbia Residential Housing. She buzzed the appropriate button. It took a few moments, but he finally answered, "Hullo?"

"Hi Zev, it's Alistair. I'm sorry for—"

The door buzzed open.

She could hear him fumbling around on the other side of the thin door. He squinted against the hallway light when he opened it, stunned to see Alistair, his bed-smashed hair made him look like a rooster. He was dressed in nothing but the boxers he'd obviously just been sleeping in.

It had been years since she'd seen him without a shirt. She spent sweaty summers riding bikes with him through Queens as a kid, his shirt stuffed into the back pocket of his shorts, her view of his perpetually pale back riding up ahead of her. But this was different. They were all grown up now.

"What's wrong?" he asked, beckoning her in immediately. The room was dark, small, stuffy. It smelled like books and good takeout and warm bedding.

"Sit down," she said.

Without hesitation, he sat on the edge of a futon, unfolded into a bed. He picked up a rumpled T-shirt from the floor and pulled it over his head. Alistair slowly paced.

Zev went to switch on the nearby lamp. "You can leave it off," Alistair said. Then she turned to Zev, his body half-lit by the dim light of the campus.

"Are you okay?" he asked.

"No."

"Are you drunk?"

"A little," Alistair conceded. "I'm about to tell you a handful of crazy things and I need you to just listen and let me get it out, because I can't keep it all straight in my head right now."

"Okay."

"You know the books? My books? The stories I told you when we were young?"

"Yeah."

"But you don't really remember the stories, right?"

"What do you mean?"

"Tell me one."

"I . . . yeah. I can't really remember. I guess my brain's still waking up."

"They're real. The books. The stories. All of it. And I'm not supposed to remember them. No one is. But I do. And it has something to do with what happened to me."

"Okay . . . Wait, what?" Zev was officially not following.

"For some reason, I can remember them. Not completely. They're in this . . . fog. Like the rest of my dark year. But there are times when I can remember, and—listen, that's irrelevant. I'll explain better, later, but right now, I need to open this box."

She pulled the now crumpled paper cube out of her pocket and showed it to Zev.

"I'm not sure what's going to happen when I open it. To me. But I need to look inside it, and I need you to look too."

"Alistair?"

"What?"

"Am I dreaming right now?"

"No."

"Okay. What do you need me to do?"

"Just be here . . . I might freak out, or hallucinate, or even black out when I open this thing. Maybe. There might be something in it that triggers me. Or it might not."

"Might not trigger you?"

"Might not be in the box."

Alistair put the box to her ear and shook it a little, but she heard nothing rattling inside.

"I'm not sure if what's inside is real or not."

Zev looked at her, slack-jawed, "Okay ..."

"Ready?"

"Wait," Zev suddenly stood up and approached her. "I . . . have Popsicles."

"What?" Alistair asked, as if *that* was the craziest thing that had just been said.

"Popsicle sticks are like tongue depressors. In case you black out?"

"You can't really swallow your tongue, Zev. That's a myth."

"Oh. Okay. Then, yeah, I'm ready."

Alistair held the box in her left hand and put her right hand on the lid. She looked at him, into his big brown eyes.

"I don't understand, but I'm here," he said, reassuring.

She nodded, took a breath, held it, and pulled the lid off.

Inside was the plastic figure of the little girl with the bow and arrow. And nothing happened. Alistair let out the breath with a vocal sigh.

"What is that?"

"I think it's part of a game based on the books. I found it in an old house upstate. I was . . . drawn to it. It triggered these weird memories and I sort of got lost in them, but now . . . nothing."

Alistair wondered if maybe the effect had worn off. Like the nostalgia triggered by an old photo that dissolves with exposure to it.

"They're real, Zev, all of them. They're real. And I'm the only one who can remember them."

"Who is she?" Zev asked, looking at the figurine.

"I don't—Iris. Her name is Iris." The memory was coming back without the fear and pain. "She's . . . industrious and fair, and she swore an oath to seek beauty and justice and balance in the world."

"Kinda sounds like you."

"I think she was my favorite character."

Alistair found a nearby desk chair and sat in it. Zev returned to his futon, crouching on the edge.

"Are you okay?"

Alistair carefully took Iris out of the box.

"Everybody thought the books were coping mechanisms, not memories. A way to protect myself from the truth of what really happened. A way to hide it. Even I started to believe it after a while. But if this is real, then *they are* real. Maybe there's a way to unlock what happened to me, what I lost, and finally figure out who I am."

She didn't want to tell Zev about the call with Bolden. It was one unbelievable hurdle too far, even for her. Alistair looked up to Zev, expecting him to look at her like she was insane. Instead, his expression was soft, caring.

"I'm sorry you've had to go through all of this."

Alistair wanted to look away but couldn't.

"I know, it sounds—"

"So, where do we start?" Zev smiled. She wasn't alone. She wasn't crazy.

"I need to figure out how this, how Iris, can lead me to . . . the truth. If this exists, there might be more. I think I need to find more things connected to the books."

"But this is the first thing you've found in almost two decades. Where do we look for more?"

"I have no idea."

Alistair turned Iris over in her hand.

"But I think I know where we start."

Imprinted on the base of the figurine was a date and the name of a company.

Ackerly Green Publishing. 1958.

Alistair wanted nothing more than to be burritoed under blankets in her cave, fortified against a cold front that trailed along with the miserable week of rain, but instead she'd spent most of the week in libraries around town looking for books from Ackerly Green Publishing. Meanwhile, Zev used his connections in the Columbia literature department and their web of libraries to help her out as best he could. Alistair had made several deep dives online from the Seward Park Library, partly to look for mention of the company, partly to look for a woman who had hired her a few years back to find anything released by Ackerly Green.

Ed often referred people to Alistair (or, more specifically, a cheap ad she used to run in a few local papers) when he didn't feel the stakes were high enough to be worth his time. Alistair had spoken with Deirdre Byrne on the phone once and only remembered bits and pieces of their conversation. Deirdre had a gentle Irish lilt but had just come to the States from London. She'd been staying in a house her family still owned somewhere in Manhattan. She'd intimated that finding books published by Ackerly Green might help her find out more about her family. Looking back, it seemed like Ackerly Green was the key to Deirdre's mystery too. After the call, Alistair had occasionally looked for anything from the small New York company, which had, from what she gleaned, gone belly-up in the early '60s. Alistair had been hired by more than a few genealogy nerds over the past few years who had stumbled over a bump in their family's history and wanted to find a keepsake or two, and it seemed at the time that Deirdre was just the latest, but who knows? Maybe she was looking for the same thing Alistair was. *No one remembered the books but her,* but maybe that wasn't true after all. After that call, Deirdre Byrne never reached out to her again, and Alistair had long forgotten about the job. But now she was back on the trail.

Who originally published *The Chronicles of Narnia,* or *Alice's Adventures In Wonderland*? Alistair had the answer to both because she was a book hunter and an avid reader, but as a child, she had no clue. Kids don't care about companies and the grown-ups who own them. Ackerly Green Publishing didn't even sound familiar to her. But as far as she knew, Ackerly Green published *the briar books,* or at least the product tie-ins, like the board game to which Iris had once belonged. There was very little information about the company online, and what she did find had nothing to do with *the briar books.* Her web search turned up a hit for a website in search results called "Ackerly Green's Guide to Magiq," which at least sounded like it was in the same fantasy genre, but the site wasn't functioning, the search engine didn't have a cache of the site, and the "WhoIs" information for the domain had been made private.

With no other leads, Alistair started digging into the mystery of Deirdre Byrne. Who also apparently didn't exist, at least not online. There were plenty of Deirdre Byrnes, but not one who fully fit the bill of the chatty, inquisitive young woman she had spoken with on the phone.

Alistair was waiting out another booming downpour in a cluttered, bay-windowed East Village book and coffee shop when Zev texted. He'd found something but wanted to share it in person. She replied, carefully navigating her demolished screen, asking him to text whatever he'd found. He insisted that they had to go over it face-to-face. She knew he was dangling information as bait to meet up, probably to check in on her. After showing up at his apartment, she'd fallen off the map. She acquiesced, sending him her location. She should've offered to meet uptown or at least halfway, but it was cold, it was wet, and anything above Fourteenth Street felt like a world away.

Zev showed up less than an hour later, drenched to the bone. He sheepishly waved from across the shop as he barged in through the door, grabbing a handful of paper napkins to dry his face and glasses. He plopped down on the other side of the bay window seat, practically panting.

"I couldn't find my umbrella." He huffed through heavy breaths.

Alistair moved her messenger bag, making room for her soppy friend.

Thunder exploded in the gray air outside and they both jumped.

"It's crazy out there," he muttered, rubbing a handful of crumpled napkins over his wet nest of hair.

"Are you okay?" He backpedaled, "Is everything . . . cool?"

"Everything is reasonably cool, yes." Alistair answered with a smile. "You want coffee?"

"I'm fine. So . . ." he started, "first, I have a list of books published by Ackerly Green. None of which have anything to do with "briars" and none of which are children's books. I don't know if Ackerly Green had a children's division, but . . ."

"It's unlikely," Alistair interrupted. "They were only around for seven years."

Zev paused mid-gesture, handing a folded sheet of paper to Alistair. "You knew that already."

"Yeah. I hope you didn't come all the way down here for that."

"I didn't. Here's the list of books they published. Kind of all over the place, genre-wise."

Alistair took the sheet. She'd found all these titles in her research but pretended to scour the page for clues.

Zev dug through his bag for another printout.

"So I started looking into who owned the company. Two guys, Ackerly and Green, obviously. I found that the son of Warner Green went into publishing with his father for a blip of time in the '70s. Sullivan Green?"

Alistair took the sheet of paper, reading over it. It was an obituary. This, she hadn't found.

"He died in 2016," Zev said.

"In Central Park," Alistair answered as she read the passage. "That's weird."

"I know. No mention of relatives, which is also kind of weird, or the company, but it might be a start. Or the start of a start."

"2016. I wonder if this is what brought her to the US."

"Brought who?" Zev asked.

"Deirdre Byrne. Turns out, weirdly, I was hired to look for books published by this company a couple years ago. I'd completely forgotten about it because the company didn't ring a bell, I didn't find anything, and she never followed up."

"That's . . . a weird coincidence," Zev said.

"Yeah."

"You think it's not? Or it is? What are you thinking?" Zev rattled.

"I'm thinking . . . who posted the obituary? They usually mention kids, spouses . . . This seems so . . . I don't know . . ."

"Impersonal." Zev finished her thought.

"Perfunctory. Guarded. Yeah. This Sullivan guy was apparently a lifelong New Yorker . . ."

"Well, dying in Central Park is ultimate New Yorker vibes," Zev said.

"But . . . he maybe has a daughter living in the UK, who was looking to find out more about her family, which means she didn't know a lot to begin with?"

"So *she* didn't post the obituary."

"Right. But obituaries don't just happen. They get submitted. So someone called the Times."

"Right," Zev said, working a wet smudge off his glasses with a shirttail.

Alistair pulled out her half-shattered phone and succeeded in dialing a number.

Zev whispered, "Who're you calling?"

"The Times," Alistair whispered back before someone picked up on the other end of the line, and she affected a brighter tone. "Hi. Good morning. I'm hoping you can help me. It's a bit of an interesting story. I own a storage facility in Jersey City, and we've been clearing out some delinquent units. I found one for a man named Sullivan Green, and his information fits an obituary your department published in the summer of 2016? I know it's a long shot, but there are items in the unit of rare and well, *significant* value and we're just trying to track down who submitted the obituary in the hopes that they were at some point managing Mr. Green's estate."

Zev stared slack-jawed at Alistair's immediate and intricately woven lie.

"Yes. It's quite a trove, actually. Really. Really? That would be incredible. Yes. Thank you."

Alistair gave her number and hung up.

"They're gonna dig into it."

Zev continued to stare at her in silence.

"Oh. People love being part of a mystery. Don't judge me," she said.

"Judge you? That was *incredible*. All this microfiche printing and secret identities . . . It's like we're living *A to Z*."

Alistair was about to ask what he meant, but then it all came back to her. "Oh my God. A to Z Investigations."

They were twelve or thirteen. They'd both been readers and loved Hardy Boys, Nancy Drew, Harriet the Spy. They'd traded books, knocking Morse code on their shared wall at night, asking and answering what page they were on. One summer they decided they were going to open their own detective agency. They'd painted a sign for "A to Z Investigations" and put it on Zev's attic door.

"We're living our dream!" Zev said, enthusiastic, his hand landing on her knee under the café table.

"We're late-blooming teenage detectives," Alistair said with a laugh.

"As far as first cases go, this seems like a good one," Zev replied.

Alistair felt a sudden twinge of sadness. There's this thing that happens, that only people with the shade of gloom perpetually hanging over their head can understand. When the gloom clears momentarily, and you allow yourself to enjoy the light, and hope it stays, you feel guilt for wishing away the gloom that's been your constant companion.

"So what now?" Zev asked.

"Probably nothing," she answered, retreating into herself a little.

"Do you do that a lot?" Zev asked, and Alistair felt herself bristle at what she assumed was a pry at her defense mechanism, which yes, she was highly aware of, and desperately wanted to avoid discussing.

"Do what, exactly?"

"Pretend to be other people."

"What?"

"For work, I mean. The storage-unit-lady thing. Do you have to do that a lot?"

At first, Alistair didn't answer. Zev's eyebrows began to raise in a concerned arch, reacting as if he was sure he'd said the wrong thing but didn't know which part was wrong. Alistair wanted to say she was always pretending. Instead, she managed, "It depends."

Which was like saying nothing at all.

Zev looked out the window. "It's crazy out there."

She thought he was probably thinking it was crazy in here too. Pretending to be other people didn't come easy to her, but it was better than the alternative. This. Feeling like your mouth was sewn shut, trying to come up with something to say, something that would emulate *human*. Most of the time, she didn't feel the need. But it was different with Zev. He knew the awkward, gangly girl she used to be, and she knew the chubby, bespectacled boy he was. She wanted to be her when she was with him. A to Z.

Zev piped up, "Oh! And speaking of weird phone calls, I got one about you. Some guy called the department office asking for me, saying he was a recruiter. He wanted a reference, about a bookseller position you applied for. He asked about where you lived, about the books, *your books*, and it seemed kind of weird, so I pressed him about who he was and he . . . hung up."

"Huh. Did you get his name or number?"

"Ben something. When I called it was a hardware store."

Alistair wanted to ask more questions but didn't want to make the call seem suspicious. She was scared of roping Zev any deeper into the past week's events. Maybe someone had called him on behalf of Bolden.

"You know what, I *did* apply for something, a while back, when things were a little leaner. Sorry if it was out of the blue."

"It's fine. But—you listed me as a reference?" Zev asked, eyebrows arched in a kind of funny way.

Shit.

"Yeah. You—know me better than most."

Zev gave a little laugh. A laugh that, to Alistair, meant that if he knew her better than most, what did that say about everyone else?

Alistair missed the call from the Times. She'd stuffed her phone into her messenger bag when she ran home in the rain. It no longer received cell signal and was essentially useless without Wi-Fi. She'd left Zev in the coffee shop, feigning an appointment uptown, then stumbled on her lie when he said they could ride the train up together. She dribbled rainwater through the restaurant kitchen as the line cooks *tsk-tsked* with clucking tongues. She shrugged off her wet coat and hung it over the tub, saw the missed call, and, hijacking Danny Chen's "private" Wi-Fi, checked her messages.

The woman at the Times had left a phone number for a law firm.

Alistair dialed, wringing out her hair. A baritone woman with a heavy Queens accent answered.

"Office of Orvin Wallace."

"Is Mr. Wallace available?" Alistair tossed the request into the dark, hoping she'd just be patched through.

"Mr. Wallace isn't in the office right now. He's not in the *country* right now, actually. Can I take a message?"

"Uh . . ." Alistair froze for a second. Her meeting with Zev had frazzled her and knocked her off her game.

"Hello?"

"I'm sorry. I was calling about Sullivan Green. I think Mr. Wallace managed his estate. Sullivan's daughter, I *believe*, hired me to . . . hunt down a series of books. I'm a book dealer, sorry. I found the books, but I misplaced Deirdre's contact information. I was hoping you could lead me in the right direction."

A quiet beat on the other end of the line.

"What is it you have?"

"Books."

"And you need an address?"

"Address or a phone number where I could reach her directly. I don't want to be a bother."

"Mr. Wallace manages the Green family's dealings. You can send whatever you have here, and I'll forward it on."

Alistair wound her hair into a knot, trying to gain control of the call.

"That . . . sounds great. I have . . . twelve boxes. So far."

"Of *books*?"

"Yeah. And they are *heavy*."

Quiet.

Alistair prodded. "Okay, I'm ready. What's your address?"

"Hold on . . ."

The assistant put Alistair on hold. Alistair mentally crossed her fingers while trying to figure out the name of the instrumental song playing on the other end.

"Hello?"

"Yes?"

"I have an address for you. It's Deirdre's."

"Oh! Perfect. That's perfect. Thank you so much."

❧

Alistair checked her sliver of window. Still raining. She couldn't bear to go back out there. She flopped onto her bed, sticking her chilled bare feet under the crumpled blanket at the bottom of the mattress. As soon as the rain stopped, she'd be back on the case.

Was this how Bolden planned for her to follow? Or was Alistair on her own, groping in the dark for answers she wasn't going to get? Were there really others out there like her, who remembered what she remembered? It couldn't be true. She'd been alone for so long. She felt the familiar needles of despair prodding at her again, but then she thought of "A to Z" and for a moment the pain disappeared.

❧

She woke up in the dark from her overlong nap, groggy, grumpy, and unsure what day it was or even what bed she was in. Her lone window was dark so it could have been late night, early morning, or a heavily rain-clouded afternoon.

She heard music blaring on an old radio in the kitchen downstairs, which meant the restaurant was closed and Danny Chen's three uncles were cleaning up for the night. Which meant it was after 9 PM. Which also meant she'd missed dinner. Again. Her stomach growled on cue. *Who cares?* she would usually say to herself, trying to minimize the impact of that angry gnawing hunger in her belly. She could eat in the morning and veggie egg roll and

126

mu shu herself to death.

But Aunt Kath would care, Ed would care, and Zev would definitely care. Some other part of her echoed back. Hell, maybe even Bolden would care as much as she could, in her own weird, nonsensical way. The past couple of weeks had shown Alistair just how un-alone she really was. She knew it, she understood it, she accepted it in an objective, external way, but knowing how much she wasn't alone actually had the adverse effect of forcing her deeper down inside herself. Down where the gnawing was. She feared what would happen if anyone saw it. That's probably why she hadn't texted Zev when she heard back from the attorney's office. Probably why she hadn't asked him to come with her to see Deirdre. She liked the way he looked at her. She didn't want to change that.

An hour later, Alistair crossed over the freshly rain-washed streets intersecting St. Marks Place on her way to the West Village. Alistair didn't know what to expect, but the fact that the address had no apartment number and was in a *particularly* desirable location of the West Village meant it was probably a brownstone or a townhouse at the very least. The two words, *townhouse* and *brownstone*, had become fairly interchangeable, but Ed had lived in a brownstone, his bookstore on the first floor and apartment on the second. He'd told her that only houses built with the brown sandstone from a formation they'd found a couple hundred years ago in New Jersey actually qualified as a "brownstone." To everyone else Ed probably seemed pedantic and prickly, if not downright snobbish, but Alistair knew that his mantra, or at least what he always said, was: "Right is right." Right is right. Facts are facts. Black or white. Ed cared too. The way he looked at her in the hospital waiting room. Alistair physically shook the thought out of her head as she crossed Seventh Avenue and soldiered onward into the winding, gridless streets of the West Village. The rain had cleared, leaving a deep wet chill, and puffy streaks of mist in the sky, lit by skyscraper light, drifting by like parade floats.

She wasn't sure when, but at some point on her way to the

address, Alistair thought she could feel that feeling again—the one she'd felt in the house on the Hudson. The feeling that called her to the pink and lavender bedroom. Not nearly as intense, though. More like a secondary breeze in the air, one only she could feel. It was gentle, but with enough metaphysical momentum that it felt less like a breeze, and more like a current. She felt it pulling at her several blocks before the address. The hairs on her body bristled at first in alarm, a knee-jerk but understandable reaction. There were moments when Alistair thought she saw things that weren't there, or rather, *were* there, in some capacity, but only she could see them. An animal scurrying past in the corner of her eye. Possibly a rat. A glittering purple leaf tossed about in a pile of orange and yellow ones. Maybe someone lost a mitten. A thin, golden trail of light, flickering from puddle to puddle, only its reflection visible. Light pollution. She felt the wind off the Hudson when her own private current seemed to fade like a figment. She turned the corner to her destination, left with nothing but the mundane breeze everyone else could feel.

Turns out, Deirdre lived in an *actual* brownstone. A big one. On a narrow, treelined, cobblestone street hidden in the heart of the West Village. The streetlamp outside barely worked and the building had been drenched in days of rain, giving it a slick, shiny, monolithic vibe. It was beautifully untended, rickety and crumbling in places, and very dark inside. Six steps lay behind an iron fence, which led up to the black door, adorned with a tarnished brass fish for a knocker. The windows, three levels' worth, not including the dormers in the roof, were all leaded. The front bay window bulged out over the sidewalk with panes of wobbly glass fixed together with strips of metal like a stained-glass window that at some point or another had been drained of all its color.

Alistair unlatched the gate and took the steps to the door. She peered through the bay window but couldn't see much. It looked empty, or at least mostly unfurnished. She listened at the door for a moment but heard nothing. She felt strange using the knocker, opting for her less official knuckles instead. She knocked a few more times but no one answered.

Alistair quietly tried the doorknob. To satisfy her curiosity, she told herself. Locked. Maybe Deirdre was just out, or maybe she was back in Ireland. Maybe someone came by once or twice a week to check the mail for her and make sure the house was in order. All this to say, Alistair was convincing herself that if no one was home, then no one would know if she popped in just to check on Deirdre Byrne's possible book collection. Maybe she'd never followed up with Alistair because she'd found what she was looking for. Regardless, this place, one time home to the Greens of Ackerly Green Publishing, might hold some secret or clue.

After a beat of consideration, Alistair swept her hand along the pediment above the door. No spare key. Emboldened by the quiet, the dark street, and even darker windows, Alistair peered over the edge of the porch to the lower level of the brownstone under the stairs, below street level. This separate entrance was once used for staff in homes like this, but now it was mostly used to store garbage cans or to split these monsters into several apartments with separate entrances. Alistair climbed back down to the street and checked the second gate, the one leading to the service entrance. Unlocked. With one more glance at the empty street, Alistair took the steps down to the dark recess under the main stairs. A thatch of moldering leaves was piled against the door. It was locked, and there was no spare above the door, or hidden in the old gaslight sconces.

Alistair pulled her wallet out of her coat pocket and, with a slight regretful grimace, produced a metal card that held the pieces of a lockpicking kit. It lived tucked away among expired licenses and spent Metro Cards; she'd only ever used the kit to get into estate bedrooms or library cabinets. Yes, this felt much worse, but she wasn't going to steal anything. Probably. And yes, this, unlike the house on the Hudson, was *officially* breaking and entering, but she just wanted to have a look around. See what there was to see. She'd come all this way. Well, thirteen east-west blocks. But to a New Yorker, that was "all this way." Finally, she knelt, trying to remember the lockpicking videos she'd studied when she bought the kit. She had the door open in less than five minutes.

There'd be no lying her way out of this if she was found in the house, so she waited a few minutes in the dark of the basement before investigating, listening for footsteps, voices, a TV, anything. It was deathly quiet above. The lower level ended up being mostly empty. A washer, dryer, and hot water heater were tucked in a closet, but there was nothing else. She crept up the thankfully uncreaky stairs and tried the basement door. At first, she thought it was locked, but she leaned into it with her shoulder and the wedged door slammed open. It made a good bit of noise when it finally gave and Alistair could see, in the scant light coming from the kitchen window, that the edges of the basement door and framing were scorched and charred black, like they had at one point withstood some strange, highly localized fire. The black marks spread across a couple feet of wallpaper before dissipating back into images of odd flowers and mythical birds carrying ribbons in their claws.

Alistair switched on her phone's flashlight, which was the only feature that still reliably worked. She kept the beam low and made sure to keep it out of view of the front windows. The place was largely unfurnished. There were stacks of unremarkable books, an old armchair, and a few pieces of furniture that seemed like relatively new purchases, but they were all just . . . deposited in corners of various rooms. Nothing to signify that anyone was living here. On the mantel in the living room she found a bottle that was half full of fine soil or ash, with a berry-laden plant growing out of it, pushing at the cork that kept it closed. Someone had been here recently enough to keep a plant alive. Alistair continued creeping around the first floor, through the other unfurnished rooms, becoming more confident that no one had been there in a while, and that no one was going to surprise her.

That was, until she wandered into the dining room.

There was a long, dark table and several chairs, but the entire room had been set up like an impromptu base of operations. The far end of the table was anchored by three side-by-side computer monitors, with cables curling across the table and under it, to a black PC tower on the floor. There was a dry-erase board on wheels, and markers strewn across the table, along with piles of legal pads with their top pages torn off. All blank. But dust-free. Even though she had only spoken with Deirdre once, Alistair just couldn't picture the cheery woman on the other end of the line living like this, but someone had been, and fairly recently.

Alistair tapped the space bar on the computer keyboard and all three monitors lit up. She was suddenly bathed in blue-white light, but she'd grown confident that no one was inside with her and no one on the outside cared. Password. She flipped the keyboard over to see if someone had perhaps taped it underneath. Nothing.

She moved around the dining room table, looking for the stairs to the upper floors. As she passed, she trained her light on the dry-erase board and noticed faint residual marker at the top left corner of the board. She looked closer, squinting to assemble the half-gone marks into a word. Her face went slack. It couldn't be. She was seeing things where they weren't. Maybe it was an anagram or some kind of programming language, maybe it wasn't a word at all. But if it was, what other word could it be . . .

BR R

Briar. She could hear her heartbeat, and a whining grew in her ears like the buzzy aftermath of a grenade going off nearby. She was so overcome she almost missed the sound of someone sliding a key into the front door's lock.

She leapt out of the room like a startled rabbit, intending to leave the way she came in, but found that the front hall separated her from the kitchen and the basement door. She'd have to run headlong past whoever was about to walk through the door. She scrambled back into the dining room, considered ducking under the table, or unlatching the window, but it was too late. She wasn't alone. And from the sound of footsteps and voices, there was more than one person in the next room.

The new arrivals started flipping on lights and Alistair backed further into the dead end of the dining room. Next to a built-in mirrored buffet, she found a door. She had no idea where it led, but she carefully twisted the crystal knob and slipped through it, pulling it closed behind her. It was a linen closet, lined with empty shelves, which pinned her against the door, preventing her from latching it shut. Lights went on in the dining room and someone was within a few feet of her. She had to hold the knob to keep the door closed.

No one remembered the books but her.

A wave of dizziness rolled through Alistair, crashing against waves of adrenaline. She felt all at once like she might tip over, spilling out into the dining room. Something about the word on the board, or the dual shock of almost being discovered, or this place. She didn't know, but she felt like she was falling down the hole again. She began mouthing her mantra.

On the other side of the door, voices . . .

"Hey . . . I think someone was here."

Another voice, a woman: "What do you mean?"

Another: "That's not possible."

"Yeah, I know, but my PC was on. I didn't leave it on."

"Are you sure? Maybe—"

"No. It's set to sleep on its own. Someone woke it up. Like, a minute or two ago. They didn't get in, but . . ."

Alistair felt beads of sweat trickling down her forehead, her knees going weak.

"They might still be here. . ."

On cue, like a terribly telegraphed sitcom entrance, Alistair's legs gave way and she spilled out of the closet, onto the floor, at the feet of three startled people.

"It's okay . . ." she tried to explain, but the rest of the words wouldn't form. The thoughts couldn't coalesce. All she saw were boots, a blur of bodies in surprise and defense, and a bespectacled fox sitting quietly behind them on the floor.

One of the people, a young man, fell over a chair, then in his shock, yelled a word so loudly that Alistair felt like it had rendered her deaf. Then everything turned to inky black.

❦

"Alistair? You can open your eyes."

Alistair felt a chair beneath her, and something solid behind her head. She couldn't move her arms. She wanted to keep her eyes closed forever—just stay asleep until the impending problem went away. The fox. She'd found it again, or it had found her. Was it still waiting? Her eyes were sticky with sweat, and sleep. She tried to crack them open, but she feared she wouldn't be able to open them enough to try and see what situation she'd gotten herself into without also giving away that she was awake to whomever was in the room with her.

"Alistair. It's okay. You can open your eyes now," the woman's voice repeated.

Alistair's eyes creaked open. She'd been propped up in a kitchen chair with her hands folded placidly in her lap. At first, she thought she'd been bound, but her arms had only fallen asleep. She was still in the brownstone. The kitchen of the brownstone to be exact. A young woman knelt beside her, wrapped in a black cardigan, her pale face framed by long, vibrant, blue-green hair. Even her eyebrows had a tinge of the shade. Alistair's first thought was that she looked like a mermaid.

"Hi. It's okay. My name's Endri."

Alistair tried to speak but words still weren't forming.

"That's Bash . . ."

Alistair looked over at Bash, slumped on the kitchen table— dark-skinned, with long dreads pulled to one side, trickling down a shoulder that stuck out of an oversized sweatshirt. They gave a quick nod back to Alistair and chewed at their fingernail.

Behind Bash was the young man who'd shouted at her. He was now retching into the kitchen sink. "That's Aether," Endri pointed out.

Alistair cleared her throat and eked out, "Is he okay?"

"He's fine," Endri answered.

"I'm fine," Aether yelled back, his voice echoing from the sink basin.

"He's just . . . sick."

"Guess she's not a Mountaineer," Bash mumbled.

"A what?" Alistair asked.

"You're . . . Alistair? Right?" Endri asked.

"How do you know that name?"

Endri held Alistair's wallet up. "Here's the thing . . . I know you're not here to do something bad . . ."

"How?"

"What?" Endri asked.

"How do you know that? I mean, I'm *not*, but how do you know that from looking through my wallet?"

"Well . . . it wasn't your wallet that told me."

Endri tucked the wallet back into Alistair's coat pocket.

"But what we don't know is why you *are* here?"

Alistair's head was still foggy. She couldn't remember what she remembered last . . . breaking in, the computer, the closet . . .

"Deirdre. She hired me. This is her house, right?"

"Hired you to do what?"

"I'm a bookseller. She needed help finding—"

Briar.

"Alistair?" Endri waved her hand in front of her.

"Yeah. Books. She hired me to find some books for her."

Endri looked back at Bash, who was listening intently.

"Did you find them?" Bash asked.

"No. Who are you?"

"Why did you break into her house?" Endri asked.

"It's kind of a long story."

"We're all about long stories."

"It's more of a client-dealer privilege kind of thing. Can I ask *you* a question?"

"Sure."

"What are *you* doing here?"

"We're . . . subleasing, while Deirdre's away."

"This is quite a base of operations you have here. What are you working on in the dining room?"

"A website," Endri answered, cold.

"What kind of website?"

"Fan fiction," Bash interrupted. "What are we doing here, En?"

"Yeah, why didn't you just call the police?" Alistair asked.

"Who says I didn't?" Endri asked. "Who says they're not on their way?"

"Let's just cut to the chase," Alistair said. "Why do you have the word *briar* half-erased on that board in the dining room?"

"Crap," Aether choked out. "Sorry, that's my bad."

Endri smiled and stood. "What does that word mean to you?"

Alistair wondered if this was some kind of test. *Were* these the people Bolden had told her about? Were they the ones like her?

"Do you remember them?" Alistair asked.

"Remember what?"

"*The briar books?*"

Endri was bereft of reaction, and then slowly a smile brightened her face.

"Is that what you came here for?"

"I told you, I just want the truth."

Endri leaned in. "There is a lot of weird shit happening in the world, and the more you know, the more dangerous it becomes. Knowing that, do you still want answers? Real answers?"

"Try me."

Endri turned to Bash. "Would you mind grabbing my bag out of the living room?"

"Yup," Bash replied, hopping off the table and out of the room.

Endri turned back to Alistair "No one remembers them. That's kind of the thing. I can share everything we know, but the truth depends on you, and what you're willing to believe."

Bash came back with Endri's bag. Endri stood, took the bag, and pulled out two paperbacks.

"Here's the big question . . ." Endri tossed the books into Alistair's lap.

Alistair looked down at the two dog-eared books and the bold lettered titles: *The Monarch Papers: Volumes 1 & 2.*

"How fast can you read?"

PART III

Chapter Thirteen

The fathers called it the "old fort." Ilya had imagined it as gray and dusty, lined with garrisons of soldiers, and holes for shooting arrows from, like a castle in a story. But the fathers reassured the children in the train car that the fort had everything they'd need to start their new lives and return to normal. Schools and warm beds, gardens and libraries, parks and performance spaces. A synagogue. And great big strong walls all around it to keep them safe. It would be even better and safer than home. The other children believed it, because all children begin by believing their fathers. But Ilya saw the look on *her* father's face when the other children looked away. The big smile and soft eyes he'd so naturally worn in the past were now like a costume mask, as if he couldn't bear to wear it any longer than he had to do.

There was no room to move in the dark of the cold train car, so most of the children sat restlessly in the laps of one parent or the other, squirming endlessly and fiddling with their coattails or shoelaces, humming the same few songs they knew from school. The endlessness was interrupted only by days and days of intermittent wondering when they'd arrive at the old fort. When they'd finally be home.

Ilya was one of the oldest children in the car. Her classmates had either already taken the train to the fort or had been delayed in the cramped pens that had been erected for them after they'd been evicted from their homes. Pens like the kind the farmers on the edge of town had for their cattle. On the first day of their eviction it had been a kind of grim joke among the families, but as the weeks dragged on, and more and more families were crammed into the filthy, freezing space, calling them *pens* became a polite alternative.

Ilya recognized two children from her school—when it was still a school and she still attended class. They were distinct because they were twins, one boy and one girl, and because they both had wonderfully bright red hair, which was not something you saw every day back in the city. They huddled together, alone, because their mother, like Ilya's, had at some point completely lost herself to endless silent tears, staring blankly at the flickers of light under the train's chained door. Ilya couldn't remember the twins' names. She wanted to catch their attention, offer a reassuring smile in the dull lamplight, but she soon realized they were very brave together, whispering things to one another that made them laugh, and playing games Ilya didn't recognize. Games that involved clapping their hands together, then each other's. She watched the twins play until they seemed to remember where they were, and their game turned to holding hands and waiting quietly for what came next.

Ilya's mother had been quiet since they left the city, but Ilya's father had been whispering with other fathers the night before, and Ilya had been pretending to be asleep. The fathers discussed many things. The route they were traveling never used to make it all the way to the old fort, and the fathers believed the new rails might have been laid by boys like her brother, Isaak—boys who'd been rounded up first and sent away. They said it was a blessing, a mitzvah, that they wouldn't have to walk the remaining miles with their weary children and all their belongings in their arms. The fathers wondered if their boys were waiting for them at the end of the line. Ilya wondered too. Was Isaak waiting in the fort, a brave soldier, watching the horizon for his family to finally join him in the castle?

They arrived in the night. They took gulps of clear, fresh air when the doors were finally rolled open, and exhaled thick white puffs in the cold. The children did not see how wrong their fathers were about the fort that night. It was too dark, and they only spent a few moments outside. They wouldn't fully see the truth for weeks.

Fathers were separated from families that night. The soldiers waiting in the old fort told them they would be reunited soon, but for now, they must separate for reasons no one knew. The children stayed with their mothers. Ilya felt her breath hitch in her throat as her father disappeared in the crowd of other fathers, and into the dark. She hadn't said goodbye. He hadn't looked back. Maybe he was looking for Isaak.

Ilya took her mother's hand and joined the women and children. Everything happened so quickly, no one had time to gather their belongings. She looked back and saw luggage being tossed from the train, onto the frozen ground. Her diary had been in there. All her thoughts and stories. Just behind them, Ilya saw the red-haired twins, their fingers entwined in their mother's hands. Her face was lifeless, but her little son and daughter reassured her in small, trembling voices as they were all hurried along into the dark.

—

Weeks passed. Ilya wasn't sure how many. It was hard to keep count in the cold, gray, third-floor room where the mothers and their children had been led that first night. The space had once been several rooms in a large brick building but most of the interior walls had been torn down, leaving only trails of broken brick and plaster on the floor and ceiling to show where they had once stood. There were a few dozen cots, not nearly enough for everyone that had been crammed in there, so almost everyone slept on the floor, leaving the cots for the babies, the grandmothers, and the infirm. There were a few candlesticks and lanterns propped on old produce crates to light the room at night, but the days had gone so cold and dark, and most of the windows were either shuttered closed or boarded up, so it wasn't easy to tell when it was daytime at all. Some of the mothers, the ones with older children who had been taken to "the school," as the soldiers in the fort had called it, were roused from the floor every morning and led to work in a cafeteria somewhere else in the fort, one that Ilya and the others had never seen. The women would return at night, weary, aching, with crates of leftover food. The mothers moved like cattle to the women carrying food, weary from bad sleep and hunger and oversaturated with fear and worry. They helped to dole out the scraps to the children and the nursing mothers first, then themselves, if any food remained.

The mothers were smarter than the fathers had been on the train. At night, they put the children to bed on the far end of the room, so they couldn't hear the mothers whispering and crying on the other end. Ilya could only peek at them by dim candlelight. She was sure they were talking about the fort, and how nothing about its promise had come to pass. The children whispered too, but less effectively. The older children reassured each other and the younger ones, sure that they just had to wait until the rest of the fort was "cleaned up" before they were able to move into their own homes again. Homes with gardens and beds and food and light.

But Ilya knew it wasn't true. She couldn't quite explain how she knew, and after several children had become cross with her for saying so, she kept it to herself. But deep in her gut, in her heart, she knew that something was wrong, beyond this room, beyond what was happening. It wasn't an instinct so much as the reflection of a memory. As if all of this had already happened and everyone had forgotten but her. It was how she'd felt when she saw the path in the woods—the one she couldn't reach. Like a memory you knew was there but escaped your efforts to recapture it. A longing for something she'd never known.

Memories you almost knew.

Nights in the fort always brought a deep and aching fear of what was to be, and all that was unknown. But Ilya had a secret for keeping the fear at bay, a secret that allowed her to escape to the brief but welcoming peace of sleep. There was a place that Ilya imagined only when her head was on her pillow, a place that only existed in the space between awake and asleep. She wasn't sure when she'd first invented it, she'd gone there as long as she could remember, but it had become especially useful there in the old fort. Imagining herself there, in a space that was neither in the waking world nor the dream world, helped calm her fears, her overactive mind, and allowed her to rest. She would sometimes add strange or interesting elements from her life to that world, and after her last birthday, she had added the path in the woods. That was now how she got to the world of her twilight imaginings.

So Ilya closed her eyes, and even though she could hear the hint of whispers from the mothers wondering where their sons were, the sniffles of children who didn't want to know the truth, and the laughter of the soldiers keeping watch on the floor below them, Ilya was free. For those fleeting moments before sleep would take her. She might have pleasant dreams, or she might dream of the fort, and Father, and gates closing and walls closing in, and the needling fear of how she had memories of things that never happened, but for that brief in-between moment, when she was neither here nor there, she was free from fear and darkness. The path was waiting for her again, and it didn't run away from her, and at the end of it was light.

Chapter Fourteen

Ben had drawn a dotted line across the country, each dot representing some iteration of a ratty, dank, and dust-ridden motel. His pickup started billowing chugs of smoke if he spent more than ten minutes above sixty miles an hour, so it had taken Ben just under four days to get to Phoenix. He'd had countless hours of dry blinding white and endless black to think, his deepest wonderings surfacing on those long, post-midnight stretches between barren farmland and shuttered roadside gas stations. Where there was nothing beyond the emptiness that your headlights showed you. His mind primarily bounced between two powerful poles. Alistair and the Six. It was easy to think of them as existing only on-page. The lot of every writer, worrying yourself dead over invisible people who don't know you exist. But these people were real. And they were the key to everything. The truth was waiting for him in the darkness just beyond his view. So Ben drove on, through the dark, knowing he had what maybe no one had. A secret he kept with him always. A way to find the Six.

Truth be told, they were all real now. Alistair was actual, real-life Alistair. Having the chapters cut off when they did was cruel, but probably on purpose. She had a path, he had a path, and maybe in their search for whatever "the truth" was, they would meet. He'd had many moments of doubt on the road west, but although he felt like this was the thing he was supposed to do, he still wasn't sure *why* he was doing it. Honestly, he tried not to think about why for fear he'd turn around and head back to the rotting cabin where it was cold and solitary, but simple. Ben was there, somewhere outside Phoenix, because he was the only one who would, who *could* pursue this. The manuscript, Alistair, Bolden, Frank, Cor, his own book—it all put him on a path where a dozen things that never made sense began to hint at some kind of symmetry. Ben didn't want to think it, but maybe somewhere in Palomino Palms, California, was the reason for all of the turmoil of the past five years. The reason and, yes, maybe the truth.

Ben laid out the two towels from the bathroom over the motel bedspread to sleep on. At least he could count on them having been washed recently. He knew he'd make it to California tomorrow and the thought sent a brick down his gullet, where it sat all night in his gut.

Ben pulled out his phone. His advance hadn't been hefty, but it paid for gas, food, and his phone. It was more than he'd had in his bank account in months. He once again googled Jeremy Newhouse. Not much. No social presence. Made sense. If Aaron really wanted to leave his old life behind, he had to keep a low profile. The internet was a world of jagged points waiting to burst the bubble he hid inside. Ben would have to win Aaron's trust to get what he wanted. Aaron's entire life was manufactured exactly to hide from people like Ben.

Ben woke up a little later than he'd intended, showered, ate two crumbly granola bars from the gas station where he filled up (thanks, fake book advance) and started the last eight-hour leg to

Palomino Palms. He didn't know what he was going to say, or how he was going to approach Aaron. He just assumed he'd figure it out on the way.

He didn't.

It was 4:30 PM when Ben pulled over, across the street from the small, pennant-strewn used car dealership. Two guys in shirtsleeves and ties sat on the steps of the dealership's office, which looked like a double-wide trailer upgraded with a wall of floor-to-ceiling windows. The two smoked, kicked rocks across the customer-less lot, and generally shot the shit. One was round and Latino, shaped like a punctuation mark, and the other was thick but tall, with dark skin made darker by days spent carnival-barking at would-be car owners. Neither of the men was Aaron Haim.

As a teenager, Aaron had been blond, fair-skinned, an athlete, basically a cliché of small-town handsome, high school A-group. The kind of guy that Ben would've joked about the biology teacher's speech impediment with or talked sports with, bonding over some team, then been summarily ignored by outside of class. Aaron was the kind of kid who people basked in the light of, then shivered when the light turned away. Ben couldn't help but feel a twinge of schadenfreude at the idea of this blond, onetime paragon sweating his ass off on an overheated lot of used cars.

That was awful. This guy was hiding. The truth is, Ben was the massive crumbling failure. If Aaron had been a normal teenager with a normal teenage life, he'd either be a quarterback or the governor of California. Ben, on the other hand, would have probably ended up where he was no matter what. The only reason he was on his mysterious little adventure was *because* of Aaron Haim. Ben rolled down the windows of his airless truck.

Then Aaron stepped out of the office and suddenly, Ben didn't feel so sickly satisfied. Aaron was fit, broad, and built in the places that guys like Ben—guys who occasionally bought sheet cakes for one—would kill to be. And Aaron was five years older than Ben. Aaron's blond hair fell to his forehead in the warm SoCal wind, and he swiped it back. He looked cool. Even with a name tag. He didn't own the place, but he damned sure held himself like he did.

Ben suddenly had a pit in his stomach. He hated talking to guys like this. Ben had always been slightly below average height, and now he was slightly above average weight, and even though he refused to look, he was also pretty sure a worn-bald spot was beginning to show on the top of his head like an old stuffed animal who had done one too many head spins. Ben shook it off, adjusted his Henley, which he'd pretty much sweated clean through, and got out of his truck. He stood behind it, realizing all the opening icebreakers he'd conjured up over the past few days had completely left his brain. He watched Aaron chat with the other guys, shake his head at the offer of a cigarette, buff the corner of a hatchback with his shirt cuff, look up at the shimmering sun, shining back at it, hands on his waist. Ben saw the peaceful look on Aaron's face. He got back in his truck. He couldn't pierce the guy's bubble. Not yet. He wasn't ready.

Ben waited in the truck until the right time. The right time never came. Aaron was the last on the job, switching off the floodlights, locking the office and the gates to the lot. He got in a nondescript blue four-door and pulled down the road. Ben watched the taillights fade. Then he started up the choking pickup and followed Aaron, hanging a block behind. Ten minutes passed, Aaron making a beeline home.

Aaron finally pulled under a covered carport that leaned, rusted, against a green bungalow. The building was small but sweet, purposefully nondescript, like Aaron's car. Aaron jogged from the car to the front door, where a little blonde girl ambushed him. He grabbed her up and reached out for someone as he closed the door behind him. His wife. Holy shit. Janie Grant. The first and second of the Six, not only still together after twenty years, but now with a seventh.

Ben parked the truck and sat outside Aaron and Janie's house most of the evening until all the lights in the house went off. He tried to figure out why he couldn't do it. Why he couldn't approach Aaron. Why he couldn't have just gone up and knocked on their door. He could've calmly explained to them why he was there, how he found them, what he needed from them. Ben certainly didn't look like a threat—not any more than anyone else. Aaron seemed . . . safe? That's what it was—the look on his face, for that beat in the car lot, when he looked up at the sun. It was peaceful. Aaron felt *safe.* He felt that he, his wife, and his baby girl were safe. Ben had come to blow that up. And now that he was there, he realized he couldn't.

🦅

Ben couldn't sleep, so he drove around Palomino Palms the rest of the night, patrolling the ghostly, barely-there town. It was the West Coast equivalent of Crystal Ridge, New York. The kind of place that was loaded for bear with natives who had been sucked into the entropy of this little life, stuck inside the bubble. Who in their right mind would move here? People who wanted to disappear. Ben maintained the strict thirty-five mile per hour speed limit until the sun came up. He was at a red light, pointed back at the East Coast when a bird landed on the hood of his truck. It hopped a couple of times until it was right in front of him. A crow. It opened its broken beak.

Follow.

The crow shook its head, like it itched, or was saying no. Then it flew away. Ben whipped to the rearview mirror and watched the bird sail over the road he'd just come from and turn a corner. The light turned green. Ben didn't move. That couldn't have . . . it couldn't have been the same bird from the cabin. Birds all sound basically alike, right? He was tired. He'd been up all night. He was in the middle of nowhere and just wanted to go home.

He'd planned on parking the truck somewhere and taking a flight back, leaving the old beast to rot in the desert. Instead, he pulled into the intersection, and when the time was right, he made a wide U-turn. He was going back to the Newhouses'. Worst-case scenario: they tell him to get lost, he does, he goes home.

❦

It was 10 AM on Saturday. As Ben pulled up, he saw that Janie's back was to the street. She was on her knees digging into the flowery landscaping along the house, her daughter by her side, the little girl's tiny purple pants already filthy. Ben eased back into the same spot and parked. The front door opened, and Aaron emerged in shorts and a T-shirt, holding a towheaded baby in his arms. Eighth. Aaron bounced the little boy up and down, watching his girls dig in the dirt. Then he handed the baby to Janie and headed toward the sidewalk, looking right at Ben. They stared at each other for a beat before Aaron finally smiled, waved, and beckoned him over. Ben's brow burst with sweat. He got out of the truck and circled to the front. Janie turned, holding the baby, rubbing the little girl on the back. She was smiling too.

"Dan?" Aaron asked. Ben couldn't answer. He'd left all the words in the truck.

"You're here about the ad, right? The golf clubs?" Aaron asked, still smiling. Perfectly imperfect teeth. When was the last time Ben wore shorts? That's what he was thinking when he nodded, crossed the street, reached out his hand, and said, "Hi. Dan."

Aaron grabbed Ben's hand, shook it like a car dealer, then moved to the carport. "Come on back."

Ben followed like he was under a spell. He heard a sound and turned, and, for a second, he saw the crow with the broken beak watching him from the mailbox as he crossed the sidewalk. A wave of something like nausea washed over him. He shook his head to right himself, and then the crow was . . . gone. And the mailbox was a different . . . shape? Color?

He turned back to Aaron, who was already behind the house.

Ben crossed the lawn. Janie nodded, smiling, and turned back to the flowers. Which were red, but hadn't they been purple? And the house, it was blue, not green. Even the grass had a different tone from a moment ago. Ben looked up. The sky looked like someone had screwed the wrong sun in today. Everything had a slight yellow-orange cast, like looking through a glass with a final sip of orange juice at the bottom.

Ben stepped under the carport and followed Aaron around the house. Past the car was a gate to the backyard. It swung open. Beyond, Aaron unlatched the door to a small prefab shed. Ben's nausea was gone, but his hand trailed the side of the car—the blue on the body was darker here. What was going on? Was he sleep-deprived? Why the hell had he said he was Dan? *What happens if Dan shows up?* Ben passed through the fence, across the small, brown backyard, and up the two steps to the shed. Inside, it was maybe ten feet long, crammed with boxes, yard equipment, holiday decorations, and toys their little girl had outgrown. Aaron pulled the clubs out from behind a few garden tools.

"They're just a little dusty. And the four-wood got chucked into a pond last year. I mentioned that in the ad. Have a look." Aaron stepped aside.

Ben nodded and walked to the clubs, fondling them like he had a clue about golf.

"This your first set?" Aaron asked.

This was it. He couldn't keep going on like this. He had to stop lying if he was going to earn their trust.

"Actually, I'm . . . I'm not here for the clubs," Ben stuttered as he turned to face Aaron, who, in the second Ben's back was turned, had pulled a long, silver sword out of thin air.

"No kidding," Aaron answered.

Chapter Fifteen

Alistair was surrounded by takeout boxes, soda cans, pencils, paper, and her phone. She hadn't worn pants in twenty-four hours, hadn't left her bed in twelve, and hadn't seen direct sunlight in almost forty-eight. At some point, she started taking notes to keep track of everything she found interesting, relevant, or worth further research in the two volumes of *The Monarch Papers*. At first read, the series seemed like a strange, heady mix of real and fictional, actual locations and real people mixed with make-believe supernatural events and histories. Just enough reality to ground it, and just enough magic to stick it in any bookstore's fantasy section. The gist of the story was that magic used to exist in our world, then *something* happened to erase it and our memory of it. Left with only scraps of memory and magical power, a ragtag group of people from around the world banded together to unlock a mysterious book/website called "The Book of Briars," which promised to tell them the truth about what happened to magic if they could unravel its mysteries and insanely complicated puzzles. At the center of the history-altering mystery?

A series of books called "the lost collection" or just . . . *the briar books.*

No one remembered the books but her, but *The Monarch Papers* proposed that there *were* people around the world that remembered the book-shaped hole *the briar books* left behind, if not the books themselves. Alistair knew the site for "Ackerly Green's Guide to Magiq" no longer worked from her previous search, but in *The Monarch Papers,* that site had been the doorway to what seemed like some kind of interactive experience. A gamified marketing campaign for a book called *The Book of Briars.* But she couldn't find the forum where the readers, or "Mountaineers" congregated, and it was unclear if it had been taken down after the experience had ended in 2017, or if it had ever existed at all. A quick search on retailer sites proved there was no book called *The Book of Briars.*

Her phone buzzed. It was Zev. They'd been texting on an off, first about Ackerly Green, then about finding Deirdre's brownstone, and the people she'd met there. Their texts were a welcome respite from the books, though while their talks helped keep her in the shallows, they weren't without their own strange feelings and odd revelations. She found herself drifting from online searches about the people and places in *The Monarch Papers* to searching for information about the process of pursuing a Ph.D. so she could ask about Zev and his life without seeming completely uneducated. Alistair had never gone to college, had no idea how higher education worked, and the realization that she kind of cared what he thought about her was not-so-slowly dawning on her. That was a new feeling for her, and even more surprising was that she didn't seem to mind. After hours of texting him questions that vacillated between him and his rigorous collegiate pursuits—

—which means I have essentially zero personal life, not that I would otherwise. But I manage to make time for stuff that's important to me. :)

—to the earliest mentions of magic in literature and the epistolary format of narratives told through correspondence, like *The Monarch Papers.* A half-day into her delve, Zev downloaded copies of the two books and was feverishly trying to catch up with her.

I just got to where Deirdre wrote about you. You're the book dealer! And she went to Cumberland Books? What the hell is going on?

It gets so much weirder.

It's like they were written for you to read. An 800+ page encrypted message in the form of a roman à clef.

Alistair had to look up what a "roman à clef" was before responding with—

Yes! Totally.

Their exchanges evolved into trying to separate what was definitely or most likely true, from what was definitely or most likely make-believe. As Alistair read, she found her list of "definitely fiction" was getting shorter and shorter. It was becoming impossible to dismiss the books because so much of their narrative connected with fragments of broken memory *she* still had about *the briar books*. Things she didn't realize anyone else remembered. Zev texted:

I'm 75% done with volume one. I would ask if any of this rings a bell but at this point, the better question is just how many bells are ringing?

Too many to count. The six guilds, "neithernor" (just the word, not the pocket world), the chronocompass, which, in the briar books was like a watch, a compass, and a magical divining rod all in one. A million other things. Just wait till you get to volume two and "the little red house."

Alistair recognized the name immediately. *The Little Red House* was the title of the first of *the briar books*. Although, she half-remembered the title being longer, or maybe there had been a subtitle, but regardless, someone else knew the name. Not just her. Characters in *The Monarch Papers* had even found a copy of the book, although it had been turned to ash in a climactic Central Park battle where they confronted a sentient storm front. Alistair called them "characters" just to keep her head on straight, but many had real-world counterparts. Alistair had been researching and texted Zev with the results:

There's a real reporter/author named Martin Rank, a real Howard

Doshen at the Times, a kid who died (or didn't) back in the '80s named Brandon Lachmann.

And the Silver.

Wait. What? The Silver?

Well, I don't know if they're a nefarious supernatural sect bent on collecting every scrap of magic left in the world, but there are a lot of historical references to clandestine guilds in Anne of Brittany's court, as well as literary secret societies that fit the bill and the name "the Silver." These smaller societies usually die off or get swallowed up by bigger "mother societies" but they often have religious or political goals. The Silver sounds the same, but with magic.

Her phone buzzed and buzzed, Zev regaling her with centuries' worth of lore and history about secret societies. It made her smile, thinking about him sending her reams of texts about hidden libraries, secret languages, and globe-spanning cults. In his element. Not only was this right up his alley, but he also uniquely understood what this all meant for Alistair.

You're not alone.

She wasn't alone. Not in her memories or beliefs, not in her exploration of this seemingly endless rabbit hole . . . even the date she came back was a touchstone she shared with six other people. They all got a buried mention in Volume Two regarding *children who went missing and came back.* A group of teenagers called the Santa Colette Six, along with "the girl in Jersey," which is where Alistair had lived with her parents before she vanished. Alistair googled the Six and found a few old articles about them disappearing, the search, and then coming back a year later, on *November 11, 2004.*

The date of their shared return was irrefutable. Alistair could deny just about every other strange thing in the books: spells, alternative timelines, evil shadow societies, living storms—but not the date. The internet had preserved that date in digital amber. It was real.

Were the Six the ones that Bolden mentioned, the other ones

who remembered? Or had she been referring to characters in the books, like Martin Rank? And if this was what Alistair was supposed to do, find and read these books, then why hadn't she heard from Bolden? The trio she'd met in Deirdre's brownstone, Endri, Bash, and Aether, were all characters in the book, but also real. She'd seen them, spoken to them—were they sent there by Bolden to meet her? There were multiple references to figurative roads and paths in *The Monarch Papers*, just like Bolden had mentioned. Was this hers?

Endri had written her number on the inside cover of Volume One. Alistair called it after she'd finished Volume Two. No answer. Voicemail. She wasn't sure what to say, what to ask, so she simply said she'd read the books and then hung up, unable to bring herself to say that she believed the story. Otherwise, she'd done everything Bolden asked her to do. If the trio were actually working with Bolden, they would have told her Alistair had the books and read them.

Alistair had kind of gone numb from revelation. There was so much symmetry in the story, and the rush of emotions had worn her out. But above everything else, there was one piece of lore in the books that stuck in Alistair's mind.

There were places called *wells*—rare, important places where memory and magic hadn't been fully erased. These "deep places" still held on to lingering scraps, both nebulous and physical. Thoughts, memories, and objects could sometimes be found in these hinterland spaces. The books stated that libraries and old places were often wells, and the description of what they were made Alistair think of the house on the Hudson, where she'd been drawn to Iris, a toy that shouldn't exist, and then to her previous episodes as a child. The bike shed at the old library and the field trip to Ellis Island at twelve, Central Park the year she came back. She couldn't remember *all* of her episodes, the times she'd gone so deep into the dark that she saw the bespectacled fox and the thing in the black that it heralded, but the ones she *could* remember all happened in old, strange places. She didn't want to believe anything in the books, but she was already instilled with a grain of belief in the unbelievable simply because she remembered *the briar books*. She held on to impossible memories and had an impossible toy on her nightstand. Would it be too far a leap to take to believe that impossible places existed? Especially when their existence would turn the scope of her life into some kind of strange focus? The truth is that she *wanted* to believe, even in the most fantastic elements of the books, because believing in *The Monarch Papers*, and everyone within its pages, meant everything else she believed was true. Zev texted:

You said the guy yelled something at you before you blacked out and then when you woke up, he was puking in the kitchen sink. Spell sickness?

I hadn't even thought of that. Good catch. Endri did say she knew I wasn't there to cause trouble, and now I'm thinking . . . Joradian Safeguard? The spell they cast to test people before letting them in?

Right! We're basically the best supernatural teenage detectives ever.

Zev was still understandably skeptical and more firmly on the side of "mostly made up." Alistair felt strangely wounded by his continuing incredulity, even though she objectively understood. He hadn't shared her experiences over the past fifteen years or seen the strange things over the past few weeks. But she had. In *The Monarch Papers* there were different kinds of "magical people," but there was one kind that wasn't exactly gifted, but was instead "sensitive" to magic. What if . . . that was Alistair? It seemed ridiculous, but would that be why she "felt" the toy Iris under the shelf in the closet? Felt its wrongness, its doesn't-belongness? Alistair remembered that on her way to Deirdre's brownstone, she'd felt wisps of those same feelings, like the house on the Hudson—maybe she could go back and find it again, test her theory. Apply a sort of scientific method to the magic. Not enough to slip into the dark, but enough to . . . know. Bolden had said that Alistair wouldn't believe her if she just outright told her the truth. But Alistair also wanted to prove to Zev that there was something supernatural going on, because she really wanted him to be completely on her side of the fiction/nonfiction divide.

She flipped through her notes. She'd written down any real location or address in the series. Works of art, sculptures and fountains, Deirdre's brownstone . . . *the bottle of ash on the mantel in Deidre's brownstone. Was that what was left of* The Little Red House? *Is that why Alistair had seen the fox there? Had she sensed the book?* With nowhere else to turn, and still no word from Bolden, Alistair decided she'd get out of bed and go back to the brownstone. Deirdre's house had led her this far, and armed with everything she knew now, along with a *willingness* to believe in the supernatural if not an outright belief, maybe she'd find her next step on the path. Maybe Bolden would be waiting on the front steps to tell her magic was real. She slid into her coat and made sure she had her phone. It was like she was bringing Zev with her. Two days of complete isolation and she'd never felt less alone. Alistair had always seen her past, her memories, as dark and terrifying. Isolating. Things to fear, and work to hide from. But *The Monarch Papers*, and Bolden, and maybe even Zev, now posited that there was light in the darkness. Hope in the despair. Not only beauty in the blackness, but a possible way out. Alistair had never once looked at it that way. The idea that she didn't have to be broken. She could be special.

◈

The fall air had turned sharp and raw, but the sun would still occasionally break through the heavy clouds and Alistair appreciated the juxtaposition of sunny warmth and stinging cold. Bolden wasn't waiting at the brownstone. No one was. Alistair had knocked a few times, but no one was home—or no one was answering. She didn't want to break in again. Now that she'd met the trio, it felt especially inconsiderate. Alistair knocked a few more times, then with an eye roll, she put the palm of her hand to the door, trying to *feel* anything. She mostly felt door. She laughed to herself at the absurdity of trying to test out her potential magic superpower.

She checked her notes. The next closest location was a building Deirdre visited near the end of Volume Two, where a company called A&L Printing used to be. It was where Deirdre's father and grandfather worked for a time in the '70s before the fire that ended their paperback printing business. It didn't seem especially "magical," but the weather was turning icy and raw, and the address was basically on her way back home. She should've worn a sweater under her coat or at least a scarf. She turned her lucky coat collar up around her neck and trudged on.

She was there in fifteen minutes; her nose and cheeks now numb to the touch and tingling. Alistair huffed, a white cloud escaping her mouth. The building wasn't so much a building as it was a building-shaped gap where a building had recently stood. A tall green plywood barricade wrapped around the construction site where a backhoe occasionally rose up like a dinosaur, spitting out dust and broken bricks.

A few feet down the block, a tall, grey-haired man in a suit and overcoat huddled outside the barricade with a group of layered-up construction workers. There was lots of pointing and showing of plans. The workers eventually disbanded through a makeshift door in the barricade, leaving the guy in the suit alone. Alistair figured he was worth a shot.

"Excuse me?" Alistair called to the man.

He turned to her, seemingly unsure if she was talking to him. He had ice-blue eyes and a neatly trimmed silver-white beard.

"Yes?" He asked.

"Was this A&L Printing?"

The man approached with a bit of a proud swagger. His cologne arrived first.

"It was most recently a co-working space—you know, glass walls and beer taps—but it was a printing house in the '70s or '80s. Some of the old equipment was still down in the basement. Hi, by the way. Derrick Shane. I'm the architect on the project."

Alistair shook his hand.

"What happened to that stuff? Everything that was left behind?" Alistair asked.

"Landfill, I'd wager.

"What's going up here? Lemme guess, another bank?"

Shane laughed, "Actually, we're not building anything. We're *moving* a building here. From Philadelphia."

"How do you *move* a building?"

"We number every brick, every beam, every floorboard, and put it all back together like a bunch of Lincoln Logs. You're probably too young to know what those are."

"Definitely." Alistair barely succeeded at suppressing an eye-roll. "But why would you move a building instead of building a new one? And why move it from Philly?"

"Well, we're moving the building *back* to New York. It was a publishing house down in the Financial District sometime in the late 1800s. The firm I'm working with wants it home," Shane said with a raised eyebrow.

It sounded like something straight out of *The Monarch Papers*. A mysterious organization tears down an old publishing house just to replace it with an even older one from a city a few hundred miles away. And the site's connection to Ackerly Green . . . could've been a coincidence, but it didn't *feel* like one. It was worth a shot—

"Sounds like we'd have a lot in common," said Alistair.

"Who?" Shane asked with a smile.

"The firm and me. We're both interested in old publishing companies," Alistair said, hoping it would be enough bait to hook Shane's interest. It seemed he only wanted to talk about himself, so Alistair jammed the hook in herself.

"My . . . family owned it for a while. A&L Printing. The building that used to be here. My father, grandfather . . . they both worked here. I'm sorry, I didn't introduce myself. I'm Deirdre. Deirdre Green."

"Beautiful name."

"Thank you. My mother was Irish. Our family had a long history in books. My grandfather started his own company back in the '50s. Ackerly Green Publishing?"

Shane smiled. "We bought that building, did some pretty unique refitting and restoration, and had it listed as a historic site almost fifteen years ago. It was quite an ordeal. Beautiful old thing."

"What building?"

"Ackerly Green Publishing. Its old offices."

"You're kidding me. I didn't know it was still standing."

"Wanna see it?"

It took ten long minutes for Alistair to convince Derrick Shane that she could make it on her own and to just give her the damned address. The sun had set, and the air had turned biting. She was a few blocks west of the Jefferson Market Library, back in the West Village, when she felt the first currents of that *feeling*. The same one she'd felt at the house on the Hudson and the night she first went to Deirdre's brownstone. She imagined the currents were guiding her to the address. Even with the strange feeling urging her on, if she hadn't had the address, she would've walked right by. It was an impossible-looking sliver hidden in the shadow of two townhomes (not brownstones.) A fraction of a building set back from the sidewalk that looked like it was being consumed by the towering houses on either side. Nothing but a dark stone façade, a black door at the top of eight steps, and two tall, narrow windows on either side. Alistair crept up the steps to the door. The currents she felt were pouring out of this building, but instead of pushing at her, it was pulling, like a riptide.

She steadied herself, then reached for the door, checking to see if it was locked. Touching it delivered the same electric, icy zing of a limb falling asleep, and there was something odd about the material it was made from. She pulled out her phone, turned on the flashlight, and as she looked closer, she realized the door wasn't a door. It was a sculpture—door and doorframe, knocker and knob, all carved out of a single piece of black matte stone. There was no way in. Alistair leaned over the railing, looking into one of the windows. There was nothing inside. A void of black without corners or edges, as if more of the impenetrable stone was pressed behind the glass. Like it wasn't a building at all, but a solid icy monolith. Was this the "restoration" Derrick Shane claimed to have done to this place?

She took a step back, training her flashlight beam up the building. On the overhang above the door, she found a carving. A strange chimeric creature, like a horned ram's head with a limbless torso that melted away into a half dozen coiling tentacles. She could almost see them writhing, the carving was so well-defined. The creature took her breath away because she'd seen it before. Tattooed on the arm of Ed Cumberland.

Chapter Sixteen

"How did you find us?" Aaron hissed, snatching Ben by the shirt collar, his other hand extended behind him, gripping the hilt of the sword, pointing it into Ben's gut.

"Wait!" Ben gasped, Aaron now looming over him. Ben sucked in his stomach reflexively, out of fear, out of lingering flecks of ego that felt stupidly inappropriate at a moment like this.

"How did you find us?!" Aaron asked again.

"It's . . . it's complicated," Ben whimpered, his hands raised in surrender.

Aaron was in Ben's face, seething.

"Have you been following my family?"

"No. I'm not a stalker. I came here—"

"How?! How did you find us?!"

Ben felt the blade tip scrape against the skin of his stomach. It had pierced his shirt. "There—was a newspaper ad. For your dealership. You used your mom's maiden name."

A look of disgust twisted Aaron's face.

"You're sick. How do you know that?"

"No, please, I'm *not* stalking you. I was . . . I was working on a book. About missing people. A long time ago. You and the rest of the Six were what inspired it, but—I didn't put you in the book. I knew you wanted to hide, and I let you."

"You *let* me?"

"I mean, I mean I let it go. No one else knows. I swear. I just need . . . I need help. I need answers."

Ben could see that Aaron's eyes were still enraged, but they were also brimming with tears.

"Do you have a family?" Aaron asked, his lower lip shaking.

Ben shook his head.

"My family's happy here. Finally. My daughter loves her school. She has friends. We have friends. Please . . . please, don't take that away. It's not her fault. None of this is."

"I'm just trying to figure out what's going on, because people I care about have been hurt too. I don't want to screw your life up here. I swear. Please put the . . . sword down, Jeremy." Ben thought if he said *Jeremy* and not *Aaron*, it would drive his point across. He wasn't here to expose him. To hurt him. Ben's stray cognitive reasoning was a pinball in his brain. Anything could be the best, or worst, idea. He was just saying whatever bounced out of his mouth. It was better than a blade in his belly.

It seemed to work. Aaron let go of Ben's collar, still digging the end of the blade against his stomach. Ben could see the exhaustion on Aaron's face now that the facade of Jeremy Newhouse had fully cracked open. He was weary. Standing on the edge, about to run someone through.

"Who are you?" Aaron asked.

"Nobody."

"What's your *name*?" Aaron spat in reply.

"Ben—Ben Kriminger. But I'm nobody. That's why none of this makes sense. I don't know why I've been dragged into this. That's why I need your help."

"Just leave us alone, and I won't hurt you. I promise. Please. Go," Aaron answered, almost pleading.

"I want to. Just give me five minutes, and you'll never see me again." Ben was pleading back, realizing he had no idea what he was going to ask or say, even if Aaron afforded him five more minutes.

"What do you want?" Aaron asked, finally inching the sword away and leaning against the wall of the shed. Ben slowly lowered his arms. He grabbed his stomach, and without looking, knew there was blood on his hand. Not a lot, but enough to make his stomach turn.

"I'm . . . not sure. I mean, I don't know where to start. There's a young woman that I'm connected to in some weird way, I think, because I wrote that book, not about you, but about other missing people, and where they went. It was all fantasy. But some people thought I knew something, about alternate histories and lost memories, and, well, this woman also went missing when she was a little girl. But then she came back. And someone started sending me stories about her."

Aaron had an appropriate look of confusion on his face.

"I know, I know . . . none of this is making sense. That's kind of the problem. But . . . the thing is . . . she came back home, a year later, on the same day you and your friends came home on the other side of the country. I'm trying to help her, I guess, I think, and figure out what I did to get roped into this, or what I'm supposed to do. I honestly don't know, man, but I know this is all connected, and the sooner I know, the sooner I'll know what to do," Ben said. "I know you made a promise. To your friends. And I don't want to make you break it, but if there's anything you could tell me about what happened to you. Where you went—"

"What do you think is happening here?" Aaron interrupted. "You think I've been dragging my family back and forth across the country just because people like you have bullshit theories and excuses for needing to know what happened to us? You have no idea what you're asking."

Aaron was away from the wall again, taking slow steps toward Ben, sword twisting in his hand. "There are people out there . . .

people working together, in the dark, looking for us, hunting us. People that would hurt everyone I love just to know what we know, to try and get at something they think we had and never really did. I'm doing you a favor by not telling you, because if you dig any deeper, if you look any further . . . You don't understand what you're asking me. And if you did understand . . . you'd beg me not to."

"Try me."

"I couldn't if I wanted to . . ."

Janie called to Jeremy from the front of the house.

Aaron opened the shed door. "Be right there!" Then he turned to Ben. "Go home."

"Who are these people? The ones in the dark? Maybe they're the ones sending me this shit."

Aaron said, "You're leaning over a dangerous rabbit hole."

"And you think I'm gonna fall in."

"You don't *fall* down this one. It drags you in."

Ben realized this was his last shot, his last chance to turn the conversation around. If not, all of this was for nothing. The pages, the trip, the lies, the last three years . . .

"Is this about the books?"

"What books?" Aaron asked.

Ben almost couldn't say it, because he knew *not saying it* might be his only chance to walk out of this shed.

"*The briar books.*"

Aaron's sun-tinged face went pale. The look of whitewashed shock flooded over Aaron's face so quickly, so dramatically, that Ben felt chills running up his sweaty back.

"I don't know . . . what you're talking about."

"Yes, you do." For the first time, Ben felt like he had the upper hand, but it made him feel nauseated. He was lying, co-opting someone else's story, and hurting an innocent person, all for reasons Ben couldn't even articulate. The truth. The stupid truth.

Aaron shook his head, "Sorry, buddy, I can't help you . . . It's time to go."

Aaron was shaking.

Ben leaned into the lie. "Iris with her bow and arrow."

Aaron shook his head harder, his head bowed, eyes low.

"Stop," Aaron whispered.

"I remember all of it."

Aaron rushed him so quickly that Ben yelped. The sword clanged to the shed floor as Aaron slammed his hand over Ben's mouth, the other behind Ben's head, like a vise. He was begging Ben with silent head-shaking to stop talking.

After the shock wore off, Ben gave a short nod and Aaron uncovered his mouth. In the silence, Ben realized that rain had started pattering on the aluminum roof of the shed. Another long moment of quiet passed, then Aaron spoke in a voice so quiet Ben strained to hear over the growing taps of rainfall.

"This is impossible. It's supposed to be impossible."

"What is?" Ben answered, matching his quiet.

"The books," Aaron answered with a monotone chillness.

"So they're real. They're part of your secret."

"They *are* the secret. I've never even talked about it with Janie. Not really. We swore . . ."

The rain was falling harder now. Ben took a step closer to Aaron, scared to ask him to repeat himself. Scared he'd shatter this moment.

"Never?"

"We couldn't risk it. We thought we were the only five people in the world who could remember, and it had to stay that way. If we said it out loud, if we let that word back into the world, everything we lost would be for nothing, and everything left would be lost."

"What word?"

Aaron looked at Ben, tears now running down his cheeks. He looked like he was seventeen all over again.

Aaron spoke.

The sound that escaped his mouth was short, strange, and indecipherable. Whatever it was, it wasn't a word that Ben had ever heard before. Aaron covered his mouth, a mask of fear washing over his face.

Then the sky tore in two. Thunder cracked the silence of the strange scene, rattling both of them, ringing Ben's ears. He couldn't hear anything but a staccato siren howling in the distance.

Not a siren. A scream. Ben realized just as Aaron did, but Aaron was already out of the shed, sprinting to the source of the screaming. The front yard. Ben took off after him, shocked by how much faster Aaron was.

Ben was drenched with icy slices of rain by the time he rounded the corner of the house, his hand still covering the wound on his stomach. Aaron wasn't there. Neither was his family.

"Aaron?"

Ben saw that the front door was wide open. A scream bleated out from the house, a little girl's scream. Ben stumbled to the front porch and saw Aaron sitting on the carpet inside the house, holding his daughter to his chest. Janie was pacing the living room, on the phone, telling someone to hurry, hurry, hurry. Aaron was stroking his daughter's head while their other child cried in the next room.

Ben saw the edges of the little girl's yellow hair. It had been freshly blackened and curled into knots. Then the smell came to him, acrid and sharp. She had been burned.

Aaron looked at Ben once more, that same pleading in his eyes, like this happened because he tried to tell Ben. Then Aaron kicked the front door shut with his foot.

Ben stood in the rain, confused, the adrenaline from the shed dissipating into his limbs. He felt like puking. He turned toward his pickup and found a foot-deep black hole in the lawn, at least six feet across. The grass was gone, burned down to dirt, smoke still curling off the edges of the hole.

Lightning. Aaron's little girl had been grazed by a bolt of lightning.

Ben's blue-green pickup turned blue again as he got closer. He barely noticed. The crow was gone from the mailbox, the little door hanging open. He got in the truck, started it up, and pulled away, taking the first turn he could, his hand still on his stomach. It wasn't deep, but his hand was sticky with blood. He was two blocks away before he noticed the envelope stuck between the windshield and the wiper.

He pulled over, got out, and grabbed the letter. The envelope was returned mail. A letter sent from Janie to Los Angeles, then returned by Veronica Morrow. Janie's best friend. And another of the Six.

The crow on the mailbox.

He had left the letter for Ben.

Chapter Seventeen

Alistair had first seen the creature, the ram with tentacles, four, maybe five years prior.

She couldn't remember the specific book, but she did remember finding something special in the first haul she'd made on her own, or maybe it was the haul that inspired her to eventually set out on her own in the first place.

Ed hadn't been answering his phone that night, so she'd taken the train up to Morningside Heights, to his brownstone despite the late hour. The find was too exciting not to share right away. It was raining. A thick, loud, New York City deluge, the kind that flushes rivers of old garbage and black soot down the gutters, giving the place a much-needed bath.

The downstairs shop was closed so she knocked on Ed's apartment door, huddling under the small awning to stay out of the rain until she saw a light pop on in the window looking out on the street. Then Ed answered the door, still dressed from the day, his reading glasses inched down his nose, a book in his hand. No shoes, just socks. He looked vulnerable, older than usual. Caught off guard.

He'd urged her up the stairs, into the cluttered house, and out of the rain. His sleeves had been rolled up, exposing his muscle-roped forearms, which were covered in old, faded tattoos. She'd never seen them before that night. Not more than a fleeting glimpse here and there, peeking from behind a shirt cuff when he reached up to a tall shelf or sweating through a white dress shirt after he'd carried boxes down to the bookshop basement. Never so clearly, and never all at once. She'd assumed they were collected during his time in the military—a time in his life he never discussed, so she never asked. There were skulls and swords and barely dressed pinup girls, the winking kind you'd find painted on the side of a warplane in movies. Almost ironically dated.

Ed had ushered her into the living room. Thinking back now, she remembered that when he joined her, uncharacteristically emphatic in his welcome, his sleeves had been rolled down again. She assumed he'd been ashamed or embarrassed by the ink. That was the first time she'd seen the creature—next to a serpent and a book with branches growing from its pages, etched into his right arm: the chimera.

Alistair's heart raced as she sat in a booth in the back of the all-night Morningside Diner. She'd found Wi-Fi, called Ed, and told him she wanted to meet for dinner, to really catch up. She tried not to sound dramatic and over-the-top. It worked. It was almost 7 PM and Ed was never late so she knew he was on his way. She tried to formulate what she would say, or ask, but her mind had gone blank. Zev texted:

He just left the shop. Let me know when he gets there.

Alistair had come up with the perfect plan and had easily roped Zev into it. But now, she was in the midst of a blind, white panic at the thought of what she was doing and what she'd asked him to do. The plan was thus: Alistair would call Ed, urge him to meet her, and when he got to the diner—the Formica-clad relic that they always used to eat at after working in the bookshop—Zev would use the spare key Alistair still had for the shop to see if he could find anything in his back office, or maybe a key to Ed's apartment. They were looking for anything related to Ackerly Green, anything connected to the toy Alistair found at the house on the Hudson, anything related to Bolden, or Deirdre Green, or Alistair herself. She didn't know what the hell Zev should be looking for, honestly, but Ed was somehow connected to that door, to that building, and maybe to this mystery, and she needed to know how. She wanted to be in the lead for once, instead of following blindly behind. It seemed like a perfectly "A to Z" plan when they were hatching it on the street corner and in the cab uptown—distracting their mark with banal conversation while your partner secretly infiltrated their lair. Now, in the fluorescent glare of reality, Alistair was having significant second thoughts, and her brain, aching with stress, had decided not to cooperate. The third cup of coffee she was cradling wasn't helping her agita.

She could hear her heartbeat pounding in her ears as Ed turned the corner and approached the bank of windows overlooking 140th Street. He didn't see her yet. She quickly keyed a text to Zev, her thumb hovering over the send button for a second before she finally hit it:

He just showed up. Go for it.

In truth, there was a drop or two of excitement mixed in with all the tension and anxiety. The mission, the secret plan with Zev, it was scary, but also kind of fun, benignly treacherous, and strangely flirty. They were now co-conspirators. Alistair just had to remember that if she didn't convincingly stall Ed long enough and her phone didn't stay connected to the diner Wi-Fi long enough to get Zev's eventual, hopefully "all-clear" text, then, well, who the hell knows what would happen? She took a long, deep breath, and smiled as Ed sank into the booth across from her. She set her phone on the table, face down, her hand perched on it.

"On the list of things I didn't expect . . ."

"A dinner invite from your old work friend?" Alistair answered.

"Fully recovered?" Ed asked, waving for a server to come over.

"Oh, from . . . yeah. I'm good."

"What do you think it was?" Ed asked, and then, "Did you order?"

"No, not yet."

A scruffy, beleaguered server loomed over them, pencil and pad at the ready.

"Steak and eggs, over easy, medium-rare, rye toast, and black coffee," Ed said.

Alistair's phone buzzed. She flipped it over to check the notification. Zev:

I'm in.

"Got it. How about you? Anything besides coffee?" the server asked Alistair.

Alistair fumbled, turning the phone over again, "Uh . . . grilled cheese and tomato soup?" She was too stressed to eat, but the stock image of a crosscut grilled cheese and tomato soup on the cover of the laminated menu looked like . . . food.

"Got it. I'll get your coffee right out."

The server slumped away.

"So?"

"So what?" she replied.

"What do you think it was, your blackout?"

"Honestly? Hunger, lack of sleep . . ."

"All basic human requirements. You taking care of yourself?"

"I am now," she said, sipping her coffee as the server returned with Ed's cup.

"I don't like worrying," Ed muttered. "Don't make me worry."

Alistair smiled, the stress melting a little as she remembered: this is Ed. Her old boss. As close to a friend as she could claim, and as close to a father figure as she ever had. More than kind-but-never-wanted-kids-to-begin-with Uncle Gus at least. Not that she ever needed a father. Not that either Ed or Alistair were capable of expressing that kind of connection, but there was something there, sometimes strangely akin to brothers-in-arms, and Alistair suddenly felt guilty for this plan. She couldn't even remember *why* she'd gone to Ed's house that night, years before in the downpour. How the hell was she so sure she remembered one of a couple dozen tattoos she saw for thirty seconds, nearly five years ago? She wanted to text Zev and call it off. Maybe she'd overreacted.

"I thought you gave up red meat," she said.

"I did. But this is a special occasion."

"Special enough to risk another heart attack? I'm honored you missed me so much."

Ed smiled, took a swig of coffee. "I *have* missed you."

Alistair's heart sank. Ed was being completely sincere, open, heartfelt. She'd never seen him like this. Her plan now felt cruel.

"But that's not what this is about, is it?" he said. "This is about the books."

"Right. Books," Alistair answered, distracted. "That reminds me. I have to follow up about one."

Alistair picked up her phone, starting an abort message to Zev: *Doesn't feel right, maybe we—*

"To be specific, *the briar books*." Ed continued.

Alistair looked up, stunned. "What?"

No one remembered the books but her.

She'd never, ever mentioned *the briar books* to Ed. She suddenly felt like *she* was the one in the dark, again, not him.

"It's okay. I've been expecting this for a long time," Ed said.

"How—" Alistair stammered.

"How do I know about the books? Or how do I know about you?"

"What do you know about me?" Alistair asked, a slight but sudden flush of anger washing over her.

"I knew someday I'd have to tell you everything. I just hope you'll hear me out before you react. Deal?"

What choice did she have? "Okay."

"Everything you know about me is true. I've never lied to you. I've been in the book business for decades. I was a marine. I enlisted the day I turned eighteen, spent fifteen years abroad. Was always looking for something else. Married once. Divorced. No kids. That's all true. But there are other parts of my life, and our friendship, that you don't know. But it's not because I wanted to lie to you. Far from it. I was trying to protect you, in more ways than one."

Her phone buzzed. She still had it in her hand, mid-text. She glanced down to Zev's message:

Front counter is clean, office locked, but I think I can fit through the transom window over the door.

"I know you figured it out, but how did you figure it out?" Ed asked.

Alistair looked up, stymied. What *had* she figured out? Ed had a strangely similar tattoo to a pediment in the West Village. What else? She was trying to catch up while also suddenly playing as if she knew far more than she did.

"The tattoo."

"Which tattoo?"

"The chimera."

"Ah. You've got a good eye. It's an ovihydrus. I got it in this stall in Can Tho. Surprised my arm didn't rot off. That was before I knew what it was. I just knew I was drawn to it, and everything it represented."

"Which is?" It seemed like a reasonable question to ask without giving away her ignorance.

"It . . . represents the collection and preservation of rare and lost things, which is how we met, remember?"

"What does that have to do with me?"

"Do you *remember* how we met?"

"The old bookstore? The fire sale."

"Right. I saw you at Jaime's. You were asking about . . . some obscure book. I can't remember now, but I couldn't believe somebody your age even knew about it. Turns out you knew more about obscure books than I did," he said with a little laugh. "But the truth is, I'd already been asked to hire you, and Jaime's seemed like the right time to do it."

"Who asked you to hire me?"

"We'll get to that. They . . . we'd been looking out for you for a while."

"Looking *out* for me?"

"Since you came back."

"You've been following me all this time? Even before I worked for you?"

"It wasn't like that. You might not know this, but a nonprofit worked with your aunt and uncle to place you with Bolden after you came back."

"You—you know Doctor Bolden?"

"Bolden and I are both members of the same organization. We all wanted to protect you, look out for you and others like you, and also, if possible, shepherd you and your . . . unique abilities."

"What are you talking about?"

"I know that you can see things other people don't. You can remember things and places that other people can't."

"I don't remember anything."

"We both know that's not true."

Alistair's mind reeled. "Your little club has been keeping tabs on me since I was a kid? Why?"

"Bolden was trying to help you control your memories. She was either more successful than she expected to be . . . or they faded away as you got older. We just wanted to be around if they ever emerged again."

"And that's why you hired me?"

"Yes."

"That's why you were at the hospital. So it was all a lie, working with you. Being—"

Alistair's phone buzzed in her hand.

I think I found something, A

"No, Alistair. Please, hear me out. It *was* a job, an assignment, a mission. I was asked to do it and I did. But I did care about you. I *do* care about you. I've been a part of your life for a long time, and I know that sounds scary—"

"*Sounds* scary?" Alistair bit back, bubbling with briny anger. Zev texted, Alistair barely glanced down:

It's a journal. About you.

"—and unfair, but I only ever wanted what was best for you. That's the truth. I wanted to keep you safe, and if you ever needed me, needed *us*, I would bring you home."

"'Us'? 'Home'? Who *are* you?"

It goes back years.

Ed sighed. "When you've been around as long as we have, you pick up a lot of names. The Silver is as good a name as any."

He's been keeping tabs on you.

Alistair couldn't help but laugh. "The Silver. You're kidding me."

"What?" Ed asked.

"From the books? From *The Monarch Papers?*"

Ed sat back, his back going stiff at the mention.

Says he was ordered to.

"Those books are exaggerations at best." Ed nodded to her phone, "Is that really more important than what I'm telling you?"

Alistair put her phone on the table, her hand still on it. She was overwhelmed with information.

"What exactly *are* you telling me? You're claiming that you were tasked to stalk me my whole life by a secret cult who believes in magic, parallel universes, and among other things, once controlled a living storm that could time travel and erase people's minds. *That* Silver?"

Ed tried to answer but Alistair could see the words wouldn't come. He looked out the window, "The Silver is woven into a tapestry made up of many societies, each with their own purpose, belief system, and . . . set of ethics. The nonprofit Bolden worked with is one thread in that tapestry. If you read the books, you've heard of Kemetic Solutions, or the Cagliostro and his keepers. All part of a larger piece of art. I'm ashamed to say that we benefited from the Storm, but it answered to others, not us."

He turned back to Alistair.

"What you think you know about us is not true. Not all of it. And what *was* true has changed in the past couple of years. That's not who we are. Not anymore. Come on, you know me, Alistair."

"Do I?" Alistair wanted that to come out like she was spitting venom, but her voice cracked. She wished she'd never come to Morningside Heights.

"Alistair—"

"You're telling me *The Monarch Papers* is true. You're telling me—"

"It's a lot of things. Myopic and incomplete, and also true. It all happened. In retrospect, it was the best crash course you could take, to explain almost everything, though I wish you would have gotten here another way. I told Bolden that she could lay a hundred paths for you, but you'd still find your own."

She could hear her phone buzzing on the Formica tabletop. Zev was freaking out.

So was Alistair. Ed had been the one touchstone in her life, the one person who felt grounded, real. But not only was he a liar, but he was now trying to sell Alistair a fairy tale. She had to leave. Call Zev. Tell him to get out. He'd have time before Ed got home. She began to slide out of the booth when Ed put his hand on hers.

"Please. Don't leave."

Alistair stopped, looking him in the eye.

Ed looked toward the server who was bringing their orders. "Not yet," he said. "Five minutes. Food's coming."

Alistair slowly sat back in her seat. The server seemed to notice the tension: the old man's hand on the young woman's. He looked at Alistair as he set their plates on the table.

"Is there anything you need, ma'am?"

"We're good. Thanks," she said, barely acknowledging him as she quickly texted Zev:

Get out now.

"Okay, just yell if you change your mind."

Alistair and Ed nodded in agreement and the server walked away.

Ed took his hand back and began rolling up his sleeves, exposing his ink-covered forearms.

"It looks good. Dig in."

She looked at him like he'd asked her to pour the tomato soup in her ear.

Ed continued. "I'd first heard stories about the Silver on my second tour. This guy from St. Louis saw all the books I had shipped over, all the books I spent my money on . . . We started talking philosophy, obscure texts, speculating on the library of Alexandria . . . but he was also into out-there stuff like alchemy and secret histories and this secret group that sounded, well, like a cult . . ."

Ed took the steak knife the server brought, flipped it over, and slid it across the table to Alistair, handle first.

She looked up at him, confused, and saw that he had a finger to his lips, his eyes begging her to stay quiet. He urged her to take the knife.

Ed went on. "He said the difference was that cults recruit, but you had to *find* the Silver, which he said had endless libraries of secret books. He said it was more like a brotherhood. A group of people from all over the world, all walks of life, who believed in the same thing: the beauty of art, the potential of words, and the magic of belonging. He wasn't a member, but he said they'd set out 'a path of silver' around the world. A secret trail hidden in artwork and literature, that if you could find it, and follow it, you'd learn all the secrets of the world, and the world that existed *before* this one."

As he spoke, Ed pointed to a tattoo on his right arm: a pinup girl dressed in a hypersexualized postal worker's uniform, a mailbag slung over her shoulder. He pointed to the bag, which Alistair could now see had writing hidden in its folds. *For A.* For her? Ed moved his finger to the inked rope that held the bag closed and tapped it. Alistair didn't follow, until Ed looked down at the steak knife, and then pointed back to the rope on his arm, inching it closer to her and the tip of the knife.

He wanted her to cut the rope.

She stared at him, then his arm, dumbfounded. He continued to talk, about his time in the military, about his search for the works of art and locations that eventually led him to the Silver, but Alistair couldn't hear anything. He put the knife in her hand, then gently took her wrist and pulled it to his right arm. The tip of the blade brushed against his skin. She tried to pull away, but he pulled back harder as he continued to speak in a calm, mundane tone. His hand around her wrist, all at once scaring her and offering her comfort in its strength. And then Alistair's heart stopped for a moment. The tip of the blade brushed against the tattooed rope that held the mailbag closed—and the rope moved. Not like it was made of ink and flesh. It moved like rope, like a knot resisting coming undone. She felt his grip on her loosen. She moved the blade against the knot and saw it lift away from his skin. And then the blade slipped behind the rope, obscured by it. Even though the texture of the rope looked just like a painting on skin, it behaved like it was real. The dangling ends of the knotted rope hung limp against the silver steak knife. All Alistair had to do was turn the blade and cut it.

"Alistair?"

She looked up at Ed.

"It's going to be okay."

She looked back to his arm and cut the rope.

The ends of the cord fell away, sliding down Ed's arm as if they were still embedded under his skin, passing the other tattoos until they settled as his bent wrist.

The mailbag unfurled, and there was space inside it, a dark recess that opened into Ed's arm. Inside, it looked as if it had been inked that way, gray shadow and canvas texture. Alistair could see the corner of something inside the bag, barely peeking out. A letter in the mailbag.

She looked to Ed again, and he nodded as he placidly talked about meeting his wife in Manila on New Year's Eve.

Alistair put the knife down and reached for the tattooed envelope. For a moment she felt the hair on his bicep, the skin and muscle, and then the corner of the letter. She could feel it between her fingers. She worried it might hurt him to pull the envelope out, but he didn't react, didn't flinch. Ed continued talking and behaving as if it wasn't happening.

So Alistair pulled the letter out.

Chapter Eighteen

Ben had gone from slavishly following the whims of a book to slavishly following the whims of a bird. Anyone in their right mind would have abandoned the mission at the point of "recurring bird leaves clue on windshield," but for the first time in nearly five years, things were starting to make sense—in the sense that everything was supernatural, he'd been wrong all along, and nothing made sense. For the first time, there seemed to be a *reason*. Veronica had always been his "favorite" of the Six. Aside from Billy Holtzman's meteoric rise to self-help evangelism, Veronica was the only other one of the Six to have been in the news at all since they all came back and then disappeared again. According to the address on the letter, Veronica had never changed her name. Ben knew it wasn't because she sought the spotlight. She had no problem bloodying the noses of nosy people who didn't screw off when she told them to screw off. After years of altercations, people must have finally decided to leave her the hell alone, and she'd essentially slipped off the grid. Ben definitely expected to be popped in the face at some point, but what other choice did he have? It was his only lead. The crow had spoken. It was Veronica and the threat of violence, or nothing.

After finding a beach-adjacent motel, showering, and changing out of his ripped Henley and into a flannel button-down he'd bought at a roadside shop, Ben spent most of the day vacillating between watching people on the Santa Monica Pier and knocking on the screen door of an apartment a few blocks east. Back and forth, over and over. He felt like a kid waiting for the only other kid on his block to get home from school. He kept touching the cut on his stomach, which had stopped bleeding, but strangely still felt like the tip of the blade was piercing it. It hurt.

The sun was bright but not too hot—late afternoon, long shadows clawing away from the east, sinking into the hungry, cold Pacific. Ben walked back to the apartment, climbed the cracked concrete stairs to the third floor, the breeze from the ocean cooling his sweat-stained back. He knocked on the screen door. Knocked again. Waited. Knocked again—

"What the hell do you want?!" a raspy woman's voice called out from the other side of the building. Ben turned and found the short, round silhouette of a busybody neighbor looking back from behind her torn screen door.

"I'm looking for Veronica Morrow. Does she live here?"

"Who are you?" the shadow asked.

"A friend of hers and her sister's."

Quiet from the dark doorway.

"Bullshit. She ain't got no friends. Is she selling drugs? I'm the eyes and ears for the landlord . . . If she's selling drugs here, I'll get her kicked out so fast—"

"She's . . . not a dealer. Do you know where she is?"

"Probably work."

"Do you know where she works?"

"I do. But her friend don't, huh?" she asked, catching him.

"Well, we—haven't been in touch in a while."

He watched the coal of a cigarette glow behind the woman's screen door, then a billow of smoke poured out.

Silence.

"Backwater Bill's," the woman answered.

"What is that?" Ben managed to get out before the woman flicked her cigarette butt through the hole in the screen and slammed her door closed. Ben sighed. What the hell did . . . He pulled out his phone and searched.

It was a crappy bayou-themed bar about a quarter of a mile away. Ben started walking and was there in less than ten minutes. The tables all looked like docks, the walls were smeared with crudely painted banyan trees, and fake moss hung from the ceiling. Music blared. It was packed with a toxic, overloud mix of regulars, irony-seeking after-work drinking buddies, and absolutely no one who actually came for the atmosphere.

He found Veronica washing glasses behind the bar in what must've been a tub of Bill's actual backwater. Her dark, wavy hair hung over her shoulders. The holes in her vintage T-shirt looked like they were from actual wear, and the two smears of black liner under her eyes looked like they'd been applied yesterday. Her eyes flicked over to Ben and saw him watching back. He had to approach now. She went back to wiping things down and doling out watered-down short pours. Ben felt a combination of feelings akin to dread, nausea, and preparing to ask out a woman way above one's pay grade.

"Thirsty?" she asked without looking up.

Ben cleared his throat. "What's on draft?"

Veronica walked to the beer pulls. "You want me to read them to you?"

She was exactly as terse and sharp-tongued as he imagined she would be. He approached, read them, then pointed to another IPA with a clever name. "This guy. Thank you."

He squeezed between two suited men at the bar and watched her masterfully pull a full-headed mug. She set it down in front of him with a heavy *thunk*. He couldn't think of a damned thing to say so instead he slipped cash across the bar and drank the beer in three long tips, ashamed by how attractive he found her, and how flustered it was making him. *Come on, Kriminger. Grow up.* Yes, she was stunning. Something about her raven hair, all-black clothes on rich brown skin with eyes to match. She was a shade, a spirit, an ornery wraith in combat boots. But his enamored reaction was more than hormones or id. To him, this was like meeting a celebrity. Not that Janie and Aaron weren't, they were just a little—white bread. This—this was *the* Veronica Morrow. He put the mug down, nodded for another, and when she brought it back, he piped up.

"You from around here?" Ben asked.

She leaned against the bar to hear him better against the music. "What did you say?"

"Are you from around here?" he called out. The guys he was sandwiched between shared a look over his leaned-in head and stifled laughs at his expense.

"Are you trying to hit on me?" Veronica asked.

"No! The Cramps! Your shirt! Big East Coast band!" Ben shouted, course-correcting.

"That where *you're* from?" Veronica asked.

"New York City, yeah . . ."

"I lived there for a while," Veronica explained.

"Yeah?"

"Yeah. You're not originally from New York, though, are you?"

"What makes you say that?" Ben asked.

"You have a little bit of an accent. Somewhere South."

Ben felt blood rushing to his cheeks.

"That's—wow, yeah. You have a good ear, especially while Seger's blasting in the other one!"

Veronica nonchalantly rattled a shaker for another patron.

"Don't tell me where. I like to try and guess. No hints."

Ben nodded, swigging his beer, a smile on his face. Were they flirting? Was she flirting with him?

"You look . . . coastal for some reason. Salty. So Tennessee is out. Missouri and Mississippi, out. But you're not trashy Gulf coastal, so that also rules out Louisiana and the panhandle. Basically rules out Alabama . . ."

That's right, Ben thought. Her family had moved to Santa Colette from just outside of New Orleans. She knew her Southern shit.

"You're right so far," Ben confirmed.

"I said no hints," she replied with a wry smile.

He raised his hands in surrender, his smile matching hers. He'd completely forgotten why he was there. Her bottom teeth were a little crowded. Braces probably weren't her primary concern as a teenager. It was the sort of flaw Ben found himself drawn to, and hoped women saw his flaws in a similar light.

"No one who's moved to New York from Virginia or DC would say they were from the South," she mused as she squeezed a lime into a copper cup. She set it on the far end of the bar for a server to pick up and wiped her hands on a bar rag. "So we're down to Georgia or one of the Carolinas. Right so far?"

"Am I allowed to answer?"

"Just this once."

"Right so far."

"You seem . . . liberal. And you're rocking the hipster fisherman vibe so I'm ruling out South Carolina altogether. My vote is . . . North Carolina. Nags Head, to be specific."

Ben's mouth hung wide open.

"Holy shit. Edenton. But that's only like . . . thirty minutes inland from Nags Head. How the hell did you figure that out?"

"Well, the secret is . . ." she leaned in, "aspiring author Ben Kriminger, who says he's from Edenton, North Carolina when he really grew up poor as dirt in the sticks about forty-five minutes east with his alcoholic father, isn't the only one who's done his research."

Shit.

"Wanna do me now?" she asked as Ben felt himself turn paste white. "Go ahead. I'm waiting."

Ben felt his throat closing in.

"Fine. I'll start you off. Veronica Morrow, smart but never really managed to set the world on fire the way her parents hoped she would. Her twin sister was always the star anyway, truth be told. Veronica had some friends back in the day. Made the news for a while, but tried her best to settle into a quiet, unbothered life of mediocrity and Moscow mules. Finally had a good run at it until some guy decided to start poking into a part of her life she didn't feel needed another goddamned poke. That's you, in case you didn't realize."

"Yeah . . . I assumed," Ben muttered.

"How's Aaron, by the way?" she asked.

Ah. It made sense now. The Newhouses must have called ahead.

"He's good. He's . . . quick to threaten people with swords," Ben said. "Understandably, I guess."

"He's got a lot to protect, doesn't he? Never met the kids. We don't really . . . keep in touch. You said you wanted another?"

Ben had nervously finished the second beer. "Yeah, please. Thanks . . ."

She poured another and put it down in front of him. "Janie tries —" Ben said.

"Tries what?"

"To keep in touch with you. That's how I found you."

Ben dug into his back pocket and pulled out the crumpled, rain-warped letter Janie tried to send to her. He slid it across the bar. Veronica read the address but refused to touch it.

"You didn't open it?"

"Of course not."

"You've obsessed over us for fifteen years and you have the

chance to read a private letter between two of the Santa Colette Six and you thought . . . nah?"

"I've had a weird couple of months."

Veronica stared him down, unblinking.

"Yes, you have."

"What?"

Veronica leaned against the bar, arms crossed, changing the subject. "So what do you want? An interview?"

"Uh, no. I mean, sort of. I'm here to help somebody. Someone who—"

"Came back the same day we did. Alistair."

Ben was stunned. Everything else, the Newhouses knew, but that, that they couldn't have known.

"How do you know that?"

"Know what?"

"That name? Are you—did you write the pages?"

"No, I just have a habit of . . . finishing people's sentences."

"She doesn't remember where she was. And she needs help."

"See, you're telling the truth, technically, but that's not why you're here."

Ben hesitated, then, "No. It's not. For some reason, I'm a part of this story now. The Six . . . you. This woman who remembers books that were never written."

"What books?"

"She calls them *the briar books*."

Veronica returned that same, intense, unblinking stare.

"She your girlfriend?" Veronica asked.

"Who?"

"The woman you're trying so hard to help, but not really."

"Oh! No! Not at all. She doesn't know I exist. Hell, at the end of the day *she* might not even exist. She's just pages in a book as far as I know. A different book. It's a long story."

"Defender of man."

"Who is?"

"That's what *Alistair* means. But isn't that a—" Veronica stopped mid-sentence.

"Boy's name? Yeah. Usually—" Then he saw it. The look on her face. Different. "Do you know her?"

Veronica said something, too quiet to hear over the din.

"What?" Ben leaned in.

She leaned over the bar, her mouth at his ear. It gave him chills. "See that hallway?"

She nodded to a dark hall past the bar.

"Yeah."

"Get up and go to the back door. I'll meet you there."

"What? Why?"

"You wanna go back to my place, don't you?"

Ben responded with three stone-faced blinks, then, "I'm sorry, what did you just say?"

"You heard me. Go."

Veronica grabbed the envelope Ben brought off the bar and bolted for the far hall. Her sudden departure startled Ben. He jumped up, knocking over his barstool in the process, pushing through the crowd to catch up with her. He had definitely sensed a flirtation but assumed it had been solely in his head. Veronica took his hand and pulled him down the hall, leading him out a back door like a mom dragging a bad kid out of church.

They cut across the promenade and down a side street. Veronica was hoofing it.

"Just to be clear—" Ben mumbled, a little out of breath.

"Don't talk. You'll ruin it."

"Right. Okay."

He had this feeling, this tingling rush, an urge that got stronger every time he got close to Veronica. Like she was mentally willing him to follow faster. The street they turned onto was familiar. Her street. Her apartment on the left.

Veronica walked through the courtyard and bounded up the

metal stairs, pulling Ben behind her. She shook the key in the old lock and let them in, slamming and locking the door behind them.

They stood in the middle of her tiny, barely furnished living room, just staring at each other.

"So?" Ben asked. His heart thumping out of his chest.

"Take your shirt off."

"Uh—okay . . ." Ben began unbuttoning his shirt. "I've been through a lot of stuff lately, so I'm not in the best shape right now . . ."

Veronica walked over to him and yanked his unbuttoned shirt down so that it hung around both wrists. She found the blade wound on the side of his belly and jammed her fingers against it.

"Jesus!" Ben yelped, pulling away.

"Hurts, yeah?" Veronica asked.

"Uh—yeah."

"Goddammit, Aaron."

"Aaron?"

"He can't let it go. He's still looking for shit from—" She stopped herself.

"From what? From where? What's wrong with the sword?"

"It's touched. Now, *you're* touched."

Veronica was pacing the small room.

"Touched, like how?"

"That sword isn't . . . from around here. It touched your blood and . . . now you smell like it. Not literally, but—"

"Can you slow down? I have no idea what you're talking about."

"Come on, Kriminger. You know something's not right with this world. You have for a long time."

Ben suddenly felt vulnerable, unsafe. "Can I put my shirt back on?"

"You don't know about the Silver," she said, mostly to herself, exasperated.

"Maybe I do, I don't know."

"No, you don't. I know you don't. You have no idea. They followed you."

"Who?"

"The Silver!"

Ben fumbled his shirt back on, embarrassed.

"Who are *they*?"

"They're the bad guys, Kriminger."

"And what . . . I led them to you?"

"Not me. They got the scent off that sword and sent these assholes after you. They want *you*."

"Me?"

Veronica was still pacing, talking to herself. "This isn't like them. Out in the open. Like they're . . . desperate."

Ben moved to stand in the way of Veronica's frantic pacing.

"Please tell me what's happening."

"I can't."

"Why?!" Ben asked, pleading.

"Because they're here."

As if on cue, there was a long, slow knock at her front door.

Veronica dug through a small wooden box on her lone bookshelf, pulled out a small silver coin, and tossed it to him. He fumbled to catch it, but succeeded. The coin had writing on it, but Ben had trouble reading it—not really reading it so much as *seeing* it. Like something in his peripheral vision, but also right in front of him. He looked back to her as she swiped everything off her coffee table, which he now realized was a large wooden chest. She pulled off the lid.

"Get back, in the hall, now," she told him.

He backed away, gripping the coin.

The knocking was getting louder. Ben could see shadows beyond the curtained windows. The sound of cracking wood shocked him as the frame of the doorway itself began to give way against the force of their knocking.

Veronica reached into the open chest and pulled out a long

wooden rod. It was tapered at the bottom, round at the top. Long and narrow, like a beautifully carved walking stick.

"What are you—"

"Back in the hall!" Veronica shouted as she readied herself for whatever was outside the door.

Ben retreated, but not far enough to hide.

The people on the other side finally broke the door down, rushing in, rushing for Ben. They looked like they'd been randomly picked off the street. An assortment of feral pedestrians who were suddenly willing to tear down a door to get to him. Veronica held the walking stick out, closed her eyes for a long beat, said, "I'm sorry," then shouted a word Ben had never heard before.

White-hot light blasted into every corner of the room, and every hair on Ben's body stood up, surging with electricity. He was blown against the hallway wall, then slammed to the floor. The light faded until Ben could finally see Veronica's vague form, still standing where she had been, but the pursuers were gone. No. Not gone. He could see them now. They'd been scattered across the room. Five of them. Unconscious. They clung to the walls, ceiling, and floor, pinned like magnets drawn to metal.

Ben took a breath as the room's light returned to normal. "What did you just do?!"

Veronica held the stick out at arm's length. "Don't look," she whispered, but Ben couldn't look away. The room suddenly vibrated, hummed, and then the stick in Veronica's hand shattered outward into a thousand pieces.

She bowed her head.

Ben realized his left hand hurt. He opened his palm and found that the little coin he couldn't read was smoldering. A puff of smoke rose from the surface, a little red circle singed into his skin.

He looked up at Veronica.

She looked up at him, cold.

He said the only word that came to mind.

"Magic."

Chapter Nineteen

Magic.

The moment the letter was free from Ed's skin, it was real. No longer freckled and made of flesh, no longer faded and outlined in ink. It was paper. No bigger than a postage stamp, folded in half.

Alistair turned it over, found the flap on the back, and peeled it open. Inside was an even smaller sheet of paper with microscopic writing on it, impossible to read. Alistair felt like exploding. She'd just seen magic. Whatever else she doubted, about herself, about *The Monarch Papers*, about Ed, it was all blown away. She was pulled from her trance by Ed tapping the table with a finger. She looked up and saw he had rolled his sleeve down again. He was telling her to put the letter down. She did. He picked up his glass of water, downed three quarters of it, then put the glass on top of the letter. It was like a magnifying glass. Ed took her hand, holding it tight. She gripped his in turn, for security, for fear that if she didn't hold on, she would slide off the world.

She leaned forward and looked down through the glass to the letter.

"Only you could open this. It's how the magic that made it works. It's bound to you. Please forgive me. For everything. I am not your enemy. Neither is the Silver. The true enemy is what hides among the threads of the tapestry. Everywhere and nowhere. Binding the world. Always listening. Even here, now. PS 1. Go there. Bolden is waiting where they can't hear you."

Alistair had no intention of going to PS1 down on Henry Street. After the diner, she found she was rattled, shaken in a way she'd never been before. Not even her slips into the dark had made her feel quite this way. At least what she saw in the dark was nothing but visions, illusions. The letter she pulled out of Ed's arm . . . *that* was real. Which meant the rest of the world, and all the boring, mundane, things in it . . . *those* were the lies. She had so many questions she wanted to ask Ed, but he had made it clear that someone, somewhere, was listening to everything they said. He finished his steak, asked her to consider what he'd said—how the Silver had changed—and to reach out to him if and when she was ready. Now, Alistair was standing outside Lucky Golden Wok trying to force herself to go inside and hide. Back in her box, like Iris. Just go to sleep and forget. But PS1 and Henry Street were only ten blocks west. Just past her favorite library. She felt so naive. So . . . common. Magic was real, but Alistair had *a favorite library*. How quaint.

It was almost 9 PM when she got to the school. She wasn't sure if it was, but PS1 definitely *looked* like the first school in Manhattan. It was a block-wide wall of gray stone, pocked with windows, reaching up four stories to tall ornate dormers and a copper roof. The plaque above one of the two entrances read *1897*. Both entrances were locked, there were no lights on inside, and every window was barred. Alistair hoped to find Bolden waiting for her on a park bench, but she was mostly alone on the quiet stretch of Henry Street. She could barely even remember Bolden. In Alistair's memory, Bolden was nothing more than a brown, sleek triangle of hair with foggy bits of verbose-but-kind grown-up underneath, so Alistair probably wouldn't recognize her unless she walked up and introduced herself.

Alistair followed the sidewalk around the school, searching for any sign of Bolden, now looking at every passerby, wind-skipped leaf, or dark corner as potentially supernatural. Her phone buzzed and she cringed, realizing she hadn't followed up with Zev since she texted him at the diner. He was probably worried out of his mind. She dug her phone out of her coat pocket and found that it wasn't a text waiting for her, but a call with no number, which was already connected. She lifted the phone to her ear.

"Hello?"

"Hello, Alistair."

"Doctor Bolden?"

"Inside the school, quick as you can."

"It's locked—I checked."

Silence on the other end.

Alistair checked the screen. The call had been disconnected. She looked back down the block to the front facade of the school. One of the entrances was now standing open and the light above it was glowing.

"Shit," was all Alistair could say.

The front hall of the school followed the outer perimeter of windows before turning a corner into darkness. The diffused light from outside reflected on the highly polished tile floor, making it look like glassy water. Another hall led deeper into the dim center of the school. From the entrance, Alistair could make out the edge of a flight of stairs near the back of the second hall. The school was quiet and felt eerily frozen in time. The drawings pinned to the bulletin board by the front door didn't flutter in the breeze from outside. The clock above the entrance didn't tick. Only the sound of a small *click* behind her as the front door of the school closed on its own, enclosing her in the dark. Her phone buzzed again. She checked. Another automatically connected call. Alistair raised the phone to her ear.

"Are you here?"

"In a sense. No one can hear us right now. It's safe."

"Where are you?"

"I hope to see you soon, but for now I need to know about your last episode, at the house. Did you use the mantra I taught you?"

"I did."

"Did it work?"

"No."

"Of course not. Those memories have only grown more potent while they waited down in the dark. I tried to help you dampen or suppress them with tools like the mantra, but in doing so, I think I failed you."

"No. You didn't, you're the only person who ever helped . . ."

"I didn't help you. I placated you. That mantra was meant to remind you that the ephemera hiding in your mind was a lie. But it wasn't. It isn't. It's real. What you see in the darkness really happened and you know it, Alis."

Alis. That's right. Alistair had created the concept of the "alternate Alistair" during their sessions. That's where it had come from. The name. The persona. The "true" Alistair that she sometimes fantasized about. Bolden was reminding her of Alis.

"What if we could take that ephemera, all the imagery that blocks you from the truth, and instead of pushing the fragments back into the dark, we drag them into the light? We accept that they are real, but they're just harmless, broken pieces of some forgotten thing. Like the pages in the box you made for me. What if I could help you learn to look at them and realize they can't hurt you because you can shape them into something else, something useful? Make them links in a chain that reaches back to who you truly are."

"I d-don't want to go back there," Alistair stammered.

"It isn't going back, Alistair. It's going forward. Don't you want that?"

"I don't know what I want. I just wanted . . . to talk to you again. I don't—"

"No, no, no. You want more than that." Bolden's voice was fierce, impassioned. Alistair was overwhelmed, but she was also touched that this woman was still so determined to help her.

"You want the truth. About your life. About the night you came back. You want to know how this is all connected, don't you?"

"How can I do that?"

"With me by your side. By repurposing your pain to help you, instead of haunt you. Don't you want that?"

"Yes." She wanted out of the dark.

"Then it's time to begin. It's time to go upstairs."

Alistair looked toward the edge of the stairs in the dark center of the school.

"What's up there?"

"The next step on your path. I'm with you."

Alistair stalled, then took a deep breath, walked to the stairs, and ascended into the dark. The stairs reached up into a four-story void of black. Alistair took the steps one by one as Bolden continued to talk to her.

"Over the years I've come to believe that memory is a kind of magic, or perhaps a *part* of magic. It's what connects everything. It fills the emptiness. When someone holds an object and remembers something, it isn't just chemicals in their brain stirring. It's the remnant of that memory reconnecting, traveling from that object back to the person it belongs to. Memory is all around us, reaching out to us, but most people are blind to it, and if they *do* somehow stumble upon it, they only see their own memories. But you see more. You sense more. You hear its call."

"How?"

"We don't know, but this school is a well, and I think you're sensitive to deep places. I believe it's why you sometimes see manifestations of your guilt, the fox, or why you have resurgent memories of the cold night in the woods, in the snow. I know this is difficult. It took me decades to open my mind enough to let it in. But this is the work I want to do now, with the resources the Silver provides. I want to help you."

"Why?"

Alistair.

Alistair's blood ran cold. The voice wasn't Bolden's. The urgent whisper called from somewhere else, deeper in the dark school.

"What are you doing?" Alistair asked, turning in all directions, and found she was no longer on the stairs. She had stepped off onto one of the higher floors without realizing and was now standing in an empty classroom, one she couldn't quite remember entering.

"It's not me. I only told you to go upstairs. But look, you've found your way. To that room. To that desk."

Alistair turned and found a single desk behind her.

Click click click.

"No," Alistair muttered.

She turned away, fear radiating out from her chest to her extremities.

"Why would you do this to me?" Alistair whispered.

"It was the only way to show you."

"Please . . . please. I don't want—"

Click click click.

"Let me help you. Open the desk, Alis, and look inside. It's the way through. It's the path out of the dark. Take control of your past, take control of your power."

Alistair felt as if she was being torn apart at an atomic level, half of her wanting to run, the other half trying desperately to get to and look inside the desk. She turned and took step after begrudging step across the room. She slowly placed her hand on the hinged desktop, teeth gritted. She watched as her hand reached to lift the lid until it locked in place, then it reached inside. She was a puppet on strings.

She bowed over the desk, eyes closed as she felt her fingers wrap around the sheet of paper inside, her fist crumpling it as she pulled it out.

"Open your hand, Alis."

Alistair tried to fight back, but her fingers unwound, and although she tried to look away, through the windows into the black night, she couldn't resist looking down . . .

She was holding a drawing done with colored pencils—a line of trees, a forest, and six children standing bravely on the edge of it, holding staves and sticks and swords. Iris with her bow—and in the woods, a creature, a beast, towering in the treetops, its red-orange eyes burning, looking down on them. Alistair whispered a word to herself, barely audible.

Timber.

A wave of disorientation raged through her like the school had been flipped upside down. She collapsed onto the slick floor. Alistair pulled herself toward the door, unable to look up, the nausea overwhelming. Behind her . . .

Click click click.

The harbinger fox.

"Alis, listen to me. Let my voice be your anchor. I can help you through it. Tell me what you see."

Alistair took deep gulps of air as the room continued to spin out of control. She realized she could still hear Bolden even though her phone was at her side. More magic.

A cold wind began to blow through the outer hall and into the classroom, chilling Alistair and dampening Bolden's voice. Behind her, the *click click click* and in the corner of her eye . . . the fox was there. Alistair scrambled to her feet, slamming into the doorframe, clawing at it to stay upright.

Muffled, Bolden called to her.

"You have to go through the dark to the other side. You have to face it first."

"I can't!"

Alistair raced out of the classroom, trying to find the stairs, trying to outrun what she knew was coming, what she felt reaching for the back of her neck. *The cold. The fox. The thing that follows.*

Tree boughs now lined the black hallway as if they had just burst through the walls. The walls were coated in patches of scaly bark, and snow lay in deep drifts in the corners. The school was now a maze of consumed, wooded corridors, turning darker, more dangerous. The floors creaked, and wind whipped like a storm from some cold place. She turned another corner, and the fox was waiting for her.

She slid against a wall, half hiding behind a snow-covered water fountain. A sepia photograph of an old graduating class hung on the wall across from where she crouched. It had been torn open, and inside the photograph was another world—black, with stars in the darkness and snow blowing in from it.

Alistair started mumbling her mantra to herself, a whisper that grew louder as the wind howled. The black brimmed at the edge of the photograph frame, then poured over. The dark consumed the hall, eating the walls and tree branches. Those weren't stars beyond the photograph. There was nothing in the black but the glimmer of countless animals' eyes. And there was something larger perched just on the other side of the frame, looking down at her, preparing to emerge.

The thing she hadn't seen in years. The thing that always followed the fox. The thing with the alabaster claws.

Alistair scrambled to her feet, rushing past the photograph. She took the steps two at a time then spilled onto the floor at the bottom of the stairs, lost for a moment, before finding her bearings and racing for the exit. She threw the door open and charged through, finding herself not outside, but in the school's cavernous auditorium. She'd gotten turned around. The door behind her was now an inky void that grew up the walls of the room, spreading. Twinkling eyes in the black.

Click click click.

There was something else in the sound of the howling wind. Bolden.

"You have to face it, Alis!" Bolden's disconnected voice echoed above the wind. "Whatever it is in the dark, you have to face it!"

Tree branches ripped through the walls of the auditorium. The heavy, crimson stage curtains billowed in the hail of snow and wind. Alistair stepped away from the expanding portal where the door once was. The darkness grew closer, filling her vision like horror-filled oblivion. She stumbled backward through the narrow rows of seating.

Bolden's voice was distant now, fading, succumbing, but not gone. Not yet.

"Alistair! I'm here! What do you see?"

"Dark . . . It's all dark," was all she could muster.

"Look into the dark. Look *through* it."

"It's there. It's in there."

"You have to face it, Alis."

In the void, something bigger, darker than the black, was approaching. The thing from the photograph had made its way down to her. Strands of gray hair like spiderwebs whipped out from the black, and white claws perched on the edge of the dark.

"My name is Alistair . . . I am twenty-six. The only thing that's real is whatever I can feel. Nothing more, nothing much—"

"No, Alis! No. It's real. It's all real. You have to see it."

"No! My name is—"

"Alis!"

Alistair stopped her desperate recitation. Her eyes clenched shut, she was willing herself to open them. Her face contorted, body shivering, as she fought her every instinct to finally face the thing in the dark.

She opened her eyes—

Alistair.

She whip-turned and found the fox staring back at her from a wooded path at the end of the row of chairs, all whiskers and cracked glasses.

It's okay. Come with me.

It spoke. The fox spoke.

"What?"

Come with me. This way. The voice was small but sure, like a clever little child. *Everything's going to be okay. I found the way out. Follow me.*

The fox tilted its head, motioning her to follow as it sped off down the path. It was dim, but inviting, warm. Lined with trees so densely packed together they looked like walls. The leaves were still and glistening, untouched by the void of wind howling at her back. She didn't know how but something in her was sure it was the way out.

Alistair followed.

But the thing in the dark was behind her. Reaching now. Alistair felt its cold claws hovering above her shoulder. The darkness closed in and the howling reached a fever pitch. The claws took hold.

Then it all stopped. Alistair fell to her knees. It had her and she was helpless to fight it.

"Ma'am?"

A man barely squeezed into a security guard uniform was standing over her, almost as scared as she was.

The fox, the snow, the thing in the dark, all gone.

"Are you okay, ma'am?"

৩৯১৩

Alistair sat in the tub in the corner of her room for an hour, trying to drain the cold from her body, until the hot water ran out and she felt limp from crying. She'd faced the dark and it almost dragged her down with it. Her mind was fragmented and fluttering, worse than any post-episode she'd ever had. She dried off, slid into a T-shirt and shorts, and slumped into bed. She couldn't do it. She couldn't fix herself. She couldn't look into the dark and change like Bolden swore she could. She wasn't strong enough. Bolden hadn't called back. Even *she* knew it. Alistair was too weak to get better. Too hollow. Even the security guard at the school had pitied her, helping her out of the building instead of calling the police.

Follow me.

Alistair shuddered at the knock on her door. She wiped her eyes, staying silent. Danny Chen had come to complain about her using all the hot water.

Another knock.

"Who is it?" she asked in a broken whisper.

"Alistair, It's Zev, open up—"

Something rang out in her when she heard Zev's harried voice. She leapt to her feet, stumbling over the coat and shoes she'd dumped on the floor. She unlocked the door and let the light of the stairwell in. Zev was waiting on the other side, disheveled and stressed. He saw her tears, her shaking body.

"Are you okay? You didn't text back, and I thought—"

The look on his face, the tenderness, the caring worry. It was more than Alistair could stand. She bowed her head and laid it against his chest, a heave of fresh tears shuddering through her. He grabbed her instantly, his arms holding her to him, holding her up.

"It's okay. It's okay. Whatever it is, whatever happened, I'm here. I'm not leaving."

She felt his stubbled chin against her head as he whispered to her, then felt his lips kiss her forehead. She wiped her tears against his rumpled sweater and looked at him, their eyes meeting in the half-light between her room and the world beyond. Then they kissed. She didn't know who kissed whom, but it felt like the electric culmination of years of wanting, waiting, and never being able to connect. Then finally letting go. Once. Twice. Again and again. Tenderly at first, then overwhelming.

"Wait," Zev tried to pull back. "Should we take a breath—"

She yanked him into her room, and without protest, he kicked the door closed behind them.

They stumbled over her coat, but he caught her as they both fell.

They never made it to the bed.

Chapter Twenty

Ben drove east out of LA. He drove for two hours, Veronica sitting on the other end of the cracked blue leather bench, only speaking when she told him to take an exit, or merge left, this right turn, that left. Ben held the wheel with his left hand, his right hand resting on his leg, feeling the coin in his pocket. He'd tried to give it back to her at the apartment, but she ignored him, told him to wait for her outside. He'd protested, concerned about the people pinned to the walls and ceiling and floor all around them. What happened when they got down? It was absurd, surreal, but he wasn't about to let her get thrown into mortal peril because of him, even if it seemed she was the one in control, not them, and certainly not him.

So he'd waited outside. He'd sat on the bottom step and watched pedestrians pass by, completely unaware that some kind of wizard was two flights up from them. Ben had wanted the truth, truth above fantasy. Turns out the truth *was* the fantasy. The world was magic, which didn't make anything better. You might think magic would make the world more whimsical. It didn't. It made it feel darker.

Now, they were two hours out of the city, in the middle of a dark, desert wasteland. Ben wondered if Veronica was hungry. *He* was hungry. Which felt weird because who's thinking about roadside bacon cheeseburgers when they're probably being led out into the desert to die at the hands of a wizard. Veronica was despondent. She seemed somehow collapsed, both inside and out. The silence was crushing. Turning on the radio felt inappropriate when you and a wizard were evading the Los Angeles branch of some kind of secret society.

"I guess they were the ones sending me the pages. The Silver. To try and . . . I don't know. Get the sword, or get me to find Alistair. Or you."

She didn't reply. He'd broken a perfectly good silence. He wanted to ask a thousand questions about her, about what happened back at her apartment, but it felt somehow inconsiderate. There was an energy rolling off of her, darkness. Mourning. At this point, Ben didn't know if it was metaphorical energy or legitimate magical energy.

He couldn't help himself. "Are you okay?"

"It doesn't matter," she said matter-of-factly.

"That . . . thing you did, back at your apartment . . ."

"It was my sister's," she interrupted. "The stick. It was my last connection to Marjory."

Ben nodded like magic sticks were commonplace mementos. So Marjory was gone. "When did she die?"

"No. *Literal* connection," she responded, correcting him.

"Oh, like . . . okay," Ben mumbled, scared to say the *M* word.

"It was her stave. It was bonded to her. I could tell she was still alive through it. Now I don't feel anything," Veronica said, staring out the window at the dark, flat landscape.

"Where is she?"

"She went looking for answers, like you, and ended up finding the Silver instead. I have no idea what they did with her. That stick was my last line to her."

"I'm sorry. Sorry you used it for me." Ben cleared his throat, then, "So you're both like wizards or something? I mean, I'm cool with it. It actually explains a lot of stuff that's happened recently . . . you know, that there's magic in the world."

"There is no magic in the world."

"But—"

"Not anymore. Only the garbage left behind."

"What about the stuff I've seen—"

"Scraps." She turned to him. "Shadows."

"So the world *did* change. It's why—"

"It's why the stick shattered," she said. "It's not supposed to be here. Not now."

"Like the sword?"

Veronica gave a short nod.

"Why not? What happened?" he asked.

"I can't tell you," she said, turning back to her window.

"You can trust me. And also, they were trying to get to me, not you. I feel like I deserve—"

"Deserve *what?*"

Her sharp tone shut him down completely. A long, quiet stretch, then she said, "I mean I literally can't tell you. None of us can. And Marjory—Marjory doesn't remember."

"So something happened when you all came back? Or when you left? While you were gone? You . . . learned something? You experienced something?" The crumbs of story she'd scattered had lit up the writer node of Ben's brain.

"You have to stop," she said with authority.

"I'm just trying to understand. I've seen . . . unbelievable things. I need to know why, how. I deserve *that*," Ben said.

She turned to him. "Ask me."

"What—what happened to you while you were gone?"

Then things got weird. Veronica opened her mouth, and a dim yellow glow appeared on her face, then grew brighter and brighter as her lips moved. The words came out like hissing whispers, backward, twisted, like he couldn't comprehend the English language, or she wasn't speaking it. She nodded toward the road, still talking. Ben looked up ahead and saw they were in the oncoming lane, and a semi-truck was bearing down on them. He tried to turn the wheel, but some other force pulled them back into the lights of the semi. He looked back at her. She seemed unfazed.

Ben reached out and put his hand over her mouth, silencing her as the force let go of the steering wheel and he finally cranked it back, ditching them off the road, the pickup almost overturning. A wall of dust surrounded them as the truck barreled past, maybe also controlled by whatever force was going to disintegrate them both against the semi's grill. Veronica took his hand from her mouth. Ben was pouring sweat.

"Don't ask me again," she said.

Ben nodded.

"Let's go," she said.

Ben took a breath and tried to pull back onto the road, but the pickup had stalled. He turned the key and started up the engine again, and they were back on the road. He remembered the lightning strike in Aaron's front yard when Aaron tried to tell Ben something Ben couldn't understand. The Six were bound to their secret in deeper ways than he ever imagined.

Neither Ben nor Veronica spoke until they passed a sign for a town called Needles, when Veronica told him to pull over into a gas station. Ben hadn't noticed the blinking dash light or the intermittent ding of the low fuel warning. He'd almost died, for the third time in as many days. A sword, a pack of rabid maniacs, and the universe itself—all trying to keep him from the truth. Veronica pumped gas, filling up the tank, then directed Ben to pull into the adjacent parking lot, across from the truck stop's diner.

"Are you hungry?" she asked.

They ate their obviously microwaved breakfast sandwiches and drank their day-old coffee in silence. There were a handful of patrons, huddled quietly over their plates, but it was quiet except for the occasional clanging in the kitchen and the hunched server floating back and forth behind the counter like a ghost as she hummed the same three notes over and over.

Ben could feel Veronica's eyes on him. Felt that same energy coming off of her. The one that drew him to her when they left the bar. It was exhilarating then. It made him sick now.

He kept his eyes on the town outside their booth window. It was a weird little space out on the desert. The oasis-like trappings of Palm Springs: sprawling houses, palm trees, strip malls. And on the other end of the spectrum, you had truck stops and low-income housing and homeless people and graffiti and run-down bus stops. No one had come to refill their coffee in an hour, which was fine by Ben. His gut was still churning. Maybe it was the sandwich. Maybe he was allergic to magic. The sky was purple, turning lighter by the moment as the sun slumped across the desert on its way to Needles.

"What are we doing?" he asked.

"We're waiting," she responded.

"For what? I'm assuming we're safe? That's why we're here? Is this some special place? Or is it because we're just in the absolute middle of nowhere?"

She didn't answer. He turned back to the window and watched a passenger train pull into town, stop at the station, which was basically a double-wide trailer, then chug away two minutes later. Even the train wanted to get the hell out of there.

Veronica glanced out the window every now and then, usually to the closed garage across the street, but mostly she just stared into her empty coffee cup and ran her fingers along the warped tabletop. With nothing better to do, Ben watched her fondle the table. Then he realized she wasn't just drumming the table, she was . . . writing something. Spelling out letters, or symbols. She finally stopped, and as she pulled her hand away, Ben noticed she had a small gold key in her hand. Had she just made that appear? It wasn't particularly magical looking. Just a house key, but—*Scraps. Shadows.* A bolt of nausea came along with the thought. Ben stood up and walked to the bathroom. He needed space. He needed to not see things appear out of nowhere. He was disappointed in himself. This is what he had been looking for. The unveiling of what was behind the curtain, and it made him sick.

In the hall leading to the restrooms was an old payphone. He stopped and checked the receiver to see if it worked. It clicked and hissed, but it had a dial tone. He dug into his jacket and thumbed change into the box. He dialed, waiting as it rang. An old answering machine picked up.

You've reached Crystal Ridge Hardware. We're not in right now, but if you call back during operating hours, we'll be happy to help you out.

Ben hung up. It was after 9 AM Eastern time. Stevie must've been helping a customer. Without Ben there, there was no one to answer the phone. The thought made Ben sad. He'd abandoned the trappings of his normal life for mystery and adventure and now he missed it. Now he wished he had it back.

"What are you doing?" Veronica asked, from over his shoulder.

Ben was leaning his forehead on the payphone box. "I don't know," he replied.

"So, you can come with me and not ask any more questions, or you can stay in your truck until I get back."

He wanted to wait in the truck. He also wanted to say he was going to wait in the truck but actually drive home and leave the wizard and whatever the hell else was in Needles, California. He wanted to not care.

Ben answered without looking at her. "I know you can't tell me anything, but can you at least tell me what we're doing?"

"No."

"I figured."

"Listen, dude, I know this is a lot," she said with a tone that sounded like she was going to continue, but she didn't.

"So, where are we going?"

"It's a few blocks away. We can walk."

۞

The sun was up, warming the cold desert. A young couple passed Ben and Veronica on the sidewalk, tossing newspapers into people's dusty yards. Veronica led him left and right and up this block and down that one. He wondered if she was lost or possibly keeping people off their tail, but she eventually led him up a walkway to a small house that stood in a little courtyard of other small bungalows. Veronica pulled out the key she'd conjured in the diner, and let herself in. Ben followed, another wave of nausea battering him as he did. The little place smelled like fresh coffee. Someone had just been there. Or was *still* there.

"Who lives here?" Ben whispered.

"No questions," she answered back.

Ben sighed.

"Wait here," she said as she disappeared through the kitchenette, into the back of the small house. The living room was sparsely furnished, and the furnishings looked mostly like second-hand finds. A lone plate sat on the glass coffee table, holding crumbs from breakfast, or dinner the night before.

Ben hung by the front door, nervous sweat beading on his forehead. It was warm in the house, but the sweat beading on his forehead was mostly anxiety-induced. Ben could see the morning light slashing through the front window across the living room. It had a slight but sickening yellow-orange tint to it, almost imperceptible. But Ben could see it. He opened the front door and stepped outside. The color of the morning sun changed immediately. This is what had happened at the Newhouses'. The colors, the nauseating feeling. Ben walked back into the vaguely yellow-glowing room and shuffled through mail on a nearby table. All were addressed to a "Gary Buxton."

215

Veronica walked back into the kitchen, which was only separated from the living room by a half wall and two mismatched barstools tucked under the counter. "What are you doing?"

"What are *you* doing?" Ben shot back. "Who lives here?"

"What did I say about questions?"

"This is Wyatt's house. Isn't it?" Ben asked.

Her expression was stony.

"Billy certainly wouldn't live in a place like this," Ben explained. "I know where *you* live. I know you don't know where Marjory is. And I've been to the Newhouses'. So?"

She didn't answer. She didn't need to.

"Is that why you were watching the garage? I know they both know cars. Their dad was a mechanic in Santa Colette. And they also have these . . . walls around their houses, that change color."

"How do you know that?" Veronica asked, surprised.

"I can *see* it. I saw it at Aaron's too. What is it?"

Veronica sighed.

"Is it magic? Is it you? Is it protecting them? Is that why they didn't just go for the sword Aaron found, instead of going for me? You're protecting them with magic. So how did the bad guys get in your apartment?"

"Scraps. I told you. There isn't enough magic to go around anymore," she finally answered. "I can handle myself, but I can't keep worrying about them."

"So you keep *them* safe instead of yourself."

"No one can keep them safe. I try to keep them . . . hidden."

Ben looked around the living room, thinking. "But *somebody* found them. Somebody called me, a few years ago. They led me to Aaron and Janie."

"Because Aaron can't let it go. He keeps trying to dig up old bones. Like that stupid sword."

"Do they know what you're doing? Aaron and . . . everyone? Hiding them?" he asked.

From her reaction, it was a solid *no*.

"They don't want anything to do with me. Not really," Veronica answered.

"Why?"

"I feel like you might've misunderstood the *no questions* rule of this field trip."

"I just—I think it's great, that you're looking out for them, but if we're just here to hide Wyatt and move on, what are we going to do *next*? Those people are still coming for me. And Alistair! They might be looking for her, and they're probably coming for you now because once those guys fall off your ceiling, they're gonna tell whoever they're answering to that your magic wand exploded all over the place and we just ran out the door. So—"

"So?"

"So what do we do *now*?!"

"Now, I take your truck and you get on the next train that goes wherever you plan on hiding for the rest of your life."

"What? Why? Where are *you* going?"

"Uh. Also hiding forever. I have no more power. I have no connection to my sister. I tried to protect the rest of them, but I can't save them from *themselves*. Bill's a megalomaniac, Aaron won't stop collecting souvenirs that could *kill him*, and Wyatt . . . is Wyatt. I'm just done. I saved your life, and your truck is payment."

"I'm not giving you the keys."

"I already have your keys," she said, dangling them in front of him.

"Those are mine! And also, if there's no magic left how do you keep conjuring keys?!"

"There's enough for minor magic. That's it. But these you left on the table at the truck stop."

Ben slumped, "This can't be how this ends."

"It isn't," said a voice from the other side of the room.

They both turned to find a black crow sitting on the top of the old TV in the corner, an open window behind it.

They stared at it in silence. It tilted its head in return.

Ben finally muttered, "Did that bird just talk?"

The crow opened its broken beak and answered, "It did. And you . . . are running out of time."

"What the hell are you doing here?" Veronica asked the bird.

"You know him? Her?" Ben asked, still staring at the fat crow.

"No. But I know talking animals aren't supposed to be on this side of the veil."

"The *what?*" Ben asked.

"Am not from veil," the crow croaked.

"Then how can you talk?" Veronica asked.

"I eat the words. I speak the words."

"What does that mean?" Ben asked. The bird just tilted its head in response. Ben looked to Veronica, "Does that make sense to you?"

"No."

"Words . . . don't matter. *Book of Briars* matters. Must continue. Must finish story."

"What's *The Book of Briars?*" Ben asked. "The book about Alistair?"

"This story. This time. You. Her. The girl . . . the girl who remembers."

Ben approached the crow, crouching to its eye level. The crow flapped its wings for a second before settling again.

"Who's writing *The Book of Briars?* The Silver?"

"No. The *writer* writes."

"Who is the writer?!" Ben asked, losing his patience.

"Seems you guys have some stuff to work out," Veronica said, walking to the front door.

"Sister," The crow croaked. The word stopped Veronica at the threshold.

"What?"

"Sister. She is next part of the story."

"Marjory?" Veronica asked, her voice cracking.

"Yes. Her. Can show you. Follow me."

Chapter Twenty-One

Zev and Alistair were still on the floor, half-under the quilt she'd pulled off the bed. Face to face, their clothes littering the shadows around the room.

"It's all true," Zev whispered, staring into the middle distance, his arms still around her. "And they've been keeping tabs on you this whole time. That's why he had the journal . . ."

"Yeah . . ." Alistair answered, oblivious to what he was saying. She was soaking in the details of his face in the dim light of the window.

"You think they're telling the truth?" Zev asked.

"About magic? I saw it—"

"About the Silver? About being reformed or whatever."

"Oh. I don't know. They didn't seem like the Silver in *The Monarch Papers*, but . . . whatever path they made . . . whatever test they had for me, I failed it, so it doesn't really matter now."

Zev looked at her, without his glasses she could see how deep and piercing his eyes were, even in half-shadow.

"Are you kidding me? You didn't fail. You were scared and you still walked into the dark. The path you saw, the one with the fox,

219

that was the way out. The way through. Just like Bolden told you. I don't think you failed at all."

He reached up and brushed a few strands of Alistair's hair out of her face.

"I think you took a big first step, and if . . . Bolden or whoever doesn't see that, well . . . that's their problem."

"Your inclination to see the best in people is very annoying," she said with a wry smile, hoping to change the over-serious subject.

"I don't have to try with you," he answered, pulling her to him, "You know, I wanted to tell you for years, your aunt was right. I don't think I would've ever gotten into literature the way I did if it wasn't for you. I wasn't a big reader until you moved in next door. I wanted to impress you, and you loved books so much."

Alistair didn't know what to say. Normally, she would proverbially pack up and bolt in a situation like this— but now that feeling wasn't even a feeling. It was a *thing* that she could objectively see and put away instead of being overtaken by it. Which is what Bolden wanted Alistair to do with all those things in the dark.

Zev was quiet.

"Are you okay?" Alistair asked.

"Me? Oh, absolutely not. I'm freaking out. I'm worried this is all some kind of dream and I'm going to wake up without you. What about you? I mean, magic aside . . . how are you feeling about—"

"Us? Good," she answered.

"Alistair."

"Okay," she acquiesced. "I'm good, and also worried you're getting sucked into the black hole of my life."

"Hey. Your stuff might be a lot different than my stuff . . . Like, *a lot* different, but I got stuff too."

"Yeah? Like what?" she asked.

"Family stuff, work stuff. And I'm a mess. I'm hyper-neurotic, guilt-ridden, and blindly aggressive in my overachieving self-flagellation."

"Yeah . . . that's basically you describing good things with bad words. I think I still win."

They laughed together, then he kissed her, and she melted all over again. That's what she wanted right now. What she needed. Tangible. Contact. The reality of skin on skin with someone she knew she could trust.

Alistair's phone started buzzing. A call. She and Zev stared at each other for a moment before she scrambled to grab her phone off the mattress and check the screen. Zev sat up. "Who is it?" he asked.

"Unknown caller," she said.

"Maybe it's Bolden?"

"I don't know—"

Zev took her free hand. "You can do this."

Alistair looked at the screen again and then answered.

"I'm so proud of you, Alistair."

Bolden.

"What do you want?"

"All I've ever wanted is to help you. And you're ready. I'm waiting. There's an address on the drawing. The boy still has his father's car, I believe."

The call disconnected.

Alistair started throwing their strewn clothes around, looking for the drawing.

"What's wrong?"

She found it under her coat.

"She wants to meet," Alistair said.

They both watched as an address appeared in the corner of the drawing, like it was slowly surfacing from the depths of the paper.

"Holy shit . . ." Zev muttered.

Alistair input the address into her phone. It returned a field in the middle of nowhere, two hours north of the city. She was staring at the destination on the screen, but her mind was a million miles away and in a hundred different places.

Follow me.

That's what the fox had told her. She'd stayed in the dark longer than she ever had before, and for the first time, she saw that the fox wasn't a harbinger of the pale, white thing hiding there. It was trying to lead her out, to a place that felt safe and warm.

She looked up at Zev, who was putting his glasses back on.

"Do you still have your dad's old car?"

❦

Bolden was right. Zev's dad had gifted him a yacht on wheels from 1989. Zev rambled while squinting to see the speedometer because, according to Zev, the dashboard lights had stopped working sometime in the early 2000s,

"Dad wouldn't let me leave for college without 'a way to get back home.' I tried telling him that the L train's faster. Hell, a Midtown rickshaw is faster, but he had it in his head that he was gonna pass this thing down to me, so, here we are. I can't afford parking, so I have to schedule my day according to the street cleaning schedule. Four times a week I have to find space for this thing on the other side of the street, then back, then up the road and down, or else I'll be ticketed for leaving a pile of metal garbage on the street unattended. Tonight's the first night this monster has ever been useful. I'm sorry, I'm rambling. I ramble when I'm nervous. How did they know I had this car?"

"I don't know," Alistair answered from the passenger seat. Maybe they'd been watching him too. Watching anyone she knew or cared about. Alistair had initially refused to let Zev come along, attempting to convince him to let her take the monster by herself. Zev reasoned that since the car was basically a death trap for anyone uninitiated with its specific challenges, it meant Zev had to come with. They struck various deals as they made their way uptown and back to Columbia from her place: He would stay in the car. She would stay in sight of the car. If she didn't, he wouldn't. On and on.

In the midst of all this insanity, Alistair was filled with a warm wash of emotions, and Zev seemed to be feeling it too. He offered a little smile as they walked from the train to his place for the keys—a nudge against her arm, comforting her as they started upstate. In another world, they would be spontaneously driving somewhere dark and canopied with stars to talk all night and huddle together under a jacket or one of those blankets that always seem to be in trunks of cars like this one. But tonight, she was taking the next step on the path that had been blazed for her by unseen forces and she had no idea where it was heading, aside from what looked like an empty field in the middle of nowhere. The Taconic Parkway was a dark, winding two-lane road through the countryside and the quickest way upstate. Zev's eyes were trained on the road ahead. Driving headlong into God-knows-where with her. For her.

Alistair watched the passing woods outside her window. She could feel Zev turn to her every now and then, his eyes giving off an intangible energy, a heat. She probably looked lost in thought, distant. But, really, she was looking for something out there past the cold glass. Certainty. For road signs of her own, telling her this was where she was supposed to go. She was *looking for the fox now*, instead of running from him—a creature that used to conjure dread and fear, knowing that a nightmare was to come in its wake. Back at the school, Alistair felt for the first time like the fox was leading her away from danger, not toward it.

"The little red house," Zev said out of nowhere.

"What about it?" Alistair asked, startled by the sound of the book title.

"The book the Mountaineers found in *The Monarch Papers*. You told me about it when we were kids."

"Yeah, that was the first book. It was about . . . a place outside our world—somewhere I can't remember.

"Like Neithernor?"

"Maybe. It was like a playhouse, and six kids from around the world found it in six different ways, I can't . . . really remember all of it now. But they would find the house hidden in the woods behind their back yard, or in a park in the city . . . and they'd all meet there. That's how they became friends. And then . . . I don't know . . ."

"And that toy you found was one of them?" Zev asked.

"Yeah. Iris. She was Greek. And Sam and Scarlet were twins from America, and Franklin . . . I—think he was from India. But I'm not sure. What made you think of it?"

"I just . . . these books are all about kids who go to some magical hidden world, but to everyone back home, they would've just . . . disappeared. Like you did."

"Yeah," Alistair answered.

"And I'm pretty sure this is something you've already considered. That maybe you went to a place like Neithernor."

Zev was right. This *was* something Alistair had already considered, especially after learning from *The Monarch Papers* about Neithernor, which, allegedly, was a magical pocket dimension that people on Earth could escape to by knocking on doors. Alistair wanted it all to make sense when she'd first read about it. She wanted it to help patch over the missing places in her, but Neithernor just didn't *feel* right. It felt like a key that fit a lock but wouldn't turn.

"I can't believe how long you've had to deal with this. It must feel crazy, but also kind of a relief, yeah? You might have an answer soon."

"More like . . . I have hope that there might be hope."

Alistair realized that, for the first time, recalling the characters and the stories in *the briar books* hadn't summoned the apprehension she usually felt when reaching into the dark of her past. She took Zev's hand and held it tight.

They pulled off the Taconic and followed her phone directions down paved and unpaved roads until they crossed a long stretch of cold, dead, moonlit farmland. She put her hand on Zev's arm when his phone told them they had reached their "final destination."

"What a comforting turn of phrase," he said.

He steered over onto the shoulder. Crisp, recently beheaded crops scratched at Alistair's door. They both looked out the windows. Nothing but a field in a sprawling, shallow bowl of land, rimmed by ink-black woods.

"There's nothing here," Zev whispered.

Alistair cranked her window down. A whip of crystal-cold air sliced through her, easily twenty degrees cooler than in the city.

"Do you . . . feel anything? Like you did before?" he asked her.

She scanned the field. In the distance, something wide and jagged jutted up from the ground.

"There," she said as she opened her door.

"Wait. Remember, if you can't see me, I can't see you," Zev said.

Alistair turned to him and saw the furrowed brow, the set jaw that tried to mask his worry. "I remember."

She hesitated. She wanted to kiss him. Instead, she squeezed his hand and then let go, stepping out onto the frozen ground, the shorn crops shattering under her step, all the louder for the silence around them. She'd taken ten steps when she heard Zev start the boat up again. She watched him reverse and then pull forward, changing the angle he was parked, training the headlights on the "something" she was headed for. She could now see that it was a small structure that had been demolished, or burned, or consumed by time. Four fieldstone corners and a wall of jagged wood beams reaching up to the black sky like ribs on a carcass. She nodded to him. He flicked the headlights off, then on. She turned back. The winking of the headlights made her smile—she didn't know why.

She crossed the field, slow, sure, until she could see the structure even without the headlight beams. It was an old shed that probably held farm equipment, or a well at some point, but had long been left to decompose. The stone foundation framed a wooden floor that was still intact. She could climb onto it from any direction, but she took the two wide stone steps up through a doorless doorway. She was "inside" now. And there was nothing there. She pulled out her phone, flicked on the flashlight, and aimed the beam along the floor, the shattered walls. She had that vague sensation. But the cold wind bit into her, blinding the flicker of feeling with it. Whatever had been here at some point, was gone.

Alistair scanned the surrounding field. Was Bolden going to meet her here? Alistair raised her phone to turn the flashlight off when something on the wood-planked floor caught her eye. A shape half-covered in grime and caked mud.

Alistair knelt, training the flashlight as she swept the dirt away.

It was the half-ram, half-squid Ed had called an "ovihydrus," scorched into the floorboard, like it had been branded.

Alistair touched it. It was deep. And maybe she was just imagining it, but it felt warm. As if the residual heat of the branding was still simmering in its depths. Alistair heard quick footsteps crossing the frozen field. She turned to find Zev approaching, panting. "I couldn't see you," he lied with a shrug.

She aimed her flashlight at the symbol to show him. Zev climbed the steps, circling around to kneel beside her.

"That was the thing on Ed's arm," he said.

"Yeah."

"Maybe she's going to meet you here."

"That's what I was thinking, but there's something else."

"Maybe there *was*. But now it's—" Zev stopped mid-thought.

Alistair looked up at him. Zev was sheet-white and staring at something over her shoulder.

She turned. They both stood up, slow, careful.

Standing in the broken doorway was a door that wasn't there before.

Alistair and Zev leaned around the just-appeared door and found a wooden structure behind it, leading down at an angle into the ground. It reminded Alistair of the older subway entrances in the city.

Alistair approached the door. She tried the knob. It turned.

Zev cautioned, "Do you think maybe . . ."

Alistair opened the door and looked down at the entirely unmagical wooden stairs, which led into immeasurable underground darkness.

"Never mind," Zev said as he joined her side. "I guess you wanna go down there."

"You don't have to come with me," Alistair replied.

"Shut up," he replied with a nervous smile. "Let's go."

The stairs were narrow. Alistair and Zev descended single file, slowly, both gripping the wooden railings bolted to the walls, walls that turned from wood to striated stone as they went deeper into the earth. The stairs continued downward until Alistair could no longer look back and see the dim headlights through the doorway above. She pulled out her phone and led them down with the flashlight. She couldn't see more than two steps ahead of her at a time. The cold from above faded the farther down they went. Billows of warm air brushed against her face, growing stronger, occasionally tossing the stray strands of her hair. Great, they were walking to the center of the earth.

Zev whispered, "How far are we going down before . . ."

Something caught Alistair's attention.

"Look," Alistair whispered back.

Zev peeked over her shoulder. Below and beyond them, light. Flickering.

Twenty-or-so steps later, Alistair stepped down onto a glossy wooden floor, in a room with flocked ornamental wallpaper, ornate rugs, and gas lamps on the walls. It looked like a Victorian funeral parlor. Instead of a coffin, a single tufted armchair sat in the middle of the room, its back to Zev and Alistair. A shiver ran through Alistair as she wondered if someone was sitting in it, waiting for them. She rounded the chair, glancing over the top. Empty, and coated in a thin layer of dust, like everything else in the room. Two of the six wall-mounted gas lamps in the room were broken, their globes shattered and lying on the floor.

"What is this?" Zev asked.

She picked up a small, dusty card from the side table near the chair. It simply read: WELCOME. SOMEONE WILL BE WITH YOU SOON.

"It's a waiting room. Or was. I don't think this place has been used in a long time," said Alistair.

"Unless they like it like this—you know, the haunted mansion vibe. It does lend an air of mystery to the whole thing," Zev said.

Alistair smiled at his earnest enthusiasm. It felt like they were laughing at a funeral. Slightly inappropriate, but what were they supposed to do? They'd just walked down a marginally magical stairway to the center of the earth and found a vampire brothel waiting at the bottom.

"So now we wait?" Zev asked.

Alistair shook her head, "Why wouldn't Bolden be here? They're expecting me."

"Maybe it's because I'm here?" Zev asked.

"No, she knew you were coming."

"Right. Maybe it's another test—"

A short, muffled sound drew Alistair's attention to the other side of the room.

"Zev," Alistair interrupted, "did you hear that?"

"Hear what?" he asked.

They both fell quiet. Alistair crossed the room, listening. Zev followed her as she approached the wall that the armchair faced. She put her ear to the wall, the fuzzy flocking on the wallpaper tickling. A quiet moment, then she heard it again, behind the wall—

Click click click.

"You're right. It's a test," she whispered to him.

"What? How do you know?"

"The fox is on the other side," she answered matter-of-factly. "There must be a hidden door."

Alistair stepped back, searching the wall, looking for a seam or hidden latch. She ran her fingers along the textured floral pattern, black flocking on a blood-red background.

Zev followed her lead, checking the gas lamps for switches.

Alistair took another step back and fully took in the pattern of the wallpaper for the first time, endless oval frames of black flowers circling six-pointed stars at their centers. All except one oval in the middle of the wall. In the center was what looked like a small hoop at the end of a chain. She might never have noticed it if not for the sound of the fox. She looked closer and found the hoop and chain were flocked like the rest of the wallpaper, but when she touched the hoop, it slipped between her fingers.

"Zev," she called out. He rushed over, his eyes on the ornament she'd partially pulled away from the wall.

"It's like Ed's tattoo," he said.

"Exactly."

They looked at each other, nervous, then he nodded a sweet, apprehensive little nod, and Alistair pulled the hoop, dragging the flocked chain with it.

A bell rang out somewhere behind the wall, and all at once, shuddering sounds began reverberating from all around them, shaking the parlor. A cacophony that sounded like immense and heavy objects sliding, turning, slamming, and locking into place behind all four sides of the room.

Alistair let go of the hoop. The chain pulled it back and it was instantly wallpaper again. They scrambled to the middle of the room as the sounds around them grew deafening. One of the gas lamp globes shook loose and shattered as one final, resounding *thud* shook the floor, then the room fell silent again.

"What the hell was that?" Zen asked, a whiff of panic in his voice.

"Doorbell?" Alistair wondered in response.

They both heard a succinct *click* and turned to find the wall with the "doorbell" now had a wallpapered door in the middle of it, which slowly swung open, revealing a long, dark hall beyond it, with the ebbing glow of warm light at the end.

Alistair approached the open doorway. Streams of sweet-smelling air blew in from the long hall beyond it. Vanilla. Alistair was drawn to the smell and the light at the far end. The fox was there.

"Alistair," Zev called out from behind her.

He was still standing in the middle of the room.

"Are you sure you want to do this?" he asked her.

Alistair could see he was shaken by whatever had just happened behind the walls.

"I can't go back now. Not yet. They know the truth." Alistair answered.

"Right. But they're also . . . the Silver. What if we walk through that door and the walls start turning and we can't get out?"

He had a point. "I don't know," Alistair answered. "But the fox is down there. What if it's like you said, about the path he showed me? Maybe it's the way out. The way through."

Zev seemed to consider her words, then he began to nod, "Okay. I just—it needed to be said."

"If you want to go back to the car, or the city, I'd . . . I'd understand."

Zev approached her, gave a final resolute nod, "Let's go find your fox."

Alistair turned back to the doorway and, without hesitating, stepped through. Zev followed her. The hallway had been carved through cold, solid stone. Alistair could feel Zev close behind her. The hall grew slightly narrower and shorter as they approached the light at the end and the dark rectangular doorway that framed it. Zev put his hand on her shoulder. It made her knees go weak.

The glowing room beyond came into focus as they approached, the stone hallway narrowing more, now requiring them to turn slightly sideways to reach the far end. At first, all Alistair could see through the doorway was a wooden table with stacks of books on top, sitting in the middle of whatever still-unseen room lay beyond, but when they finally made it to the doorway, they stopped, both frozen, Zev peering in over Alistair's shoulder.

They were unable to move, unable to comprehend what they were seeing.

Beyond was the grandest library either of them had ever seen. Towering walls of books reached to coffered ceilings that had to be seven stories tall, or taller. Rich oak stairs led up and over and around, balconies bulging out every now and then along the railings. Massive dark-stained tables were set out on the marble of the ground floor, littered with piles of books so high Alistair couldn't imagine how they could've been stacked by human hands. They both stepped through the doorway and took in the nauseating vastness of the room above them. It was as if a mountain had been hollowed out and the library and its ornate, impossible woodwork were now holding it up.

Above the wonder and spectacle of it all was the realization that the entire endless room was illuminated by a towering, floor-to-ceiling wall of looming windows. The wall's individual panes, each taller than a person, were rimmed with cold, silver light. Moonlight. Alistair walked toward the windows, weaving through the tables and stacks of ancient books. How was this possible? She knew how far down they were. Was it some kind of trick, or spell? A projection?

As she approached, Alistair could see an endless expanse of blue-white beyond the glass. A snow-covered plain, with tall shards of blue-white ice reaching up like fingers from a grave. Beyond the miles-wide plain were blue-black mountains, and beyond that, hanging just over the edge of the mountain crests, the fullest moon she'd ever seen. She touched the glass. It was freezing. Frost rimmed the edges of the windowpanes. She turned to Zev in astonishment, but he wasn't there. She glanced around the first floor of the sprawling space. He was gone. She called out to him—

But no sound escaped her lips.

Alistair called again. Nothing. As if the room were a vacuum. She looked left, right, but couldn't find him. She now realized her shoes made no sound on the marble floor. She rushed to the closest table, grabbed a book, and slammed it into the marble. Silence. She screamed for Zev. Nothing came out but cold quiet. She ran across the floor, searching the upper floors, the balconies. She climbed the stairs and ran up one aisle, down the next, oblivious to the wonder around her. She felt like she was suffocating in the silence. She ran up and around stairways, through arched, book-lined corridors, up and down book-littered halls, getting lost in the stacks. Her heart pounded silently. She couldn't hear her own heaving breath, the silence of swallowing, clearing her throat. Her vacant screams. Most unnerving, that persistent voice in her mind was dampened. The one that fears and needs and overthinks. Alistair found herself unable to articulate the feeling into inner words. That's how quiet it was. She wanted to curl into a ball and shield herself from the overwhelming nothing, but she had to find Zev.

There he was.

Across the open air of the library's center, one floor down, hunched over, as if he'd been hurt.

She raced to him, knocking over stacks in her path. As she approached, she could see that Zev was moving, breathing, lucid. He wasn't hurt, he was reading—crumpled up, holding a massive old book in his lap, entranced. He jumped when Alistair approached. He called out in surprise, and for the first time realized he couldn't hear his own voice, or hers, or anything. She grabbed him by the arm, but realized she had no idea how to get back to the waiting room. They were lost.

She mouthed "Let's go," and tugged Zev up from the ground. They both ran, looking for any way out, but Alistair wasn't sure if they were getting closer to the entrance or slipping deeper and deeper into the stacks.

Click click click.

She stopped cold, Zev colliding with her.

In the eerie, deathly, din of nothing, she could hear the fox. She took Zev's hand and led him toward the sound, a calm washing over her. She followed the sound down the aisles, past the stacks, up the stairs, further and further into the depths of the library. The sound of the fox growing louder and clearer until they came upon a door in the distance.

Wooden and beautifully ornate, it began to open as they approached, and Alistair felt that familiar current calling her toward it. They rushed for it, and as they crossed the doorway's threshold, the sound of Alistair's panting and Zev's pleading to slow down came flooding back. They fell into the small, wood-paneled room behind the door, which was no bigger than a closet, and was lit by a single flickering sconce.

"What were you doing?!" Alistair screamed, not realizing how loud she'd been yelling in the vacuum of the library.

"Did you see what's in there?! What those books were?!"

Zev's knees buckled, his back against the oiled oak wall as he slid to the floor, pulling his glasses off. He had tears in his eyes. "There were bound papyrus—from the—" he was overwhelmed and stammering.

Alistair turned back to the library and slammed the door shut, then slumped against it, panting.

"They have—I don't—pieces from—" Zev was struggling to get it out. "From Pergamum. I was holding a volume of the Pinakes. It was just sitting on the floor like—like an old paperback. Just sitting there . . . on the floor. What if your books are in there? What if that's why you're here? What if every book that was ever lost is in there?"

Zev had looked behind the curtain and seen the face of his own personal God. All the lost words were here. "Alistair, how is this possible?"

Alistair wanted to give him an answer or comfort him, but she didn't know what to say. It was all too much to absorb. She took short, fast breaths, trying to regain her composure. She realized that the small dim room they were in was slowly growing brighter. The back wall was now gone, and a room was "fading in" in its place. The light seemed to come from nowhere, slowly pushing back the shadows, and Alistair could see that they were in a small entryway that led to a long golden gallery. Filigree crept up the sand-colored walls and across the ceiling, curled together, and continued on like it had grown that way. The room had dozens of matte gold pedestals laid out in a grid, with etched glass cloches sitting on top of each of them. Shafts of light shone down into each cloche, illuminating whatever was inside.

It was a glittering, gilded museum.

Alistair got to her feet and took one step into the large gallery. If the library had been carved out a mountain, the gallery had grown inside a flower. The rounded walls sloped inward and joined in a soft peak at the ceiling, and gentle swathes of light peeked in from the folds the walls made when they met. Alistair cleared her throat, checking to make sure she could hear it. The large round room smelled sweet, floral. It felt warm and safe. Alistair took a few more steps, despite her apprehension, drawn to look into the cloches. The displays held the strangest things. A child's backpack covered with dirt. A crumpled stack of notebook paper. A shattered hand mirror, its glass pieces spread out beautifully, as if it were a work of art. There was part of a strange, horned skull, a little girl's shoe, a candelabra shaped like an octopus, its arms reaching out, holding eight small lanterns. A small, broken pair of glasses that looked like the pair the fox wore.

"What is it?" Zev asked from the other end of the gallery. He'd gotten back on his feet and followed her into the gallery, slipping his glasses back on.

"I don't know . . ."

Alistair approached a case that contained a single sheet of notebook paper, its edges curled. On it was a drawing made in crayon, or maybe the smeary oil pastels they used to pass out in elementary school, she wasn't sure.

It was a drawing of a house, narrow but tall, with several floors and rooflines jutting out and sloping off in different trajectories. Ramshackle and rough, the turret that topped it leaned out precariously, seemingly weighed down by the chimney stack on the right of its peak. There were other chimneys on other roofs, six in total, some stone and cobbled together, others smooth black, like metal, with little triangle caps on top. A small broken fence surrounded the house, with little gray pickets drawn at different angles, and tufts of blue-green grass growing in between. The drawing was lovingly illustrated and beautifully detailed, as if whoever had drawn it had been sitting in front of the actual house, marveling at its impossible structure and scale.

At its rich, red exterior.

The artist had signed the bottom of the work in a beginner's cursive.

Alistair Mead.

Chapter Twenty-Two

Ben's upper body was shielded from the chilly and unexpected Northern California rainstorm by the raised hood of the pickup. His lower half was already soaked. He shivered, his head wobbling as he poured the second bottle of oil down his truck's gullet. A quarter of the oil puddled on the pavement somewhere under the engine. His beloved truck was bleeding out. Every two hours or so the oil light would come on and the engine would start chugging and slurring. The truck was not prepared to traverse the country and back again. She had planned to die a peaceful death hauling sheets of plywood from the hardware store to Ben's cabin. Easy, fitting, an honorable death for an almost forty-year-old pickup. Doing what she was built to do. This, though, this was just cruel.

"Sorry," Ben whispered to his truck's assorted under-hood parts as he filled her with oil again. He tossed the empty oil bottle in the bed of the truck and slammed the hood shut. He looked up and saw the crow circling above them in the rain, a black smudge against the gray clouds hanging over the desert. Ben climbed back in the passenger seat of the truck, his jeans sopping wet. Veronica had slid back into her leather jacket while he was working under the hood. The desert was turning colder. She started the engine and pulled onto the road. The truck's "check oil" light flickered and went out, sated for now.

They'd followed an old dry highway that split Death Valley and the Sequoia National Forest, where it had been clear-skied and quiet. But they'd started inching closer and closer to the misty woods outside Yosemite and still had no idea where they were going, other than "north." That's the direction the crow had been flying for nearly seven hours, leading them away from Needles. Two hours out of Carson City, Nevada, the crow had descended level to the horizon and veered right, signaling, they assumed, for them to get off the highway and continue on desolate back roads. The heavy rain turned the twisting unpaved roads to mud, slowing them down.

Ben had spent the early hours of the drive thinking about when he had first met Veronica back at the bar. How she'd somehow known he was from North Carolina, down to the town. It had then dawned on him that she said she wasn't talking to the Newhouses, so they didn't tell her about him, and she most likely hadn't done any research. He was a nobody to her. Which made it all the more embarrassing that he'd rushed back to her apartment under the assumption she felt anything but disdain and pity for him. No, it was magic. It had to be some kind of magic. That's how she knew so much about him.

She could read his mind.

It's why she broke their silence to ask about the book pages on the road out of Needles. It's why she pulled into a truck stop in Barstow because he really had to pee but wasn't going to say anything. It was hard not to stare out at the cold, dark desert and stop his mind from wandering. He was already conscious of what he was doing and saying, or not saying, but now he was hyperaware of what he was thinking. Thoughts, fears, urges, song lyrics, and his mind kept wanting to think about the one thing he didn't want anyone to know.

"Who's Frank?"

Shit.

"What do you mean?" Ben asked, grim, knowing exactly what she meant.

"You already think I can read your mind. That's all you're thinking about."

"So I'm annoying you with my thoughts?"

"I'm not *trying* to read your mind. That isn't even really what it is . . ."

"I thought you said you didn't have any more power. Reading my mind is probably a waste of good energy."

"All the other magic, the flashy stuff, is shit I learned along the way. But I was *born* with telemancy, a type of it. I unlocked it later in life. I'm not trying to read your mind, but when someone's . . . vulnerable, their thoughts kind of leak out and I can get lost in them."

"Awesome," Ben answered, trying not to . . . think. "Frank's . . . a guy who harassed me and my girlfriend for years."

"Because of your book."

"Yeah." Ben leaned in toward the windshield, checking for the crow in the night sky.

"What happened to him?"

"Don't you already know?"

"Actually, you're weirdly good at *not* thinking about the night he came to your apartment. Or at least how it ended."

"That's not fair."

"I'm just trying to make conversation," Veronica said.

"You know, given your whole . . . vibe, I thought you'd be more comfortable with silence."

"Well, what the hell else are we gonna do? No reception, no radio, and we have no idea how long we're gonna be following that bird. We're stuck together until he takes us where we're going, and frankly, I was hoping your *talking* would drown out your *thinking* for a change because your brain never shuts up."

"Why don't you try to read *his* mind instead, then?" Ben pointed in the bird's general direction.

"I can, kind of, which is all kinds of weird because I can't read minds of simpler animals, even though crows are smart as hell. He can't naturally speak. He was right that the words aren't . . . his, if that makes sense."

"Oh yeah. Total sense." Ben's anxiety and discomfort had brewed into one hell of a bad mood. "Sorry. This is just weird piled on weird. It would be like me asking what . . . happened between you and your sister? What happened with you and Wyatt? It's weird having someone you don't know pry into your private thoughts without your . . . consent."

Veronica watched the road for a while, then, "I loved Wyatt, for what it was worth. As much as I could. Then I lost him like everything else. We tried to make it work after we came back, but I was like a curse. Bad things and bad people followed me everywhere I went. Couldn't keep my friends, couldn't keep my sister safe, couldn't even keep a real job without people coming to pick apart my past. And Marjory . . . she doesn't remember what happened. She's the only one of us who doesn't. But we couldn't tell her. Literally *couldn't*. Over time she became obsessed. Kinda like you, except she half lost her mind looking for the truth, and then found the path of Silver. She was broken by then. All I know is they took her, from what I could sense from her stave. The . . . walking stick. She has power too, like me, but not exactly the same. We both get sucked into other people's heads, but she can't read a weakened mind, so much as *control* it. God knows what they have her doing. If she's—" Veronica cut herself off.

Ben felt guilty for bringing it up. He realized how scared she was for her sister. "I'm sure she's okay. You said you felt her out there up until the stick broke . . . Also, that's one trustworthy bird up there. If he says he's taking us to her, he's taking us to her."

A long quiet stretch. Nothing but the ticking of the pickup's engine.

"I lost someone I care about too, because of that guy. Because of Frank. She's around, Cor, she just doesn't want anything to do with me. At least not like it was."

"He's the reason you stopped writing."

"I guess," Ben answered simply, betraying the flood of painful and humiliating thoughts that swept through his mind, aware she could sense all of it.

"I won't ask you about him again," was all she said in response.

"Thanks."

Ben felt relieved and guilty all at once. She was trying to reach out to him, after all. It wasn't the most orthodox way to go about it, but she was trying, if for no other reason than to pass some of the grueling hours on the road. He wondered if it would feel like a relief, telling her the truth about Frank, letting that burden off his shoulders.

"Why'd you leave North Carolina?" Veronica asked, interrupting his thought.

"I . . . don't know. I never felt like I belonged there. I grew up poor, in a farming family, which I had no interest in. Dad didn't want kids, or at least not a kid like me. I was . . . more imaginative than he was willing to accommodate. He worked his ass off, drank his brains out, got in fights everywhere he went, but my mom thought she could fix him. Then Mom *died*, I was—geez, maybe nine or ten. I stayed as long as could. I tried to help him, but once someone's determined to blow themselves up, there's not much you can do."

"I hear that."

"Right, yeah, you get it," Ben answered. "So, he got worse and worse. I stole his truck, *this* truck actually, when I turned nineteen, figured I was doing him and everyone else on the road a favor. I went to college for a while, then worked a bunch of crappy jobs, and when I had enough time and distance away, I eventually remembered what I loved doing—making up stories—so I started writing."

"What happened to *him*?"

"He fixed up an old junker truck we had in the barn, and a year after I got to New York he hit an ambulance head-on."

Veronica sighed. A moment of quiet, then Ben glanced over, and Veronica looked back. They both started laughing. A good, deep, gallows laugh.

"We're a couple of nightmares," she said.

"It's funny we have so much in common. That's why I first got interested in your story. I was Wyatt's age when you guys disappeared. To me, in my life, that sounded like a dream. Just getting up and vanishing."

"In some ways, it was. In other ways, I'd do anything to take it back."

"Did you know about magic then? Before you . . . you know, whatever?" he asked hesitantly, trying not to trigger another run-in with a semi or a lightning bolt.

"Sort of? That year, the months leading up to us . . . *whatevering*, we learned a lot. It's part of the reason . . . well, yeah."

"What other kinds of powers are there? You said some people are born with them?"

"You're asking because of the book pages. Sorry, your brain is pretty loud."

Ben had never felt more seen. "Whoever wrote the pages can basically see into the future, at least from what I can tell. They were writing things that hadn't happened yet."

"It's definitely in the realm of possibility."

"At this point, what isn't?"

❧❧

It was nearly 3 AM when the crow descended again, guiding Veronica and Ben along the outer perimeter of Carson City, Nevada, a bland civic center in the middle of the desert. Darkened strip malls, schools, and prickly desert underbrush were barely visible beyond the dark curtains of rain draping the truck. The passenger side windshield wiper had stopped working in the deluge, but the crow was now at eye level again, barely steadying itself against the rain.

The crow led them to a left turn, then a right, past corporate parks and old factories, to a wide one-story building set out by itself on what Ben assumed was considered "prairie." There were lights on inside, and the sign on their muddy approach read EAGLE VALLEY PSYCHIATRIC HOSPITAL.

Veronica pulled into the near-empty parking lot and shut the engine down. The crow landed on the hood, nothing more than a flat, dripping mess of feathers. It walked to the windshield and tapped it with its beak. Ben rolled down the window and the crow clumsily flew in, splashing rainwater everywhere, perching on the dashboard. It was shivering, water pouring off its drenched body.

"You okay?" Ben asked, having left behind the shock of wizard twins and talking birds somewhere around Death Valley. The bird shook its head, preening its sopping feathers. Ben reached under the seat, sifting through junk he'd left under it until he found an old oil-stained T-shirt. He tried to help dry the crow, looking over to Veronica who was staring at the clinic.

The rain had become a drizzle.

"What are you thinking?" Ben asked.

Veronica didn't answer.

"I mean, this could actually be *good* news. She's not with . . . the bad guys. She's getting treatment. Maybe she wouldn't do what they wanted or maybe she got away and ended up here?" said Ben.

Veronica continued scanning the building. "Maybe."

"Can you . . . hear her?"

"We can't affect each other," Veronica answered.

"Oh, that's good. I mean, that means she could be in there even if you don't hear her," Ben said, then turned back to the crow. "Is her sister in there?"

"He's too tired to speak. He's almost run out of words anyway . . ."

"Okay," Ben answered, as if that made sense. "So, what's the plan?" Coming from him, it did not sound as cool as he imagined it would. Veronica pulled her jacket tight around her and stepped out of the cab. Ben grabbed his hoodie and opened the door to follow. He turned back to the bird. "Stay in there. We'll be right back." He realized he was talking to the sentient crow like he talked to Volley the super mutt. He shut the door and hustled to catch up with Veronica. They took the cracked concrete path between the lot and the clinic, then Veronica tapped the button next to the double doors of the building. With a sharp buzz, the doors unlocked.

Inside was a long, low-ceilinged waiting room bathed in sharp fluorescent light. The walls were green, the floor tile was green, even the metal grates on the outside windows were coated in a sickly mint. Beyond the glassed-in reception desk, Ben could see a thick, cotton candy sphere of white hair. The head it was attached to looked up from her book. She was in her seventies at least. But not what seventy looked like now—seventy from sixty years ago. She could've been a mascot for pancake syrup or boxed cake mix. She smiled at Ben and Veronica and waited for them to approach the window. When they did, she flicked a switch with a flourish and leaned into an old microphone. The plaque facing the window read FAYE.

"How can I help you on this dreary evening?"

Ben and Veronica looked at each other, then back to Faye.

"We're here to see someone," Veronica said.

Faye smiled, pulled a pamphlet out of a nearby drawer, and slid it through the slot of her window.

"Visitor's Day is every other Wednesday. You'll have to come back next week. This pamphlet will explain everything including visiting hours, what you're prohibited from bringing—"

Veronica pushed the pamphlet back through the slot, letting it crumple before falling onto Faye's desk. Faye seemed unnerved.

"I want to talk to whoever's in charge here."

Faye smiled back, placid, unblinking, then, "What is this in reference to?" She took out a pencil and notebook. Veronica leaned into the microphone and spoke in a slow cadence like she was giving aggressive dictation. "It's in reference to the thrift store couch cover of a dress you're wearing."

Faye managed to write *In reference to* before her face fell at the landing of Veronica's insult.

"Also, my sister, Marjory Morrow. That's M-A-R-J-O-R-Y Morrow. I'm here to take her home."

Faye put her pencil and paper away and stood up, brushing the creases out of her floral print dress. "Have a seat," Faye offered through a gritted smile.

Veronica took three steps back until she was shoulder to shoulder with Ben.

"You said that to get in her head, didn't you? About her dress. To make her vulnerable . . ." Ben whispered.

"Yeah. It worked. Listen, Marjory's here. Also, Faye's working for the Silver."

"What?" Ben yell-whispered.

"She's going to tell them that we found Marjory. We have about —I don't know, twenty seconds—"

"*To do* what? *Before* what?"

Veronica shrugged. "Why don't you go start the truck?"

"I'm not leaving you."

"You can't do anything."

"Neither can *you*. You don't have any magic."

"I don't need magic to make a mess," Veronica said as she let the crowbar Ben kept under his driver's seat slip out from her jacket sleeve. "You *sure* you don't want to leave?"

Veronica was putting on the same aggressive stance she'd had when they first met, but Ben could also see the fear in her eyes. The fear she'd been carrying since Needles. Not for them, or at least not *just* for them. This was about her sister.

"I'm backing your play," Ben said.

"Thanks," Veronica replied, then she approached the reception window and slammed the crowbar into the glass, exploding it into countless tiny pieces. An alarm immediately began to scream. Veronica grabbed the edge of the broken window and hoisted herself through the shattered gap. Ben wasn't quite as agile but made it through without a cut. He followed her as she tore an adjacent door open, both of them sprinting through a back hall of empty administrative offices before bursting through a security door and finding themselves in a network of mint-covered halls dotted with what looked to be patient rooms. They both looked one way, then the other, unsure where to start.

"Marjory!" Veronica screamed.

Nothing but the echo of her voice and the Klaxon alarm. Ben went to the nearest patient room door, which was locked. Beside it was a handwritten name tag with the last name "Adler."

Ben yelled back to Veronica over the alarm. "They have names. Check that end of the hall. I'll check this one, then we'll meet back here."

Veronica sprinted down to the opposite end of the hall. Ben went door to door, checking names, looking in the small observation windows of every room. The lights were all out. He could now only barely make out Veronica yelling her sister's name down at the other end of the hall as he came to the end of his. No "Morrow" on any of the rooms. The alarm was deafening, but where was security? Where was anyone? He howled in surprise as someone grabbed his shoulder from behind.

It was Veronica.

Ben looked behind her. The hall now extended the length of the building.

"Was that a dead-end a second ago?" she asked.

"Uh-huh."

"Shit," Veronica said. "They're changing the building."

"They're *what*?"

"You gotta get out of here." She handed him the crowbar. "Tear your way out if you have to."

"I'm not leaving!" Ben yelled as he pushed the crowbar back into her hands. "What do we do now?"

Veronica clenched her eyes closed.

"Veronica?" Ben asked, frantic.

She held up a *gimme-a-second* finger, then opened her eyes.

"Thoughts are coming from there," she pointed to another hall that led into the center of the building. She started sprinting down it, and Ben followed. At the end of the hall was a door, different from the others—ornate stained wood. Ben looked back and saw that the hallway behind them was now another dead end. They were being corralled.

"Veronica," Ben called out, but she wasn't stopping. He kept close as she turned the knob on the wooden door and walked through, crowbar poised to strike. Ben rushed in behind her and slammed the door, the crowbar in his hand vanishing just as the door latched shut. The alarm stopped immediately.

They were now in a strange museum-like room. A grid of pedestals was laid out with objects on them, each ensconced in a glass dome. The entire room was ringed in gold filigree.

And they weren't alone.

Standing on the other end of the room was a scared young man in glasses and a young woman with brown skin and a camel-colored coat.

All Ben could say was, "Alistair?"

PART IV

Chapter 23

A year had passed in the old fort. Perhaps more. It had been the mothers' unofficial responsibility to keep track of time, whispering endlessly about the many weeks and months that had passed since they'd arrived. But as a windy autumn came to the old fort, Ilya and the other children were separated from the mothers. From then on, time felt both endless and like nothing at all without the mothers to mark its passage.

There was no reason given for the relocation of the children. At least not to the children themselves. On the rainy day the families were separated, Ilya looked back over her shoulder, hoping for her mother to nod her on with a stern but reassuring look, but her mother's face had lost all its light. Izaak had been that light. It was not to say that Ilya's mother loved Izaak more, only that Izaak had been their mother's impossible boy. A child who came when her mother had resigned herself to never being able to have a child. When Ilya was conceived, some five years later, it was merely a surprise, not a miracle.

Izaak was the light. Ilya was the daughter.

As she passed through the doorway, Ilya saw her mother look to her as she left—possibly for the last time—without a tear or a blink. The children around Ilya, mostly younger than she was, cried and screamed, but Ilya noted a strange feeling beginning to unfurl inside her. She felt as if she grew an inch or more in that moment she passed from her mother's unflinching view. Ilya couldn't explain it, but in that instant, she felt strong. Like iron beams had grown inside her bones. Ahead of her were the ginger-haired siblings she'd met on the night she and her family had arrived at the fort. She took their hands as the children were ushered like sheep to their new accommodations on the other side of the old fort.

The children were brought to a moldering assembly hall that had been filled with hastily hammered-together bunk beds. There were older children there. Izaak's age. But all girls. And they knew nothing about the boys who'd come first to rebuild the fort, then vanished. The older girls were meant to tend to the younger children.

They did not.

They, instead, lived in daydreams. They repaired their dress hems and braided their hair into ornate wreaths on their heads. They recited poems to one another and hung up sheets to block their corner of the hall from the younger children. They did not see what was going on all around them. Like Mother, they had gone away. So Ilya—and the other children who, like her, were not quite old enough to care for younger children yet not quite young enough to be cared for by children themselves—took care of those who were squarely young. Fed them, cooked for them, told them stories to help them sleep.

That was Ilya's most important responsibility, telling all the children wondrous stories before they drifted away for the night. It wasn't long before Ilya had told all the stories she herself had been told by her father, and so she began to tell her own stories. There was one about twin dragons who shared a tail and couldn't manage to get along, which was directed mostly at the ginger-haired siblings. There was the story about a fancy chef who'd been captured by cannibals, who demanded they prepare a complicated recipe that would feature him as the main course but would also aid in his clever escape. And there were many stories about the "impossible path" she saw in the woods on her ninth birthday. What it really was, why it would sometimes disappear, and where it might lead. The children were happy to hear the stories and telling them made Ilya feel as if it wasn't just her body and her small, worn hands that had a purpose in the old fort, but also her mind. Her imagination.

When the children were first moved, Ilya asked the soldiers for medicine when children fell ill, but no medicine ever came. The sick were simply swept away and never seen again. When the ginger-haired girl never came back, Ilya stopped asking for medicine. She took the lonely ginger-haired boy under her wing. She showed him what she'd learned from the books she read in her old life, like how to find the herbs growing outside the hall that helped with tooth pain or stomachaches, or which weeds and flowers the children could boil and eat when food was scarce. The boy never left her side. She saw that same strange strength growing in him too. Now, in the bones of someone else, Ilya finally recognized it. It was the quality her father often spoke about as the days grew darker in their old home in the city. A quality he respected and valued in others.

Fortitude.

Autumn ended, and a quiet, steely winter began, with razor-sharp wind and nothing to eat but potatoes left too long in the frozen ground. After ages and no time at all, the snow became blackened, muddy puddles formed, and winter turned to a rainy spring. And Ilya, as far as she knew, had at some point turned eleven.

Every night, once the children were in their beds and all the stories of far-off places and interesting characters had been told—and the older girls had finally ended their singing and preening for the night—Ilya would crawl into the pallet of blankets she'd made on the floor by the ginger-haired boy's bed. Her back ached. Her feet throbbed in time to her heartbeat. Her head ached as she laid it down on her pillow made from old newspapers. It was then that she would soothe herself by imagining the "impossible path." She would envision finding it, walking under its gently swaying, sun-dappled trees. The only respite from the dark of the old fort. The uncertainty and pain. The worsening living conditions, the overcrowding, the neglect. The trains that would take thousands away at a time, perhaps even Father and Mother. Eerie hours of shuffling footsteps outside the hall windows, heading for transports, then quiet—only to be replaced with countless strangers' footsteps shuffling in when the next train arrived. Strangers who whispered outside their windows about the horrors in "the east."

The sunlit path was Ilya's only way out, but she would always fall asleep before she reached the end. On her way, before Ilya's mind drifted away from the pain of her body, she would see Izaak there, waiting for her, just ahead. Smiling. A light.

The early spring rains passed. The weather turned warm. Summer came soon after. And with summer came the tours.

The children weren't told who the inspectors were, only that the children were to repeat the answers they'd been told to memorize if anyone asked them questions. Walls were freshly painted, flowers planted, derelict rooms were made up into mock schoolhouses. Even a synagogue was built. The suitcases that had disappeared on the night the children arrived suddenly reappeared, and the suitcase contents were distributed among the children. Frilly dresses and shiny shoes. Trousers and crisp, white shirts. Ilya saw girls wearing dresses that could've been her own, not that it mattered. They didn't fit her anymore. The older girls fawned and showed off their new frocks as if they were the spoils of a day at the shops, not the remnants of someone else's life, of *all* their former lives. After all the suitcases were returned by the soldiers, and all the clothes were handed out, the children beamed and laughed, overcome with happiness to have something familiar, something from home. To Ilya, it was confirmation that they were never going home again.

When all the suitcases were empty, Ilya sifted through the errant belongings left strewn on the floor. She found her suitcase in a corner, and near it, her diary. She slipped it under the apron she'd taken to wearing to protect her dress from stains and spilled food and sick children. When the ginger-haired boy was asleep, she went out into the weed-strewn moonlit garden behind the hall. She sat under the great gnarled oak and flipped through the pages. She found the last thing she'd written before they were put on the train.

> *If you're walking in the wood one day*
> *And feel a wind from far away*
> *That carries scent of spice and dew*
> *Of memories you almost knew*
> *Then look around, beyond the haze*
> *To knotholes that go on for days*

She took the short, dull pencil out of the notebook's pen loop and began to write.

> Or you might glimpse a wreath of thorns
> And through it, things with crooked horns

She was startled at how quickly and easily the words came. These were not words she'd made up. They were words that she'd somehow remembered, although she'd never written them.

> *Then rest assured, for without fail*
> *You've found a path—*

Try as she might, the last words wouldn't come to her. There was a wall there between her and the final rhyme. The same wall that had haunted her since her first night in the fort—earlier even, when she first saw the path in the woods. A wall through which she could see slivers of memory, of all of this having somehow already unfolded.

With clenched-shut eyes and balled fists, she attempted to drag the last words of the poem through the cracks in the wall, only to have them retreat further and further into the dark beyond.

Ilya believed that her fortitude had come from her unexplainable knowing that this had all already happened, and no matter what she did, it would happen again, different in some ways, in many ways precisely as it had before. Mother, Father, Izaak, the fort. She couldn't explain how she knew, but she knew, with both steely certainty and heart-rending fear.

She had already sat beneath this old oak tree and cried like she cried tonight. Tears that came from endless depths of hopelessness, because, through the wall, Ilya saw glimpses of a time when she was slightly older, and she was not in the fort. A time she had lost almost everything, but not *everything*, and more importantly, she was free. And Izaak was there. Ilya cried because somewhere inside she knew that whatever events had set her freedom and her reunion with Izaak into motion, had never come to pass.

She let them go that night, the memories. She decided they were nothing more than make-believe. Fortitude wasn't born from hope; it was strength born from pain. And if she was going to stay strong and find a way to be free, she couldn't count on make-believe anymore.

Ilya cried one last time, until the tears stopped falling. Then she went back inside. She left the diary in a rooted crook of the old oak tree.

Summer passed, blistering heat, and the tours. Officials from countries with languages Ilya couldn't understand came to assess the conditions at the fort. Children who misbehaved or squirmed during the visits disappeared when the tours were over. Ilya held tight to the ginger-haired boy, always seeking him out and standing with him when the soldiers brought the nurses and the official-looking men in shirtsleeves and ties. They looked the children over, examined the hall and the grounds. Then once the soldiers had asked the children questions and the children gave the answers they'd been told to give, the group moved on to other parts of the fort, satisfied by what they saw and what the children told them.

Near the end of summer, the oppressive heat pushed the tours outdoors, and the children were led to a garden park in the middle of the fort and told to play while the tour groups watched from beyond the garden gates. It only took a few moments for the children to forget that they were pretending to play before they were simply playing. Gardeners tended to the flowers and trimmed the tree limbs as children raced around and below the trees, recalling all the games they'd played before the fort. Ilya had grown too fortitudinous to allow herself to play. To play was to bend and sway, and the iron beams in Ilya had made her rigid. Today, her rigidity was a blessing, because while she was pacing instead of playing, she also watched the gardeners. One of them was thin, his face hollowed and pale, but she knew in an instant that it was her father.

She rushed to him, wrapping her arms around his waist as he flinched and pulled away. "Father, it's me. It's Ilya—" she cried out to him.

Had she changed so much that her own father didn't know her now? He didn't look at her. His eyes stayed on the tour beyond the garden fence, and to the soldiers surrounding the tour.

"You'll give us away," he answered in a whisper, his lips barely moving.

Ilya stood rigid, her feet planted in the ground as her father moved away from her, pulling dead leaves from tree limbs as if they'd never met.

"Father . . ." was all she could whisper. She wanted him to pick her up and hold her. Those on the tour hadn't noticed her rushing to him, but he was right. If they had seen—seen evidence that the children never saw their parents—both Ilya and her father might have been made to disappear, like all the others who misbehaved.

Ilya felt her lip quivering, but she held back her tears. She wanted to show her father the strength she'd discovered in the year they'd been apart.

"Are you eating?" he whispered as he went about his business, tending to the plants. Ilya followed behind; only occasionally did he have to hold his arm out to keep her at a distance.

"We have food, more when the tours come. Where is Izaak?" she asked, trying to be heard over the laughing children.

"Gone. On to another encampment in the east. Mother is there too. I saw her leave."

"Perhaps they're together," Ilya whispered.

"Ilya, you must stay useful here. Be good. Quiet. Strong. Don't give them a reason to send you away. It is bad here, but it is better."

"Better than the east?"

He didn't have to answer.

"You too, Father. Be strong and useful. And we will be together." He didn't answer. "Father, please look at me," Ilya pleaded.

Her father stopped his tending and looked over her, beyond her. She turned too and saw that the older girls had called the children to them to line up. To leave.

"Go now," he whispered.

Ilya turned back to her father. She wanted to tell him that she would see him in the garden tomorrow, to reassure them both, but somehow, she knew it wasn't true. The older girls called her name as the last of the younger children joined them. She turned back to the children, anguished, and saw—just beyond the older girls and their ornate wreaths of braided hair—was the impossible path. The path that only she could see. Far off at the edge of the fort's enclosed walls. It looked inviting as ever. A breeze cut through the leaves on the tree-lined path, and Ilya saw it billow the hems of the older girls' dresses, although they didn't seem to notice. She felt the cool air brush against her neck in the sweltering heat of the garden.

It was calling her. Calling her to disappear amidst the trees. To be carried away by its gentle wind and the comforting rustle of its leaves.

But she turned away.

She saw her father and the other gardeners being ordered by soldiers out of the garden through a back gate as the tour began to move on. He was leaving, as were the children. Ilya ignored the older girls. She ignored the path. She ran toward the back gate. Toward her father. She reached for him as soldiers closed the gate. She called out for him, hoping he would look at her one more time, but he didn't turn back. He kept walking with the other men dressed just like him.

A soldier snatched Ilya up by the arm and she learned with a snap that her bones were not so strong that they couldn't still be broken.

The soldier carried her away like a doll. Away from her father. Away from the children and the garden and the tour. Ilya called to her father, ignoring the blinding pain in her broken arm. "I see Izaak every night. We are on a path out of this darkness. It isn't make-believe, Father. It is memory!"

He never looked back.

Ilya saw the other soldiers usher the tour away from the garden, around a nearby building, and out of sight. She saw the gardeners being marched away. One of them put a hand on the shoulder of a man she thought was her father.

Ilya was dragged away to where they disappeared children to. The other children watched from behind the garden fence with cold, unflinching eyes. They, too, had grown iron in their bones.

There was no certainty in the moment. No final cry. No last time she heard her father say her name. It was simply the last she ever saw of her family.

And the last time she ever saw the path.

Chapter 24

Alistair and Zev backed away as a frantic bearded man and a woman clad in black denim and leather burst through the other door, into the gallery. Alistair thought he heard the man say her name in the chaos after he slammed the door shut behind them. They were both panting and tense.

"What are you doing here?" the bearded guy asked Alistair, out of breath.

"Who are *you*?" Alistair asked back.

"We were looking for her sister. She was supposed to be in the clinic, but—"

"What clinic?"

"What do you mean *what clinic*?"

"What do you *mean* what do I mean? What the hell is going on?" Alistair finally snapped.

"You. Quiet one." The leather-clad woman pointed at Zev. "Where did you come in?"

Zev pointed behind them. "There. Through the library."

The woman crossed the gallery, checking the other entrance.

Zev turned to the bearded man. "What clinic?"

"I just told you—"

"I mean, *where geographically* is the clinic? What city? What state?"

"Carson City. Nevada. The clinic that—"

"That's where *you* came in. We . . . came in through a door in upstate New York." Zev took a step toward Alistair. "This is the place Augernon told Marty about in *The Monarch Papers*."

"*Who?*" the bearded man asked.

It dawned on Alistair. "The Palace of Doors. He said the Silver could be anywhere."

The woman in leather piped up, stepping back into the gallery from the library door. "We should make a break through the library back there."

"I'm not leaving," Alistair said.

"Alistair, listen—" the bearded man said.

"How the hell do you know me?"

The man slumped. "My name's . . . Ben. Kriminger. We're both looking for the same thing. What happened to you when you were a kid, the Six, everything."

"You're the guy who called me," Zev said.

"Hello?!" the leather-clad woman called out to them, impatient.

"You can trust us. You came back the same day she did," Ben said as he nodded toward the woman in leather.

Alistair turned to the woman. "Who are *you?*"

"She's one of the Six," Ben explained.

The woman sighed, still holding the door to the library open. "Yeah. My name's Veronica. I'm one of the Six, and I'm a Gemini and an eight-wing-nine and I'm not much for cuddling. Why aren't we running right now?" Then Veronica's expression went slack. She looked at something over Alistair's shoulder. "What the hell?"

Alistair turned. Behind her, standing at the far end of the golden gallery, Alistair saw Doctor Deborah Bolden, her hands clasped in front of her. A warm, gentle smile on her face.

"Hello, Alis."

Alistair had always thought of Bolden as being completely put together. Dark, tailored clothes that were both simple yet obviously expensive, and pops of bright but tasteful jewelry, one leg crossed over the other, with a pad of paper on her slim knee, and beautiful, expensive shoes. It was that same Bolden standing in front of her, but older, crumpled. Her clothes were drab, her signature blunt-cut hair was now streaked with gray, but it was Alistair's Bolden.

Bolden hurried toward her, and then wrapped Alistair in her arms and held her tight.

Bolden would sometimes hug Alistair at the end of difficult sessions, even though she said it was frowned upon. The first time it happened, she said, "Hey, you need a hug and I happen to have one."

It had been so long since that day, and Alistair's initial instinct was to recoil, but the sight of Bolden, the sound of her warm, encouraging voice, sent Alistair's lip quivering and she finally slumped into Bolden's arms.

"I am so proud of you," Bolden said to Alistair. "The journey you've taken. Who you've become. And now, you're here."

Alistair hadn't expected to react like this, to allow herself to feel so vulnerable, but something about her doctor's tone, their long history, the countless hours they'd spent together when she was a child—it was like seeing a long-lost friend again. Or a family member. It had been a long journey to get here. Bolden saw that. Saw her.

"It's all right," Bolden gently murmured over and over, before finally letting Alistair go, her hands on the younger woman's shoulders.

"Look at you," Bolden said. She turned to the others, her hands still on Alistair's shoulders, comforting her. "We didn't realize we'd have so many guests tonight, but you're all welcome." She looked at Ben and Veronica. "I'm sorry about the confusion in the clinic. Faye is very cautious, and you took a bit of a back door to get here. But you're here, in our refuge. Our *Palace of Doors* as Zev called it." She smiled at Zev. "It's nice to finally meet you, by the way."

"Thanks. Where *exactly* are we?" Zev asked.

"This is the place where we protect memories of a time that no longer exists," Bolden said proudly.

Veronica spoke up from across the room, "How though? Good to see you, by the way, been a while, but how are you doing it? Any of it? There's not enough magic left in the world."

"That's a very good question, Veronica. I hope you don't mind a dry bit of orientation. The truth is, we didn't build this place or the door network. We found them. They're relics of the lost time that have somehow survived largely intact. We don't know how they've survived, but we know they were built by a civilization that once thrived *at the twin poles of the Earth*. Isn't that incredible? They were an evolved, sophisticated, and peaceful people who seemingly vanished overnight. But that's its *own* sprawling tale. To answer your question, Zev, more specifically, or at least geographically, we are, right now, nestled in a mountain range in the Antarctic."

Bolden smiled brightly, looking at each of them and their stunned expressions. "That is one among millions of revelations we've made, and continue to make here. As to how we do everything else, the answer's in front of you. These . . . artifacts . . ." Bolden gestured to the objects under glass. "They still hold the memory of a time unaltered. And there's no greater power than memory. That's a very . . . distilled way of explaining it, but that's part of the reason why Alis is drawn to them, I believe. And why we're looking for them. Why we protect them here. Look at what we've been able to do with the trinkets we've amassed over the years."

"What you've been able to do? You mean hurt, maim, and memory-wipe countless people?" Veronica asked.

"That wasn't us, Veronica."

"It wasn't the Silver chasing us down Santa Monica Boulevard?" Veronica retorted.

"You've found us in a desperate, transitional point in our existence. The Silver wasn't always what you know us to be, and we are trying to restore what made us who we are. It hasn't been easy. We're not perfect, we've made countless mistakes, but we are fighting to be free of the changes that have happened to our world, and free of an influence that has infected our ranks and corrupted our mission for centuries."

Alistair only half listened. Her eyes, and attention, had drifted around the gallery, to the objects on display.

"Is this . . . everything?" Alistair asked, gesturing to the cloches and the artifacts beneath them.

"Oh no, my dear. This is only what you chose to show us."

"*I* chose? When?" Alistair asked.

"When you walked through the first door, when you rang the bell and chose the library, when you picked the door to this gallery. This is what you wanted at every step. Believe me, it's even stranger than you can imagine, but it will all make sense in time. Here, come with me." Bolden urged Alistair toward one of the glass enclosures.

"Do you know what this is?" Bolden asked.

Alistair looked through the glass. Inside was a small stack of notebook paper, wrinkled and covered with a young person's developing handwriting.

"It's a book report," Bolden said, answering her own question.

Alistair couldn't make out the title. It was almost as if it evaded her eyes, the words crawling up the page and behind it, too shy to be read. But the author of the report she could see as clear as morning.

"*Written by Alistair Mead,*" Bolden said.

Alistair felt a rush of light-headedness, like the room was leaning backward and she might go with it.

Click click click.

Alistair scanned the gallery, the others watching her, but she was looking for something else.

"Is he here with us? The fox?" Bolden asked quietly, so only Alistair could hear.

"I think so," Alistair answered.

"It's okay; it's to be expected. You're stronger now, and I'm here with you. You're not alone." Bolden took her hand and continued, but Alistair could barely hear. "*This* is the most concrete proof that we've ever found in our decades of searching: a report that is nearly impossible to read, and not because of the handwriting. Proof that the . . . *briar books* existed. This was it, all we had, and then you simply walked into a house on the Hudson and walked out with . . . Iris. Is that her name?"

"Yes," Alistair answered, her head swimming. "Wait." She snapped out of her trance for a moment. "You didn't know her name?"

"Not until you did," Bolden said with a smile. "Not until you found her. Our hope, with your help, is to—"

"But—no. I thought you . . . I thought the Silver knew everything. That's what you said on the phone. That's why you brought me here."

"I'm sorry, no. You misunderstood. We are all still enslaved by the same lie."

"Wait." Alistair pulled away from Bolden's hand. "You . . . don't know what happened to me?" Alistair asked.

"We know so much. And together we'll fill in all of the—"

"Answer me." Alistair interrupted.

"No, we don't know. But, Alis, we can help each other find the truth. Imagine what we could do, what we could discover, together. Buried out there is the answer to the secret. *That* we *do* know. The answer to how you were lost, where you went, and more importantly, *what you left behind there.*"

Alistair saw subtle movement above her, near the ceiling. The tips of the petal-like walls that joined at the apex of the room were slowly curling back and slipping downward as if the room was wilting. Beyond the gold-gilded petals and unfurling filigree was cold, black stone.

Bolden drew closer to Alistair. "I know what you've endured. I know that you lost something. A part of you. This, now, is not who you are. This isolated young woman. You pretend it's your choice to be alone, but you've been forced into isolation because you feel lost without what you left behind. But you don't have to be alone anymore. And never again."

Click click click.

Alistair was struck by a tidal wave of dizziness. She caught a glimpse of a fox tail darting around a pedestal behind Bolden.

"I . . . didn't misunderstand you, Doctor. You lied. You said you knew what happened to me and the Six," Alistair said, embarrassed by her voice catching in her throat. "And I believed you. I thought . . . ." Alistair had revealed herself, and now it felt like her bare belly had daggers in it.

"No," Bolden said, consoling Alistair. "No. I told you what you needed to hear most, to help you on your path. That was always my job. Even now."

Alistair slumped to the floor, overwhelmed with dizziness, bracing herself against the closest display. She could see both Zev and Ben rush for her, but she held her hand up to stop them.

"Your job? That's what this was? What I was?"

"Alis—"

"Stop calling me that. It's not my name."

"I didn't mean to hurt you."

"You only want me for what I can find for you. This was just another test."

Bolden knelt beside her, cradling Alistair's shaking hands in her own. "This was a *path*. And you walked it. Bravely. There are very old rules in place that we can't break. I couldn't tell you everything. I couldn't just bring you here. You had to come on your own. We had to be sure your eyes were open first, Alistair. So you could see what's possible. We had to show you what you're capable of. We had to see what your mind would seek out here. And look at what you found. The most important artifacts we have. It's incredible, what you can do. And we can help you do more. Unlock your potential. We can help each other. We—"

"Stop saying *we*. I don't care about *them*. I came to see *you*. I trusted *you*!"

The room was silent as Alistair's outburst echoed against the gilded walls.

"I came to see you," Alistair said again. Stupid, burning tears in her eyes.

"And I'm here," Bolden finally answered in her same calm, reassuring tone. "And you *can* trust me."

Alistair lifted her head against crashing waves of nausea and hurt. She could see the others in the distance, watching them, lined up like three pins waiting for someone to pick up a spare. It didn't matter. It hurt too much to care.

"Have you always been lying to me?"

"What?"

"Since the phone calls? Or since my treatment? Did they tell you to be in my life, like Ed? Was that your job? Were you helping me, or were you always testing me?"

"Both," Bolden said, her eyes also brimming with tears.

Alistair nodded. "Thanks for telling me the truth. I'm going home."

Alistair tried to lift herself off the floor, but she was too dizzy. Zev rushed to help her up.

"No, no, no . . ." Bolden spat, desperate, grabbing Alistair's arm.

"Don't touch her," Zev lashed back at the doctor.

Bolden let go. Alistair felt Zev's warm hands on her arms as he helped usher her away from Bolden. His body next to hers. It was cold comfort, but it was comfort.

"Wait, please!" Bolden called out. "Why does it matter why I did it, what they wanted from you? From me? You're here. We're together."

As Zev and Alistair stepped between Ben and Veronica, Alistair turned back to Bolden, Zev's arm still around her, propping her up. "It matters because, even after Ed told me—about everything, about your cult—I don't know why, but I still believed you were the person I always thought you were. Someone who cared about me. Believed in me. What hurts most is how stupid you made me feel."

"Wait!" Bolden cried, pleading. "You can't go back now, not after seeing what you've seen. Could any of you?" She looked to Ben, then Alistair, then Zev. "*All* who seek the truth are welcome here."

"Memory's the opposite of truth," Veronica replied.

Bolden ignored Veronica and moved closer to Alistair.

"Please don't do this. Please. Give me a chance. Alistair, I can keep you safe."

"How safe was my sister?" Veronica asked, looming over Bolden, getting in her face. "She went looking for your magical path and disappeared off the face of the earth. Is she safe too? Huh? Or was she not as valuable to you as—"

Bolden looked genuinely afraid of Veronica, and in that moment Veronica suddenly stopped short. She turned to Alistair, her eyes wide like a terrible thought had just occurred to her. "Run."

"What?" Alistair asked.

"What's wrong?" Ben asked.

"Never mind. Shit. It's too late," Veronica said.

"You— read her mind," Ben whispered.

"Someone's coming. Someone she's scared of," Veronica mumbled back.

"I . . . well, this has gotten out of hand," Bolden said, ignoring Veronica's comment. "This is a wondrous day, and we should all be celebrating it together, not standing apart in mistrust and anger. Please, let's take a moment before things get out of hand."

Veronica glared at Bolden. "So I guess you were the carrot, huh? Now, here comes the stick."

Click. Click. Click.

Alistair heard it again, but this time the sound was different. It wasn't the fox. The walls of the wilting gallery were now *lined* with doors, and they were opening one by one. A dozen people emerged from the shadowy portals. Not just people . . . Alistair. They all looked like Alistair.

"Am I the only one seeing this?" Alistair asked in disbelief.

"No . . ." Ben answered as several of the mirror Alistairs turned to him . . .

And like a page turning, the Mirrors *became* him. His wrinkled jacket, rumpled hair, stunned expression.

"Oh shit," Ben gasped.

The Mirrors stepped into the fading light in the middle of the room, taking a moment to look at each of them, changing into Ben, Zev, and Veronica as they went, then back to Alistair. Whoever they looked at, they became. Alistair stepped back from Bolden, Ben and Veronica now flanking her, and Zev right behind her, holding her up.

"I can't read them," Veronica whispered to Ben.

"I think that might be the point," Ben answered.

One Mirror Alistair stepped away from the rest and approached *actual* Alistair. It was an uncanny replication, but the posture, the mannerisms, weren't Alistair's. They belonged to whoever was behind the magic. There was even a hitch in the Mirror's gait, a slight limp, but still imposing, dangerous. Like a seasoned pack leader surveying prey.

"Hello, Alistair." The Mirror spoke in a sparkling echo of a voice, like a mixture of Alistair's vocal cords and static. "I wish we could've met under less chaotic circumstances, but you're here, and that's what's important."

Alistair didn't answer. Words wouldn't surface from the churn inside her.

"She's just overwhelmed," Bolden panted, joining the Mirror standing in front of Alistair. "She needs time to—"

"That's enough, Deborah," the Mirror answered, their response instantly silencing Bolden.

The room was heavy with a soupy cloud of fear, confusion, and wide-eyed wonder. Every time the main Mirror turned to look at one of them, seeming to relish in their astonished reactions, Alistair's stomach turned in concert. An illusion standing in front of her that was anything but. Smoke and mirrors without the smoke. And the Mirror was talking.

"These are just masks, and they're for our protection. To protect our identities, and our minds," the Mirror said, briefly turning into Veronica, before flipping back to Alistair. "The Silver is *not* what you think we are. Not under my leadership." The Mirror looked up at the ceiling, at the wall-petals slipping down, revealing more of the dark stone behind it. Alistair saw it too. The golden gallery fading before their eyes.

"Is this not what you want anymore? These things? Have you changed your mind?" the Mirror asked Alistair.

"I just want to go home," Alistair answered.

"When I first found this place, it was in shambles. The ones still huddling here at the bottom of the world looked to me because I was driven, like you, by a fire, to find the truth. They knew I wouldn't stop until I had it."

Alistair knew the flanking Mirrors around the room were watching her because they all looked like her. It felt threatening, cruel, and strangely humiliating. Her every reaction flickered around her in an ever-tightening circle as the reflections moved closer and closer. Corralling Alistair, Ben, Zev, and Veronica.

"You were wrong about Doctor Bolden. She *does* care about you, very much. She's tried to protect you, coddle you, if you ask me. She told me you'd be resistant. She said you're 'uniquely independent and very clever.' Is that true? Are you very clever, Alistair?"

"Are you trying to scare me?" Alistair asked her reflection. It was working. Fear and acidic adrenaline were now swirling into the mix of emotions.

"I'm trying to wake you up. This age is ending. I know that doesn't mean a lot to you, but soon we might not have the power at our disposal to find the thing we have to find. We are running out of time. Can you . . . forget all this for a second? Forget the Silver. Forget your doctor. Forget the fox. It's you, me, and the thing we want. Nothing else. Let me wake you up to the reality of our world.

To the possibility of what we could do together. And the fact that you've put your trust in the wrong people."

"What does that mean?" Alistair asked.

"Ask her," the Mirror answered, looking at and becoming Veronica simultaneously.

"Ask her about the spell she cast. Ask her why she did it, all of it, her and her friends."

"Who are you?" Veronica asked the Mirror through gritted teeth.

"You might have been the pretty one . . ." The Mirror touched its face and pulled the magic away like a veil. ". . . but I was the one with the brain." Beneath the illusion was a woman who looked almost identical to Veronica, except her hair was dreadlocked and neatly pulled back from her face. And her left eye was an opaque white orb.

"Marjory . . . " Veronica said. Her voice was not much more than a breath.

"They broke the world. They broke my body, and my mind, and they refuse to tell me why."

"Because we *can't*—" Veronica interrupted.

"Not *you*, but the others . . . if you hadn't hidden them."

"What they *remember* would be hidden from you too."

"Maybe at first."

"Would you really destroy them and their minds, their memories, just to get what you wanted?"

Marjory smiled, her eyes rimmed with tears. "In a heartbeat."

Silence settled over the gallery. The walls began to slip further down, but Marjory waved her hand and they suddenly froze in place. She looked Alistair in her eyes. "If I really wanted, I could wear you down and take control of your mind, and maybe even use your power myself. But I don't want to do this alone. I think you might be the only one who understands how cold this life is, knowing that it was better before. How lonely it is, feeling what no one else feels. Remembering when we were whole and not knowing why we can't be again."

"Marjory?" Bolden piped up from behind, "Maybe we should all take a moment. Maybe even a day or two, just to—"

Marjory stood up straight, her hackles raised.

"She's right." Another voice sprang up from one of the other Mirrors in the gallery. "It's all getting a little too heated in here. We still have time, Marjory—"

Even through the voice disguising filter of the mask, Alistair recognized the gruff, gravelly tone. Ed Cumberland pulled his mask away, taking a glancing look at Alistair before approaching Marjory.

"We don't want to make any mistakes. Not now. We're too close to screw it up like this."

Marjory looked at Ed and he managed to say, "Wait—" before suddenly beginning to spasm and shake, his hands at his throat, his mouth gaping open and closed like a fish who'd just been yanked from the water.

Marjory spoke to Alistair without taking her eyes off of him. "Did Ed ever tell you that he almost drowned when he was seven years old?"

"What are you doing?" Alistair asked, frantic.

"He was with his father at a beach in the Bronx called Orchard Park. Mr. Cumberland wasn't paying attention, and a current carried little Edward out into the bay. His legs got so tired, so fast, and he went under."

Ed fell to his knees. He was clawing at his neck, his eyes rolling back into his head.

"Stop it!" Alistair screamed.

"You see how powerful memory can be?"

Marjory released him from her mental grip, and Ed took a deep, ragged breath, falling onto his back, panting, tears dribbling onto the floor.

Alistair wanted to go to him, but Veronica grabbed her arm, whispering under the din of Ed's labored breathing while Marjory was half turned away. "She's trying to break you. Hold on . . ."

Alistair realized she already knew that. She could feel it. Beyond the crashing sea of emotions that she was drowning in, she felt a unique sensation, gentle, like something tickling the edges of her mind. Like fingers searching for a clasp to unlock. She had to keep pushing back, bearing down, just to keep the fingers from finding purchase, and a way in.

Marjory looked down at Ed like he was nothing more than a broken toy.

"They're weak, Alistair. They don't have the drive we do. The guts. The ability to cut everyone away to get to the quick. To the truth. You don't have to be hurt by their lies and deceit. They're just props, helping to play out a pantomime, believing all of this somehow matters. But none of this stupid, human mess means anything when you know it's all a lie. His life itself is a lie."

Alistair looked to Ed, crumpled on the floor like garbage, a scared little boy looking for his father. He and Bolden had both tried to step in to protect her from Marjory. As angry as Alistair was at them, it made her feel . . . no. She had to toughen up. She had to fight back. Bear down. Marjory wanted her weak. She had to focus on the anger brewing in her, the fight.

"All this power and this is what you do with it? With magic? Torture people?" Alistair asked. "You're just like the books said you were," trying to hide the quiver in her voice.

"You're still hanging on to that fiction. You want Mommy and Daddy and the boy at your back. You don't know anything, but you will," Marjory said, still watching Ed take ragged gulps of air on the floor, Bolden now kneeling beside him.

Alistair retaliated, pushing back. "I . . . know about the guilds, and Anne of Brittany, and *The Little Red House* and the Storm. I know about Neithernor and the Silver getting their asses kicked out of it."

Marjory turned and took two broad, limping steps toward Alistair.

"You think Neithernor is the secret? You think we're fighting for *Neithernor?!*" Marjory screamed the words, before regaining her composure. "That place is a sandcastle on a shore waiting to be washed away. A distraction. A graven image of something great, of something hidden on the other side of the lie. You think you know everything because you read those books? Because of the Mountaineers? What the Mountaineers *know* couldn't fill a thimble."

"So, which is it, then?" Alistair asked, "You know everything, or you know shit? Get your story straight." Alistair took her own two steps forward, mirroring Marjory now, refusing to back down. "You didn't bring me here to open my eyes and show me the 'truth behind the fiction.' You can't, because you need *me* to find it *for* you. Simple as that. You need what I can do. What I can get for you before your new age begins because, without me, you've got nothing but one good eye and a ticking clock."

Bolden reached out a protesting hand from where she sat with Ed. "Alis, don't."

Alistair turned to Bolden, snapping, "Call me that one more goddamned time and we're gonna have a problem."

Bolden fell silent.

Alistair faced Marjory again. "Was this really your plan B? You thought you'd get in my head, get me all worked up and weeping over my old boss and book reports?" The fire Alistair felt was spreading. "Everybody's trying to tell me who I am, what I can do, this . . . stuff . . ." She gestured to the objects in the gallery. ". . . has nothing to do with me. You don't know me at all, lady. These things aren't mine. They're garbage."

With the echo of Alistair's last words, the gold-petal walls collapsed like heavy curtains, revealing the empty black stone vault behind them. The gallery Alistair had wished for was vanishing, the pedestals behind the circling members of the Silver were fading away before her eyes.

"See?" Marjory said with glee. "You're fighting me, but you know it's true. None of this matters. You and I are on the same side, but the tragedy is that you don't realize it. You don't know yourself. Hell, you don't even know what the fox really is."

"Marjory!" Bolden yelled out. "Don't. Please."

"What?" Alistair asked. "What is she talking about?"

And just like that, Alistair felt the fingers suddenly find the edges of her mind and begin to painfully pry it open.

Marjory's voice echoed from somewhere inside.

I felt the pain when you saw the little red house.

Alistair raised her hands instinctively to her temples, trying to block out the sound.

It wasn't drawn from memory . . . Somewhere, somehow, you know the secret. But you've blocked it out. Why?

"Stop! Stop!" Alistair screamed. She could hear Zev yelling, saw him stepping in front of her, but she couldn't make out his words of protest. It was as if she were underwater, and the sounds above the surface were muffled and fading as she sank deeper and deeper into the dark.

You're afraid to really seek the truth, because of what you'll learn if you do.

A trench had opened in the depths of Alistair's mind, where Marjory was waiting like a leviathan.

Let me show you.

Things were happening around her body, in the gallery. Yelling, people scrambling—but her external senses had turned inward. She was sinking into the darkness. It wasn't a trench. It was the hole in her she'd always feared. The place she had avoided going at all costs. It had always been a metaphor, the darkness, the part of her that had been cut out. A way for Alistair to make sense of the pain. But Marjory was making it real.

She couldn't feel anything except the riptide current of this woman's will dragging her down. Marjory was right. None of the human connections she'd ever experienced mattered. No one could save her, even if they wanted to.

She was completely alone.

The dark consumed her. Nothing in the black but glimpses of a snow flurry, sickly white hands, and a fox tail, all caught in the current with her.

And deeper in the dark, Marjory, with burning eyes, drawing her down.

Then something in the dark took hold of Alistair's body in a grip she couldn't escape.

Chapter 25

"D id Ed ever tell you that he almost drowned when he was seven years old?"

"What are you doing?" Alistair asked, frantically.

Ben couldn't fully comprehend what was happening. His brain had gone haywire.

Marjory ignored Alistair, watching Ed writhe against an invisible tide. "He was with his father at a beach in the Bronx called Orchard Park. Mr. Cumberland wasn't paying attention, and a current carried little Edward out into the bay. His legs got so tired, so fast, and he went under."

During Alistair and Bolden's half-shouting, half-whispering confrontation a few moments prior, Ben's brain had started bouncing from one thought to the next. He imagined Zev would be taller, Alistair would be shorter, what was the palace of doors, and how the hell were they in Antarctica? It was an old defense mechanism borne from his childhood— probably in the face of his father's rage—that in the midst of conflict, Ben's brain would withdraw, resorting to odd questions, random observations, and inappropriate jokes.

So when a bunch of people wearing other people's faces showed up, and Marjory Morrow revealed herself to be the leader of the Silver and started magically choking out Ed Cumberland in front of them, Ben's brain was ready to fully activate the ejector seat.

"Stop it!" Alistair screamed.

Ben began wondering who the people that Zev mentioned earlier were. Marty and Augernon? Zev said that he and Alistair came in from New York, and Ben and Veronica had come from Nevada, but now they were, apparently, in Antarctica and no one seemed to be at all impressed or surprised by that. Marjory was watching Ed gasp for air now, wriggling on the floor.

Ben saw Veronica reach for Alistair, whisper something, then step back to stand beside him again.

They were all trapped in the center of the golden room, nudged in by the Mirrors. Everyone else was watching Alistair. All the mirrored faces became her as she and Marjory faced off.

Focus. Pay attention, Ben thought. This wasn't a drunken argument that ends when the drunk passes out. Something bad was happening, escalating, and Ben knew he would need to be prepared, ready, for anything.

Ben . . .

A bolt of lightning shot through his brain. Ben flinched in shock, hearing Veronica say his name, although her lips weren't moving.

It's me. Sorry, this is going to hurt both of us.

It was Veronica's voice. She wasn't just listening to his thoughts; she was inside his head. It felt like he was being tasered.

We're in trouble. Can you hear me?
Ben nodded, still staring at her, trying to keep his composure.
You can think and I'll hear you. And stop staring at me.

Ben looked away. *Can you . . . hear me?* he asked, the pain doubling. He winced, his hands already shaking from the pain.

Yes. I can't hear them through their masks though. It's all our own thoughts reflected back on me. But I can still hear Bolden. Faintly. Look around the room. The doors . . .

Ben did.

There are more of the Silver behind them. A lot more.

Okay, Ben thought back, his heartbeat throbbing behind his eyes. *Is that bad?*

Yes. Bolden's afraid.

Of who? Of what?

Of Marjory's plan. To get Alistair here. And wear her down.

Marjory was still staring down at Ed, talking to Alistair.

Is he dead? What's happening? I can't hear anything but you!

There was a thump in Ben's head like the brain equivalent of his ears adjusting to pressure in a plane and the pain receded to the periphery of his mind.

Marjory watched Ed's heaving body. "They're just props, helping to play out a pantomime, believing all of this somehow matters. But none of this stupid, human mess means anything when you know it's all a lie. His life itself is a lie."

Ben wanted the silence back.

No. No.
Push it back. Push it away. No time to be thinking about this. Don't go there right now. Not now. Not ever.

Not now.

Ben couldn't stop it—

Frank.

Frank had said the same thing. *What if life itself is a lie?* that night in Ben and Cor's apartment. It was that question that had set the darkest corners of his mind ablaze. The question that gave Ben the idea, the black and blood-red idea that—

Ben. Ben! Not now. I need you to focus.

It was Veronica in his head again.
Marjory knows.

Knows . . . what? About Frank?

About the spell. The memento. "Find the thing we have to find." That's what she said. New York. The broken bridge. What we did.

Ben could hear Veronica's mind ratcheting back and forth, thoughts in chaos like his. Things he didn't understand. She was scared and Ben could feel it like mercury slipping into his veins. *Veronica? You're freaking out. You can't freak out.*

We have to get out before Marjory gets hold of Alistair. I'm gonna . . . give you a signal . . . and you need to grab the coin in your pocket, then grab your friends. Like . . . skin on skin . . . grab.

The coin?

The coin she gave him when she blew up the walking stick. He still had it.

Did you hear me? The coin. Skin on skin . . .
Her voice was loud, every word a dagger in his brain.

I got it.

Veronica's voice echoed in his mind, words he didn't understand, quickfire turns of phrase that sounded half like English, half like an ice pick probing his soul. His body was vibrating. She was doing something, dialing up some kind of force, and she'd forgotten to disconnect the previous call.

It felt like the echo was tearing him in half.

Ben watched Marjory step closer to Alistair, and Alistair stepped closer to Marjory. He heard "little red house" and "Mountaineers" and "ticking clock." Alistair and Marjory stared into each other's eyes, pointing fingers, but Ben's vision was blurred, his brain flooded with Veronica's reverberating words.

What if life itself is a lie?

That night. Frank. The blood on the walls. The couch. The floor. The locked bathroom door. Not knowing whether Cor was dead or alive. Frank had asked the question, and for a brief moment, Ben took solace in it. He wanted to believe it. Because if life was a lie, the woman he loved wasn't dying on the bathroom floor ten feet away.

Or his mother. When she locked him in his bedroom while his father raged at her outside the door. He was nine or ten. He was sure the door would come down. He was sure she would die.

Veronica's voice raged inside Ben, chanting sounds that almost resembled words, and all his darkest thoughts were bubbling up to the surface. Like he needed her to know. He wanted to scream. He thought if he could open his mouth, her cursed words would pour out of him, and then he could catch his breath. But he couldn't. He would give her away and the Silver would know, and every stupid quest that sent them here would be over. Through searing, vibrating eyes, Ben could see that all the masked Silver that were watching Alistair were now flickering back and forth between Alistair and him and Veronica. No.

Alistair was on her knees, and Zev was rushing forward.

One by one, the other Mirrors focused on Ben. They were catching on. They were going to figure them out. He squinted and took a deep breath, trying to act normal, trying to drown out Veronica's voice, now a hurricane of staccato syllables, until he realized she was repeating one word over and over.

Ben!

Screaming his name. Howling it. Why? What did she want? He was about to black out when he remembered—

The coin. Skin on skin.

She was waiting for him to grab Zev and Alistair. Shit.

Ben plunged his left hand into his pocket and fumbled to pull the coin out, getting it into his palm. He lunged for Zev and Alistair, stumbled, almost hit the floor, and saw the Mirrors fill in between the cases, blocking all exits.

He got to his feet and grabbed Alistair's arm. She was cowering on her knees, hands at the sides of her head. Zev had stepped between Alistair and Marjory. Ben reached for him . . .

And grabbed Zev by the back of the neck like a puppy, the coin planted between his palm and Zev's pinched skin.

He tried to speak to Veronica in his mind. He couldn't.

He screamed. Out loud.

"NOW!"

Veronica charged at her sister, shoved her with the palms of her hands, then toppled a half-vanished glass cloche, grabbing the sheets of paper under it. She yelled a single word that sounded something like "rolomain," and the room suddenly went white and hot and metal and blood.

The papers in her hand exploded into bands of light.

Her voice left Ben's mind, but he could hear the echoes ratcheting out to Marjory and the Mirrors—and Veronica, who was unprotected by the coin. For a moment, he could *hear* magic.

Everyone but Zev, Alistair, and Ben hit the floor, unconscious, as the marble tiles below them began to melt into thick, viscous sludge, engulfing Veronica, her sister, and the members of the Silver in gold-veined quicksand.

Ben's mind was blank. What happens now? Alistair had hit the floor and Zev was picking her up. They were in the eye of the storm, unaware of what had just happened, and Veronica was being pulled under by the liquid floor.

What if life itself is a lie?

Shut up, Ben thought as he stumbled to Veronica. "Find . . . a door!" he yelled to Zev and Alistair, his head still throbbing.

The floor sucked at Veronica's unconscious body. Ben grabbed her by the arms, planted a foot against a pedestal, and pulled hard, getting her free of the sludge. He saw Marjory stirring nearby even as the lower half of her body disappeared into the marbled morass. He tried to drag Veronica away, but the floor started to take hold again. Ben picked her up in his arms—

"Hey!" Zev called from farther down the room. He and Alistair were waiting for him at an open door. He moved as quickly as he could, but he wasn't really much of a "carrying another human" type.

Alistair seemed weak, disoriented. Almost drugged. What had Marjory done to her? She took Zev's hand as they passed through the door. *Sweet*, Ben thought, with a pang of . . . something. Envy? Jealousy? Which was the one where you didn't want to lose the thing you thought you had?

Zev was on the other side of the door. His mouth was moving, calling Ben, but no sound was coming out. He was gesturing wildly and pointing behind Ben. Ben turned, Veronica limp in his arms.

Marjory was awake and clawing her way out of the liquid floor, moving toward him.

Bring her back to me.

He took two steps forward without even realizing.

Put her down.

He felt his arms go weak and Veronica began to slide out of them, down toward the floor. Marjory had slipped in amidst the riot of his mind. It hurt, but not like when Veronica was in his mind. This was pain *and* pleasure. A bite followed by a fluttering tickle. Ben wanted to go to her. He wanted to give Veronica to her. Handing her over was the only way to scratch the itch in his mind.

But how? How could she be controlling him if he was protected by—

The coin. In the frantic lunge to save Veronica, Ben had dropped it and hadn't even noticed. She had him.

Closer.

He leaned forward to take another step, and he felt another force yank him back. It was Alistair and Zev pulling him through the doorway. Veronica fell to the floor back in the gallery, the marble licking at her legs, but the moment Ben passed through the threshold, his mind was his own again.

Through the doorway he saw Marjory crawling towards him, one eye cloud white, the other now black glass. The pedestals in the room beyond her vanished one by one as the gallery disappeared, the molten marble now black stone. Marjory was free and she was almost at her sister's ankles. Ben lurched forward, reached in, grabbed Veronica under the arms, and using the doorway as a fulcrum, hefted her through. Then Ben saw it, a few feet away from him, on the floor. The coin. Without thinking, Ben reached in, and for a moment, Marjory was inside his head again—

Poor Frank.

Ben shuddered, terrified, but he managed to grab the coin just as Marjory swiped at him, her fingers momentarily transformed into talons. She narrowly missed him as Zev yanked him back and Alistair slammed the door behind them, barely staying upright as she did.

Ben tried to yell for Alistair and Zev to bar the door, but he couldn't hear his own voice. He cleared his throat, but again, no sound escaped. His first panicked thought was that Marjory must have done something to him, rendered him deaf or mute. He couldn't even hear his own struggled breathing. Then a second flood of panic washed over him as he realized his own thoughts were somehow muffled. Everything had gone quiet and the silence felt like it might suffocate him.

Zev rushed over to him, motioning to his own ears, covering them, then giving Ben a thumbs-up. They couldn't hear either and apparently that was okay? Ben nodded, trying to compose himself, then got to his knees, trying to lift Veronica again. Zev grabbed her legs and nodded for Ben to get her shoulders. They'd carry her together.

They stood with Veronica hanging limply between then and Ben finally saw that they'd escaped into a sprawling, towering, impossible library. He'd still been harboring flecks of rationality that the magical "Palace" was still somehow, at least partially, somewhere beneath or behind the clinic in Nevada, but the library blew those last few flecks away.

The ceiling of the library was ensconced in shadow above them.

It was so tall that light, or at least his mortal eyesight, couldn't reach its pinnacle. There seemed to be more books in the library than were ever actually published, and all around the immense vault, hidden in nooks, half-obscured by bookcases, and etched into walls, were doors.

They moved quickly through the library with Veronica between them and Alistair stumble-leading, knocking over book stacks and shoving away tables that were in their way. She did not seem okay. What had Marjory done to her? Ben vacillated between concern for this poor young woman, fear for all of them, and fanboying over the fact that not-fictional Alistair Mead was less than ten feet away from him.

As they approached a stairway leading down to the library's moon-dappled main floor, Ben saw motion up on a higher balcony. A dozen or more Mirrors funneled silently out of an unseen door. Their masks flickered between Ben and the others, even Veronica's sleeping face. The Mirrors rushed for the stairs. With Veronica in their arms, the group wasn't going to make it out before being closed in and trapped. Ben looked around, desperate for an alternate route, as Marjory emerged from the doorway they'd just escaped through. She shouted into the silent void, and prismatic energy spit out of the ends of her fingers, nearly hitting Zev, but instead slamming soundlessly into a bookcase behind Ben. The tall case leaned over slowly, then back, teetering one way, then the other. Books tumbled from its shelves. Ben and Zev made eye contact, and in that split-second, they knew they were having the same muted idea. They rushed the bookcase, Veronica still in their arms. Ben slammed his shoulder against it, and Zev did the same, just as the bookcase leaned away from them. It began to tilt forward, threatening to crush the three of them. Alistair rushed to it, throwing her weight into their effort. The bookcase was frozen at an angle for a moment . . .

Then it fully toppled away from them. The towering bookcase fell, slamming into the next, then the next, then the next. There was no sound but the vibration of the cases falling felt like tremors in the earth. Cartoon dominos. Dozens of bookcases toppled onto each other, creating a barricade at the large stairway leading down to them, blocking the Mirrors from the main floor of the library. Ben looked back. He couldn't find Marjory in the stacks where she'd just been standing.

His legs burned as they carried Veronica down the stairs to the main floor, then to an open doorway where Alistair was waiting for them. They stumbled to her, Ben checking over his shoulder as the Mirrors began to arduously climb over the toppled cases. The group ducked through the doorway, into a dark, narrow hall cut into bedrock, Alistair first, then Ben and Zev, with Veronica between them. They shuffled through the tight hallway as it slowly grew wider and then ended at what looked like some kind of parlor. As Ben stepped into the room, the silence broke, and the sound of his breath exploded in his ears. God, he was out of shape.

Alistair slammed the door behind them, its edges fading into the wallpaper pattern until it seemed like it was completely gone.

"Are you okay?" Ben asked.

"Hurry," was all she said as she guided him across the room to an immense set of stairs. Alistair took one of Veronica's shoulders, and Zev adjusted, taking more of Veronica's weight. The three of them hauled her up the stairs, stopping every once in a while to catch their breath, aware that the Mirrors, or Marjory, could arrive at any minute. After a few minutes, they heard them. Footsteps at the bottom of the stairs.

Alistair spat through ragged breath, "When we get to the top, get her through the door. I'll get the car and ram the door down. I'll demolish it."

"It won't . . . stop them. I saw them change . . . an entire building," Ben huffed.

Zev piped up from three steps down, "We just need a few minutes. Take side roads, get on the highway. The door's in the middle of nowhere. They'll have no idea where we're going . . ."

They were nearing the top.

Ben and Alistair both hit the closed door at the same time. Alistair reached for the doorknob with one hand. Tried it—

"It's locked."

The footsteps below them were getting closer, louder.

"Break it down," Zev panted. Ben took Veronica into his weakening arms as Zev shifted past him and he and Alistair slammed their shoulders into the locked door.

Two, three more times. The Silver were close, twenty, maybe thirty steps away——

"Hurry up, they're coming!" he shouted.

The sound of wood splintering startled Ben as the doorjamb behind him gave way under Alistair and Zev's combined efforts.

The stairs abruptly tilted up and forward under Ben, like the four of them were being flipped upside down, dumping them out . . .

Of a door, down a set of stone steps, and onto a freezing snow-swept sidewalk.

Alistair clambered to her feet and rushed back up the stairs of the old gray townhouse from whose door they had somehow just exited. She slammed the door, then turned back to the others, terror in her eyes.

"This is Ackerly Green. How did . . ."

They were somehow back in New York City.

Nowhere near a car.

Or the countryside.

In the middle of a city with a million doors.

Chapter 26

We never should've left the city.

That was Alistair's last thought before the door at the top of the stairs gave way and dumped them out in the heart of the West Village, at the bottom of Ackerly Green Publishing's old front steps.

Was that how the door worked? Had she done this? Stranded them on an island of doors? Every co-op, every storefront, every alley entrance was a possible portal for the Silver to reemerge. It was true—they weren't the Silver from the books. They were under new ownership, and they were so much worse.

It was almost 3 AM. A first snow was pelting the city, carried by a heavy, razor-sharp wind. Large, papery flakes stung Alistair's eyes and were already piling up along the frozen sidewalks. Ben waved down six taxis before an ancient, bush-bearded cabbie agreed to let three panting, scared, and scratched-up people get into his car with their "drunk friend." Veronica was still unconscious, and they'd put several blocks' distance between them and the stone door. Ben had made a harried phone call to someone who agreed to meet them across town and hide them, no questions asked. According to Ben and what Alistair overheard on his call, they were heading to a restaurant the woman managed, which was closed for renovations. They had no idea if the Silver could follow or track them, but hiding somewhere, even temporarily, seemed to be the only idea that made sense. Hide, and wait for Veronica to wake up and tell them what to do about her sister.

Zev sat up front next to the cabbie, just as detached and quiet as he'd been since they fell through the door. Ben and Alistair flanked Veronica in the back. Ben had his arm around her to keep her upright, her head lolling against his shoulder as the cab sped uptown.

"I don't know what to do," Ben whispered. "I don't know if we should take her to a hospital or just let her sleep it off. She didn't tell me this would happen. She knew what Marjory was doing to you, but then everything else happened so fast. I'm sorry, I didn't have time to explain."

Alistair didn't reply.

Ben continued, "I guess we should get to the restaurant, hide, and then hope she wakes up. If not—"

Alistair watched the white-gold lights of Midtown streak past outside the frosty, fogged-up window. She could still feel the echoes of Marjory in her head, or maybe not echoes, maybe a draft, from a window someone forgot to close. Maybe Marjory was still in there, pulling at thoughts Alistair had never let slither out of the darkness.

A chilling sickness still swirled in her stomach, triggered by the thought of how easily the woman had infiltrated her. Maybe everything the Silver had done to get her there had broken her down and made her mind vulnerable to control. Maybe Marjory knew what Alistair wanted to hear, wanted to know. *The snow. The fox. And now, the little red house.* Whatever it was, Alistair had given in completely. So much for walls.

Alistair had grown up knowing that Aunt Kath and Uncle Gus cared about her even though they'd never wanted kids, but they avoided talking about the time before. They'd trusted Bolden to fix

Alistair. But there had never really been a childhood therapist Alistair could confide in, no fatherly boss she'd really ever come to know. No Deborah Bolden. No Ed Cumberland. It was always just . . . the Silver. Watching her, following her, manipulating her, keeping journals and medical histories, waiting for her to be of use. Alistair wondered what her life might have been like if she'd had real treatment as a child, and that was the thought that finally sent her back to the brink of tears.

Zev. She wanted Zev. She wanted to feel the way she'd felt in his arms, lying on the floor of her room. He hadn't said a word since they fell through the door.

❧

Cor was the name of the woman Ben had called, and she was waiting for them at a side door when they pulled up to the corner of Lexington and 50th Street. She was dressed head to toe in cold-weather running gear. Alistair imagined she was the kind of put-together person who had her workout clothes all laid out and ready for the morning. Cor's eyes went wide when Ben and Zev pulled Veronica out of the back of the cab.

"What happened?!" Cor yelped.

"Let's get inside," Ben answered.

Ben paid the cab driver, then he and Zev carried Veronica past Cor, into the bright fluorescent maintenance hall beyond the doorway.

Alistair stood frozen in the wind and snow as the taxi pulled away. She stared at the bright hall ahead of her. Zev looked back for a moment before he and Ben carried Veronica around a corner and disappeared.

"Are you okay?" Cor asked Alistair, still holding the door open.

What would Alistair gain by going in? She told herself that maybe they'd all be safer without her. Marjory and the Silver only wanted *her*. But her reticence wasn't because of that. If they *could* hide from the Silver—if that was even possible—Alistair could make a new life somewhere, hidden, walled off again, this time forever. The mistakes she'd made were the connections she'd tried to forge. All lies. Marjory had been right. Alistair's solitude would have saved her; it was the connections she'd made that caused all the pain. She wanted to walk away but couldn't, because, at some point, Veronica would wake up, and more than solace in solitude, more than isolation, Alistair wanted answers—real answers—and she wasn't going anywhere without them.

The restaurant was in mid-construction, being renovated to give the vibe of a century-old subway station. Clean white tiles on the walls broke away into glossy emerald variants closer to the ceiling, outlining low arches and high cathedral vaults. It was a work of art in near completion. Ben and Zev nestled Veronica into a long leather corner booth in the back of the restaurant's cavernous, unlit dining area, and covered her with a clean packing blanket they'd pulled off a flat of restaurant supplies.

Alistair saw Ben quietly pull Cor aside, although she wasn't sure *what* he was going to tell her. A few minutes later they were back, and Cor seemingly launched into work mode, taking care of what she could. She brewed a pot of coffee on a hot plate, and then huddled in a corner with her phone, calling off the construction crews which would've arrived in a few hours. Zev, Ben, and Alistair sat on folding chairs in the long kitchen, out of view of the street-facing windows, warm coffee cups in hand, gripping them as if they were bracing together on the edge of a frozen mountain.

"Is she okay?" Alistair asked Ben.

Ben looked up from the contents of his cup, "I think so, she was mumbling when we laid her down in the booth."

"I meant ... Cor."

"Oh, yeah. She can handle anything."

"What did you tell her?" Alistair asked.

"I told her ... I told her I'd tell her everything. Later."

"Girlfriend?"

"Ex."

Alistair nodded and took a gulp of coffee, scalding the roof of her mouth.

She glanced at Zev, who seemed to be a thousand miles away, or at least avoiding eye contact. Whatever connection they'd made seemed frayed, or broken altogether, Alistair couldn't tell, but also couldn't blame him. But she was frayed herself and maybe now wasn't the best time to be assessing the state of her remaining relationships. Zev could just be in shock, and that would be completely understandable.

"Do you know why someone would send me book chapters about you?" Ben asked, blowing on his coffee.

"I have no idea," she answered. "What was in them?"

"Not a lot. You going to the house upstate. Waking up in the hospital. Getting the call from Bolden."

"You drove out to California because of *that?*"

"No. Well, not *just* because of that. I was getting the chapters about you *before* you were doing the things in the chapter. I called the same clinic you did, just to check and see if it was true. I got that chapter days before, but when I called, you'd just hung up. Then my editor got a chapter. About me. About something only I knew. It said I was going to California to find the Six. Our whole life, Cor's and mine, was turned upside down because of someone who believed the same stuff Marjory does. Said the same things she did. I needed to know why."

"Did you get answers?"

"Not even remotely."

"So who's writing a book about us?" Alistair asked.

"I still don't know. The bird said looking for Marjory would lead us to the writer. But, unless it's one of us . . . I feel like we did something wrong, or worse, this isn't over."

"It's definitely not over," Alistair replied. "They wouldn't have gone through all the trouble to lead me to the Palace and tell me everything they did if they had any intention of letting me leave.

Decades of lying, all to get to tonight, and then it all falls apart? Wait, did you say . . . bird? A bird told you to look for Marjory?"

"Yeah," Ben answered, then his brow furrowed as something occurred to him. "Oh shit. I left him in my truck."

A moment, then a laugh burst out of Ben, so unexpected and loud that Zev jumped.

And then Alistair started laughing too.

"We are officially in Wonderland," Ben said. "Nightmare Wonderland and the Queen of Hearts wants your head. Or at least parts of it. Thank God for Veronica."

Alistair corrected him, "If *you* hadn't gone to California to get her, I'd still be down there at the bottom of the world." A sharp shiver ran up Alistair's neck. That's how Marjory had described it.

"Glad I could help. You think the writer meant for us to meet there?" Ben asked.

"I don't know what to think anymore, I'm just . . . I'm . . . glad we did."

Ben held his coffee cup out to her and after a moment's hesitation, Alistair clinked hers against it. Cheers. Ben smiled and nodded. It felt like a small, intimate moment two friends would share, though she barely knew him. It didn't matter. He'd helped save her life. It was worth acknowledging, if nothing else. Alistair nodded back.

She noticed Cor standing at the other end of the kitchen.

"She's awake," Cor said.

They put down their cups and followed into the dim dining area. Veronica was sitting on the edge of the booth where they left her, waiting for them.

"Hi. We're fucked."

Alistair grabbed a chair parked under a nearby table and set it down in front of Veronica. Ben and Zev followed suit. They all sat in a semicircle, except for Cor, who hung back.

"Does this place have a liquor license?" Veronica asked. They all stared in silence until Veronica finally said, "I'm serious. You're all freaked out and I can't handle all the stray thoughts right now. My head is pounding."

"Oh, sorry," Ben said, turning to Cor. "Is the bar still stocked?"

"It's all in boxes but I'll see what I can find," Cor replied, before taking off to the far side of the dining room.

"Can she still control me? Is she still in my head?" Alistair asked.

"I don't know," Veronica answered. "She couldn't back in the day, not from a reasonable distance, but she's got a lot of firepower at her disposal. I have no idea what she's capable of anymore, especially now that she's a cult leader and completely off her nut." She glanced at Ben. "Tell me you still have the coin."

Ben reached into his left pocket and after a moment of fumbling responded, "Yeah."

"It'll protect you and anyone you touch, because I gave it to you. Don't pull it out, don't drop it, don't lose it. It's all you've got to keep you safe from her."

"Marjory said she needed me to 'find the thing we need to find,'" Alistair said. "It seemed like she knew exactly what she was looking for."

Cor brought back a bottle of whiskey and a glass tumbler and set them on the booth table. Veronica unscrewed the cap and guzzled from the bottle.

"Yeah . . . the memento of the spell. It's real, and apparently she knows about it," Veronica said, wincing through the fire of the rye.

"What's the memento?" Ben asked.

"Memories can't be destroyed," Veronica answered, swigging again, then offering the bottle to the rest of them. Only Zev took her up on the offer. "We might forget them, but they don't break. This memento in particular holds all of the old memories."

"How do you know?" Alistair asked.

"Because I made it."

"What do you mean, *you made it*?"

"Not directly. It was created after I did what I did. Marjory wasn't lying. I *did* this. I broke the world. I'm the one who took your memories away, and no, I can't tell you why."

"Yeah. That's not good enough," Alistair snapped back.

Ben interceded. "No, she means she literally *can't*. She tried to tell me, and we almost died. It's part of the spell. If she tries to tell the truth, bad things happen. Head-on-collision-with-eighteen-18-wheelers-and-bolts-of-lightning kind of bad."

"When did this happen?" Cor asked Ben from behind them, concerned.

He turned to her, "I . . . no, I went out to California to find her." He nodded toward Veronica. "And a lot of stuff happened. I'm okay."

"And you're Veronica Morrow?" Cor asked.

Veronica nodded.

"You're his favorite."

Ben turned red. "That's not . . . as a writer, she means. From a writer's viewpoint."

"Why?" Alistair asked Veronica. "Why did you do it?"

Ben jumped in, "Like I said, she can't—"

"I'm asking her," Alistair continued, cutting him off.

"Why? Well, to save the world, obviously. We did it—*I* did it—because the alternative would've been even worse. Worse than you could imagine. I changed the world to save it. And that change rippled forward and backward through history. You have to believe me, I—"

"Where is it? The memento," Alistair asked. "Or can you not tell me that either?"

"Your attitude's a lot, but I like that you're to the point," Veronica answered. "It's here. In New York City."

"How? Why?" Ben asked.

"How do I know or how is it here?"

"Yes," Ben answered.

"I know because I essentially made it and I'm still connected to it. Not enough to find it though, I've tried."

"The Clash. When you lived in New York. You were thinking about it in the gallery," Ben said.

"Right," Veronica confirmed, "I lived here a while back. I tried to find it, to keep it safe. From everyone . . . but especially from Marjory. These things, mementos—"

"There are more of them?"

"Tons, but she's looking for one. Mementos are after-effects of 'big' magic that change things, like time, life, memory. They sometimes have minds of their own. As to why New York . . . it's because New York's special. Geographically, magimystically."

"Magimystically?" Cor asked, eyebrows raised.

"Uh . . . that's a word that means the whole—*magi* and *mysti*, the science and rule-obeying parts of magic and then the . . . wacky, unexplainable parts of magic. The point is, most things end up here. One way or another."

"Then we need to find it first," Alistair said.

"Yeah, we do, and before Marjory finds you. She's more powerful than any of us. She just doesn't remember yet."

"I thought you were going to put up more of a fight," Alistair said.

"Listen, they're weak, the Silver, but their weakness makes them desperate. And with Marjory leading them, she's gonna keep coming for you, with every ounce of power they have left. That woman, that's not my sister anymore. She's unhinged. She *needs* the memento, and she sees you as her last chance at getting it while they still have power. She thinks she'll be made whole, that she'll know what she lost if she has it."

"Is she wrong?" Alistair asked.

"No. But, first, anyone, but especially Marjory learning what we hid, could be *catastrophic*. Second, in the hands of the Silver, or whoever's *watching* the Silver, there's nothing more dangerous than this memento, because those memories are still connected to the people they used to belong to. With enough effort, they could use the memento to sway people, control them outright—not just one at a time, but altogether. En masse. Everyone connected to magic knows a new age is on the horizon. Marjory said so herself. With this memento, the Silver, or whoever's watching them, could influence it, shape it, control it."

"So *we* find it instead," Alistair said resolutely.

"To hide it, once and for all," Veronica answered.

"Once I know. Once I know what happened to me, you can do whatever you want with it."

"It's not that easy," Veronica said.

"*You* remember. Seems pretty easy to me."

"And I wish I didn't."

"Well, I didn't get to make that choice. I'm not like you. I'm not like them," Alistair said, gesturing to Ben and Zev. "I'm stuck somewhere between two worlds and I can't go on not knowing anymore. I won't."

"How would we even find it?" Zev asked, breaking his hours-long silence, bottle in his lap. "What does it look like?"

"No idea," Veronica answered.

"You don't . . . know what it is?" Ben asked.

"No. I've never seen it. Chances are it's an object that already existed. The object *became* the memento after the spell. See, magic is kind of . . . Shit, hand me the bottle." Veronica held her hand out to Zev who forked it over. She took a long swig and continued. "Magic isn't what people think it is. It's not just fireballs and lightning and throwing shit around the room with your mind . . . although I've done my fair share of all of those, and Marjory too. Magic, at its core, is narrative. It follows the rules of story, or rather, story follows the rules of magic. It works best, and most effectively, with setup. Foreshadowing. Theme. Things that make a kind of sense in a storytelling way."

"What does that mean?" Cor asked.

"It means magimystic forces would pick something poetic," Zev said.

Alistair could tell that, while not drunk, Zev's head was

swimming with enough whiskey to loosen him up a little, and discussing literature and its structure was his favorite pastime.

"Something that would . . . make sense. If that makes sense," Veronica continued.

"It does not," Ben answered.

Zev interjected, "So narratively, or 'magimystically,' it's Chekhov's gun. She's saying that there's a good chance it would be something that has already been set up earlier. Every good ending is surprising but inevitable. All the clues were there before, so we'd know because . . . we'd know? Because it's already been established somehow?"

"Right. You get it. I like you," Veronica said, taking another swig and passing the bottle back to Zev.

"Ben said the writer who was sending him pages knew things before they happened," Zev continued. "They sent Ben to get you, and you saved us all down in the Palace, so maybe this is what we're *supposed* to do next. They saw it already. Which means . . ."

"We might already know what it is, or at least have the information to figure it out," Veronica answered.

"And someone with the ability to find it once we do," Alistair said. "Me."

A quiet settled over the room. *Something important. Something that would resonantly hold memories from the time before. Something that would hold memories from the time before—*

Zev and Alistair spoke up at the same time. "The pocket watch."

"The what?" Ben asked.

"Sullivan Green's pocket watch. It was all over *The Monarch Papers*," Alistair said.

"Right!" Zev said. "He lost it, he found it, King Rabbit stole it. The whole time I'm thinking, where is this going?"

"Same! Like, why would they leave this giant loose thread hanging? We never knew why Sullivan left it for Deirdre, why King Rabbit wanted it, why it was promised to him, how *he* lost it..." said Alistair.

"Well, he doesn't have thumbs, so . . ."

"Right."

They both smiled at each other, a glimmer of their connection restored in the haze of magic and whiskey.

"Okay! What?" Ben asked.

"It's from a book. Another book. About all this," Zev said.

"That's not a completely terrible idea, actually," Veronica said. "The pocket watch does have a kind of dramatic irony, which is very 'magic.' We were led to read *The Monarch Papers* so we see the importance of the pocket watch laid out in a way no one else would."

"And it's a dangling thread in need of resolution," Zev said.

Alistair shook her head. "But the Silver read it too. They used to *own* the pocket watch. That's where Sullivan found it. In the Palace. Which . . . shows you what you want to find."

"Which Bolden just told you," Zev said. "Do you think she was trying to help without Marjory realizing?"

"I don't care one way or the other. I never should've trusted her to begin with."

"Yeah," Zev said. "That was on me. I convinced you to go to her. I'm so sorry."

"And *I* decided to go. Come on, you know no one can make me do anything I don't want to do." Alistair smiled at Zev. "Unless, of course, you have the magical power to do so like Veronica's evil twin."

"This is probably the first time I'm not the evil one in that scenario," Veronica said.

Zev thought for a second, then, "There's a good chance the Silver doesn't know what the memento is. They had it in their possession. All the more reason for them to dismiss the idea that it's the key to everything. They can't accept that they had it and lost it. And Marjory said herself that they dismiss *The Monarch Papers* and the Mountaineers altogether. Their collective ego won't let them believe the truth. Hell, even if they do know what it is, they still don't have *you* to find it."

"So how *do* we find it?" Alistair asked.

They all looked at each other until, one by one, their gaze settled on Veronica.

"How do we find it?" Alistair asked again.

"There could be a way. You're drawn to things. I could amplify that. Maybe. But I don't have the power to do it, even if it *was* possible. All that shit they collected down there, and none of you thought to take something on your way out?"

Alistair had never taken her favorite coat off. She reached into the breast pocket and set Iris down on the table beside Veronica.

"Iris, the Ebenguard. Passionate, practical, fiercely loyal. Always willing to fight for what's right. Setup. Foreshadow. Theme."

Veronica eyed the figurine like Iris was a mix of old friend and worst enemy. "Yeah. She could work."

"I'm sorry for interrupting, but what you're saying," Cor looked at Ben. "What *she's* saying is that it's all true. Everything those people thought about your book. What you wrote. You're saying Frank was right—"

"Uh, yeah. Basically," Ben answered.

Cor nodded, "Jesus." She circled around to Veronica and pointed at the bottle. "You mind?"

Veronica handed it over and Cor took a sip, cringing like she'd just had the very first whiskey of her life.

"What about it?" Veronica asked Alistair, taking back the bottle Cor was holding at arm's length.

"What about what? I didn't say anything," Alistair answered.

"The little red house. Sorry, you can't stop thinking about it."

"Well . . . I remember it. Not the book. Not *just* the book. There's the story, and then there's my memory, and I feel like I was confusing it all, trying to make it make sense. It's all in there, in the dark. It's what Marjory wanted to show me."

Alistair could feel familiar tingles at the edges of her mind. It was Veronica. She seemed less invasive, more curious, but Alistair was too raw to let her in. "Don't."

"Sorry," Veronica said, hands up in apology. "That's not supposed to be possible, you remembering. I don't know what you lost, but I can see pieces of old memory in you, in the dark, like shards of glass."

"I don't remember though. Not fully. But . . . you know where I was when I went missing. Don't you?" Alistair asked.

Veronica looked at her awhile. "Maybe," she said before picking up the bottle and taking a swig. "Any other questions?"

"None you can—"

Veronica took another swig.

"Do— you know why the little red house looked so familiar to me?"

Veronica took a swig. *Yes.*

"Is the little red house real? Not just the book. But, the place *in* the book."

Veronica took a swig. *Yes.*

Alistair was struggling, asking questions she was slowing realizing she already knew the answers to. Answers she knew but had been unwilling to accept.

"The place in the books is real, isn't it? That's where I went. Where *you* went. A place beyond the fray."

It was all bubbling to the surface and Alistair couldn't stop it.

"It's where . . . it's where magic really comes from. Came from. It's why the world feels so— empty now, because . . . you made us forget it. Not magic. The place. The name. That's the thing that's missing, isn't it? And then everything else went with it."

Tears ran down both Alistair's and Veronica's cheeks. Veronica took a long swig on the bottle. *Yes.*

Yes, to all of it.

"It had briar in its name. *The briar books.* Briar something."

"Alistair," Veronica heeded.

"It's right there. On the tip of my tongue."

"Leave it there."

"It's always been there. Why? Why do *I* remember?"

"I don't know," Veronica answered.

"It's in the name of the book. The title was longer. *The Little Red House in Briar—*"

The bottle of rye shattered in Veronica's hand. The wall of stacked glasses at the bar detonated a second later.

Then the front windows of the restaurant exploded in on them. Frigid wind and snow blasted into the dining room as everyone scurried away from the damage.

They just stood and stared at the shiny glass fragments everywhere. No one knew what to do. A couple of pedestrians passed by the windows, barely giving a second glance at the wreckage. It was New York City after all.

"Magic?" Cor asked.

"Magic." Ben nodded.

"I'm sorry," Alistair said, to everyone really, but she was looking at Cor.

"They're insured," Cor said, fear in her eyes.

"Marjory *will* come for you," Veronica said to Alistair, "and I know what she's capable of doing to get what she wants. You caught a little of it yourself. She'll take control of you, override you. Basically become you. This doesn't have to be your fight. I could use Iris to hide you. Like I hid my friends. You wouldn't know the truth, but you'd be safe."

Alistair shook her head. "I'm not hiding again." She turned to address them all. "None of you would be here if it wasn't for me. If you don't want to go further, I get it. But I've never known a moment when my life was my own. And that ends tonight."

Zev put his hand on Alistair's arm for a brief, but comforting moment. "I'm not going anywhere."

"Yeah. Same," Ben echoed.

Veronica shook her head, licking rye from her thumb. "Fine. Let's do some magic."

Chapter 27

Alistair had been sequestered with Veronica in a storage room in the restaurant's basement for the past hour. Cor was upstairs leaving a new set of messages for workers, this time to board up the smashed windows as soon as the sun came up, and Ben and Zev were waiting in the cold, cracked-concrete basement hallway, waiting for Veronica and Alistair to emerge.

Ben had been trying to think of something to say to Zev but had been struck awkwardly silent. He just stood there, endlessly fondling the magic coin in his pocket. He'd been completely useless upstairs. The others were all working out the secrets of the universe and Ben just sat in the midst of them, probably looking like he was watching an energetic tennis match. Apparently, there was *another* book series, and everyone had done the required reading but him. King Rabbit and magic watches and more characters he'd never heard of. An expanded universe that the fandom hadn't told this casual about. Before Veronica woke up, he'd momentarily let himself bask in the idea that yes, maybe he had been the lever that had set all of these gears in motion, that it had really all been about Alistair and Ben, the two people that had started this.

Turns out, that wasn't the case.

"What exactly did Veronica say she was doing?" Zev asked.

Saved from silence by the far cleverer and less socially inept.

"Something about elemental forces and calling them, or grounding them. I'm not sure. She said a lot of stuff."

"I think I might be a little buzzed so some of it went over my head."

"Yeah, I didn't drink. Not for lack of wanting, but then the bottle exploded—"

"You think she's okay in there?" Zev asked.

"You mean Alistair? With the spell?"

"I mean Alistair, with Veronica."

"Oh, she's nothing like her sister. She's . . . cool."

"Right. But, if she's to be believed, she also changed all of time and history and everyone's memory without anybody knowing and won't tell us why."

"She *can't*, but I'm sure it was—"

"For a good reason? Must have been a *really* good reason."

Ben felt himself bristling at Zev's insinuation but knew it was because the guy was worried about Alistair. He couldn't fault him for that.

"I don't know, but she's a good person. She was trying to save her sister. She's trying to help Alistair now."

"Right. Except in both instances, she's trying to help fix a problem she created."

They both fell silent again, waiting.

Ben regularly stressed about saying the wrong thing, but after the "Palace," as everyone was calling it, then the roundtable upstairs, he felt even more jumbled and out of it. That momentary bite of Marjory in his head had left him feeling cracked. He couldn't imagine how Alistair felt.

What if life itself is a lie?

The thought slipped through the crack and sent cold fingers

tickling Ben's body as Veronica finally opened the storage room door.

"Okay," she said, "We doing this?"

Ben and Zev both moved toward the doorway as Veronica held up a hand. "I can't have the whole gang up in here, it'll be too distracting. We have one shot with Iris. I only need one of you."

Ben and Zev looked at each other. Ben felt a momentary urge to step in before Zev could, but he suspected Alistair would probably want Zev, not him.

"You should probably go," Ben finally said to Zev.

Zev nodded and ducked past Veronica, into the storage room.

Ben could see Alistair look up at Zev from the chair she was sitting in. She seemed— ready. Resolute. They briefly made eye contact, before Veronica leaned into Ben's view. "You holding up?"

"Um. Yeah? Are you okay doing this?" Ben asked.

Veronica lowered her voice, "Doing it is nothing. It's the memento that's dangerous. If we find it . . . depending on how it all plays out, I might need your help."

"Yeah, of course. With that?"

Veronica didn't answer. She took a quick glance over her shoulder at Alistair, who was talking to Zev. Ben could tell she was worried about Alistair. Worried what she might do with the memento.

"Right," Ben said.

"But first thing's first," Veronica said as she began to close the door, then stopped. "Hey."

"Yeah?"

"You're a good guy, Kriminger."

The comment caught him off guard and sent his heart into his throat. "What? Why do you say that?"

"Cause none of this has anything to do with you anymore, but you're still here."

He wasn't sure what she meant by it, but it stung. "That sounds more like a nuisance."

"You're not a nuisance. See you on the other side," she said as she shut the door between them.

Ben sighed, turned, and found Cor waiting behind him.

"Veronica Morrow, huh?" she said with a sly smile.

"Stop. It's too weird," Ben said.

"What is?"

"My ex-girlfriend is making jokes to me about—"

"About what? About a girl you like?"

"It's more serious than that. I mean—we've been through some *serious shit* together the past couple of days. That's what I mean by serious." Ben leaned against the concrete wall next to Cor with a sigh.

"I think she likes you."

"I think that's not correct," Ben replied.

A few seconds passed.

"Why though? Why do you think that?" Ben asked.

"Because she's someone who obviously knows what she wants, and she's making it pretty clear, even in the midst of all this 'serious shit', how good a guy she thinks you are."

"Hmmm," Ben nodded, "This is not getting less weird."

"It doesn't have to be weird."

"It *should* be though. I don't deserve this. I don't deserve your—kindness. From anybody really, but especially you. I've put you through—"

"Jesus. Ben. Enough." She pulled away from the wall, facing him directly, her hands on her hips like she said her dad used to stand. "I need to be honest with you."

No. Please no.

"Okay."

"I think you're still stuck back then with all the awful shit that happened. But I'm not. I mean, it's always there, but I'm doing better than I have in a long time."

"That's good."

"That's not the point."

"Oh," Ben said. He could feel his shoulders tensing, preparing for the *actual* point.

"I think I resented you for not telling me everything you have locked up in there," Cor said nodding toward Ben's head, "Because I wanted to help *you* let go of the burden. The weight of your past, that night, all those things you keep to yourself, but that's just not my place anymore. I mean this in the nicest way possible . . . I can't fix you. After I came to see you at the cabin, after you came back to the city for your birthday, it all kind of hit me, and it helped me really let you go. We're not responsible for each other anymore. We don't owe each other anything *but* kindness."

Ben nodded through the pain, "It feels like we're breaking up all over again."

"Yeah, kind of. And also . . . kind of for real this time."

"Right. I just—" He wanted to tell her that he loved the way she saw him. Good, brave, kind. Seeing himself through her eyes made him think he was better than he was. Made him feel like he deserved her.

He cleared his throat and finally continued, "All this horrible stuff is behind a door I can't seem to open. Or maybe I don't want to open. I know it was hard being on the outside, but I'm locked in here with all of it, and that's hard too. I'm just sorry I hurt you, and — I'm allowed to be sorry."

"You're right." Cor took his hand, squeezed it, then let go. "It's really nice to see you with friends."

"They're—" Ben wanted to correct her, but it felt good to feel like he belonged somewhere right now even if it was a lie, *especially* right now. "They're good people," Ben said instead.

"What are they doing in there?"

"Magic. Apparently." And Ben, as usual, was on the other side of the door.

They spent the next twenty minutes waiting and small-talking about everything Veronica had told them upstairs, what Ben had done in California, what happened in the Palace, and everything they'd learned about Veronica's sister. Magic was narrative, secret ancient cabals existed, people could read and control minds, etc. etc.

He didn't realize at first, but Ben found himself becoming more and more agitated as the conversation continued. It all suddenly felt banal and meaningless, though he'd never tell Cor that. All he cared about was what was happening behind the storage room door. He should've been the one to go in. Not Zev. He couldn't explain why. Like Veronica said, this had nothing to do with him, but Ben had to know why the writer chose him. He couldn't leave, as much as he wanted to extricate himself from the infuriating situation with Cor, and Ben knew Cor well enough to know she wouldn't walk away from him after what she'd just told him. So he stood next to her, getting more and more frustrated, his sweaty hand in his pocket, flipping the magical coin over and over, wishing the trappings of his painful, mundane life away in exchange for the magimystic beyond the door.

"Well, at least you know what your next book will be about," Cor said.

The familiarity, the flippant, innocent statement, finally triggered something. Ben's agitation exploded out of him like steam. "If you still think I could ever write another book, after everything that happened, after everything I lost, then— it's probably best we broke up twice," Ben said, regretting every syllable as they burst out of his mouth.

He could feel Cor looking up at him. He could only imagine the pain in her face. He couldn't bear to look at her. "I'm sorry," he whispered.

The lights in the hall began to hum and flicker. It was a welcome distraction. The lights went out altogether for a moment with one sharp *buzz*. Then they flickered back on. Then it was over.

The storage room door opened an excruciating minute later, and Veronica held it open for Alistair to walk through. Alistair blinked slowly and sort of floated out of the room, like a toddler who'd just woken up. Zev followed behind, his arms outstretched, ready to catch her if she fell.

"Is she okay?" Ben asked Veronica. "Did it work?" He could still feel Cor's wounded eyes on his back.

"Ask *her*," Veronica answered, pointing to Alistair. Ben could see Veronica's hands were shaking and there were beads of sweat on her forehead.

"I can see them," Alistair answered. "Connections. All over the place."

"What do they look like?" Zev asked.

"Like currents. Like the air is thicker in places. They're crisscrossing everywhere. Currents of memory."

"How do we find the memento? *Our* memento?" Ben asked, wincing at his desperate attempt to insinuate himself back into the narrative.

"I see it. It's connected to me, here," she touched her chest. "It's been pulling at me all this time."

Alistair extended her hand into the space in front of her, fingers twisting and touching some unseen string. She seemed slightly intoxicated.

"So where is it?" Ben asked.

"I don't know. I can't see where it leads. There are so many currents."

Ben looked to Veronica, "How long is this gonna last?"

"A few minutes, a few months, forever?"

"Forever?!" Ben and Zev asked simultaneously.

"This is *big* magic, and I *just* threw it together. I have no idea how long it will last. Alistair knows that. I told her. She still wanted to do it."

Ben shook his head. "How do we help? How do we weed out the other connections? I feel like we should've had a better plan in place before we did this."

"She needs to get high," Zev said.

"I don't know, she seems pretty high already," Veronica said.

"I mean *elevation* high. She said the memento, the memory is pulling at her, attached to her. Let's get her on the roof and maybe it will pull the current away from the others? See where it ends?"

"Is that even how this works? It's not a rubber band—" Ben protested.

"Hey, it's a start. We need to try everything. We have no idea how long—"

"I didn't mean it was a bad idea, Zev, I just—"

"Guys?" Cor spoke up from behind, nodding her head down the hall.

They turned to find that Alistair had wandered up the basement stairs without them.

They found Alistair outside the smashed-out front windows, standing in the middle of a small snowdrift, a thin veil of white already coating her hair and shoulders. She walked out of view of the windows, heading north. Zev and Veronica rushed after Alistair, out of the restaurant's front door.

"Wait! Where's her coat?" Ben yelled to them. "Her favorite—"

"Here," Cor said behind him. She was holding Alistair's coat. "I have to wait for the crew to come and fix the windows—"

"I'm sorry—"

"Don't be. It was honest. That's all I ever wanted."

She handed him the coat, they stood in silence for a second, then he left without another word between them. The front door of the restaurant closed behind him, waves of snow stinging his face, and Ben realized that was probably the last time he would see Cor for a long time.

Around Madison and 57th, he finally caught up with Zev and Veronica, who had in turn finally caught up with Alistair. Alistair had been crisscrossing northwest, silent, unbothered by the snow soaking into her clothes, the ice crystals in her hair and lashes. Ben handed Veronica Alistair's coat and she managed to slip it onto Alistair's arms and over her shoulders as they walked the next block and a half.

"Stay close to her," Veronica told Ben, "There's nothing that can protect her now except you and the coin."

No pressure. They kept quiet as Alistair continued walking, determined, all at once pulled by the invisible string and pushing against the frigid wind. Ben didn't want to break the spell Alistair had risked having cast on herself with his stupid ramblings, so he stayed beside her and kept his mouth shut. It was Veronica who finally broke the chilly silence made all the more profound by the sound-dampening snow around them.

"So I guess we know where she's going," Veronica said quietly.

"Yep," Zev whispered back, bookending Alistair with Ben.

Ben didn't, but it only took two more blocks for the waving, endless grove of bare black trees to finally roll into view—

Central Park.

Ben and Zev caught Alistair by the shoulder before she blindly stepped into the early morning traffic of 5th Avenue. Then, with the green light on their side, they crossed into the dark park.

☙❧

"It's getting too dense to tell them apart," Alistair whispered to herself, "but they're all pointing this way."

They passed the snow-capped carousel, then disturbed the pristine white sheet covering the Sheep Meadow as they forged a trail through it, their tracks quickly covered over by snowfall. Ben glanced back to see their trail vanishing and it gave him a twinge of comfort. It would be that much harder to track them if they were being followed.

They crossed the icy Bow Bridge, and then followed Alistair into the dark heart of the park's Ramble, a thick, acres-spanning copse of trees bound together with endless winding trails and littered with deep, dark recesses.

"This is where Sullivan Green lived," Zev whispered, to himself, to Alistair.

They walked with Alistair down lightless, snaking, tree-lined paths, leaving behind the streetlamps at the edges of the Ramble. Only the ghostly glow of snowfall reflecting the lights of the city lit their way. At a sharp turn, Alistair stepped off the trail, through the trees, into thick, dead grass. They scrambled to follow her down the steep embankment, into a small valley so deep they couldn't see the trails above, or the city surrounding them.

"There," Alistair said, pointing to a towering tree with a deep gap at the base of its trunk, partially covered by underbrush and snow. Alistair knelt at the opening, the scale of it framing her like a doorway. She shoved the snow away and ducked her head down to climb inside.

Zev managed to get out, "One of us should go—" by the time Alistair had folded her body into the narrow opening and disappeared. He followed after her, needing an extra second to squeeze through the gap.

Ben approached the gap, then looked back to Veronica, whose arms were crossed, fortifying herself against the cold. She approached the tree and knelt beside him. "Be ready for anything," she said to him quietly.

"You're not going to try and stop her, are you? She has a right to know," Ben said.

"I don't know if she can just take her piece back and leave everyone else's intact. If so, bully for her, and we're done. If not, we can't let her undo what's been done. I won't let her. I need you on board."

"I'm with you," Ben said. It wasn't completely true.

Veronica slid easily into the gap between the roots of the tree and disappeared into the dark.

Ben didn't want to have to choose between Veronica and

Alistair. He began to cram himself through the opening, unaware of which side he was taking, as he felt his legs slip out into nothing—

Then catch on a short incline as he slid into a dark underground space. Veronica and Zev were already standing, slowly sweeping their phones' flashlights around as snow continued to flurry in through the small opening above, coating everything in a thin crystalline glaze.

It looked like someone had been squatting for years in the pocket under the tree. Roots wove in and out of packed dirt walls, which were further supported by pieces of cardboard boxes and broken furniture. There was a mattress on one side of the room, but everything else was covered with junk. Old toys, moldering books, silver plates, picture frames, endless shattered tchotchkes. Hundreds upon hundreds of trinkets and broken things. With each step, Ben had to focus to keep from crushing something underfoot. He could barely stand upright without hitting his head on the ramshackle support beams that held up the hard-packed dirt and stone ceiling.

"Where is it?" Veronica asked Alistair, who was standing with her back to them.

"I don't know. It's too much. All of these things are . . ." she trailed off.

"We know what we're looking for. We just have to start digging," Zev knelt and began pushing objects aside, sifting through the garbage, looking for the pocket watch in question.

Ben knelt too, picking through the detritus, but his attention stayed fixed on Alistair. Something felt wrong. He glanced at Veronica, who was also watching her as she absently scanned the room with her flashlight.

"Alistair, are you okay?" Ben finally asked.

"She's fine. She's overwhelmed," Zev answered. "We just have to find the damned thing."

"It's not here," Alistair whispered.

"What do you mean?" Ben asked.

"It's not here. It *was* here, for a long time. Here with all of these other things . . . But it's gone now. I can barely see it, the current, here, through the wall. It's somewhere else. It's getting harder to see —" Alistair's body suddenly went limp, and she collapsed to her knees like a dropped doll.

"Alistair!" Zev shouted as he and Ben rushed to her.

"I'm okay. I'm okay," she muttered, finding Veronica in the dark room, "You have to do it again. I lost it. I can't see it."

"It's not here, you said—"

"I know it's not here! But I have to keep looking! All this stuff has power, I could see it, but the path went on from here. You have to do it again."

"It's too soon. It's too much to handle," Veronica said.

"Bullshit. Here," Alistair said, handing Veronica an ornate, gilded fountain pen. "Do it."

Veronica took the pen. "Alistair, this place is a well. It draws things to it. If the pocket watch isn't here, it means someone took it, or there's a more powerful— I get what you're feeling, but—"

"No! You don't! None of you do." Alistair answered, desperate.

"You're right," Ben interceded, swallowing hard before continuing, "We don't. But we see how much this is hurting you. Maybe in ways you don't. And we're here to help you. We just want to—"

Movement behind Alistair drew his attention.

A small, black, leather-bound book was floating in mid-air directly behind Alistair's head.

Zev wordlessly pointed to the other side of the room where a candlestick was slowly rising from a pile of trinkets, floating upward toward the ceiling.

"What's happening?" Ben asked.

"I don't know," Veronica answered.

One by one, then ten by ten, then all at once every broken, tarnished object began rising up from their piles.

There was a distinct thud behind Ben, then another. He turned in time to see a volume of books suddenly ratchet upwards through the ceiling like bullets. Dirt, stone, and snow rained down as the objects began launching out of the hovel. The sound was calamitous.

Veronica yanked Ben against the wall and Zev shielded Alistair as the objects loudly careened off the ceiling supports on their way up, the ceiling beginning to crumble.

"Go!" Ben shouted to the others, motioning toward the hole they had crawled in through.

Zev pulled Alistair toward the entrance and knelt to boost her up as the last support gave way. There was a quiet moment before the roof came down entirely. A half-ton of frozen dirt and debris collapsed in on them. Ben clenched his eyes shut against the collapse, waiting for the towering tree above them to fall in, reaching out to Veronica.

There was a terrible sound, muffled by the dirt, but loud, like a point-blank thunderclap. The tree above them exploded upward, along with its roots, the walls, and most of the fallen dirt, leaving a rain of debris in its wake.

Ben couldn't breathe, his lungs full of dirt and dust. He coughed it out, took a deep breath, and wiped the grime from his eyes. He looked up to find tree-rimmed open sky, snow falling down into the crater they were now lying in, and Marjory standing on the side of the hole, a smile on her face, her body flickering with golden energy.

"You don't think I looked here already?"

Ben looked to Veronica, panic flooding him. He saw Veronica grip the fountain pen Alistair gave her. It vanished in a quick flicker of golden light, and for a moment, Veronica's eyes reflected the same color. "Get out of here right now."

Veronica got to her feet, looked to her sister, said a word that wasn't any language Ben recognized, and levitated out of the hole in the ground, meeting Marjory eye to eye.

Twin gods floating on air, shimmering with divine energy.

Marjory clapped. "Big sis still has tricks."

Ben whipped his head toward Zev and Alistair. They were both already looking at him from across the crater. "Let's go!" he hissed, as Zev scrambled over, grabbing Ben's hand as Alistair grabbed Zev's. They struggled to climb out of the far side of the crater, keeping hold of each other as they crested the rough edge of the hole and tried to get as much distance from Marjory as possible. Ben looked up for a moment, the snow, debris, and junk from the hovel were caught up in spinning, converging rings, which orbited the sisters who were both floating at the center like powerful celestial objects.

Ben turned toward the tree line, pulling the others along, and saw, on the edges of the snowy clearing stood members of the Silver. They were disguised in their mirror masks, their faces flickered between the near-identical visages of Veronica and Marjory Morrow. The Silver were each encircled with smaller orbital rings of objects.

Ben stopped cold. They were surrounded.

"What do we do?" Zev asked.

Ben looked back to Veronica, whose focus was on her sister. She couldn't help them. Ben took two steps backward—

"Ben!" Alistair yelled as a chunk of tree that was caught in one of the sisters' wider orbital rings spun toward him. It sliced Ben's cheek open before he could react, then sped past them, already halfway across the clearing, looping up in an arc around the Morrows.

"It didn't have to be like this," Marjory called to Veronica, her voice supernaturally amplified.

Veronica yelled back through the wind, "Of course it did, because you're too goddamned selfish to let this go! All you've ever cared about is how *you've* been hurt. How this has affected *you*. All I ever wanted to do was protect you."

"Then stop. We don't have to fight," Marjory said. The spinning circles of debris slowing for a moment.

"We do if you think you're gonna take them," Veronica answered back.

Ben could see that all around the clearing, the Silver were edging in, growing closer.

"V, they're already mine." Marjory raised her hands, gesturing to the objects spinning around them. "Take whatever power you need. I don't need to fight dirty to tear you apart. But you should know, what I lack in memories you stole from me, I've made up for in practice."

"Honey . . . I changed history itself," Veronica answered.

The orbiting trinkets surrounding the sisters began to glow the same golden color as the fountain pen. The clearing was awash with light as the objects were consumed.

"This is our chance," Ben said, pulling at Zev, eyeing the encroaching Silver. They had to try and plow through the line of Mirrors.

"We have to split up. I'll give you a chance to get out of here with the coin," Alistair said.

"No!" Ben and Zev shouted back.

"We don't leave you unprotected. We don't leave you to the bad guys," Ben panted.

"This isn't a book!" Alistair said.

"I know it's not! But this can't be what's supposed to happen! I'm supposed to keep you safe!"

The glowing objects above them flickered out of existence and in their place rivets of glowing energy appeared, darting toward the sisters, infusing them with golden light.

Marjory fired first. The same prismatic energy she fired at them in the library leapt from her hands in tall arcs, like solar flares, lashing at her sister's limbs, binding them, stretching them out in four directions. Veronica howled in pain, then shouted something, and the pieces of the shattered tree that spun around them rocketed toward Marjory. The tree reformed in mid-air as if exploding in reverse, encasing Marjory inside its thick trunk.

The prismatic binds dissipated, and Veronica plummeted to the ground, hitting it hard. She whipped her head toward Ben and the others, a protesting hand up to keep them away. The roots of the floating tree began to grow, slithering downward, slamming into the frozen ground. Veronica pointed behind them.

They turned to see the roots burst from the ground at the feet of the Mirrors, flinging ten or more into the woods, their ringed orbits scattering to the ground. The circle of the Silver was broken.

"Run!" Ben shouted as he started charging toward the hole Veronica had made in the Silver, Zev and Alistair just managing to keep pace.

He looked back as the floating tree burst into flame, a black shadow at its center, like an infernal sonogram. Marjory was emerging.

"Jesus Christ," Zev panted as he glanced back. His hand was like a vise in Ben's.

Ben looked to Veronica one more time, nothing to say, no longing, resonant look. There wasn't time. He sprang for the edge of the clearing, toward the broken line of Silver, dragging Zev and Alistair with him, his left hand clenched around the piece of metal in his pocket. He couldn't look back. He couldn't worry about Veronica. He had a mission. Protect Alistair. Protect Alistair or Marjory wins. He just had to hope the coin would protect them long enough to get through the line, out of the Ramble, out of the park.

As they approached the broken line, the Mirrors on their periphery regained their composure, their orbits beginning to glow. They weren't going to let them leave. The trinkets vanished around the nearest Mirrors, their bodies glowing with golden light, their masks all reforming into Ben's face. Long glasslike shards of matter appeared above a Mirror just ahead on their left. The shards speared through the air toward them, then dissolved to sand just before they reached Ben. Ben could feel the coin heating up in his hand, doing its job. The Mirror on the right raised their hands and iron chains tentacled from their flesh, whipping toward them. The chains bounced off an invisible barrier, lashing at it over and over. A tall, broad Mirror rushed to block their path; his body covered in a shell of purple energy. The shell began to expand into an oversized suit of armor, but the Mirror, and those surrounding him, were suddenly wrenched upward by new roots exploding from the ground.

Ben dragged Zev and Alistair through the gap before more Silver could close ranks, and raced through the Ramble thicket, laterally across the paths, the echo of what sounded like thunder behind them.

And countless footsteps in the underbrush.

The thunderous echoes of the sisters fighting. The Silver in pursuit.

The snow blowing hard against their faces, blinding them as they ran.

Ben couldn't believe he'd left Veronica back there, but there was nothing he could do, nothing but protect Alistair with what little power he had. He had no doubt Veronica could take Marjory, but there were dozens of Silver back there, primed with power, ready to help take her out.

An explosion overhead was followed by showers of aqua-colored energy raining down around them like sizzling sparks. Ben glanced up through the snow to see two figures fighting across the sky, their bodies in silhouette against the blue-green fallout. The Morrows, locked in battle. One slammed the other downward behind the trees, into the ground. Tremors shook Ben's footing and rattled the trees surrounding them, casting down pounds of snow and dead branches. A fireball rocketed past them from behind, detonating on impact several yards ahead, the fire licking at their invisible barrier as they passed. Ben could barely keep his hand on the coin. It felt like a burning coal in his palm. And the Silver were still coming for them.

They burst through the far edge of the Ramble, heading north. A wide, tree-flanked bridge up ahead straddled 79th Street, which bisected the park. A dozen implausible plans rushed through Ben's head. Maybe they could commandeer a car or hide in a subway station. There was a stop on 79th Street on the western edge of the park, but he didn't think they would make it.

They sped up the bridge that straddled two busy lanes of traffic. Cars zoomed past two-stories below as the cloud-coated sun began to rise in the distance. There was a hissing sound, approaching quickly. They looked to see a comet of energy rushing at them. It passed over their heads before smashing into the far end of the stone bridge.

It was Veronica. She was writhing, smoldering with smoke, light flickering across her battered, blood-stained body.

"Christ—" Ben uttered as he pulled Zev and Alistair to Veronica's side.

"What— are you doing?" Veronica muttered, her mouth burbling blood. "Get out of here. I got this."

She tried to sit up but couldn't.

"I'm gonna get help," Ben said, taking in the injuries she'd suffered, the frightening gravity of her wounds. He wanted to brush away the thin veil of snow accumulating on her, but it was already turning red, soaking into her wounds.

"This is insane. You have to let me go," Alistair said to Zev, standing over Ben's shoulder, trying to wrench her hand free. "No one else is getting hurt because of me. I'll run and buy you time." Alistair looked down at Veronica. "I'm sorry."

Veronica tried to speak but only fresh blood passed her lips.

"Here, take it," Ben told Alistair, offering her the coin.

"I don't want it. Use it for her."

"We all came here to protect *you*."

"I don't need you to risk your life to—"

"Jesus Christ, Alistair," Ben pulled his right hand free and put the coin in Zev's palm, "Take this and the two of you run. Hide. Keep each other safe. I'm not leaving her here for them."

Zev looked at the coin in his palm. It gave off steam in the frigid wind.

There was a dull, clacking thud behind them on the bridge. They all turned. It was Marjory. Cut and bleeding, but alive.

She saw her sister crumpled on the ground behind them. "She wasn't as strong as I thought she'd be. It was easier than I—" Marjory said, a flutter in her voice betraying her bravado.

She passed them, approaching her sister's bleeding body with an expression that was a mix of amazement and sorrow.

Veronica's every breath was labored.

"I know you wanted me to kill you. I know that's the key. If you let them die directly by your hands, you lose the power. Is that what you wanted to do, cut me off from magic like you've done everything else? You'd die to do that?"

Veronica couldn't answer.

"Well, you can't anymore. I won. I— I beat you. And now I'm going to undo everything you've done."

Ben could hear Veronica struggle to breathe as her sister loomed over her.

Marjory looked over her shoulder in Alistair's direction. "Did you see it? Back there? The deeper well? The one out there calling all the mementos? It's so close." She turned away from her sister, hand outstretched. "We're almost there. I saw your memories. You've been to that deeper well. It's time to put the pieces together, Alistair. It's time to go back."

Ben stepped in front of Marjory, tears clouding his vision, "She's not going with you," he told Marjory, defiant and overwhelmed with emotion. "Get out of here, both of you," he said to Zev and Alistair without looking behind him.

Marjory smiled and reached out her hand, never taking her eyes off Ben.

There was a small, but distinct sound behind him, a familiar sound he couldn't immediately pinpoint. It didn't register to Ben what it was until he saw a shining object land in Marjory's palm. It was the sound of a coin being flicked into the air.

Ben looked back and saw his pained confusion mirrored in Alistair's face. She was still holding Zev's hand even though Zev had just tossed Marjory the coin.

Zev's voice was barely audible over the wind, his head bowed, "I first read about them in undergrad, the path of Silver. I've been following it . . . for years. But I couldn't get to them. Then— they came to me. The night you were in the hospital. They said— they said that if I convinced you to come, if I brought you with me, I could join them. I could know everything they know. Everything about the world. Every book imaginable. All the secret stories. I didn't realize. I didn't know what they wanted from you."

"What are you saying?" Alistair asked, trying to pull her hand free from his, her face contorted as she tried to hold back the tears brimming in her eyes.

He gripped her tight with both hands. "I wanted to, after the library. Once I knew, once I saw, I tried to get you out. But it was too late. Now I'm in, and I can't let you go. I'm sorry."

"She's manipulating you," Alistair seethed, "she's controlling you."

"No. For the first time in my life, I'm free. Unbound, they call it. And you can be too."

Ben lunged for the coin in Marjory's hand, but she snapped her fingers, and he fell to his knees under a crushing, invisible weight. He watched as the coin glowed orange in Marjory's palm and began to smoke, then melt down her fingers. She shook her hand, whipping strands of molten metal into the snow and onto Ben's torso and legs, burning through his clothes, searing his flesh. He gritted his teeth, helplessly bearing the pain.

Marjory stood still on the peak of the bridge, blithely watching as Alistair growled like an animal in a trap, trying to get free of Zev's hold. She hit him in the arm, the chest, the face, slamming into him over and over. She smashed her fist into his nose, blood spraying down his mouth and into the snow, but he didn't release her. Ben saw the strangely stolid expression in Zev's eyes. A mask for his pain. Was there a word to describe a betrayer's pain at having betrayed? Something better than *regret*? Ben couldn't think of one. Germans probably had one, but Ben didn't know it.

But there *was* a word. A word that Ben was suddenly preoccupied with remembering. He was doing the thing again. Where his brain checked out of a traumatic event. He was fumbling over a word he couldn't remember. A pointless word that didn't matter because he was *trapped*, helpless, halfway between Veronica dying on the frozen stone and Alistair fighting to get free of the man who'd just betrayed what little trust she'd ever had in someone else. And Ben was unable to help either of them. It had all been a *trap*.

"Come with me," Marjory said to Alistair.

Zev dragged Alistair to Marjory's open arms. Ben could see, in the distance, the Mirrors surrounding them, watching their grand plan finally unfold. Ben screamed, though it wasn't words. It was nonsense. Just pain made into sound. Words failed him. He felt nothing, nothing but his body burning from the melted coin, and his hands—

Flickering with golden light.

Like the light he'd briefly seen in Veronica's eyes after the hovel exploded.

Power. And a word. A word that Veronica was whispering in his mind. He looked to her. She was watching him. Focused solely on him. Sending him power—

And a word he didn't recognize even though he somehow knew what it meant—

Trap.

Marjory took Alistair by the arm, as Ben raised his flickering hands, no idea what would happen next, and screamed, "Thidisu!"

A thin, phantasmal wall exploded from the stone bridge between Marjory and Alistair, breaking Marjory's grasp. It was semitransparent, crystalline, and undulating with purple energy. Marjory reeled on Veronica, and another wall appeared, cutting her off from her sister. Despite having never seen anything like them, the walls were strangely familiar to Ben. It took a moment for him to realize they were ghostly replicas of his own cabin's walls.

Marjory turned to Ben, her good eye turning black as ink. Ben screamed the word again and another wall burst from the bridge to cut her off from him, but Marjory uttered a one-word response and the walls exploded into mist. Ben felt the destruction in his blood. He could barely breathe. Mirrors rushed forward to restrain Alistair, as Zev took two slow steps back into their ranks. He looked like the little boy Alistair had described when Ben first read about him in the book pages. Someone handed Zev what looked like a thin piece of fabric. Zev held it in his hands for a moment, rivulets of blood dripping from his chin.

Then he put the veil over his face and Zev was gone. A Mirror in his place.

Alistair had gone ashen. Ben's heart broke for her, even as Marjory loomed over him.

"Leave him alone!" Alistair screamed, her voice hoarse and thin.

"Stand up," Marjory said to Ben, and he felt his body rise off the ground, back onto his feet.

"We didn't really get a chance to talk when we first met but we have a friend in common."

Ben's head spun with pain and grief. *What was she talking about?*

"You knew Frank, right?" she asked. "I knew Frank. Back before the Silver." Marjory leaned in, her lips at Ben's ear. "I'm the one who gave him your book."

Ice cold lightning coursed through his ear and over his entire body. His vision narrowed.

"It was—"

Ben was back in his and Cor's apartment. On that night. He was walking out of the apartment, and Cor was in his arms, dried blood caking her body. His own hands were covered in fresh blood. He could see the bathroom door he'd kicked off its hinges to get to her. To save her. And there was something on the couch he couldn't look at. Frank. Dead. More blood than Ben had ever seen.

Marjory. She was doing this.

No. No.

"No!" Ben heard someone cry. Cor. No. Alistair. Veronica? His mother?

Ben just wanted to keep walking and never stop. Carry them all in his arms, out of the apartment, out of the nightmare. So he did. Ben stepped through the apartment door and beyond, to the edge of the bridge in Central Park. He watched his body from within a memory deep inside, trapped. The woman in his arms was Cor, and Alistair, and Veronica, and he had to save them all, so he stepped out into cold dark nothing and felt a glorious fear flood his body as gravity took hold, snatching him down, shattering his body against the frozen asphalt two stories below, right in the path of a flatbed truck.

Blood in his eyes.

Bones in pieces.

The pain was monumental, and everywhere, but fleeting. One brilliant moment, then over in an

Chapter 28

Alistair's snow-stung eyes were fixed on the spot above the railing where Ben had just been standing. The sound of screaming tires echoed from the road below the bridge. She felt her bones shudder. She shambled toward the bridge's edge, oblivious to Marjory or the Mirrors, as if another invisible string was pulling at her chest. Maybe Ben was clinging to the edge. Maybe he was floating in midair, another magic trick. Maybe he'd vanished before hitting the pavement.

He wasn't. He hadn't.

Alistair could see Ben's contorted body on the asphalt below the bridge, bloody-black ribbons beginning to spill from his head like streamers, a crooked procession of parked cars framing him, headlights still trained on his twisted body. In the blur of tears and stinging snow, the scene could have been a Renaissance painting. Perfectly lit, heartbreakingly beautiful, and grotesque.

A man stood in the way of a truck that had stopped only a few feet from Ben, its headlight beams highlighting the gore as others watched, frozen behind open car doors.

Alistair looked away, her mind as cold and opaque as the winter sky. Her eyes fell to Veronica lying flat on the bridge, draped in snow. She looked up at the gray clouds, streaks of blue morning moving through them. Not dead, not yet. But still. Broken, inside and out.

Everything, for nothing. There was only so much Alistair could weather in one night before she grew cold to it all. Numb. Zev had been a heavy, brutal hit, though dull. But Ben and Veronica, especially Ben, was a pickax blow to the chest. She didn't know him, but he had only wanted to help. He'd been roped into something he didn't understand and did everything he thought he should, just to get Alistair here.

Alistair looked away. She could see that Marjory had joined the Mirrors who were waiting for her at the base of the bridge, lined up like soldiers, or books on a shelf. Zev was now somewhere among them. They all were watching her, waiting. In the vacuum left by the sight of Ben, Alistair's mind replayed the hours she'd spent with Zev, things he did and said, looking for clues she could have picked up on, hints she should have noticed. She was lost in that moment, unsure what would happen next, when an Alistair-faced Mirror broke ranks to look behind them, then another turned. Then Marjory herself, who was anchoring the row of identical human book spines at its center. Something from the Ramble alarmed them.

Alistair felt it too. In her ears, her head. A pressure change in the air, like falling to the bottom of a pool. There was a loud *crack* and then a blast of wind split the border of the Ramble's white trees, blowing them forward like an unseen building had just collapsed behind them. A wall of violent air snatched torrents of snow and ice as it charged across the field between them and the woods. The Silver didn't have time to prepare or defend. They were like loose pages, blown in every direction as the wind wall collided with them. Alistair clenched her eyes closed as it reached her. She was shoved a good ten feet backwards, her back slamming into the edge of the bridge's railing, taking her breath away as she was pelted with burning ice and debris. Behind the initial wall of wind was what felt like every crystal flake of snow in the park. She couldn't see Veronica in the gust's blinding white aftermath, but she felt something. A hand, grabbing hers, pulling her away from the scattered Silver.

Alistair tried to pull away relentlessly while gasping for air, but the iron grip on her hand held fast. Her handler raced through the white, icy blind as Alistair struggled to both get free and keep up. A thought flashed in her mind, and she felt sick and embarrassed by it but also steeled by the shred of hope it offered her.

Zev. He was making it right. Fixing what he broke. He must have learned some kind of magic to hide them and their escape.

They emerged from the snow and Alistair took her first real breath. The blizzard hung at the edge of the park like a mile-long drape. The Mirror dragged Alistair to a car waiting at the curb, its passenger door open, another Mirror behind the wheel.

"Hurry. Get in. She'll know it was us. She'll be right behind," the Mirror said, finally letting go of Alistair's hand. Its masked voice was buzzed and obscured, but Alistair recognized it immediately, just like she had in the Palace.

Ed Cumberland removed the veil obscuring his face. "Get in the car, Alistair! Please."

Zev was still behind the white curtain of the storm, with the Silver, right where he wanted to be.

"Please, Alistair," the Mirror in the car pleaded.

Bolden. Had to be.

Ed took a step toward Alistair. She wanted to back away. She wanted to claw his eyes out. Instead, she was frozen in place, her mind detaching from her body. Ribboning out of her like the blood from Ben's—

"Alistair!" Ed snapped her back together temporarily, "This isn't what we wanted for you. This isn't how we wanted it to be. She twisted everything. All we wanna do is get you away from her.

Whatever you want after that is on you. Okay? We're out of power, and the wind's gonna die soon. You have to go."

A line of cars had formed in the street beside them, New York drivers honking incessantly. An ambulance somewhere, far off. It was all for Ben.

It was all for nothing.

"Alis, please . . ." Bolden called out to her.

That name again.

They looked like worried parents, Bolden ducking down to call to Alistair through the car's passenger window, Ed waiting impatiently on the sidewalk. In another universe they could've been trying to extricate their teenage daughter from some adolescent mess she'd gotten herself into. Underage drinking in Central Park or caught red-faced in some older boy's car. It was strange to think they had known each other all this time. A woman from the end of Alistair's days as a child, and a man who'd found her at the dawn of adulthood. Probably the closest she'd ever had to family, truth be told. At least the kind that really knew you, saw you, flaws and all.

The kind that could shatter you in a heartbeat if they wanted. Or crush you over the course of decades. Because you loved them. And you'd let them. Because you believed they loved you too.

"Give me the keys," Alistair finally said.

"What?" Bolden asked from the driver's seat.

"She wants to drive, Deborah. Give her the keys."

"Just get in, I'll let you drive when we're out of the city," Bolden pleaded.

"Why would I trust either of you? Get out of the car, and give me the keys, or I walk."

Bolden hesitated, then turned the engine off and scurried out and around the front of the car, pulling her mask away. She gave Alistair the car keys. "I know a place we'll be safe," Bolden whispered to her.

"I was never safe with you," Alistair said. She reached back and threw the car keys into the storm, as far into the park as she could. "Now, none of us are."

Ed and Bolden stared into the wall, then back at Alistair. Bolden looked completely shocked, Ed resigned, defeated.

Alistair began to back away, ignoring the twinge of regret she felt bubbling up inside of her like sewage. They didn't deserve her regret, or her mercy. They deserved Marjory.

Ed took Deborah by the arm and dragged her away down Central Park West.

Alistair didn't remember slipping into the subway station on the other side of the street. She didn't remember descending the stairs or hopping over the turnstile. She had no recollection of how long she waited for the next train. At some point the ambulance finally passed overhead, the sound of its siren ratcheting down to the platform, pulling her out of her tear-stained fugue.

A train pulled into the station. Nearly empty. It was still so early. She got on the last car and sat in the back, her body curling in on itself, wringing out endless tears. She didn't notice the Mirrors walking in from the next car until the train had already left the station.

She could've pulled the emergency brake. She could've screamed or tried to push through them to the next car. But she just didn't have it in her anymore. She felt her well-built walls collapse in on her. There was nowhere she could go where they couldn't find her, and nothing left worth fighting for. Alistair felt a weariness settle over her. Weariness wasn't the right word, but it was all she could come up with. She'd never felt what this really was: surrender.

She slumped against the rocking wall of the train and watched as the half dozen mirrored Alistairs opened worn leather satchels, producing carved pieces of dark wood, assembling them like a six-foot-tall jigsaw puzzle in the middle of the train.

She knew what it was before it fully took shape. When they were finished, they placed a tarnished brass knob into a slot and turned it. The door opened, and Marjory Morrow stepped through, onto the southbound B train. The dark stone of the Palace behind her.

A smile spread across Marjory's face like a deep, wet wound. She knew she'd won.

Click. Click. Click.

It wasn't the fox. It was Marjory, mocking her, already whispering in her mind. The witch didn't have to pry her way in this time.

Alistair had already been split wide open.

Chapter 29

Alistair rifled through a bin of yellowed discount paperbacks on the sweltering sidewalk outside Walter's Variety Bookstore. The covers didn't matter. Neither did the contents. She wasn't looking for prized books. She just wanted to find the cheapest ones with the most pages.

The school year had finally ended, and Alistair's summer plans consisted of reading, working on her papercraft objects, being dragged to the beach by Aunt Kath and Uncle Gus, and hours of bike riding with Zev along the griddle-hot sidewalks of Ozone Park.

Sweat pooled where Alistair's backpack made contact with her T-shirt as she moved on to the next bin in line, hoisting herself in, digging straight to the bottom.

"Alistair!" Someone yelled.

Alistair popped her head out of the bin, her mess of wavy, unkempt hair half in her face. It was Walter, the bookstore owner.

"I been calling your name," he wheezed from the open doorway of the bookstore, fanning himself with a magazine, only his bulbous belly breaching the threshold. "Find anything good?" he asked, nodding toward the bins.

"Just those," Alistair pointed to a teetering tower of paperbacks she'd stacked beside the bookstore door.

"*Just* those?! You're wiping me out again!"

"Can you ring them up?"

"They probably ain't worth more than five dollars. Just take 'em. I'm closing up anyway."

"You're what?" Alistair checked her watch, realizing how late it was. "Oh, shit."

"Your parents know you use that kind of language?" Walter asked with a ribbing grin.

"They're not my parents," Alistair said, smiling back. She bounded off down the sidewalk, calling back, "Zev'll be here any second for the books. Tell him to wait for me before he starts going through them. Thanks, Walter!"

❧

Bolden's office air-conditioning met Alistair's sweat sheen and gave her a ripple of goose bumps. It felt good. She glanced over at the origami box she'd made, which sat in a place of pride on one of Bolden's bookcases.

Bolden had stopped asking about the contents of the box more than a year ago. The slip of paper with the list of forbidden things. The things Alistair wanted to stow away for the hour so that she could talk about whatever else she wanted, without fear or worry that those things would come up in conversation unless she wanted them to come up. For one hour a week, they were locked away.

Bolden sat across the small, well-appointed room in a high-backed leather armchair. It didn't fit in with the rest of the pale, creamy decor, but also kind of did in a way that Alistair didn't fully understand and just assumed rich, sophisticated women did. Alistair often wondered where the chair came from. Maybe it was sentimental, or maybe it was the first chair Bolden bought when she started being a therapist.

"How was your week?" Bolden asked, a pad of paper draped over her crossed knees.

"Sweaty mostly," Alistair answered.

"How do you feel about the school year ending? I know you were concerned about staying busy. Staying focused."

Alistair shrugged her shoulders. "Fine. I've been reading a ton, making things . . ."

Alistair's eyes wandered to the abstract painting hanging behind Bolden's head. Bolden turned to look at it too.

"Is it distracting?" she asked.

"No, it's—" Alistair stopped herself.

"You can tell me."

"It looks like half of a naked lady that's got a windmill for a face."

Bolden's body bounced with polite laughter. "That's an interesting perspective."

"Is it like a Rorschach or something?"

"Have you seen Rorschach images before?" Bolden asked, writing something down on her pad.

"On TV. You can tell how people think with them, right?"

"That's up for debate. There are other ways to ask the same kind of questions nowadays," Bolden said with a smile.

"I remembered something about *the briar books* yesterday," Alistair said abruptly.

"Oh. You did?"

"Sort of. Well, it *might* be from the books."

"Do you want to talk about it?"

Alistair shrugged. "I saw this lady with this big white dog. He was like a horse, and he was dragging her around the park. Sticking his head in bushes. Sniffing for birds or something. It was funny. And I got this image in my head, or this memory, about a dog with flowers in its fur. A white dog. Big enough to ride on, at least for a kid."

"How did it make you feel?"

"The memory? I don't know, kind of sad, I guess."

"Do you remember a dog like that in the books?"

"Maybe. It's not like that. That simple. I mean, I don't know where the idea came from, but something about it *feels* like it's from somewhere else. But I can't tell for sure if it's something I made up in my imagination, or something I used to remember."

"Well, it might be either, or possibly both," Bolden said with a smile. "Have you ever heard the saying *Imagination is nothing more than memory, transposed?*

Alistair furrowed her brow, considering the statement. "No. What does it mean?"

"Well, it means that—"

Alistair interrupted, working it out aloud, "Things we make up are actually put together from memories."

"That's right! You got it. Kind of like the objects you make with book pages. Like the box you made me. It's a belief that 'new ideas' are really just combinations of different memories and experiences that are then turned into something new."

"That's depressing."

"Why?"

"Because that means there aren't any new ideas."

"Or maybe it means that the more experiences you have, the more memories you make, and the more likely you are to be inspired to have a new idea."

"I guess. Yeah. Not a lot of great ideas came from people who just sat on their couch all day," Alistair quipped.

"That's a good point," Bolden said, her warm eyes crinkling at the edges. "So, what do you plan on doing this summer? What new mementos are you going to make?"

"Memories?"

"I'm sorry?" Bolden asked.

"You said 'mementos.' I think you meant 'memories.'"

"Right." Bolden nodded.

"I don't know. I started a book club with my friend and we're gonna see how many scary books we can read before school starts and then vote on the scariest."

"Your friend Zev?"

"Yeah."

"That sounds fun. I know you like him. I don't really like scary books, but you're braver than me." Bolden wrote something, then without looking up, asked, "Were *the briar books* ever scary?"

"I don't remember," Alistair said.

"No?"

"No."

"You seem like maybe you don't want to talk about them. Do you want to put *the briar books* in the box today?" Bolden asked, looking at the paper box on the shelf.

"No. It's fine."

"Okay." Bolden wrote more, then took a moment, smiled at Alistair, and asked, "Would you like to tell me what *is* in the box?"

"The—same things."

"The fox?" Bolden asked.

Alistair felt a flush of cold wash over her. A chilly current reaching out of the dark place where her memories used to be. She responded to Bolden with a short, reticent nod.

"The snow-covered path?"

Another faint nod. The cold current wrapping around her legs, up her body.

"What else?"

"We're not supposed to talk about the things in the box," Alistair said, her voice unintentionally breaking into a whisper. "You said—"

"Whatever you put in the box is locked away while we're together. You're right. But . . . you haven't had an episode in a long time, Alis. You've grown much more confident. Maybe it's time to take them out and look at them again. Make some kind of sense of them. If you're willing. If you're ready to show me."

Alistair didn't answer.

Bolden stood and approached the shelf, picking up the box. She sat back in her leather chair and placed the box on the small coffee table between them.

"We only know where you were found that night, but nothing about how you got there, and where you were before. Where the fox was. And the path. Maybe I could help you understand more about the night you came home."

Alistair's head was throbbing. She noticed a far-off droning sound, somewhere outside the office. A rhythmic thrumming under it. Like her aunt's old dishwasher.

"This isn't—"

"This isn't what?"

"I don't know," Alistair looked Bolden in the eyes, scared, before realizing what she was trying to say was, "This isn't how this happened."

Alistair rifled through a bin of yellowed discount paperbacks on the sweltering sidewalk outside Walter's Variety Bookstore. The covers didn't matter. Neither did the contents. She wasn't looking for prized books. She just wanted to find the cheapest ones with the most pages.

"Alistair!" someone yelled.

Alistair popped her head out of the bin, her mess of wavy, unkempt hair half in her face. It was Walter, the bookstore owner.

"I been calling your name," he wheezed from the open doorway of the bookstore, fanning himself with a magazine, only his bulbous belly breaching the threshold. "Find anything good?" he asked, nodding toward the bins.

Alistair raced down the sidewalk, sucking in Ozone Park's summer miasma. Up ahead, Zev was rushing out of a bodega with two unwrapped Creamsicles, his glasses fogging in the heat. He saw her barreling toward him.

"I'm sorry!" he called out. "There was a line . . ."

He checked his watch, dripping Creamsicle on his shirt. "You're late!"

"I know!" Alistair yelled as she rushed past, then stopped and sped back, taking one of the Creamsicles out of his hand. She took a bite and mumbled over the chunk of icy sugar in her mouth. "I left a stack of books at Walter's. Most are just for origami, but there are a couple that looked really scary from the covers. He knows you're coming to get them."

"Alistair?" Zev asked with a smile, the late sun reflecting in his glasses.

"Yeah?"

Bolden's office air-conditioning met Alistair's sweat sheen and gave her a ripple of goose bumps. It felt good. She glanced over at the origami box she'd made, which sat in a place of pride on one of Bolden's bookcases.

"How do you feel about the school year ending? I know you were concerned about staying busy. Staying focused."

Alistair shrugged her shoulders. "Fine. I've been reading a ton, making things . . ." Alistair's eyes wandered to the abstract painting hanging behind Bolden's head.

Bolden turned to look at it too.

"Is it distracting?" She asked.

"No, it's—" Alistair stopped herself. A sound just outside the office had caught her attention. A far-off drone.

"You can tell me," Bolden continued.

Alistair was distracted by the droning sound. A rhythmic thrumming under it. Like her aunt's old dishwasher.

"What's that sound?"

Bolden tilted her head a little, trying to hear what Alistair was hearing. "It might be the air-conditioning. It's working hard today."

Alistair nodded, still listening for the sourceless sound.

"Are you all right?" Bolden asked. "Did you want to talk about the painting?"

"I remembered something about *the briar books* yesterday," Alistair said abruptly.

"You did?"

"Sort of. Well, it *might* be from the books. I saw this old lady with this big white dog. He was . . . like a horse. He was sticking his head in bushes. And I had this . . . this image in my head, this memory, about a dog with flowers in its fur—" Alistair stopped, her brow furrowed.

"What's wrong?" Bolden asked.

"Imagination . . . is nothing more than memory, transposed," Alistair answered.

"Where did you hear that?"

"You told me that."

"Did I?"

"Yeah. I think so. I just . . . can't remember when."

Bolden's warm eyes crinkled at the edges. "So what do you plan on doing this summer? What new memories are you going to make?"

"Memories?"

"Yes, memories," Bolden asked.

"You said 'mementos.' I think you meant 'memories.'"

"Are you sure?"

"I—I started a book club with my friend and we're gonna see how many scary books we can read before school starts."

"Your friend Zev?"

The droning, thrumming sound had grown louder, more

344

distracting.

"Zev. Yeah."

"That sounds fun. I know you like him. I don't really like scary books, but you're braver than me." Bolden wrote something, then without looking up, asked, "Were *the briar books* ever scary?"

"I don't remember," she said.

"No?"

"No."

"You seem like maybe you don't want to talk about them. Do you want to put *the briar books* in the box today?" Bolden asked, looking at the paper box on the shelf.

"No. It's fine."

"What *is* in the box, if you don't mind me asking?"

"The . . . same things."

"The fox?" Bolden asked.

Alistair felt a flush of cold wash over her. A chilly current reaching out of the dark place where her memories used to be.

Alistair responded with a short, reticent nod.

"The snow-covered path?"

Another faint nod. The cold current wrapping around her legs, up her body.

"What else?"

"We're not supposed to talk about the things in the box," Alistair said, her voice unintentionally breaking into a whisper. "You said—"

Bolden was speaking, saying something about Alistair's past episodes, but the droning was so loud now Alistair could feel the vibration in her body.

She could see the tops of several green trees framed in Bolden's office window, swaying in the hot air outside. Maybe it was the glass, or maybe it was the sweltering, hazy air, but the trees were slightly out of focus, as if they'd been smeared across the windowpane.

"Alis?"

Alistair looked away from the window and found Bolden

perched on the edge of her leather armchair, the paper box sitting between them on the small coffee table.

"The memories in this box can't hurt you anymore. Not while I'm here. I won't let them."

"I don't want to talk about them. I don't think I need to anymore."

"There's nothing to be scared of there. It's all in your imagination. It's nothing more than memories. Let's look at them together and make sense of them."

Bolden pushed the box toward Alistair. "Open it for me."

Alistair's head throbbed. The sourceless sound was everywhere, deafening her.

"Don't you trust me?" Bolden asked.

"I do," Alistair whispered.

Alistair carefully reached for the box, then stopped with one finger on the lid. "I did."

"You did what?" Bolden asked, visibly anxious.

"Trust you. But not anymore . . ."

❧❦❧

Alistair raced down the sidewalk, sucking in Ozone Park's summer miasma. Up ahead, she saw Zev rushing out of a bodega with two unwrapped Creamsicles, his glasses fogging in the heat. He saw her barreling toward him.

"I'm sorry!" he called out. "There was a line . . ."

He checked his watch, dripping Creamsicle on his shirt. "You're late!"

"I know!" Alistair yelled as she rushed past, then stopped and sped back, taking one of the Creamsicles out of his hand.

She took a bite and mumbled over the chunk of icy sugar in her mouth. "I left a stack of books at Walter's. Most are just for origami, but there are a couple that looked really scary from the covers. He knows you're coming to get them."

"Alistair?" Zev asked with a sweet smile, the late sun reflecting in his glasses.

"Yeah?"

⚜

Bolden was perched on the edge of her leather armchair, the paper box sitting between them on the small coffee table.

"I have to tell you something, Alis. This box is irrelevant. *You're* the one who keeps the memories at bay. Not the box."

"It's a ritual. You said it was like the mantra. You said it was as powerful as I could imagine it."

"I know what I said. But *you* are stronger than any ritual. You can't keep these memories trapped forever. They will find a way out of the box. They will haunt you all your life. I know. I've seen it."

"What do you mean you've seen it?"

"They won't let you go until you release them, until you fully understand them. Until you can tell me where you were and how we can get back there."

"I don't want to go back," Alistair answered, both afraid and bristling with agitation.

Alistair looked away from Bolden, up to the smudged trees in the window, which were now just a blur of green against a cold gray sky, whipping past the window like the images in a zoetrope.

The droning sound was all around her again.

"Something's wrong. Something—"

"Alis!" Bolden barked as she clapped her hands. "Stay with me. Here, in the office. Where you're safe. Where you can tell me anything."

"I always had trouble remembering the order of memories. My aunt and uncle thought it had to do with my memory loss. My missing year. I could never remember which summer came before which, or how old I was when we went on some road trip or vacation."

"What does that have to do with this?" Bolden asked, her furrowed face looking more and more unfamiliar.

"I don't remember a lot of those things, but you would."

"How—How would I know—"

"Not everything, but you'd know how old I am, right now."

Bolden sat back in her armchair.

"How old am I, Doctor Bolden? Right now?"

Bolden just stared back, blankly.

"Twelve? Thirteen? What grade am I starting next fall?"

"I see a lot of children—" Bolden began.

"What year is it?" Alistair interrupted. "What day is it? What street are we on?"

"Why are you behaving this way?" Bolden asked.

"Because this isn't happening. It happened."

"What do you mean? Of course, this is happening, Alis. I'm here with you. *Now.*"

Objects on the bookcase began to rattle gently. The drone was vibrating the room.

"No. This was the last time I saw you. This was the last time we met. After, the whole summer passed and I came by to see you before school started, and the office—was empty. You were gone."

Alistair looked around and for a flicker of a moment. There was nothing in the room but the sofa and the chair and the paper box on the coffee table between them. Then the furnished room returned.

"I played this memory over and over. I know it from beginning to end. I didn't say it at the time, but I knew I didn't need the sessions anymore. I knew I was going to be okay. And you knew it too. But I didn't want to stop seeing you. This was the day you hugged me, right over there, and let me go."

"I never should have let you leave," Bolden said. "You weren't ready. The memories you'd locked away came back. They broke you. But if we had dealt with them here, in this moment, you would have never had to suffer again."

Bolden sat forward in her chair. "Alis, I'm trying to help you. I'm trying to keep you from getting lost down a long, dark path."

"How? How do you know all this?"

"I can't explain how, but we can—we can change this moment. We can go back and fix things before you're too far gone for me to help you. I won't leave this time. I'll stay here and help you. All you have to do is open the box."

Bolden picked the box up from the table and joined Alistair on the sofa.

"Here, take it. Open it. I'm here. I'm not going to leave you this time."

Bolden took Alistair's hand and put the box in her small, upturned palm.

Alistair reached for the lid with her free hand, hesitant, touching it. Over Bolden's shoulder, Alistair saw the fox, waiting for her. An icy chill curled over her shoulders. She could feel the snowy path behind her.

"I can't," Alistair said, pulling her hand back.

Bolden's face twisted in anger as she snatched at Alistair's arm, pulling it back toward her. Alistair turned away, forcing herself free, but Bolden wrapped her arms around her, trying to force the box into Alistair's hands.

"Stop! Let me go!" Alistair shouted.

Bolden was folding Alistair's hands around the box, screaming, "You're going to open the box! You hear me?! You're going to open the goddamned thing, or I swear I'll—"

Then Bolden stopped, her arms going slack around Alistair. Both she and Alistair could see themselves reflected in the white-framed mirror hanging across the room.

And in the mirror, Bolden wasn't Bolden. Her skin was darker, her hair was wild and long, and one of her eyes was drained of color.

Nothing but a milk-white orb staring back.

❧❧

Alistair raced down the sidewalk, sucking in Ozone Park's summer miasma. Up ahead, Zev was rushing out of a bodega with two unwrapped Creamsicles, his glasses fogging in the heat. He saw her barreling toward him.

"I'm sorry!" he called out. "There was a line . . ."

He checked his watch, dripping Creamsicle on his shirt. "You're late!"

"I know!" Alistair yelled as she rushed past, then stopped and sped back, taking one of the Creamsicles out of his hand.

She took a bite and mumbled over the chunk of icy sugar in her mouth. "I left a stack of books at Walter's. Most are just for origami, but there are a couple that looked really scary from the covers. He knows you're coming to get them."

"Alistair?" Zev asked with a sweet smile, the late sun reflecting in his glasses.

"Yeah?" Alistair felt a drop of melted Creamsicle about to run from the corner of her lips. She wiped at it with the back of her hand.

A thought occurred to her. Or maybe a memory. She wasn't sure. It didn't matter. Zev was about to say something, but Alistair leaned into him and kissed him. He smelled like summer, sweat, and sugar. His lips were cool. She finally pulled back and Zev was frozen in place, his glasses slightly askew.

Alistair scanned his face like she was memorizing it.

"I wish this was how it happened," Alistair said, before taking off down the sidewalk.

❧❧

Bolden's office air-conditioning met Alistair's sweat sheen and gave her a ripple of goose bumps. It felt good. She glanced over at the origami box she'd made, which sat in a place of pride on one of Bolden's bookcases.

Alistair looked to Bolden and found her perched on the edge of her leather armchair, the paper box now sitting between her and Alistair on the small coffee table.

"We're not leaving here until the box is open," Bolden said with a smile. "I can make this feel like a second, or centuries. It's up to you."

Alistair heard the droning sound in the distance.

"It's a car. Tires on a road. We're in a car, aren't we? That's the sound. That's why the trees look like that."

"We're going to the place they found you that night, walking barefoot in the snow. Scared and ignorant."

"The memento. That's what you want. I remember now."

"Because I'm *allowing* you to remember. You feel safe here. This place, this day, it's important to you. So that's where we are, for now. But I can show you whatever I want you to see. Over and over again, until I get what I want."

Bolden glanced to the floor at Alistair's feet. Alistair looked and saw Ben's broken body there, blood running out of his head, onto the cream-and-tan rug. Alistair whipped her head away.

"It's not real," Alistair whispered.

"I'm only showing you what you've already seen. No lies. They're all gone. Everyone. They're either dead or they've deceived you. There's nothing else left out there. We're not leaving until you open the box."

Alistair looked at the box on the coffee table, "It's funny. Bolden saved me, in the end. Back in this moment, but now too. I know she was a Silver, but she also cared about me. I can't deny that. She could've broken me, forced me back there, to that night, like you're trying to do, but she didn't. She helped me. She cared about me. She taught me something valuable, but I didn't realize how much it meant until just now. She taught me that I don't have to let my past control me."

Alistair picked up the box from the table. "I am more than my memories." She looked up at Bolden. "I'm not opening the box."

A wicked grin crawled across Bolden's face. "Then we'll start all over again."

"No. We won't," Alistair answered.

Bolden looked around the room, confused.

"What's wrong?" Alistair asked.

"How are you doing this?"

"Keeping us here? I'm using my imagination, which is nothing more than memory, transposed."

Bolden leapt from her chair, yanking the box away from Alistair.

Alistair sat back on the sofa. "Only I can open the box, *Doctor Bolden*. And whatever I put in the box is locked away until I change my mind. Those are the rules here in this room. Anyway, it wouldn't help you find the memento even if I did open it, because I put something else in the box. Three little words . . ."

Bolden bared her teeth, trying to pry the paper box open to no avail.

"One. Eyed. Witch."

Bolden's face went slack as Alistair stood up.

"My name is Alistair Mead. I am twenty-six years old. The only thing that's real is whatever I can feel."

"What are you doing?" Bolden hissed.

"Nothing more, nothing much. If I fear something's real, all I have to do is touch."

Alistair stepped over the coffee table, snatching the box out of Bolden's hand as Bolden fell back into her armchair.

"Because . . . real things feel like something, and fake things feel like air. I can touch the thing that worries me . . ."

Alistair put her finger to Bolden's chest. "And know it isn't there."

352

"Marjory?"

Alistair woke up in the back seat of a sleek sedan. Ice-brimmed evergreens whipped past the heavily tinted windows. The tires droned on the blacktop. A man was driving, Alistair was in the back, and Marjory was unconscious in the seat next to her. Blood was trickling from Marjory's nose—thick, bubbly foam in the corners of her mouth. She was locked in the memory.

"We're almost there," the driver said with gruff hoarseness.

When Marjory didn't answer, the driver glanced back and saw Alistair awake. He did a double take and this time saw Marjory's state. "Shit!" he gulped as he scrambled for his mirrored disguise in the passenger seat.

Alistair reached for the door on her side. The driver yanked the steering wheel, banking too fast onto the road's shoulder, skidding the car out of his control. The car slid off the asphalt and dipped down a steep, snowy embankment. Alistair's door swung out as the car tipped over, and she lurched out of the open door, crashing knees and elbows first into the ice as the car slid past her.

She heard it slam into the line of trees and the bottom of the hill with a definitive *crunch*. She didn't look back. She turned and crawled back up the embankment, her arms and legs bleeding, burning against the hard-packed snow. She could hear one of the car doors opening. Someone getting out. Climbing the embankment behind her, getting closer. Snow crunching. Heavy, hoarse breathing.

Alistair pulled herself up onto the shoulder of the empty road. Another man was standing on the opposite side, waiting for her. Stone-faced and towering, he almost looked like a wooden totem, watching her with cold eyes, the only remaining relic from some abandoned roadside attraction.

The driver grabbed her leg, yanking at her as Alistair dug into the asphalt, growling. The man in the road took two steps toward her. She could see he was holding a rifle at his side. He lifted it, aimed—

And fired. Alistair could hear the driver's body hit the ice behind her and slide back down the embankment. The man in the road lowered the rifle and stood waiting in silence.

Alistair struggled to her knees, her jeans torn and soaked with blood. "I guess you're not with them," she said, still panting.

He shook his head *no*.

Alistair forced herself back onto her feet. "Were you waiting for me?"

The man nodded.

"How did you know I'd be here?"

The man slung the rifle's strap across his shoulder.

"The book said," the man answered with a low, clipped voice that carried a hint of an Eastern European accent.

"Said what? To kill that guy? To stand in the middle of the road with a rifle and wait for a car to run off the road?"

"It said you'd be here. It said to take you back."

"Back? Back where?"

"To the island. To the writer."

"To the place in my memory?"

The man didn't answer.

"Why?"

"To remember."

Alistair looked behind her, down the embankment. The driver's body had left a streak of red down the white hill. His mask flickered and became Alistair's face. It was like the end of one of the ghost stories where the person finds their own body and realizes they didn't survive after all. Alistair could see Marjory's head pressed against a spiderweb crack in the back window of the car.

"Did it say I go with you?" she asked, her eyes still locked on the demolished car.

"It said there was nothing else left for you now but the truth."

Alistair took in a deep, painful breath of icy air and exhaled. She turned back to the man in the road.

"Then let's go."

Chapter 30

Before they'd stepped off the road, back into the woods the man had come from, he had wordlessly expelled the spent casing from his rifle, loaded another bullet into the chamber, and handed the gun to Alistair. She didn't know if it was to offset their power imbalance, incriminate her in the murder of the man back at the car, or just because the book told him to do it. She took it anyway.

They walked for hours through dense, dark, eerily still forest. She carried the rifle in her hands for a while, until her hands were too cold, then she slid the strap over her shoulder, keeping enough distance to maybe have a chance to grab it if the man turned on her. Her old combat boots had gone soft and soaked through with snow. Icy water sloshed between her toes. She wasn't sure exactly what kind of combat they were built for if they turned to leather mush within hours of facing the elements of—wherever they were. Her aunt and uncle had once or twice mentioned she was found by a truck driver in New England. This wasn't mentioned to her, but to friends in other rooms, or on resigned, exhausted phone calls when she'd first come to live with them, but nothing more specific.

Alistair reached up to her right shoulder, past the rifle strap, with painfully stiff, tingling fingers. She'd ripped her coat in the accident. That *really* hurt. The sleeve had come half-loose and cold air was cutting through the open seam, chilling her core. She tucked her exposed hand back under her arm. She'd learned an hour or two into the walk that if she stumbled, she wouldn't have time to catch herself with her hands in her pockets. It's how she got a refreshing faceful of ice that the man had to pull her up from. She was dazed, mentally and physically fatigued. The lack of sleep, the spell the night before, the entire ordeal in Central Park, and her psychic battle with Marjory had all taken a toll. Then there was the bitter, relentless cold worming its way into her every cell.

The man forged through the endless thick of shadowy evergreen trees ahead of them, pushing back the needled boughs with his enormous bare hands. Alistair could see he was backtracking over the footprints he must have made to meet her on the road. As the time passed, and he essentially ignored her, she started creeping closer to him to keep the branches from swatting at her stinging skin, and to block the gentle, but killer breeze blowing against them. Even with his hunched shoulders, he was easily a foot taller than her. As they walked on and on through the woods, she'd memorized every abrasion and frayed edge on his canvas jacket. The back of his neck was creased and tan, like seasoned leather. His hair was neatly brushed back and almost completely silver, but she could see fading hints of the color his hair used to be at the edges. Chestnut, maybe, or auburn. He pushed another branch away and Alistair could see red-blond hair on the back of his hand, like her Uncle Gus's. He was definitely a ginger, once upon a time. And sometimes, when the branch was bigger and took more effort, she could see stains on his fingertips. Faded blue-black, like old ink.

Standing on the road, she'd never felt surer. Confident in besting Marjory with the tools Bolden had taught her. Closer to closure than she'd ever been. Even in the midst of a car crash, a murder, and the man who knew she'd be there before she did. Of course, Alistair had felt a rightful, ruddy blush of fear as she first stepped off the road and followed him into the woods. Anyone in their right mind would. But she had the gun he'd given willingly, and she also felt pricks of excitement, anticipation, even something resembling hope. She couldn't articulate it, couldn't slot the emotional responses into their proper, explainable spots, but she was going back to where she was when she was lost, and in that place she might find the key that finally fit the lock.

"Who are you?" Alistair asked, her voice quavering, shaking like the rest of her.

"I am the caretaker," the man answered.

"Caretaker of what?"

"The island."

"Where the writer lives?"

The caretaker didn't answer.

"How do they know what's going to happen? Is this what they say we do next?"

Silence.

"What if I just stopped here? What if I—"

The caretaker interrupted, "What if I turned around and went back home? What if I didn't do what the writer said I was going to do? What if I just shot you in the back? What would happen then?"

He knew exactly what she was going to say and repeated it without a hitch in his voice or pace.

She didn't ask any more questions.

A book said she'd be there on the road. *The Book of Briars*. That's what Ben had called it, in the car, on the way to the restaurant.

Bloody ribbons spilling from his head like streamers.

"There," the caretaker said, pulling her out of her macabre fugue. He pointed ahead, down the snowy forest bank. They'd been making their way to water. A pond, or maybe a lake—she couldn't see its edges through the wall of snow-covered trees. But somewhere on it was an island. The island he said he was supposed to take her to. Take her *back* to. She followed him down the hill toward the ice-crusted water. It hadn't frozen over, not yet, but the edges were riddled with fragmented sheets of floating ice. Alistair had been waiting for something to feel familiar, a trigger in the path they took, or even the man who was taking her, but this all felt new. Maybe there hadn't been snow when she was first brought to the island as a little girl. Maybe it had been night. Maybe she'd been sleeping, or unconscious.

The forest floor broke away at a short cliff near the water's edge. The caretaker stepped down, his height making it easy to clear the distance, then he held out a hand to help her. She saw his face up close for the first time. There *was* something about him that was familiar. His demeanor, his gait more than his face. He looked up at her and waited, hand outstretched. She was so numb she couldn't feel her hand in his when she took it.

They pushed through to the water's edge. It was a flat, black lake that stretched out farther than she could see, its borders obscured in all directions by a curling wall of white fog. A small green rowboat bobbed in a wash of broken ice at the rocky shore ahead of them. The early winter sun was low in the sky, and it made the fog wall ahead even more otherworldly. Silver and swirling.

The caretaker stepped into the freezing water without flinching and offered his hand again, steadying the boat with the other. Soon they were heading across the water, into the fog.

Alistair crouched on the floor at the back of the boat. Her knees to her chest, her body rippling with chills, her teeth rattling. The rifle sat at her feet, which were so numb she couldn't tell if they were still attached to her body. She could barely see the man just three feet ahead of her, rowing rhythmically at the front. The coiling mist obscured everything and cloaked them in cold and damp. The only sounds were ice chunks dully knocking against the body of the boat and the slosh of the oars as the man pulled them deftly through the water.

The weight of the situation pressed onto Alistair now that she was on the water. This could've been the person that first took her when she was a kid, and she had no idea where he was taking her now. She had a gun she had no idea how to use, and he had power she wouldn't be able to overcome if it came to it. If she tried to turn back now, there was nothing but deep, wet death waiting for her. She couldn't turn back. Answers were on the other side of the fog. The inevitable conclusion of her story. Maybe even the little red house, warm, and set on a hill, or a nestled valley, waiting for her beyond the cold dark path.

What she'd give to see the fox right now.

Alistair realized her rush of confidence after the crash was because it would've been the perfect conclusion. She'd bested the enemy on their own turf, using tools she'd been given by an unexpected mentor, skills she'd never understood or been able to utilize until the time was right. Until she'd grown. It felt like the end of the hero's journey. The end of her Act Three. But now there was a man, a gun, a boat, a book, and the promise of a surprise Act Four that she hadn't anticipated.

Nothing good ever happens in a surprise Act Four.

Alistair bowed her head, huddled so forcefully she felt like she might collapse in on herself. She clamped her eyes shut, giving them brief relief from the cold. When she opened them, she noticed some kind of oil or paint splatter inside the boat. Black and frozen solid. It ran half the length of the boat's rim on the left side, and at some point, it had dribbled down the edge into the curve of the hull before freezing. The more she looked, the more she saw. Splashed against the dark green paint of the boat's hull, she found black smudges, splatters, hints of handprints. She reached out, scratching at the frozen substance with her fingernail. It was only black when plastered against the boat's dark paint. It was, in fact, red.

A fire began to smolder in her thumping chest, spreading out through her veins. The useful but sick-inducing fire of adrenalized fear. Alistair scanned the interior of the hull. It was half covered in the frozen fluid. She knew what it was but couldn't bring herself to think the word. Couldn't bring herself to think who it had once belonged to, or where they'd ended up.

Beyond the fog probably. Like her. On to Act Four.

She looked up at the man's back and gasped at the sudden sight of a towering, black immensity rushing out of the fog toward them. The boat came to a sudden crunching stop as they made land. The fog peeled away from the edges of a narrow, pebbled shore and the wide, boundless thick of dark trees beyond it.

The island.

Alistair curled her fingers into fists, hiding the specks of red she'd scratched away, not wanting him to see that she knew. The caretaker waded back into the black water, and in one quick motion pulled her out by the shoulders onto the shore. Her body was trembling and numb, burning and frozen, seething with adrenaline and crippled with cold. He vice-gripped her by the arm. Now that she was on the island, his demeanor didn't matter, she thought. There was nowhere for her to go, no way to resist. And in the shock of it all she never had a chance to grab the gun.

He rushed her under the heavy canopy of trees. She was too tired, too sick with fear to fight him. She had to get her bearings, figure out a plan, remember where they'd left the boat. They moved so quickly she could barely register what she was seeing around them. The trees were dripping with objects of all kinds. The path was lined with them too. Clothing, books, baubles, bottles. Hanging on limbs, fluttering in winter-shorn underbrush, even embedded in the bark of thick, black tree trunks. Like it had all washed up in some giant storm. This was the place Marjory had told her about— the place where everything lost ends up.

The caretaker brought her to a small clearing on the far edge of the island, water on either side beyond the packed, snow-scattered earth. A small shack sat crooked at the far brim of the clearing. Alistair's legs went weak. A wave of dread slammed into her at the sight of the building. It was no bigger than her apartment, a glorified shed really, its windows giving away nothing but black inside. And Alistair knew, somewhere in the similarly black recesses of her shattered memory, that she had been inside it before.

He dragged her toward it, her feet scraping behind her. A heavy wooden crossbar lay across the door of the shed, secured by plates of iron that had been bolted to the doorframe. The caretaker tossed the crossbar aside with one hand and threw open the door, shoving her inside. She collapsed onto the creaking wood floor of the dark, dank room. She didn't look back but heard him close the door between them, barricade it, and then she heard his boots as they stomped across the clearing, back into the woods.

Alistair.

She didn't move for a long time. The flicker of fire she'd had in her belly had gone cold. She felt like her body might freeze solid and fuse to the floor, like the blood in the hull of the boat. Her eyes adjusted to the dark and she watched the last sliver of gray sunlight creep across the floorboards.

There was a bed frame in the corner with a lumpy mattress and a pile of old blankets tossed on top. A narrow fireplace on the wall opposite the shed's front door. Two securely boarded-up windows flanked the fieldstone chimney. A pile of firewood and kindling crouched in a dark corner. More boards battened holes where the walls of the shed had given way over time. Alistair lay her weary eyes on all of it, unsure what she would find, but also somehow certain she'd seen it all before.

Alistair.

She couldn't just lie there. She needed to move, get out of her wet boots and socks. She needed to start a fire, the actual literal fire, and get warm. She needed heat if she was going to think her way through the next steps and what they wanted with her. She pried herself up from the floor, pushing her boots off with fingers she couldn't feel. Her socks were soaked, the skin of her toes warped and peeling. If it wasn't frostbite, it would be soon. She crawled to the hearth of the fireplace on her hands and knees, unable to stand now that she had offered momentary relief to her tortured feet. Did the book say that she was going to lose her toes?

Alistair grabbed a few sheets of the old vellumy typewriter paper set on top of the firewood, and the matchbox that kept them from fluttering away in the drafts of the old shed. She balled them up and placed them in the mouth of the fireplace. Though she had no memory of ever starting a fire, this felt familiar to her, almost rote. She knew you started little and worked your way up to full-blown firewood. Her shaking hands fumbled to pull a match out of the damp box. It took several matches and dozens of strikes before one caught. The paper crackled as the sheets began to burn. Alistair added strips of bark from the woodpile, and eventually they caught too. The meager heat hurt at first, especially at the tips of her aching fingers. But pain was better than nothing. It meant nerves were still working. She couldn't let the cold take hold. She wasn't done.

She eventually managed a blaze of kindling in the hearth and carefully set three split pieces of wood around it, hoping the fire would spread to them. In time, it did. She pulled herself onto the low hearth and huddled against the heat with her knees to her chest. The room began to glow, faintly, but enough to better see the edges and dark corners. No fox waiting in the shadow. Only the incessant whisper of her name from somewhere unseen. Just outside the window, or down the flue, or under the bed. She couldn't pinpoint the source.

She spotted more firewood beside the front door, and another window to the left of the door. The light she'd followed on the floor was flickering through the boarded-up window and broken glass in it. That was west. Where the sun was about to set. There were three shelves on the otherwise blank southern wall holding what looked like canned goods. She couldn't imagine eating right now, but if her body ever soaked up enough heat, she might actually need to—

Alistair.

—consume something. Drink something. She was so thirsty. Nauseated. Her feet sizzling with the current of damaged nerves.

The bed was small, and the mound of blankets looked threadbare and moldering in the growing glow, but they also looked incredibly inviting, given her condition.

She could wiggle her toes, though it hurt terribly. She cowered close to the hearth, drinking in the waves of warmth down to her bones, careful not to get too close. She still couldn't fully feel her extremities and might burn herself without realizing.

Alistair, where are you?

A question now, not just her name. The voice was like ice water pushing back against the heat. Every time it whispered, the warmth recoiled. It feared the voice too. Alistair wanted to get into that bed, under the covers, and sleep for days, her fate be damned. She wondered if she could move the bed closer to the fire, close enough to drive the pressing cold away. Once she could move her fingers and actually *feel* them moving, she decided to try. She pushed herself to her feet, pain crisscrossing up her body like lightning bolts. She shouldn't be walking on them. Not yet. Just get to the bed. Get under the covers.

She hobbled over, grabbing a knob on the old iron frame. She was too weak to move it. She would have to leave it where it was. Just get under the blankets and hope the fire stayed lit. She grabbed at the mound of blankets to pull them back—

And realized that there was already someone in the bed.

Alistair felt what little warmth she'd absorbed flush out of her. Her hand was frozen on what she now realized was someone's body. She stood on burning feet, stinging fingers still touching whoever was hidden underneath the covers.

Alistair.

As the firelight grew, she could see the blankets moving. The subtle rise and fall of someone breathing. Not dead, only asleep. Or hiding. She waited for them to leap up from the mattress, but they didn't move. Alistair clenched her fingers around the blankets and began to creep them downward from the head of the bed. She had to know who she'd been locked away with.

A thatch of dark, wavy hair. The face of a man underneath, deathly blue, crusted with blood and dirt, but breathing. A thick, filthy beard framed his face.

Alistair couldn't believe what she was seeing, sure she was hallucinating again.

Even still, she called to him, her voice so ragged she didn't recognize it.

"Ben—" she whispered.

❦

Ignore the voice. Keep the fire going.

A clear mind. Warmth. That's what she needed, what he needed from her if he was going to survive. Water too. If he ever woke up.

Alistair had twisted open quart jars of preserved fruit in the hours after she found Ben in bed. Dark berries with thick, tart flesh. She ate a little to keep herself sharp but saved the liquid, the sweet syrup, for Ben. He would need fluids. That's always the first thing they do. Doctors. Hospitals. They give hurt people fluids.

He needed a doctor. They needed help.

Alistair perched on the hearth, watching him, waiting for every slow, labored breath to lift his belly so she knew he was alive. She'd dried her boots and socks at the fire while she waited. Her toes were torn and savaged, but intact. She'd gritted through the sick-inducing pain when she squeezed her raw feet back into the shrunken boots. She might need to run, or climb, or kick. She had to be ready for

364

anything, because no matter what, she was not letting Ben Kriminger die. Not again.

When she found him in the bed she'd yelled for the caretaker through the boarded front window, but he never came. She'd tried to force the door open, but it was barred tight. Same with the windows. There was no way out. Or maybe there was, and Alistair just couldn't see it. She ached to sleep, to prime her mind, reboot her senses, but she couldn't. Something might happen to him if she did.

Alistair, where are you?

Right here. In the shed. Waiting for Ben to wake up. The more she focused on him, the easier it was to drown out the voice haunting her. She tried to check Ben's head, his body, but darkness fell too fast that first night, and even in the firelight she couldn't see more than flickering glimpses of massive black bruises and blood. So she sat at the hearth and talked to him. Told him they knew what was going to happen, the caretaker, the writer, the book. She and Ben were both supposed to be here. They needed them both for some reason. He was going to be okay, because it didn't make sense for him to die here, not with her.

It wouldn't make a good story.

She watched morning come. A break in the roof made way for gentle snowfall to accumulate in the corner of the room. Alistair gathered it, melted it in one of the jars she'd emptied, and used it on the corner of a blanket to clean Ben's face. She was too scared to touch the wound at the back of his head, which had melded with the pillow. In the first light, she could see the blood under the skin of his chest.

He might never wake up.

Alistair.

Ignore it. No one was there. No one was coming.

"Alistair . . ."

Not the fox this time. Alistair knelt at the edge of the bed. Ben was whispering.

"I'm here, Ben. Can you hear me?"

"Alistair ..."

Alistair.

"It's me. I'm right here. It's gonna be okay. I'm gonna get you help, don't worry."

Alistair failed to choke back tears.

"Alistair Mead," Ben said, his voice trailing off.

He wasn't calling for her. He was still asleep, dreaming about a girl in a book.

Alistair, where are you?

Three dark, windless days had passed. Alistair thought she might need to tell a paramedic how long Ben had been asleep, or how long he'd gone without eating, so she used a stone from the fireplace and made hash marks on a piece of plywood nailed to the southern wall of the shed. Three days, almost four. She was the Count of Monte Cristo, counting her days.

She'd read somewhere it took three days to succumb to dehydration. In the moments Ben would stir, or mumble, she made him drink, hoping the sugary syrup was enough to keep him hydrated and fed. He choked the first few times, and she thought he would drown, but then, maybe becoming more aware of her presence, he began to drink. She cried over him the first time. Cried until she finally fell asleep beside him in the bed, spent.

He moved his leg in the middle of the night. That, too, sent her over the emotional edge. His body was working. He wasn't completely shattered by the fall, by Marjory. There was hope. She was scared to touch him, unsure what was broken. She took his socks off the next morning and warmed them next to the fire. When they'd cooled a little, she slid them back onto his pale feet. She didn't know if he could feel it, if he was aware of the small comfort, but it was all she could do. He wouldn't be here, broken, if it wasn't for—

Alistair.

She had to stay there with him, stay sharp. Drown it out. She couldn't get lost in her memories again, even though she could feel their pull, dragging her into the dark. No. She had to stay here, now. She couldn't slip back to whatever happened in the shed the last time she was here. She mumbled her mantra. She planned how she would get help if she could get out of the shed, to the boat, back across the lake. She recited poems from Edgar Allen Poe. She talked to Ben.

The front door of the shed slammed open, stopping Alistair's heart for a moment. The caretaker dumped a stack of firewood and kindling by the door and stepped back outside, pulling the door toward him. Alistair leapt off the hearth and rushed him, grabbing the door before he could lock them in again. "He's going to die if we don't get him help!"

The man loomed over her.

"Why did you bring him here?!" She screamed up to his face.

"The writer said to bring him here." His face devoid of expression.

"Why?"

"The book said."

"The book—And then what? What am I supposed to do?!"

"You are here to remember." The man looked at Ben. "He is here for you."

He pulled at the door, and try as she might, Alistair couldn't hold it open against his brute force. She heard him bar it again. She screamed at him through the door, "What happens if I can't remember?!"

"Alistair . . ." Ben mumbled in his sleep.

Alistair.

Alistair.

Alistair, where are you?

She knocked her forehead against the door, barely able to catch her breath. "It's okay, Ben. I'm right here."

"Okay. But—where's here?" Ben whispered.

Chapter 31

Alistair sat with crisscrossed legs on the bed next to Ben, who was now mostly awake and relatively coherent. He had no idea how he'd gotten to the island. No memory of the woods or the lake or the boat.

Alistair had an open jar of berries in her lap. She reached in and pulled a berry out for Ben, placing it at his pale lips.

Alistair, where are you?

Alistair nervously blinked against the now ever-present voice in her head, "You can move your legs and your left arm. That's probably good news for your spine, right?"

"Right," Ben answered, chewing, his voice not much more than a sandpapery croak.

"You *can* move your right arm, but there's something wrong at the shoulder. Also, probably broken ribs, which maybe is all the bruising and pain, along with hitting the asphalt. But you can breathe, it just hurts—"

"A lot."

"So, no collapsed lungs, probably. Maybe."

"Right," Ben answered, taking another berry Alistair fed him.

"The back of your head is—not good, but it's not bleeding anymore, and you're awake, so I'm gonna vote concussion, not brains pouring out of your skull."

"I second that vote, very much."

"Then we have . . . your pelvis."

"Yeah."

"It's broken, definitely," Alistair said.

"If I . . . try to move at all, it sounds like Rice Krispies and feels like I'd rather be dead."

"Yeah, pelvises should definitely not sound like anything. But basic body functions are still okay though, so that's a plus."

"Thank God for mason jars," Ben said with a grim smile. "It's kind of unbearable, Alistair. The pain."

Just saying it, she could hear the flutter in his voice. The threat of him being swept away in the fear and physical torture.

"I know, I'm sorry," was all she could manage to say in response.

Ben stared at the ceiling, wheezing quietly, while Alistair watched the late light flickering in the window by the door.

"Okay," she continued with a nod. "Okay. That just means I'm going to have to bring help here. To you. I'll find a way out of the shed, I'll take the boat, I'll find somebody, and I'll bring them back. Easy."

"Easy," Ben answered. "Except for the gollum wandering the island who probably already knows that's the plan."

"He was *there*," Alistair muttered to herself, realizing, "In the park. I saw him go to you in the road. He was waiting under the bridge."

"So he's a troll, not a gollum."

"I . . . thought you were dead," Alistair interrupted, ignoring his joke, her voice catching.

"I mean, give me a few days—"

"Ben . . ."

"I'm sorry. I joke in times of stress."

"Here, drink," she said as she tipped the jar to his lips. When he was finished, she drank a little too. "Cheers," she said and put the jar back in her lap. "So . . . how the hell do you outsmart someone who already knows what you're going to do?"

"I'm sure if it wasn't for the concussion, I would have an answer to that."

"They want me to remember something. He said it's why they brought me back here."

"You think he means—"

"The memento. He must. How else could I remember? I just don't get it. If they want me to find it, why the hell did he lock me in here? Why the holding pattern?"

"And if *The Book of Briars* says you find it, then why don't they use the book to find it *themselves?*"

"I don't know—unless . . . they don't know either."

"What do you mean?" Ben asked.

"Maybe they only know I'm supposed to be here. And you're supposed to be with me. What if the writer doesn't know what happens next, or doesn't know yet? Ben, what if *The Book of Briars* isn't finished?"

"Holy shit," he whispered.

Alistair, where are you?

Alistair wrenched her shoulders up close to her ears at the sound of the whisper.

"The voice?" Ben asked.

"It's fine."

Alistair was finally bowing under the full, desperate weight of the situation, and she knew Ben was feeling it too. She felt helpless, he *was* helpless.

"We're at the end," Ben whispered.

"Hey. No. Don't say that."

"I mean *narratively.* We're coming full circle. This is how we started *The Book of Briars.* Trapped in a little room, locked away from the world. In pain. Alone."

"You're not alone," Alistair corrected, "*We're* not alone."

"Ooh. Character development."

They both smiled and shared weary little laughs. Ben grimaced. He took several shallow, panting breaths, tears brimming in his eyes.

They listened to the fire crackle for a while as his flush of pain settled. Alistair noticed the berries had stained the ends of her fingers. At the edge of the blue-black stain, she found what looked like a typed letter G, and she found a word running down the back of her index finger.

threshold

It must have come off the old newspaper the caretaker left for kindling. Except it would've been backwards if it had—

"What happened to Veronica?" Ben asked.

"I don't know."

"She's tough, so . . ." Ben whispered.

"True."

Alistair offered Ben a berry, but he declined with a small shake of his head. She put the lid back on the jar.

Alistair could see the anguish just behind his eyes. Everything hurt, inside and out. She'd been dealt her own brutal blows, but her body wasn't broken into a thousand pieces. She could see him succumbing to the desperation.

"Why were *you* locked away?" Alistair asked.

"What?"

"You said we started the story locked away? Was it Cor? The breakup?" Alistair asked. She wanted to take his mind off his plight, even if it meant dredging up bad memories. Bad was all they had at the moment, but he needed distraction.

"The . . . breakup was more of a by-product, though I very recently learned it was kind of deeper than that. It's kind of a part of this, in a weird way. I wrote a book about people like you. Like . . . the Six, Veronica. People who disappeared. Some readers got kind of weird about it. Now I know why, but at the time there was this guy. Frank. From Maryland. A doctor. A dad. He was obsessed with the book. He wouldn't leave us alone, Cor and me. Calling us nonstop, sending deranged letters, showing up outside the apartment, outside Cor's job, following us everywhere. Begging for me to tell him "the truth." We called the police so many times. It got worse and worse, and we were worried he would do something drastic, to himself, or to us. But there was nothing the cops could do unless he outright threatened us. It got to where we were scared to leave the house. Scared to answer our phones. Living in constant fear and it was breaking us down. Then it all stopped. He just vanished. We were looking over our shoulders for months before we finally started to think things might be normal again. Then he broke in. I was gone. He hurt her. Cut her arm open to make me tell him what I knew. He thought I knew what happened to "the real world." He locked her in the bathroom, bleeding. I didn't know if she was dead or alive, and he wouldn't let me go to her. Wouldn't let me get help. He just kept begging me to tell him the truth. But I didn't know anything. I'd just made it all up."

Tears streamed from Ben's upturned eyes, trickling down the sides of his wounded face. Alistair wiped them for him.

"I've never told anyone this," he said in a choked whisper.

Alistair wanted to tell him he didn't have to go on, but it was obvious he needed to get it out, painful as it was. He'd been saddled with other people's stories for so long, including her own, she couldn't bear to stop him, even if he was telling her because he didn't think he was going to—

"I tried to go to Cor, but he had this knife. This crazy sharp knife. He said he'd kill her. It was hours. I barely remember. Just . . . screaming. Crying. Begging. Both of us. And Cor's blood all over the living room floor where she'd been sitting when he broke in. Then Frank said it. 'What if life itself is a lie?' Just like Marjory said. Like, it didn't matter if Cor was dead or alive because *none* of this was real. And it got me thinking. How I could get us out of that apartment, Cor and me. A lie. A story. I mean, I was a writer. I knew what he wanted to hear. I could tell him a story where I *did* know the truth. Where I *could* see pieces of his hidden world, but not completely. A story where . . . only people who *die* get to really see the truth. I—I told him it would be okay, because life was a lie, like he said, and death uncovered the truth. I could see he wanted to believe me. So I kept talking. I kept telling this story. Giving him everything he wanted. And I convinced him. Told him it was all going to be okay. Told him I wrote the book to call people like him to me, and someday we'd all be on the other side where it was true and full of wonder. He was so scared. I told him we could go together. I'd make sure he crossed over, and then I'd follow him. I told him—I told him that I hoped Cor had already gone ahead of us."

Ben lay there, silent, as the sun set in the window by the door.

"He put the knife to his neck, but he couldn't do it. So—so I helped him. I put my hand on his hand. I felt this flood of rage when I did. I wanted to kill him. He'd made our lives hell. He hurt Cor. I— I don't remember who moved the knife first, how hard I pushed—it all just went white, but I remember when it was done and the look in his eyes when he knew that I'd lied to him. I just ran to Cor. I never looked back."

Silence swallowed them both as they sat together in the light of the snapping fire.

"So, there's my absolution. For what it's worth."

"You saved her, Ben." Alistair said.

"No. I wanted him dead. I wanted to let the anger in me out. I killed him."

Alistair bowed her head, not sure what to say. Then something occurred to her.

"No, you didn't. People who kill can't use magic. You did magic, on the bridge, to save me. You couldn't have done that if you'd killed him."

"That was Veronica."

"That was *you*. You said the word. You built the walls."

Ben took a long, rattling breath and sighed, fresh tears rambling down the sides of his upturned face. "She knew. Veronica. She told me—that last night. She told me I was a good man."

"Well, I'll always bet on Veronica Morrow being right."

They smiled at each other and Alistair took his hand.

❦

Ben couldn't keep his eyes open, but Alistair didn't want to let him sleep. She kept talking, longer than she thought she was capable of talking, but in the end, the pain and exhaustion were overwhelming, and Ben finally closed his eyes against it all.

She tried to wake him up later to drink, but he was unresponsive. She watched him as long as she could. Then when she couldn't keep her own eyes open, she crawled into bed beside him, to share her warmth, to feel him breathe. To be with him if—

Alistair, where are you?

A loud, sharp sound made Alistair shudder and her eyes flick open. She wasn't sure if she'd dreamed the sound or not. Something like a distant door slamming. Or a gunshot. It was dark in the room, but she could see her own breath in the glow of moonlight slicing in from the window. The fire must have died while she slept. Her back was pressed against Ben, under the blankets. She could feel his labored breathing.

Alistair, where are you?

She had to get the fire going again before the embers died, if they hadn't already. She gently slid out from under the blankets. The room was freezing. The fire had gone out hours ago.

She quietly rounded the bed in her socks, toward the fireplace, brushing her hair out of her face, when she felt something wet and sticky at her temple. More on her ear. Even in the dark, she knew what it was.

Blood. Not hers.

Alistair.

She went back to Ben and checked his pillow, careful not to

wake him. It was wet. The wound at the back of his head was bleeding again. It could mean anything, she thought. Maybe he broke open the wound in his sleep, or maybe more fluids in his body meant more fluids leaking out. Or brain swelling, or internal bleeding, or—

Stop.

She whispered, "Ben?"

Alistair.

He didn't answer. She didn't want him to, really. She wanted him to sleep. Heal. Wake up better. But a thousand bad things could happen at any moment and her chronicle of his ailments was probably incomplete, definitely uninformed. If she was honest, the list was nothing more than a way to keep them both calm in the face of a grave situation that neither of them could remedy.

Fire. She could do fire. She turned to the fireplace and froze at the sight of something draped in black, crouched on the mantel above the hearth. It was watching her with pinpoint eyes like shining beads. It then unfurled two black wings, spreading them out on either side before they came to rest again.

A bird.

Alistair heard a gentle clacking.

"Eat," said a whisper coming from the dark.

"What?" Alistair whispered back, half a question, half a response of complete shock.

"Berries," answered the whisper in the dark.

"You want—" She stopped herself, realizing for a second that she was talking with a bird, before, "You want something to eat?"

The bird spread its impressive wings again.

"Okay. Um—okay."

Alistair went to the wall lined with jars, pulled one down, and unscrewed it. She was about to offer it to the bird, but instead set it on the floor near the hearth.

The bird leapt down to the jar, pecking ravenously at its

contents, digging its face into the depths of the jar. Alistair could see in the moonlight that it was a glossy black crow.

It feasted until there was nothing left but syrupy liquid. The crow clacked its beak, preened its feathers, then looked up at her.

"Good," the crow said, its voice was a barky simulation of human speech, but completely understandable, and louder now that it had eaten.

Alistair crouched where she was standing. "You're Ben's bird. The one that helped him."

The crow clacked its beak, nodding in response.

"You flew all the way back here?" She asked quietly, as Ben took a deep, rasping breath, then settled.

"Help," the crow answered, lowering its volume to match Alistair's.

"You need help? Or you came to help Ben."

"Yes." The bird clacked its beak, pecking at the jar.

"You want more?" Alistair asked.

The bird nodded its little head up and down. Alistair went to the shelf, unscrewed another jar, and set it down. The bird emptied the second jar as quickly as the first.

"Not write. Book."

"What? The book? *The Book of Briars?*"

The crow nodded up and down and did a little shuffle with its feet.

"Not write. You mean it isn't finished?" Alistair asked.

"You. Been. Here. Is all."

"Me. Ben. Here. Is all. That's all they know. I *knew* it."

More nodding, more shuffling from the crow.

"That's good. I just have to get to the boat. I have to get out of here and—"

The crow shook its head.

"What?" Alistair asked.

"Drown."

"I'll drown?"

"Water. Under."

"Yeah, I know drown. But I don't know—I'll drown if I—"

"Man," the crow answered with a flustered flap of its wings.

"I'm sorry. I'm trying to understand. The man, water, under, drown . . . he drowned? He'll drown me, or I'll drown if I take the boat. He . . . he drowned the boat?"

The crow nodded furiously.

"Son of a bitch. He sank it," Alistair huffed, sitting down on the floor, thinking. "The boat's out of the picture. But they don't know what happens next. If I could find a way out of this room, I could cross the lake when it freezes over, if it freezes over in time. I don't know . . . Ben's really hurt, and—I don't know if he has time—"

"Remember," the crow whispered.

Alistair.

"Toy. Thing. Hold."

"Remember the toy? Just tell me what you're trying to say, please."

"Can not."

"Okay. Okay. Remember . . . you mean the memento? Is that what you're talking about?"

The crow nodded furiously.

"They want it. If I knew where it was, maybe I could trade it to get Ben off the island. Maybe that's why he's here. They *have* to have another way off. Another boat. Or some way to call for help. But I have no idea where it is. Do you?"

The crow shook its head, then said, "What is. Can help?"

"Uh . . . well, it's a pocket watch."

"Many."

"There are a lot of pocket watches here. Got it. Yeah, of course."

Alistair rubbed her chin in thought, and the crow copied her with its wing. She rambled as she thought to herself, "I have no idea what it looks like. I know Sullivan found it in the Palace. I know he said he took it because it belonged to the Greens—"

"G," croaked the bird.

"G, yeah, Green," Alistair said.

"Saw G. Saw," the crow answered.

"You saw G? The letter? On a pocket watch?"

The crow nodded and danced.

"Sullivan knew it belonged to his family because it was monogrammed!" Alistair winced as she realized how loud she'd yelled.

The crow winced too, mimicking her.

"Can you bring it to me?" Alistair whispered.

The crow shook its head. "In the briar. No go in the briar alone."

"Why? It's stuck?"

"Man."

"The caretaker."

"Always looking. Hunt. Waiting. Watching."

"Okay. If I can get out of here, will you come with me? Show me?"

The crow flew into the air, over her head, landing on the edge of the front window's broken pane, before squeezing through it and disappearing.

"Wait," Alistair whispered, getting up and rushing to the door. "I can't get out," she whispered through the broken window.

There was a rattling racket of wood against metal, and the furious flap of wings. Then a loud *thunk* as something hit the ground outside.

Alistair grabbed the dented metal knob and pulled. The bird had unbarricaded the door. She found it just outside, proudly marching in circles with wings outstretched around the plank of wood it had just dislodged.

"*Good* bird," Alistair whispered.

She quietly squeezed into her shrunken boots and grabbed her coat off the floor. She checked Ben one more time, his wan appearance dropping a stone into her stomach. Then she stepped out into the freezing night, barred the door behind her, and followed the crow into the dark heart of the island.

֍

The air outside was frozen still. Alistair's torn coat offered next to no defense against the heavy, pressing cold. Back in the city, she would have already hung her favored coat up for the winter, opting instead for the ugly but insulated parka her aunt and uncle had bought her a few years back. The cold felt like endless needles digging slowly but effortlessly inward, straight to the bone.

Every footstep and flap of the crow's wings rang out on the otherwise silent island. The black, moonless sky loomed over them like a domed lid, spattered with endless flickering stars. It was all Alistair could see. The crow hopped down one path to the next, luring Alistair away from the shed, into deeper icy black. She had to listen for its scratching footfall or feathery flapping. She'd sometimes see a glint in the blanket of black as her weary eyes struggled to adjust, a small, inky silhouette pulling her back from the wrong path, or helping her avoid low-hanging branches. She'd never see the caretaker coming like this. She would walk right into him.

But the caretaker didn't know what would happen next. Neither did the writer. For the moment, they were as blind as Alistair was. Unless this was also part of the story and they were letting her play out these events. It didn't matter. She couldn't let that possibility stop her. Ben could die if she did.

The crow drew her into deeper, denser vegetation that brushed and scratched against her. They were going away from the water, into the center of the island.

Light ahead.

Alistair thought she imagined it at first. A flicker through a veil of bushes. Warm, golden light, which cast the countless trinkets scattered and hanging all around her into black relief. She followed the crow toward the flicker. It was an old iron and glass lantern sitting on the ground in a large clearing. And the caretaker was sitting beside it in a chair. Alistair froze. She couldn't see him, only the black edges of his body, his outline cut out like a paper silhouette by the light.

He was slumped in the chair. Still. She could fully see the crow now, just ahead of her, inching ahead, beckoning her around the bushes with a wing, into the clearing.

"Sleep," the crow whispered.

Alistair. knelt, scrambling along the path, her hands numb against the packed earth. She breached the edge of the large bramble-lined clearing and could see the caretaker was asleep just like the crow had said, his rifle in his lap.

In the low light, Alistair thought the flat ground was dotted with large, dark stones or broken paving, but as she inched closer, she could see that the clearing was strewn with the bodies of birds and other small wildlife. Alistair stopped cold at what looked like a badger at her feet. Or had been before the caretaker blew a hole through its head.

The crow hopped around the bodies, beckoning her somewhere behind the caretaker, whose chin was resting on his thick chest as he snored softly.

Alistair stepped over and around the dead animals, never taking her eyes off the man with the gun. If she woke him up, she might survive a rough-handed haul back to the shed. He needed her after all, as far as she knew, but the crow who brought her here might end up another blasted-open body on the ground. And no one else was coming here to help them.

She followed the crow into the tall, dancing shadows cast by the man in the chair, to what looked like a well-tended garden of brambles behind him. Garden implements were propped about, along with baskets of the same purple-black berries she'd been living on, countless more growing on the thorned branches all around them. The crow waited at the edge of the overgrowth, pulling back a branch with its broken beak. Finally, at the crow's side, Alistair could see just how tangled, thick, and prickled the bushes really were. Deep in the exposed growth offered by the crow, in the black soil, among a dozen other barely visible artifacts, was something small and shining. Gold maybe, or brass.

"Yesh?" the crow whispered with the branch in its beak.

"Maybe," Alistair mouthed back.

She tried to put her arm through the bramble, but the nap of her coat caught immediately on the thorns. She had to slink out of it carefully, quietly, as the crow held the obscuring branch back for her. Alistair looked back at the caretaker, watching his shoulders rise and fall, then she rolled up her sleeves, her quickened pulse pushing back the oppressive cold with fear-drenched blood. The shadow of the sleeping gollum flickering over the task at hand.

She reached into the bramble with her bare arm. The thorns were dagger-sharp and hungry, sticking in her skin, tearing at her as she reached in. She leaned forward, the thorns biting her all the way to her shoulder, her arm pushing deeper and deeper, her numb fingers barely registering what they were brushing against. The thorns were a thousand guards, pulling her back as she reached as far as she could, fingers clawing—the hint of something at their tingling tips. A vine. Or a root. Or a chain.

Alistair's head was bowed in concentration and effort, her face pressed to the edge of the bushes, and in the flickering light she could just make out the roots of the nearest berry bushes in the dirt. And the typeset letters and words climbing up the bark from the frozen soil, onto the branches, into the leaves.

F. Q. A. Falling. Meadow. Thornmouth.

Printed on every part of the bush, as if someone had pulled the plant through the bail of a typewriter.

threshold

That's where the word on her finger had come from. Not the newspaper. From the berries themselves.

The island had words growing out of the ground.

The sound of fluttering wings first snatched at Alistair's attention, but it was the thorned branch swatting down on her bare arm that finally shattered her fixation on the words. The branch the crow had been holding.

Alistair looked up at the caretaker towering over her, one of the crow's wings in his unyielding hand.

"Did you find it?" the caretaker hissed through clenched teeth, pitching the frantic crow onto the ground behind him.

"Find—what—" Alistair stammered, trying to figure out what to do.

"The memories!" he bellowed, his maniacal voice echoing across the island.

The crow leapt off the ground, digging its claws into the caretaker's neck, its wings beating at his anger-wrenched face.

The caretaker wrapped his hand around the crow's body and yanked it away from his head, ribbons of blood instantly curling down his neck. He marched back across the clearing, the crow frantically fighting in his grip, back to the lantern light, to the chair. The rifle.

Alistair instinctively lunged toward them, the thorns tearing away shreds of her exposed arm. The pain took her breath away and stopped her in her tracks.

"Please," the crow yelled out in the distance, its breath short.

It knocked Alistair out of her shock. She scramble-ran, getting to her feet when she was halfway to the caretaker and the crow. The caretaker pitched the bird into the ground and pressed a boot against its black body. He was going to crush it.

Alistair charged him, spotting the rifle in the seat of the chair, grabbing it with one arm as she howled, "Stop!"

The rifle was backwards, but she swung the stock down one-handed like a hammer into the back of the caretaker's head. He stumbled forward two steps, releasing the crow. The bird hobbled and hopped behind Alistair.

The caretaker reeled on Alistair as she fumbled to flip the rifle around with one arm limp at her side. He swatted the rifle out of her hand, almost knocking her off her feet.

"Get out of here!" she yelled back to the crow who was struggling to fly as the caretaker grabbed hold of Alistair's shoulders and slammed her into the hard-packed dirt.

"Where is it?" he spat back.

She shouted back defiant obscenities, but he'd knocked the breath out of her.

He knelt over her, grabbing her bare, bleeding arm with one hand and wrapping his other around her clenched, blood-soaked fist. She screamed, in pain, in desperation, punching him in the side and back with her free arm, unable to breathe, all the while trying to pull herself away from him as he pried her fist open to get to the memento—

And found nothing but a handful of black, sodden soil.

"He told you where to look, didn't he? DIDN'T HE?!"

Alistair couldn't answer.

The caretaker tossed her arm aside, stomping toward the bushes, pulling at the vines and branches, yanking entire plants out of the ground, digging in the dirt for the pocket watch.

Alistair couldn't move. She just watched him tear the garden apart. Her breath finally throttled back into her chest with a loud, wet gasp.

They didn't know any more than she did—at least the caretaker didn't. But he wanted the memories back so badly, Alistair had every confidence he would kill her for them if it came to it.

Unable to find the watch, the caretaker howled into his own bleeding, filthy hands and leapt back up, grabbing her by one arm and dragging her away from her coat and the crow, away from the words and the lantern light, back into the frozen dark.

She didn't know up from down. Her legs trailed behind her. She couldn't get back on her feet. He was pulling her too quickly down path after path. It wasn't until she felt the wooden *thunk* of the shed's porch under his boots that she knew where she was. He unbarred the door and dragged her through the threshold, tossing her across the floor like a bowling ball. The corner of the fireplace hearth caught her mid-back and she screamed from the pain. A twinge of embarrassment snaked through her at the sound of her own weakness. The man stood in the open doorway for a moment, nothing but a shadow in the dark. He took two steps toward Ben, who was still asleep, looking him over.

"Don't touch him . . ." Alistair hissed.

The caretaker took another step into the shed, towering over her.

"I don't care about the book, or what it says, or this island. Or you. I will tear it all apart to find the watch and the memories." The caretaker spoke calmly, quietly. "And when I find them, I'll put you both in the water. If he's still alive by then."

He turned and walked out, barring the door behind him again. A few moments later, thundering bangs began reverberating from the other side of the closed door. Alistair watched the wood of the door splinter and split in several places as the caretaker drove nails into it and the frame.

Then quiet.

Alistair listened to the man's footsteps fade, then she finally exhaled and rolled onto her stomach, writhing in pain, her right arm coated in streams of blood. She hobbled to her feet and brought kindling and wood to the dark hearth. It took a long while to start, with the damp air and her frozen, aching body, but when it finally caught, she sat at the hearth and used her other arm to reach over into her right hip pocket.

Just before she rushed to stop him from killing the crow, she'd grasped and grabbed at whatever she could.

And she'd found it. The memento.

In the firelight, Alistair could see that the pocket watch was tarnished brass, the cracked glass on the lid beveled at the edges like a cut jewel. There was a small clasp on the top, and when Alistair pressed it, the lid flipped open, allowing access to the hands and face of the watch. She tried to wind it up, but it didn't work.

She closed the lid and turned the pocket watch over with her shivering hands. On the back was an inscription to "WG" from someone initialed "IC." The inscription read:

Time enough for everything, but above all, wonder.

Alistair closed the lid, the burgeoning warmth of the fire only pulling away the numbness to reveal how much pain she was really in.

The ceiling of the shed was reflected back in the surface of the cracked lid of the watch. Strange, it would show the wooden slats above her, but not—

She held it up to her face, sure she was wrong, but no. She was not in the glass. She had no reflection.

Alistair?

She shuddered at the sound of the voice, but her attention snapped back to the reflection as something rushed past the tiny portal of glass. Alistair turned the watch one way, then another, trying to see what she thought she'd seen.

She stood, holding the watch up like a hand mirror, her own face still nowhere to be seen. But finally, on the foot of the bed, waiting, watching, she found it. The bespectacled fox. She craned her head back to see that no one was in the bed but Ben. The fox only existed in the glass. She turned back to the reflection as the fox nodded to her gently and said—

It's time.

Chapter 32

It's time.

Time didn't pass in the glass of the pocket watch. Days didn't change. It was one moment, eternally, played over and over in reverse. Alistair's last night on the island as a little girl. After this moment, she knew she followed the fox down the path. Alistair watched the glass, waiting to see what to do, where to go, unaware of just how much time had actually passed on the island. How many suns had set. Her world was now only what the pocket watch showed her, drawing her deeper and deeper into her fractured memories and one never-ending moment—Narcissus without a reflection.

Alistair.

She found the fox in glimpses; furtive peeks as it bounded behind her, darting away in surreal reverse every time she heard the voice, catching sight of its fiery fur in the cracked face of the watch. The jars of canned berries weren't there in the past, but she found origami boxes scattered on the crooked mantel of the fireplace, made from the paper she'd been given for kindling when she was a child. The first time she was on the island. The pocket watch held all the lost memories, and the longer she looked into its face, the more she recalled. It was all repeating—the island, the shed, the caretaker with his firewood, food, and kindling. Back then, just like now. Again, and again.

But not always.

As the gray light of winter dimmed and the fire faded, the reflection returned to *now*, as it was on the island and the otherwise inescapable reality of Alistair's situation. Reflections require light, so Alistair would look away long enough to build and tend a sweltering fire to douse the shed in the feverish glow, to try and catch sight of every corner as it used to be. To find the fox. Fleeting and reversed, but true.

The bed was there in Alistair's looking glass, but empty, which was better. Better to be alone here, feeling the silvery slip of her sanity as she grew more and more transfixed on the past. Sanity wasn't a cliff to which she was desperately clinging. In the glass of the pocket watch, it was a ribbon wrapped around a gift.

Pull it loose and see what waits inside.

It was far less frightening, less painful in the reflection, where Ben was not in the backward bed. In the memory realm of the watch, in the moment the fox came to the shed, Ben wasn't on the island with her. He was a teenager somewhere out there in the world, maybe just deciding he wanted to be a writer. Years before the book he'd written, and before *The Book of Briars* came to him. It was a seductive comfort to think of him somewhere in there, alive. Awake. Unbroken.

Ben never woke up after she found the watch. His consciousness had taken flight with his crow. She didn't know how many days it had been since that night, since the caretaker made his promise to her.

She'd tried to wake Ben, tried to make him drink before she lost herself in the watch. But he was unresponsive, ashen, barely breathing. He was going to die, again, at her hands. Again, and again.

But in the pocket watch, somewhere, he was safe.

It's time.

The fox in her ear, then appearing, running backwards in the glass, then gone. She ached to find him, catch him, even though every sighting brought along a feeling of dread that tugged from somewhere in the dark. Something about her newly surfaced memories was wrong. The night she disappeared. How she first came to the island. Not the memories *themselves*. They were just . . . misremembered somehow, and she couldn't work out how. No amount of time lost holding the memento and looking into its glass made it right. Again, and again, she watched the fox appear in the shed, call to her, and tell her it was time. She knew she followed the fox into the dark, to the snow-covered path. Where the thing with white claws waited, along with a way out, a way off of the island. But in the reflection, the fox could not be caught. It never led her down the path. It was all wrong. It was stuck. It was backwards.

The story was unraveling. *The Book of Briars* coming unbound. What poetic fate, growing old in the shed, Alistair's whole life spent eating black berries, ripe with words, staring into her broken mirror. She wasn't the Count of Monte Cristo. She was Miss Havisham. A cursed woman, drowning in her own memories.

Footsteps outside. Alistair retreated to a blanket by the hearth, her body crumbling to the floor, exhausted. She stuffed the watch in her pants pocket and listened for the caretaker. She'd heard him since their altercation in the garden, passing by the shed, stomping through the underbrush, looking for the watch.

He wouldn't find it, but eventually the writer would know Alistair had, and she'd hear those footsteps just outside the door. But this time, the footsteps faded, disappearing down a path somewhere.

A whistling, winter wind had finally arrived, singing through the gaps in the shed walls. Contrasting eddies of hot and cold undulated across her skin. Her legs were shaking from pacing the shed. Her arm ached from holding up the watch. She needed to sleep. Rest her mind. Maybe then the memories would right themselves. She slid her hand into her pocket, holding the watch in her palm, and her eyes fluttered closed in seconds.

She heard a sound as she slipped into the dark of sleep, distant but distinct amidst the crackle of the fire and the whistle of the wind.

A *clacking* sound, again, and again. She recognized what it was the longer it went on, but by the time it had finally dawned on her, she had already been swept away in the current of her dreams.

Typewriter keys.

The writer was writing again.

She felt like she'd only just closed her eyes, but her body felt rested and light when she woke. The fire was still burning. The windows were slowly letting in the light of the cold winter sun. More light sifted down through a crack in the roof of the shed.

Had that been there the night before?

She followed the jagged hole to the edge of the wall where she saw that someone was in the shed with her, looking out the front window, in silhouette. She flinched, grasping for the watch. It was gone.

They knew. They took it.

"It's okay," the man at the window said, without looking back.

"Ben?" Alistair whispered.

Ben looked back to her; even in shadow, she could see the warm smile behind his beard.

"How— I'm dreaming," she realized.

Ben nodded, "Maybe? After I fell asleep, I could hear you. I could still think, but everything hurt so much it was like my mind refused to go back. Then something happened. I ended up here a while ago. It's not quite dreaming, whatever it is. Maybe I'm dying. Maybe this is where you go when you go."

Alistair got off the floor, Ben's face fading into view as she approached the window. They stood at it together in the gray light, looking at each other.

"But I'm here too," she said.

She looked out at the swirling mist beyond the window. The fog cleared for a moment, revealing a long path leading away, lined with tall thin trees. Then it curled closed again.

"That's not the island," Alistair said.

"No. I don't know what it is. *Where* it is. I tried to go out there, but the door won't open. Sometimes I hear voices, but they're too far away.

Alistair could see that the panes of glass in the window were beveled at their edges, cut like jewels.

"Were they always like this?" She asked as she ran her finger along the glass.

"I don't remember."

"This feels—"

"Weird?" Ben asked.

"Familiar."

"But you've never been here."

"What do you—"

She looked back and found herself in a room she'd never seen before. A broken fireplace, cold and black. A recliner in the middle of the room, with nothing but the glow of an old space heater to light it. And sheets of paper scattered across the floor. She knelt and picked up a page.

"I thought Alistair was a boy's name," the lanky train conductor mumbled with a smug underbite smile as he checked Alistair's state ID and scanned the digital ticket on her phone. Alistair pointed at the chunky headphones she was wearing. She wasn't listening to music, but he didn't need to know that."

"Is this your cabin?" Alistair asked.

"Yeah. I've been here awhile. I even started rereading the chapters."

"But we're still in the shed—"

As the words left her lips, a shadow passed over the room, and when it was gone, the shed on the island had taken the cabin's place.

"Wow," Ben muttered, looking around the changed room.

Alistair stood. The sheet of paper now gone from her hand.

"It's like when Marjory had me locked in my memory."

"Do you think she's here?"

Alistair looked back to the window, to the bevels at the edges of the glass. Then to the roof, and the long, jagged opening in it. Just like the glass in the—

"I think this is the watch."

"The what?"

"The memento."

"You found it?"

"Yeah. Your crow was here."

"I *thought* I heard him."

"He came to help you. He took me to the watch. The longer I hold it, the more I remember. I can even see a memory in the glass. Backward, but . . . something must have happened when I fell asleep."

Alistair thought for a moment, then said to herself, "The caretaker was sleeping in the garden. Maybe dreams get mixed up with memories when you're near the watch. Maybe that's why he's so crazed about it."

"They think that might be what dreams are, actually," Ben said. "Our brain's way of processing memories. What to remember—"

"What to forget," Alistair said.

Alistair.

"Is that what *you're* trying to forget? The voice?" Ben asked.

"You heard it?"

"Yeah."

"I can't make sense of it." Alistair said. She saw an apprehension in Ben's eyes. "What?"

"It's what you left behind," Ben said reluctantly.

"What does that mean?"

"I've been thinking, remembering, I guess. That's all there really is to do here. That's what Bolden told you the night in the gallery, when we met. She said there was something you left behind."

They were suddenly back in Ben's cabin again.

Ben walked around the recliner in the middle of the room. "Why me? That's what I keep asking. Why, of all people, me? I'm nobody, but they wanted *me* here. Or . . . there. On the island. The book said I had to be here with you, *for* you. But I'm dying. Obviously. So . . . unless it's now, here, in this place that I matter, what was the point of any of it?"

"You're not going to die. I can still get you out of here. I just have to remember—"

"But you can't remember. Not until—I need you to listen to me, okay? No matter how hard it is." Ben picked up a handful of stray pages from the floor. "If they had this whole book about us, why were they only supposed to send me a few chapters, out of sequence, to start it all? Why not everything they had? What made these chapters different?"

Alistair shook her head.

"What color socks did you wear the day you went to the house on the Hudson?"

"I . . . have no idea," Alistair answered, not following.

"Neither do I. You probably wore socks, but that wasn't in the chapter because it didn't matter. That's what writers do. We take the important parts, the parts that mean something, that support characters or narrative, and we weave them through the story, hiding them, and cutting out things that don't matter—paying off things that do. People do that with memories too, now that I think about it. The point is, those chapters mattered."

"I'm not following."

"Your aunt at dinner, with Zev."

"What about her?"

"She couldn't remember your name."

"She was drunk."

"The train conductor. What did he say?"

"The—I don't know."

"You just read it. You know what he said."

"So what? It doesn't matter."

"Exactly. So why keep it in the book? What about how you secretly wished to be someone else, someone with a different name."

Alistair bristled. "That's personal."

Ben approached her.

"I know. I'm sorry. But why is it in the book? Why would the pages they sent me point out your name every time? That it didn't fit or didn't belong, or they couldn't remember what you were called? Or you didn't want it. I—I have nothing to offer this story but the fact that I'm a writer. Even if I never write another word, it's what I am. That's why I'm here. That's why I'm in the book. A writer would wonder why someone would leave these loose threads hanging unless they'd all be important later. Unless those moments were going to make something down the line make sense, make something surprising, but inevitable. Just like Zev said."

Alistair turned away as the cabin became her apartment above the Chinese restaurant. Alistair and Zev's clothes still littered the floor.

"There's plenty of things in books that don't mean anything. We both know that."

"No one remembered the books but *her*. Not *Alistair*, just 'her.'"

"So what?!" Alistair yelled, turning back on him, pain and anger she couldn't explain spilling over.

"It all means something. It all leads somewhere," Ben said.

"This isn't a book."

"Yeah, you've said that already, but . . . it is. Didn't you wonder why Marjory taunted you about the fox? About not knowing what it was? Why Bolden tried to keep her from telling you?"

"I—I don't know."

"I think you do. I think part of you has known since you got here, at least. Since you started hearing that voice again. I think you lost more than a year's worth of memory on the island, but you can't bring yourself to remember what it was you lost."

The room fell dark for a moment, and when the shadows withdrew again, the sunlight outside the room was gone. Alistair approached the window and outside she found a sidewalk leading away through a quiet suburban neighborhood, which stretched off into the night. A nearby streetlight flickered on. Ben approached, looking over her shoulder.

"What is this?" Ben asked.

"It's New Jersey," Alistair answered with a sigh. She looked over to a compact two-story home across the street—one light beaming back from a second-floor room.

"That's the house I grew up in. With my mom, my dad, and—and me. Before I disappeared. Before they died. I couldn't remember what it looked like, and then once I found the watch—it just came to me. I can almost remember this night. The night I disappeared. But what I remember . . . is wrong. It's memories and made-up things overlapping, like I don't want to see it. I don't know why I remember things that no one else does, but . . . there's something here—that I won't let myself remember." Alistair leaned into the windowsill. She couldn't take her eyes off the light in the upstairs window. "No one took me, Ben. I left home that night on my own. But not alone. Not exactly. I was following someone."

"Who?" Ben asked.

Alistair put a finger to the glass, pointing down to the sidewalk, where the fox was waiting.

"Him. He's not a figment of my imagination. He's a memory, hiding in a fairy tale."

The fox sat on the sidewalk and tilted its head, listening, waiting. Its cracked and crooked glasses glinted in the light of the streetlamp.

"Who are you?" Alistair whispered, her breath fogging the windowpane.

"Alistair," the fox said. *Not in Alistair's head, but there, beyond the window. From the fox's own mouth.*

Alistair stepped away, startled, her legs buckling under her before Ben could catch her. She collapsed, hitting the hearth of the fireplace instead of the floor of Ben's cabin. Back in the shed again.

"The truth was always in that dark place. That's where I put it."

Alistair took several deep breaths, just trying to get out the words. "It hurt too much to remember. He could've been anything, but I made him a fox. Memory, transposed."

Alistair looked into Ben's eyes, saw her pain reflected back. "The voice isn't calling me. It *is* me. It's always been me. I just couldn't bear to remember . . . I'm not—I'm not—"

Ben took her hand and said what she couldn't. "You're not Alistair."

Alistair shook her head and answered, "No, I'm not."

She folded in on herself, grief thundering over her.

Ben wrapped his arms around her, and through a wash of tears, she saw the fox over Ben's shoulder, sitting on the bed with his crooked glasses.

She held out her hand—

The fox hopped down and nuzzled its nose under her palm.

"I followed him here that night. I lost him here. And when I came home . . . no one remembered my brother but me."

The fox rested his fuzzy chin in her hand.

"His name was all I could say. When they found me. It's all I said for a year."

Alistair.

"But no one else remembered him. So . . . I lied. I put him in a box, with the books, in the dark. When they asked me who Alistair was, I told them it was *my* name now. And eventually, I forgot too. Everything except his glasses," Alistair said, smiling down at the fox's face.

Something caught the fox's attention, its head turning to the shed's south-facing wall, to the corner closest to the fireplace. He walked over, sniffing the floor, then he crouched and started digging at the planks below a chunk of boarded-up wall.

Watching him, Alistair felt bristling chills begin to swirl up her spine. A memory surfacing out of the depths, amorphous and dim, but rising slowly to the surface. She stood up from the hearth, watching the fox paw at the floor. She turned back to the fireplace, to the stack of gray stones that formed the chimney.

"I remember . . ." she muttered as Ben stood with her. "The night we left. That's why I kept seeing him, over and over. We'd been planning our escape. He'd been sneaking out to the shed for weeks."

"From where?"

"From the house. There's a house on the island. That's where he led me. That's where I have to go." She looked to Ben. "But if I wake up, you're—"

"Listen . . . Alis," Ben eked out a sad little smile. *"Alis and the Looking Glass.* I think I did what I was here to do."

"No. No more character arcs. Just . . ." she looked up at the shed window, the faceted glass around its edges. *"Through* the looking glass. It's a window."

"What is?"

"The pocket watch. The past. I've been looking at it the wrong way. It's not a mirror."

"I wish I could write that down," Ben said, conjuring up a turn of phrase. *"The past can't tell you who you are. But it can show you where to go. It isn't a mirror. It's a window."*

Alistair woke up on the floor of the shed. It was still night. Nothing was left of the fire she'd built but embers. She reached down to check that the watch was still in her pocket, then pulled herself off the floor, still wrung out from days lost in the reflection of the watch. She went to Ben's side, struggling against the pain to kneel next to him. His breathing was labored, skin icy and gray. She had to rebuild the fire, keep him warm, keep him alive the only way she knew how.

The embers she left were so hot the firewood caught without

kindling. She set enough wood on the blaze to last for hours, then she pulled out the pocket watch. This time, instead of looking into the glass on its face, she flipped the lid open with a click of the clasp and *looked through it.*

Like a telescope lens into the past, she could see the shed as it was, not fractured or backward. Just exactly as it was. *The past is a window.*

Click-click.

Alistair heard it, somewhere near, but muffled. She hesitated, in disbelief that she was about to utter the words, then asked—

"Alistair, where are you?"

Quiet for a moment, then, "Here," a voice whispered from outside the front door. Alistair hobbled over and held up the glass of the watch to the window, and there it was, waiting for her through the lens. The fox.

"It's time. Can you get through?" he asked.

"I—wait a second," she said.

"We have to hurry. They'll know I'm gone," the fox said in response.

Alistair scanned the room with the lens. In the southern corner that the fox had been digging at in the dream, she noticed a discrepancy in *now* and *then.* A pile of firewood *then* where the boarded-up wall was *now.* She could barely see behind the pile of wood in the past that a hole had been gouged into the wall there. Big enough for her to slip through when she was eleven, but in the present, it had been boarded up with plywood and screws.

"Hurry," whispered the fox from just outside.

"I'm trying," Alistair said, realizing she was talking to a memory that couldn't hear her.

She pivoted to the fireplace. The stone of the chimney stack. Her memories righted, she could now recall the feeling of her bare feet on the edge of the hearth in summer, socked feet warmed by fire in winter. Feet on the hearth, tippy toes, reaching up to something. She'd done it over and over as a child. Again, and again.

She climbed onto the hearth and her fingers found the large, loose stone in the chimney. She pulled it away and reached into the hole it left behind. On the soot-soaked ledge of the chimney's interior she found a stash of rusty tools she'd hidden there fifteen years before. They were scalding hot from the fire, and Alistair had to throw them onto the floor to keep from burning her hand. A broken piece of a hacksaw blade, and a rusted woodworker's file.

She tested the file, waiting for it to cool enough to hold, then stumbled back to the corner where she'd originally escaped, jamming the file between the wall and the plywood board that covered it, prying it back. The file sunk deeper and deeper as the board began to give. Finally, there was a resounding *crack* as the old plywood splintered, revealing half of the hole behind it. She was out of breath and energy but couldn't stop.

She planted her feet into the plywood sheet and pushed, finally bending it back, wrenching it from the wall. She stopped and listened, realizing how loud her breakout had been.

No footsteps outside, yet.

She lay on the floor and looked through the hole in the wall, but there was nothing to see outside but snow-covered underbrush and night. She held the glass of the pocket watch to her eye, looking again, and found the fox waiting for her on the other side.

"Come on," he whispered to her, before turning and running off into the night.

"Wait," she whispered back.

She tied the belt of her torn and filthy coat tight around her waist and slid an arm through the small opening, then a shoulder, panicking for a moment when it seemed her torso might not make it through. She took a moment to compose herself, and with every breath that she exhaled, she slipped through bit by bit, finally shimmying her hips out through the hole and crawling out into the snow.

It was deathly cold outside the shed, and now the wind was blowing hard, flash-freezing the sweat on her exposed skin. She waved the watch around her, looking for the fox, her teeth already starting to chatter. She caught a flip of his tail, whipping through the brush, and ahead of her she found paw prints in the snow.

She followed them into the dark with no idea what would come of this, or where she would end up, but everything that had happened so far seemed to be leading back to this. To the path, and the dark, and the fox.

Though the night was ink-black, the island in the past was lit with the chilly glow of a heavy, near-full moon. Brighter than she remembered, and no alabaster claws waiting to snatch at her shoulder.

Alistair's legs burned as she tried to keep low, both to stay hidden, and to keep track of the prints in the snow. The fox was moving too fast to find and she only had his tracks to lead her.

The paw prints disappeared over an embankment. Alistair hesitated for a moment, then slipped her legs over the edge. She slid down the rocky incline to a deep, narrow creek bed. A shallow stream of frozen water cracked to pieces under her hands and knees as she landed roughly at the bottom of the ravine.

Alistair looked up and down the length of the creek. No more tracks. She didn't know which way to go, and the sides of the creek bed were too tall to see over, and too icy to climb.

"This way. . ." a small voice whispered from behind her.

Alistair looked through the lens and saw the fox passing through a small stone culvert that ran under a crumbling footbridge farther down the ravine.

Alistair steadied herself on the ice and began inching toward the bridge, when a loud *snap* echoed behind her, then a succession of quieter *snaps*. The sound of branches breaking underfoot. Someone was walking along the lip of the creek's edge above, every snap immediately followed by a heavy, thudding footfall.

The caretaker.

Alistair flattened herself to the ground. The footsteps above her were coming closer, falling harder, and she swore they were picking up pace. She was close enough to the culvert to hear the echo of wind bouncing through it, felt it blow her hair into her face. She pulled herself along the ice, careful to keep from cracking it, trying to reach cover before he found her. She felt the edge of the culvert at her fingers when a *resounding thud* rumbled behind her. He'd just leapt down into the ravine with her.

Alistair grabbed at the stone arch of the bridge and yanked herself inside, ducking in as the ice of the creek behind her shattered under the caretaker's approaching footsteps. She crouched into a ball and slithered into the shadows, lifting the watch to her eye, looking deeper into the black tunnel. There was light on the other side, some ten feet away. She needed to move, put distance between her and the caretaker. She carefully shifted her body further into the culvert, and then began blindly crawling, the lens her only sight. He would either give up, thinking it was an animal or a trick of the howling wind, or he could come for her through the culvert, which would give her the advantage because she was sure he couldn't move through it as quickly as she could, even in her exhausted state.

Or he would be waiting on the other side.

She could hear him behind her at the mouth of the tunnel, but she refused to look back. She was overwhelmed with adrenaline and exertion, and at one point she thought she might faint as a brief but intense surge of vertigo rushed through her. Then she heard commotion behind her and footsteps on the bridge's cobblestone above. Then they stopped. Seconds passed, then the footfall picked up again on the other side of the bridge. He'd just crossed over her. She scurried to the end the culvert, looking through the watch glass and the light ahead. She heard him getting quieter, moving in the direction Alistair had come from.

She finally collapsed under the far edge of the bridge, the cold air scorching her lungs as she tried to quietly catch her breath. She waited until she couldn't hear him anymore, then glanced back down the tunnel. Without the lens of the pocket watch, she saw that the culvert was *completely blocked with branches, bushes, and debris.*

She held the watch up again and saw that the culvert was clear in the past, but completely impassable now. It was as if she'd slipped into her own memory, for a moment, via the watch glass. The realization was too much for her to process and a flicker of the same vertiginous feeling resurfaced. She sat at the far edge of the culvert, shivering from the deadly cold, staring at the watch in her hand. Willing herself to stay conscious, Alistair peeked her head out from under the bridge.

A vague black shape, like a tapered monolith, rose above the fortification of shadow-veiled trees in the distance. Alistair held the pocket watch up and through it saw the spindled peak of a roofed tower, bathed in silver, moonlit memory, and the fox waiting at the base of the tree line.

The house where the writer lived. Where her brother was leading her.

Where *The Book of Briars* was bound to end.

Chapter 33

Alistair followed paw prints from the bridge up a rutted, overgrown path, and into a densely wooded grove where she finally caught up with the fox. She could hear him whispering, speaking with her in the past. She struggled to get closer to hear what he was telling her.

"I was right about the books. Wait 'til you see. You won't believe it," he whispered back.

That's right. That was the truth. Her *brother* had loved *the briar books*, not her. It felt like memories were leaking out of the fracture in the watch's glass: drips and drabs of everything that was. Alistair remembered the books, even without the watch, but not indelibly, not in detail. She remembered characters, like Iris, and places, like the little red house, but the sinew that connected the details had always been missing. Why didn't she remember more? Maybe it was a trick of the spell the Six cast. Maybe she'd heard them second-hand or—

She could feel the memory break through the surface—the words of the characters. Not hearing them, not feeling them silently speed past her mind's eye and burst into images, but speaking them herself. She'd read *the briar books* to her little brother. She could remember focusing more on her performance than what she was actually saying. She'd read them to him until he'd learned to read himself. A pinch of pain, but also pride. The day she found him reading on his own. She couldn't see the memory, where he was when she found him, but she could *feel* it.

Watching the fox scurry ahead of her, the pain returned. The last moments she spent with him, walking this path years ago. Here on this island, then saved, then lost forever, somehow, somewhere, all because of the books. Maybe it wasn't the truth she was ever really seeking. It was the unburdening of guilt that she never understood.

She wanted to call out to him, stop him from disappearing again, but if she let him lead her, if she let this all play out like it already had, for a moment she could pretend it was now, he wasn't gone, and the world hadn't forgotten the little boy she'd tried to protect.

The path grew steep, and the grove finally broke at the edge of a patchy clearing. The fox crawled under the little wooden fence at the end of the path, and when Alistair reached it, she saw they had made it to the writer's front yard.

It was emphatically not the little red house.

It was a rotting, gothic relic, the kind of house you'd imagine when someone said a place had "some bad history." It loomed over the trees, perched on the peak of the hill, reaching into the dark sky like a claw from a burial mound. Roofline after roofline angled upwards, dripping broken remnants of ornate iron filigree, the final tower on its fourth floor was a long, accusatory finger, the half-intact weathervane like a fragment of exposed bone.

The icy wind was painful on her exposed skin, but when it picked up on the house's hill, it was unbearable. Through the watch, she could see the fox waiting for her on the house's wide, crooked porch. She opened the creaking gate and took two reluctant steps along the broken stone path before the house's front door opened. Alistair could just make out a figure waiting on the other side. A woman, silver-haired and holding an amorphous bundle of something in one hand while waving with the other, calling Alistair to her, hurried.

The woman was saying something, short and sharp, over and over. Even with the distance between them and the hissing wind, Alistair knew what it was. *Quickly.* She wanted to check the watch again, to see that the fox was still there, reassuring her about this house, this woman, but she couldn't risk revealing the memento. Instead, she put her hands and the watch in her pocket and began to climb the steep yard.

The woman was paper-thin and just as stark white. Shriveled with age, her long silver hair was pulled up tight, stray pieces falling around her face, whipping in the wind that buffeted the hill, like a witch from a fairytale. She held a heavy gray blanket and a sheet of paper and was emphatically gesturing for Alistair to hurry. Her urgency had Alistair checking over her shoulder more than once, afraid the caretaker had found her.

"Come. Inside. Quick. He's not well," Alistair could hear the woman say as she finally approached the house's front porch, carried on numb, buckling legs.

"Who's not well?" Alistair asked as she clambered up the uneven stairs.

The woman rushed out and pulled her into the dark house with a surprising show of strength that set Alistair's already twisting stomach into somersaults.

"The caretaker," the woman said, closing and locking the door behind them. She threw the blanket over Alistair's shoulders, fussing with it until Alistair was tightly wrapped up, "I pray something will happen to him, though I know it isn't kind. Nothing terrible, just that maybe he'll fall asleep and stay that way."

The woman peered through the small window in the door, continuing on in a voice that hinted at an unplaceable accent but belied her advanced age with its warmth and sweetness, "He's haunted by this place. It's twisted him. You were clever at the bridge. Using the pocket watch," she glanced back at Alistair for a moment, "It's all right, you're safe," then she resumed her watch. "He doesn't know you have it. That's good. We'd all be in trouble if he knew."

Apparently satisfied that the caretaker wasn't coming, the woman turned from the door and took Alistair by her blanketed shoulders, gently but assertively urging her down the unlit house's main hallway, "Come, get in front of the fire. You could've died out there. I only just saw what happened, or else I would have met you at the footbridge."

Alistair could hardly make sense of the house's layout as the woman pushed her into its belly. It was dark, full of doorways that broke off to even darker rooms, and nearly as cold as it was outside. They quickly passed what looked like a dining room, and inside it a room-long table covered with stacks of paper, all weighed down by stones. A room at the end of the long hall was flickering with the glow of a fire and radiating warmth, and Alistair was drawn to it despite her exhaustion and apprehension, every atom in her body spiked with ice.

The woman set Alistair onto a tattered sofa opposite the fire in what looked like a decayed parlor, then sat in a nearby leather armchair and smiled, "I'm so glad you're here. Would you like some tea to warm up? Or—" the woman gestured to a small bowl of the purple-black berries on the spindly coffee table between them, "I wish I could offer more, but it's all we have, I'm afraid."

"It's—all you—eat?" Alistair struggled to ask, her body shaking, her teeth chattering.

"It's the only fruit this place will bear. The berries and the animals who come to eat them. We used to let them have the berries, goodness knows we had more than enough, but then . . ." The woman trailed off, lost in thought, "Something happened . . ."

"To the animals?" Alistair asked.

"Yes, yes, sorry," the woman said, shaking her head. "They began to speak. It must be something to do with the words that grow in the ground here."

"Is—Is that how the crow can talk?" Alistair asked.

The woman nodded with a smile. "I read that you met the fat little thing. We almost starved in those days because I couldn't bear to let the caretaker slaughter them. Why, I don't recall. No, I *do* remember. It wasn't just that they started talking. They began to beg for their lives."

The woman's eyes all-at-once went glassy and unfocused, caught up in her own words. "Terrible days, then, forget all about it. He kills them first now before they get to the briars. It's a kindness, but that isn't why he does it. There's no more kindness left in him. He doesn't know what he forgot, only that he forgot, and the island won't let him remember. Cruel. Terribly cruel."

Alistair wanted to bombard her with questions about the island, the book, her brother, but the old woman continued to fade away, lost in memory, her face slack and expressionless. She looked like a spirit from an old Victorian ghost story, sitting silently in front of the fire, her white skin melding with white licks of flame, almost translucent, like one upsetting or inappropriate word might turn her to mist.

"What's . . . your name?" Alistair asked quietly.

The spirit turned to Alistair, slowly coming back to *now*, "It's— Ilya, I'm sorry, I was lost for a moment. *His* name, the caretaker, I— don't recall now. However, I do remember his face as a child. And his sister. But only he came here with me."

"To the island?"

"To the country. And yes, the island. I knew it was here before I knew it was here. The moment I stepped off of that ship into the city, I knew where I had to go. You know a thing or two about that feeling, don't you?"

"Do you remember me? When I was here before?"

"I think I do. I mean to say, this island has a way of . . . not just making you forget, but making you lost in the remembering. If that makes sense."

"It does."

"Memories drift here, away, and back. What I remember and what I read of the book, maybe even what I knew before, all the stories mix together now. I *believe* I remember you, but I certainly know who you are and why you're here. We've been waiting for you to come back for years."

"You knew I would come back."

"Yes. Well, the writer knew," Ilya corrected.

"You—You're not the writer?"

"Oh my, no. I was known to spin a yarn as a child, but I didn't write *The Book of Briars*."

"Then who did?"

"The *writer*."

"Who is he? How does he know what happens before it happens?"

"I—don't know, not exactly. Magic, I assume," she said with a knowing smile, "Would you like some tea? To warm up?"

"No. Thank you. I just want—"

"It was the storm," Ilya said out of the blue.

"What was?"

Ilya's eyes went soft again. "Oh. Yes. A terrible storm came to the island, perhaps twenty years ago. I wrote it down somewhere, but— afterward, very strange things began to happen. Stranger than had already happened."

"What does he want?" Alistair asked, trying to keep Ilya focused on her and her questions.

"Want? The writer? Nothing. It's the island that really knows the story. The writer simply tells it. And we all move around the little board game like playing pieces. Like your . . . Iris. With the bow and arrow?"

"You're saying the *island* knew I'd come back here?"

"The storm came, then the words in the ground, then the writer. Then you."

"Do you remember my brother?" Alistair asked, her voice catching.

Ilya leaned in closer to Alistair. "The boy who loved the books. That's why he came here. He was looking for the place in the books. I don't remember where he went or what happened to him. I know other children were here on the island. Searching, maybe. But that was another time, wasn't it? Before everything changed." Ilya squinted and gave a weak smile. "Despite what the writer claims, you're not the only one who remembers the books. Or the boy. Or even the little red house."

"You remember."

"Sometimes. Not always. And less often as my life grows long," Ilya said to herself, lost in the spirit world for a moment. "Maybe that's where he went."

"Where?" Alistair asked.

"You know where," Ilya answered.

"The little red house."

"They all came here to find it. But it's not here, not *exactly*."

"Then where is it?"

"It's down a path. A secret, hidden path. One I have seen throughout my life but could never reach. Or did I? Did I find it?"

Ilya drifted away again.

"So what happens now?" Alistair asked sharply, calling her back.

Ilya considered the question for a moment, then answered, "We wait."

"For what?"

"For the writer to tell us what happens next."

Ilya nodded toward the sheet of paper she'd set on the coffee table. Alistair leaned in to see that it was a manuscript page about her following the fox through the culvert and hiding from the caretaker. It stopped at the moment that Ilya opened the door for her with a blanket and a sheet of paper in her hand.

"We're supposed to sit here until the writer tells us what the island wants us to do next?"

"Until the writer tells us what we *will* do next."

"Ilya? How long have you been waiting for this book to be finished?"

"As long as I can remember."

"Why?"

"There's something I forgot. Something very important that I lost. If I can just hold on . . . a little while longer, the writer will tell me what it is."

"Well, I'm running out of time. I'm sorry you forgot. I'm sorry you're stuck here, but I can't wait. I—" Alistair stopped herself.

"What is it, dear?" Ilya asked.

"There's something I have to do, but I—" Alistair found it hard to catch her breath, "but I can't remember what it was."

"It happens to us all here on the island."

"No. It's important. It's—"

Alistair held her icy hands to her temples, trying to pull the memory back to her. She was starting to panic. It was one thing to learn she forgot something she might have once known, but it was something else to feel her memories of here and now begin to slip away as she reached for them.

"Ben. It's Ben. He's dying," Alistair looked to Ilya. "Where is he?"

"Ben?" Ilya asked.

"The writer," Alistair spit back.

"You can't see the writer."

"Why? Where is he? *Who* is he?"

"Alistair, now is not the time—"

"Screw this. I'm not sitting here waiting and forgetting everything while my—my friend dies in that shed," Alistair stood, but Ilya stood faster, her hands darting out to Alistair's shoulders like harpoons, pinning her in place.

"No!" Ilya barked, startling Alistair.

"Let go of—" Alistair looked down, and for the first time, in the light of the white fire, Alistair saw Ilya's hands. Spectral thin, nails long and glassy, reedy bones and sinew pushing through the vellum skin—

Skin as white as alabaster.

Alistair felt a chilling breath escape over her lips, and her lungs collapse in her chest. She was staring down at the hands she'd been running from her entire life.

Ilya was the thing in the snow, in the dark. In the memory. The creature that reached from the void, clawing at her shoulder as she fled with her brother down the long, dark path.

"Alistair, please, it won't be much longer. You've come so far," Ilya entreated, lowering her voice.

Alistair was frozen in place, the claws still at her shoulders. All she could do was stare, trying to maintain her composure.

"Sit, please," Ilya said with a kind smile.

Alistair felt Ilya's hands lower her back onto the sofa, then Ilya looked in Alistair's eyes, her head tilted.

"It must be the pocket watch," Ilya said, finally letting go but still standing over her, now a black shadow blocking the light of the fire. "Being near it. All the things I'm remembering just now. May I see it? Not to take it, or even touch it. It's yours. You were meant to come here and find it. I just want—to look at it."

Alistair hesitated, but the fear of this woman now clouded her every thought. She reached into her pocket, sticking her arm out of the blanket, still gripping the watch tightly.

"Just as I pictured it from the book. Beautiful. May I see the back?"

Alistair turned the watch over without answering, her hands shivering.

Ilya squinted, reading the etching in the firelight, leaning closer, coming into view, "Time enough for everything, but—"

Ilya's eyes went wide and wet.

Ilya recoiled from the watch, caving in on herself as she retreated to the far corner of her armchair, hair falling into her face.

"What's wrong? What's—" Alistair asked, afraid but uncoiling a little now that Ilya was further away.

"That's it. Yes. Childress. Childress. Clear as day. I know why I know what I know." With a gasp, she said, "Ilya Childress."

"What's—" Then Alistair remembered the initials on the back of the watch, "You're— 'I.C.'? You gave this watch to Warner Green?"

"All the lost time," Ilya whispered to herself, "Everything made, then unmade. Forgotten," she whispered to herself, tears beginning to slide along the creases at the corners of her eyes. "Not forgotten. No. Forsaken."

"Who are you?" Alistair asked.

"No one, now. But then, I was glorious. I was—"

Ilya stood up so quickly that Alistair almost screamed, pulling the watch under the blanket. She was a little girl again, and her childhood nightmare was looming over her.

"Would you like some tea? To warm up?" Ilya asked, flipping her tone like a switch. "I think I'll make some tea. Help yourself," Ilya said, nudging the bowl of berries closer to Alistair, the alabaster claws glowing in the firelight.

"Dear," Ilya whispered, brushing strings of silver hair out of her face, "What is it?"

Alistair gave a single slow nod, "I'm—just cold. Tea, please," she whispered.

Ilya watched her for a moment, then disappeared from the room, into the dark of the house.

A deep, fluttering breath finally filled Alistair's half-empty lungs. She felt numb, disconnected from her body. There was nowhere left to go. Nowhere safe. The caretaker, the cold, the witch who'd waited years for Alistair to come back to the house. She let the blanket slide off of her shoulders and pushed the watch back into her pocket. She had to get up. She had to go. She couldn't just sit on that sofa and wait for Ilya to remember. Alistair snuck to the doorway, looking into the black for the old woman, but Ilya was gone, off to the kitchen for tea, or god knows what. The cold of the house kissed Alistair's face as she slipped into the dark. She kept her back to the hallway's paneled wall, inching toward the direction of the front door. Ilya was either a convincing liar or unaware of her part in Alistair's fractured memory, but as long as Alistair had the pocket watch and memories continued to surface for both of them, she wasn't safe. Soon, Ilya might remember why she so desperately pursued them down that dark path, if she didn't already remember.

Alistair stopped at the edge of the main entry, the front door fifteen feet away, a lone candle lighting the room from a crooked hall table. She listened for Ilya but only heard the wind and its occasional serpentine currents weaving through the bones of the old broken house.

She took a few steps into the entryway, stopping to listen, then a few more. Her fingers reached the lock of the front door. She tested it to see how hard it was to unlatch, how loud it would be when she did.

Then Alistair pulled her hand away from the lock like it burned. The fox had led her here tonight, just like she'd come here with her brother years ago. Somewhere in this house had been the key to their escape. *Where was the fox now? How had they gotten off the island?* She had to get off the island, didn't she? She couldn't stay, could she? Wasn't there something important she had to do? Wasn't there something else, someone else, on the island? She came to the house to do something, help *someone*, but in the moment, at the door, Alistair couldn't remember anymore, and she wasn't sure if she was safer leaving or staying.

Click. Click. Click.

Alistair didn't want to look back. She wanted to run. She wanted to lock herself back in the shed, or hide in the culvert, or drown in the lake—anything to never see those hands again.

"This is the only way out," the fox whispered from behind her.

She knew he wasn't there. Not anymore. She knew it was nothing but a ghost talking to a little girl. But it was all that was left of him, and the sound of his tiny voice was a vise on her heart. Alistair looked back to the staircase that led to the dark-draped floors above. She reached for the watch in her pocket, flipping the lid open, already knowing where the fox would be, sitting on the bottom step, waiting for her to follow, just like it had before.

The fox perked up as if it had lost her a moment, then found her again.

"Don't be afraid. It's gonna be okay," the fox said, "it's just a little bit further. We're almost there."

"But I know what happens next," Alistair whispered. "She follows us, and—"

The fox stood, circled, and began to climb the steps, looking back at her. "Stay close. We're almost there," the fox said before stepping out of sight around a corner upstairs.

A grueling mix of fear and sadness took hold of Alistair at the sight of the little fox disappearing into the dark. She couldn't let him go alone and didn't want to be left behind. Then Alistair heard a faint *click click click* coming from somewhere in the upper floors of the house, but it wasn't the fox. It was a typewriter. The writer was upstairs, in the house. And the fox was leading her to him.

One by one, Alistair took the creaking stairs as carefully and quietly as she could, and in seconds she was gone, swallowed by the dark, consumed by the call of typewriter keys.

The staircase spiraled ever upwards. Even through the pocket watch, all Alistair saw was black. But she could hear the typewriter and the reassuring sound leading her on as if the *click click click* that had haunted her life had always been the call of the writer and the strike of ink-stained metal on paper. The wind whistled through the broken walls. The house's upper floors were frigid and exposed, broken panes gently rattling in their window frames. Tattered drapes slithered against her exposed skin, broken railings waiting to send her back to the witch, three stories down.

Somewhere on the first floor, muffled by the howl of the winter wind, a whistling sputter pierced the quiet, then was suddenly silenced—a tea kettle. Ilya would be back at the fire with the tea soon, carrying the pot with her claws, wondering where Alistair had gone with all her memories, and she'd come to find her. Follow her. It was all repeating.

Again and again.

Alistair ducked to avoid the low, angled ceiling of the fourth-floor hall. It was a cramped little space, not much larger than the shed, lit by a dark gray sky visible through the broken roof. It was oddly nauseating to see a rattling weathervane spinning just above her head, evidence of how high up she was and how the house was barely standing. The edges of the sky were lightening. The sun was rising. Another pang of fear bit down on her. There'd be nowhere to hide from the witch once morning came.

"Alistair?" She heard faintly from downstairs.

Ilya must have brought tea and found Alistair missing from the living room. Alistair looked around the fourth floor, weaving under the odd pitches of the ceiling. There were four doors branching off the hall. She tried them all. Locked or jammed shut from neglect and rot. Alistair held her breath, homing in on the direction of the slow, methodic clicking until she found the door that stood between her and the writer.

"Alistair? Where did you go, dear? The house isn't safe to wander alone," Ilya called back from downstairs, louder now, more anxious.

Alistair crept to the writer's door and listened. The brush of the door against the tip of her frozen ear felt like a knife. She couldn't hear anything behind the door except for the wind and the pecking of the typewriter.

"Alistair!" Ilya called from below. She was closer now, at the bottom of the stairs or already on her way up, calling in a panicked, hissing whisper. "You didn't go upstairs, did you?"

Alistair tried the doorknob again, it turned, but the door was locked. Quickened footsteps on the creaking steps echoed up the stairwell. Ilya was coming quickly, feverishly calling Alistair's name. Alistair looked through the glass of the watch, trying the door handles, looking for the fox, or another way out short of climbing out of the broken ceiling onto the roof. She could hear Ilya panting as she reached the upper floors. Every door in the past was just as locked in the present. Then Alistair froze in place as she noticed one slight but distinct difference. There was a skeleton key sticking out of the lock on the writer's door.

"Alistair! You mustn't go up there! You hear me?!"

Alistair focused on the key through the watch's lid. She knew it was impossible, but so was the culvert, the debris that had blocked her way, then vanished. She reached for the key. She knew it wasn't in her grip, not really—

But she could feel the key there, nonetheless.

She turned it and felt the satisfying *click* from the past as the door unlocked inside the lens of the watch. Ilya was close, her footsteps at the top of the stairs. Alistair let go of the key, turned the knob, a wave of vertigo assailing her as she rushed into the narrow hall on the other side of the door. She lowered the pocket watch from her eye, turned around, and the locked door was once again closed, now between her and Ilya.

Ilya violently shook the doorknob from the other side.

"Did you steal my key?" Ilya muttered from the other side. "How could you—Listen to me. You have to come out." Ilya beat against the door, pleading as Alistair backed away.

"You don't understand, Alistair. It isn't safe in there. Do you hear me? It isn't safe!" Ilya cried out from the other side of the door. Alistair's heart was thundering in her ears. What was Ilya so afraid of in the room?

On this side of the heavy door, Alistair could not only hear the sporadic *click* of the typewriter keys behind her but a kind of *jangling*. Like a keychain on a belt or a broken wind chime.

She looked over her shoulder, down the short hall, through the far doorway to the writer's room, which was swathed in brimming pre-dawn light. She could just make out what first looked like some kind of massive spider's web. A thousand thin strings crisscrossed the room ahead. A single thread of the web fluttered, and the metal jangling sound followed, then a single click of the typewriter.

"Hello?" Alistair called out.

"Alistair!" Ilya yelled, pounding on the door. "Unlock this door right now. You have no idea what you're doing!"

Alistair inched down the hall toward the room, seeing now that the taught strands of webbing were actually made of twine that had been nailed, tacked, and tied to the walls, the floor, even the ceiling, all terminating at a single location just out of view from her vantage in the hallway.

Another thread fluttered, and a key clicked out of view as Alistair neared the doorway to the room. There were gray-black patches on the walls that looked like paint splatters or ink stains. It was still too dark to see clearly, but the edges of one of the stains spread out on the faded, yellowed wallpaper near her and dissipated into clouds of *typeset letters*. Closer, and she could see a pool of letter 'A's near the floor, a splatter of 'T's above a broken wardrobe.

She leaned through the doorway and saw feathers and bells and pieces of tin hanging at the far ends of the strands, all terminating at an incomprehensible wooden contraption that surrounded a black typewriter. It sat on an old, warped desk in the middle of the room. The device looked like a dozen ramshackle looms all cobbled together, built with painted planks of fence, stairway spindles, thread bobbins, bent wicker reeds . . .

Ilya continued to bang on the door. "Please come out of there. If you break it, we'll never know—"

The tall, door-like windows that once led to a long-rotted balcony had been propped open by two wooden chairs. Currents of air made their way up to the tower, curling through the opening. Alistair heard a flutter above her head and looked up to find a black feather flitting in the wind, surrounded by a stain of lowercase 'h's. The feather worried the thread it had been tied to and the thread, in turn, tugged at a delicate little dowel in the contraption, which moved another, which struck a key on the typewriter.

Alistair knelt under and stepped over threads, approaching the machine. A stack of blank paper sat beside the typewriter, and one sheet was in the bale, already half-filled in with prose she was still too far away to read.

She leaned in to see that a fresh lowercase *h* had been added to a sentence on the page.

Alistair *heard a flutter above her h—*

She could still hear Ilya on the other side of the door, though her frantic yelling had weakened into a monotone muttering. "It took so many years to understand. What was happening, what the island wanted. The letters, the words, so much time wasted before I understood. I'd never be able to fix it if it broke. I don't have any more time. Please, Alistair . . . "

"You made this?" Alistair asked, raising her voice enough for Ilya to hear over the wind. She could hear Ilya's body slide against the far side of the door.

"Yes. I built the writer, and when I was finished, it began to write *The Book of Briars*. It's so fragile, Alistair, and I have to stay here and tend to it, keep it oiled, change its ribbon, feed it paper. Even then, the writer only writes when the briars grow sharp, and the fall winds blow, and by spring, the letters fade . . . Alistair? Will you please let me in?"

"I—I know who you are."

Silence from the other side of the door.

"You've haunted me my whole life."

"I know," Ilya answered quietly after a moment of hesitation.

"Why? Why were you trying to keep us here? Keep us from leaving?"

"I wish I knew why. Why I did what I barely remember doing, but I would never hurt you. Anyone. I swear. I don't know that woman. She is lost to me."

Alistair could hear the pain in Ilya's voice.

"I can't let you in. I don't have the key."

"How did you—" Ilya gasped, "the pocket watch, like the culvert—"

"There was a key in the lock, in the past."

"That is very clever, dear."

Alistair felt an odd rush of pride triggered by Ilya's words.

"Would it be all right if I went to get my key? To let you out?"

"Yeah, it's—" Alistair heard something over the wind and the clack of the typewriter. She turned back in time to see the typewriter carriage reach the edge of the page and push against a wooden spring-mounted cabinet knob, which pushed back, returning the carriage, sending it to start the next line.

"How did you manage to make—" Footsteps. That's what she heard. Heavy ones. Coming up the stone path to the house, below the writer's open window.

"Ilya!" The deep, tattered voice of the caretaker howled from below. "She's gone!" His voice grew louder, closer.

"Ilya," Alistair yelped quietly.

"Oh no. Stay quiet, dear," Ilya answered back. "He may not know you have it. I'll keep him away. Stay still. Don't move. The writer will tell us what to do next."

"Wait—" Alistair called back to the old woman through the door, hesitating before she finally whispered, "Be careful."

Alistair heard Ilya slip away down the stairs, her already small footsteps growing smaller. Then the quiet was suddenly shattered by a series of thunderous *thuds* as the caretaker pounded on the house's front door.

Alistair strained to hear what was happening, almost sure she could hear the unintelligible staccato of voices below. Then a sudden crash shook her, the sound of wood breaking, maybe glass too. The caretaker had broken down the front door.

She could hear Ilya's voice now, wild, screaming at the caretaker, more heavy thuds, a struggle, then it was quiet again.

Alistair wove through the web of twine, back to the room's hall, every step creaking on the hardwood. She listened at the locked door. She could hear heavy boots downstairs, moving through the house, looking for her.

"Where are you?!" He yelled out. His voice was closer than she anticipated.

He was already coming up the stairs.

This way.

Alistair whipped around, startled, before realizing—She fumbled the watch out of her pocket and flipped it open. She found the fox standing at the end of the hall.

"Everything's going to be okay. I found the way out. Follow me," the fox said.

She could hear the caretaker's steps behind her, through the door. She could hear doors being thrown open, slammed again. She tried to focus on the fox in the lens and followed him back into the room.

The web was gone. The room in the past was tidy and maintained. The wallpaper unpeeled, the furniture neat and clean. It was made up for a child. Alistair could see a small bed, the edge of a little writing desk, and book pages littering the floor. She approached the doorway leading into the room and stopped short at the sight of the window.

It wasn't a window anymore. It was a doorway. Its frame was wreathed in hundreds upon hundreds of folded-up, interlocking book pages. And beyond the frame, where a view of the black island should've been, was an inviting, endless, summer path lined with white trees.

The fox was waiting by the window. "I finally figured it out. I was right about the books. I'll explain everything once we're safe. Trust me."

Alistair approached the fox, stunned by the sight of the endless path.

"Where does it go?" she whispered, to the fox, to herself.

"You know where," the fox answered with a whisker-trimmed smile.

"To the little red house," she said, breathing back tears.

"We have to hurry. Go on ahead. I'll stay back to close the door," the fox said.

"No. You have to come with me," Alistair said.

"I'll be right behind you," the fox reassured her.

Alistair approached the window's threshold. She could feel the warm, sweet air, like a mix of spice and dew—

and memories you almost knew.

Alistair put one boot onto the low paper-covered windowsill and realized with a shiver that she would have to step out of the window to step onto the path.

There was a startling *thud* as the caretaker arrived at the door.

"You have it, don't you?!" he seethed from the other side.

"Hurry," the fox said.

Alistair put the other foot on the windowsill, standing on the edge. One more step through the lens was all it would take—but she hesitated.

Over the rim of the watch's lid, Alistair could see the edge of the island in the distance, the sun moments from breaking the horizon. The wind swayed the snow-covered treetops, but the water beyond the trees was still. And white.

The lake had frozen over. Something about the sight of the frozen lake—

"Ben," Alistair whispered. The name seemed unfamiliar at first, and then the memory came rushing back to her. "I can get him across the ice," Alistair said to herself.

She could get him off the island, get him to a road, to a hospital.

"Hurry," said the fox.

"I—can't. I can't leave him."

The caretaker was pounding at the door, twisting the doorknob back and forth.

"Hurry. I'll explain everything once we're safe. Trust me," the fox implored from the past.

Alistair shook her head then stepped off the frame of the window, "I can't."

She knelt in front of the fox. "You have to go without me this time," she reached out and touched the fox's furry ear. "I'm sorry I lost you, but you're already gone, and I might still be able to save my friend."

Alistair closed the watch's lid, and the fox vanished, replaced by the web and the loom and the monster at the door. Alistair leaned out of the window, looking out for a roof slope she could reach or a ledge she could climb onto. There was nothing but four stories of open air.

She would have to climb up, onto the tower of the house, then maybe she could crawl through one of the holes in the roof—

The door caved in behind her, the caretaker in the doorway, his eyes bloodshot, his hair unkempt. Freshly bleeding scratches at his face and neck. Ilya had fought him.

"What did you do to her?" Alistair asked.

"Give it to me."

"Let me go," Alistair approached the web of twine, putting her hand on one of the strands, "or I'll tear this whole thing apart."

"You think I care about your story?"

Alistair looked back to the window and hefted the watch, "You seem to care about this. I'd hate to see it lost in the woods again—"

The caretaker rushed her without expression, without hesitance. Threads pulled taught against his body, then snapped in half or ripped from their moors. He reached her in three steps, his hand around her throat before she could react.

She fought against him at the edge of the window, as hard as she could, but on her best day she would've been no match for him. He pried the pocket watch from her clenched fist with rough, iron fingers. She fought back, but her fatigued mind was now starved of oxygen and slipping into a deep and comforting void. From somewhere in the sinking dark, she felt her arms go slack as he took the watch, her knees buckle into unconsciousness as she tried one last time to push him away.

Then, with one deadly-swift motion, the caretaker shoved Alistair through the open window.

PART V

Chapter 34

The *snap* of a crackling fire woke Alistair.

She was back on the floor of the shed, one blanket under her, the corner gripped in her fist, another blanket half-hanging off her body. She felt numb. No, not numb exactly. She felt warm, a little too warm actually, but the feeling she'd first mistaken for numbness was just a lack of pain, like nothing hurt for the first time in a while. She took it slow, pushing herself up from the floor and away from the fire until she was sitting upright.

She could tell from the light in the boarded-up windows that it was morning, maybe even afternoon. But the light was crisp, clear, not dull, and muddled like winter light. Alistair couldn't remember how she'd gotten back to the shed.

Back to the shed . . . from where?

The caretaker. Her foggy mind was clearing. He must have brought her back.

A breeze blew in from a gap in the wall or past a broken windowpane. It was cool, sweet, and smelled like black tea and cloves. It felt good on her neck but too warm to have a fire burning. Why had she built such a raging—

Alistair looked over her shoulder to the iron bed in the middle of the room. It was empty, and the front door of the shed was open.

Alistair got to her feet and approached the open door. Outside, the snow was gone. So was the rest of the island. Instead, Alistair found a wall-like thick of birch trees just beyond the clearing, with heavy green canopies swaying in the breeze, scattering sourceless light in every direction.

Splitting the wall of birch was a mossy cobblestone path that wandered away from the shed until it eventually dipped out of sight beyond a misty vanishing point. Alistair could see objects on either side of the path, spaced perfectly apart. From the shed, they looked like thick fence posts or tree stumps.

This all felt familiar, but Alistair couldn't place where exactly she'd seen it before. She stepped through the doorway and felt the air swirl against her face and hair. The leaves rustling above her sounded like the sea. The warm light of morning or maybe midday on her skin was soothing. She took in the calming moment.

The shed was at the center of a clearing, with birch trees all around and more cobblestone paths breaking off in other directions, disappearing behind the dense tree lines. Alistair walked to the path she'd first seen through the door. The "tree stumps" were carved pedestals made of oiled wood. And on each one, or at least the few Alistair could see, was a book, bound in leather. The closest book to her, which was thirty feet or so away, looked like a thick encyclopedia volume, and the next closest, another thirty feet away on the opposite side of the path, was thinner by about an inch but still big enough to make out from where she stood.

The sky above was bright, blue, empty except for a long, thin cloud that zigged like lightning across it. Alistair reached to her pocket, though she wasn't sure what she was looking for once she realized she was doing it. She looked at her upturned, empty palm. Staring at her hand, she had the distinct feeling that she'd forgotten something in the shed.

She turned back, but the small clearing was empty now. The

shed was gone, and she could now see more cobblestone paths cutting off in all directions through the surrounding birchwood.

Alistair noticed that the disappearance didn't seem worrying, though it *was* strange. She just wished she could remember what it was she'd forgotten inside before it had disappeared.

❧

Alistair began to follow one of the paths, unsure if it was the one she'd first seen, but figuring it didn't really matter since she didn't know where she was going anyway. As she approached the first pedestal, she saw that the book on it had a gold filigree title pressed into its cover's dark brown leather. It was called *The Book of Robert.* Alistair wanted to open it but was concerned whether it was for her to read or anyone else but Robert, whoever Robert was.

What if the wrong Robert found it, though? Alistair wondered as she continued along the path, warmed by the sourceless sunlight, cooled by the gentle breeze, eventually passing *The Book of Sebastian, The Book of Hazel, The Book of Seth, The Book of Trevor...*

The path stretched on without turns or corners, only gentle, meandering curves as it wove this way and that through the trees. Alistair peeked between the tree trunks, but they were planted too close to slip through, and she couldn't see anything beyond them except more white trees dipped in sharp shadow.

Sometime later, Alistair sat on the side of the path, wondering if she should continue or turn back and try another way, not at all concerned that she had no idea what she was doing there or even where she was. She even noted her distinct *lack of concern* as not concerning. She decided she'd sit for a while, then walk to the next book, and then she'd go back to the clearing and decide what to do next. She brushed the palm of her hand over the fuzzy moss that snaked between the path's worn stones.

Above her, the same jagged cloud hung high in the air, stretching from one unseen edge of the sky to the middle. It looked less light lightning now and more like cracked glass.

⚭

The next book's title curled across the cover in a dramatic typeface —*The Book of Sel*. Alistair touched the lettering, feeling the swirling indentations. She would try and remember that she walked until *The Book of Sel* and then turned back, though she couldn't remember now where she'd come from in the first place. Something else she forgot. No, she didn't forget. She was just—

Lost in the remembering.

Where had she heard that before? It took a moment, but an image started to appear in her mind like an old photograph developing, submerged but fading into focus.

An old woman waiting for her, *standing in the doorway of a house on a hill.*

Ilya.

The gentle, ever-present breeze picked up, brushing against Alistair's back and pushing her hair into her face. She swept the strands away, and when she could see again, she discovered a new path now crossed the path she'd been walking along. She walked to the spot where they intersected.

Down the new path, Alistair saw a woman sitting on the edge of the cobblestones near an empty pedestal. The woman had a book in her lap. She was leaning over the large tome, looking at the cover with a great deal of focus.

"Hello?" Alistair called to her.

The woman didn't answer or even look up from the cover.

Alistair approached the woman, and after a few steps, she looked back and saw that the path she'd been on before was gone, just like the shed. *The Book of Sel was off on more important business*, Alistair thought to herself.

"Ma'am?" She called out to the woman again, who finally, slowly, looked up.

"How long have you been there?" The woman asked, her voice soft and tinged with an Eastern European accent.

"I just got here, I think. I'm not sure. What about you?" Alistair asked.

"I don't know either, now that I think about it. A good while," the woman said.

The woman looked familiar to Alistair but not completely recognizable. It was like seeing someone for the first time in years and knowing them even through all the changes and growing older they'd done, except the opposite. Alistair remembered the woman being older, not like she was now, which was not quite young, but certainly not the elderly woman she half-remembered her being.

"I didn't know if we were allowed to read the books," Alistair said, coming closer, looking around at the other pedestals, "or if we needed to ask whoever they belonged to first."

"Hmm," the woman considered, "I haven't seen anyone here except for you, and I've been here for a long time, so I don't know how I would ask—" the woman looked down at the cover, "Ilya, if I could read her book."

"Ilya?" Alistair interrupted.

"Do you know her?" The woman asked.

"Isn't that you?" Alistair asked.

The woman thought about the question for a moment, "Oh, I think so. Then, I suppose it would be all right if I read this one."

They shared a smile.

"What's in it?" Alistair asked.

"I don't know. I haven't opened it. I can't explain why, but it sets me on edge. I'm quite nervous."

"About the book?"

"About the truth," Ilya answered, barely loud enough to hear. She looked up at Alistair's face and, after a moment of study, said, "Alistair?"

Alistair thought for a moment, then said, "No, sorry. That's not my name."

"Then what should I call you?" Ilya asked.

"I'm— not sure. Isn't that weird? I *did* see a book with the name Sel earlier, and I thought it was pretty, but I don't think that's my name either."

"Well, I'll call you Sel until we get to the bottom of it."

"Okay," Alistair answered with a nod. She looked further down the path, endless trees and pedestals and unread books and warm light and cool air.

"For some reason, I thought I'd find someone else here," Alistair said. "When I woke up, the door was already open. I think he might've gone on ahead of me."

"Who's 'he'?"

"I— can't remember."

Ilya was looking back at the book in her lap. "Sel, would you do me a favor?"

"What's that?" Alistair asked, looking back to Ilya.

Ilya lifted the heavy book up to her, "Would you mind opening it?" she asked. "Reading it to me for a while?"

"Not at all. I'm pretty curious to see what's in it, to be honest," Alistair replied.

Alistair took the book with both hands and sat on the other side of the path, setting the tome in her lap. "If it gets to be too scary, just let me know."

She opened the leather cover, and the spine gave a small but satisfying *crack* as the book fell open in her lap.

Then Alistair began to read—

The Book of Ilya

ILYA'S NINTH BIRTHDAY

On Ilya's ninth birthday, she first sees the path while playing with classmates in the woods beyond the village.

She follows the path.

She finds the little red house.

One month in the place beyond the path.

ILYA RETURNS HOME

Missing her family, and yet unaware of the concept of temporal dilation, Ilya returns home, carrying the promise made to her that she would be able to return.

Ilya goes home and finds her parents distraught.

She learns that her brother has been transported to the "old fort," and she's only been gone a matter of hours, not weeks.

. . .

She believes she may have fallen asleep in the woods and dreamed the place beyond the path.

THE OCCUPIED VILLAGE

While crowded into a makeshift encampment with other families waiting to be taken away, Ilya secretly practices "finding" the path again.

On three occasions, she is able to see the path beyond the walls of the camp.

Ilya continues to practice, believing it requires a relaxed mental state often associated with idle daydreaming and a focus on the path itself rather than where it leads. She calls maintaining and combining those separate thoughts at once "magic."

She does not try to escape the encampment by taking the path. She is worried that someone might notice her absence, or worse, her mother and father will be taken while she's gone.

TEREZÍN

The train arrives at the old fort on a cold night. Ilya watches her father vanish in the crowd of fathers separated from their families.

Ilya's ability to find the path fades.

. . .

Ilya is eleven when she is taken from her mother. Living with other children, she takes two young, red-haired siblings into her care.

They are the children she saw on her first night at the fort.

When the little girl dies, Ilya spends many nights trying to console the red-haired boy.

She tells him a story about the little red house.

The path unfolds just outside the window of the room.

The boy becomes frightened. He refuses to follow her.

Ilya does not stay.

Four months in the place beyond the path.

Ilya studies many things, magic, history, and the natural time dilation between her world and the place beyond the path.

Ilya returns the following morning, as planned, only to find that soldiers came in the night and took several children.

. . .

She never sees the red-haired boy again.

Ilya does not find the path again until the following summer.

❧

Ilya discovers her father tending a garden in the fort's square. He tells her that Isaac and her mother have gone east to another camp. Ilya refuses to leave his side, even as the children are called away. Soldiers come to take her from her father, and the path unfolds for her in the distance.

She does not want to leave him but cannot let the path vanish again.

Ilya vows to come back for her family.

She escapes to the path.

Seven years in the place beyond the path.

AUSCHWITZ

Ilya returns after learning to control where she will arrive.

She finds her brother, Izaak, huddled with hundreds of other young men, worked to the threshold of death.

. . .

Her mother is not there. Izaak tells Ilya that train after train arrives where no one on board survived the journey, but her father arrived one week prior, barely alive.

Izaak takes Ilya to him.

Their father holds them, tells them he loves them.

He will not survive the night.

Ilya knows she may lose the path forever if she is there when her father dies. The pain would be too much to overcome.

She and Izaak tell him goodbye.

Ilya takes Izaak beyond the path.

They learn that the dilation does not affect their age, which remains bound to the place they come from.

Twenty-seven years in the place beyond the path.

A VILLAGE NOT FAR FROM PRAGUE

Izaak misses home and asks to return to see if anything remains.

. . .

The war continues. Izaak wants to stay and search for his friends and the girl he loved before he was taken from the village.

Ilya refuses to stay.

Izaak feels he is beginning not to recognize himself or Ilya. He tells her that he isn't going back.

Ilya explains that he will not be able to return to the place beyond the path without her, and there will be no way for him to reach her once she leaves.

Izaak understands.

Ilya takes the path, leaving her brother behind.

Two-hundred-and-seventeen years in the place beyond the path.

CENTURIES

Alone, Ilya grows in power, learning all she can about magic and the history of the place beyond the path.

She uncovers secret stories that were meant to remain hidden. Histories about the place beyond the path and its connection to the world she left behind.

. . .

Ilya dreams about her family, her brother, who she never forgave for not returning with her.

NEW YORK CITY

Ilya wakes from her dream in a New York City apartment, where Izaak fled to escape the war.

Ilya has been gone nearly a decade. Older now, bereft of the wonder she once had as a child, she finds is no longer able to find the path.

Ilya can perform minor feats of the magimystic, but fears in time, her power may fade in this world altogether.

A hand-delivered letter arrives for Ilya. It is an invitation to join an organization called the Briar Society. They know about the gates, the magimystic, and the place beyond the path. They also know she has performed magic since her return. Ilya eagerly responds with many questions, hoping they can help her return, but learns that she knows much more than they do, and all their well-intentioned attempts to explore the space between worlds, or cross it, have failed, sometimes dangerously so. As far as they know, there is no way back.

Lost, Ilya finds work as a seamstress in a garment factory in Manhattan's Lower East Side. She helps repair the factory's complicated machinery. She cries at night, her hands aching from the grueling work. She does not speak to anyone but her brother. Her every thought is focused on somehow finding the path again, but she is beginning to forget about her time in the place beyond the path.

Ilya writes down everything she remembers. She sometimes uses magic to help her write her notes, because the pain in her hands is always present now, but also to write quickly so that she doesn't lose more memories.

The notes become stories.

The stories become a book.

A book Ilya calls *The Little Red House.* Once it is finished, Ilya asks other women in the factory to read it to their children. Many of these women have never heard Ilya speak. One by one, the women borrow the manuscript, each of their children falling in love with the story.

A woman returns the book, now stained and tattered, and offers to give it to a friend whose son owns a publishing house.

Weeks pass, then Ilya receives a letter in the mail from a man named Warner Green. He would like to meet Ilya and discuss the book.

ONE YEAR PASSES

Ilya sees a pocket watch in a shop window and has it inscribed for Warner. She pays for it with the advance from her book.

. . .

Warner gives Ilya the first bound copy of *The Little Red House*. She opens the front cover but quickly closes it until she is alone.

Inside, there is a handwritten message from someone beyond the path.

The Little Red House is released and becomes a spectacular success.

Warner Green asks Ilya to write a second book, a continuation of *The Little Red House*'s story.

Subsequent printings change the title to *The Little Red House in the place beyond the path—*

Ilya plans to create an ongoing series of books about the place beyond the path.

Ilya begins the second book, *The Articulated Beasts of—*

ONE YEAR PASSES

Eager to hold her readers' attention while she continues the second book, Ilya works with Warner Green to pen the novelty book, *Ackerly Green's Guide to M.A.G.I.Q,* which includes references to the first book and subtle clues about future stories and the place beyond the path.

. . .

Ilya finishes the second book before the end of the year.

TWO YEARS PASS

Ilya begins the third book. With her popularity growing, she uses her wealth to purchase a secluded island on a New England lake to escape the city and unwanted attention.

She wants to focus on the books.

She calls the island *Neithernor,* naming it after a beloved object from the books. Like its namesake, the island is a safe place and a respite from the world. It is *neither* where Ilya is heading *nor* where she came from.

Ilya and Izaak move to the island with Izaak's wife and their newborn baby.

TWO YEARS PASS

Ilya begins the fourth book, now exerting complete control over the story, illustrations, advertising, related merchandise, even the peculiarities of how the books are edited, bound, and published.

Children around the world now eagerly await the books.

THREE YEARS PASS

Ilya begins the fifth book, growing more and more reclusive. She no longer leaves the island.

To employ Izaak, Ilya allows limited tours of Neithernor. Children come to see statues of characters and wander the island, designed to resemble places in the books. Ilya has no need for grown-ups but spends time with every child who comes to visit.

Izaak's fourth child is born, and his wife wants to leave the island. Izaak refuses to abandon his sister there.

TWO YEARS PASS

Ilya begins the sixth book. Her hair is graying, and her hands ache as they peck the typewriter keys.

Izaak's wife leaves him. She takes their children from the island.

ONE YEAR PASSES

Ilya completes the sixth book. It has taken her much longer than she planned.

Izaak returns to the island after sending the sixth manuscript to the publisher. Ilya and her brother toast to another finished book.

. . .

Ilya tells Izaak this will be the last book in the series, and he should go to his wife and children. There will be no more tours. She won't need him to care for her or the island anymore.

Izaak does not understand.

Ilya explains that the sixth book will complete a spell she's been crafting for over a decade. She tells him that she made mistakes while she was in the place beyond the path, terrible mistakes she is still paying for, but when the sixth book is finished, she'll return there to make amends. She won't be coming back to the island.

Ilya reveals that the six books, when finished, will have a secret gate hidden inside them, leading her back to the path. She had to hide what she was creating deep inside the stories so it wouldn't be discovered by those who she believes have barred her from coming back.

Izaak tells her that he doesn't know nearly as much about magic as she does, but he knows that wars were fought over the old gates because they were so precious. A spell to build a new gate would be impossible. It would require more power than exists on this side.

Ilya confesses to Izaak that only children can first find the path. To see it requires not just innocence but innocent *intent*, and above all, wonder. Imagination. It is the most abundant source of magic, but so often, adulthood steals that magic. That is why they had to be children's books. Ilya has spent years capturing the imagination of millions of children, infusing the books with it. As more and more children dreamed of that faraway place and imagined themselves walking the path, the spell grew stronger.

When the sixth book is bound and published, all the children that have loved the books over the past twelve years will have helped her return.

Izaak doesn't know what to say to his sister.

The following morning, Ilya watches from the shore as Izaak leaves the island.

They will never speak again.

THE SIXTH BOOK

The sixth book is published.

The first copy arrives on the island, and Ilya begins the arduous work of opening the gate hidden within the books, but her hands are now gnarled and useless from years of work and writing. The delicate, complicated process of finishing the spell is nearly impossible.

She tries to find Izaak, to ask him to come back and help her, but the letters she struggles to write to him go unanswered.

. . .

Her readers finish the sixth book and the series, some of them now adults themselves. The attention of her readers begins to wane, as does the power they granted the books.

Ilya is unable to open the gate. She is consumed with regret and sadness, all alone on the island. She decides she must continue the story to recapture the imagination of her readers.

Ilya records herself dictating new books about the place beyond the path, sending them to the publisher to be adapted into manuscripts by other writers.

The new books are nearly as beloved as the original six, but her aging body and mind are beginning to fail her.

DECADES

Ilya does not write anymore. She still tells the stories aloud, but only to herself, her recorder long broken.

Her house is rotting, and the island is overgrown, reclaimed by nature. The small welcome center now nothing more than a derelict shed. The follies children used to explore have succumbed to hundreds of harsh seasons.

Ilya is alone.

The Letter

A young man from the nearest town brings her groceries and mail by boat when she leaves the light on at the end of the island's dock.

He tells her he used to love her books when he was a kid.

In a batch of mail left on the dock is a letter from a child.

Dear Miss Childress,

I love to read and I love the books about the place beyond the path. They are my favorite. Your books are why I learned to read. My favorite characters are Franklin and William Fayweather, and Endri. My sister's favorite character is Iris. I have two questions to ask you.

Do you plan to write any more books about the place beyond the path?

Did anyone ever solve the puzzles in the books?

I would love it if you wrote me back.

Thank you very much,
  Alistair Mead, eight-years old.

Ilya reads the letter again and again. The only thing hidden in the books was the spell, which itself was a kind of puzzle, but would be impossible for anyone to see, least of all an eight-year-old child with no knowledge of the magimystic.

. . .

Ilya remembers the day she first saw the path. How little she knew then. Her 9th birthday.

Ilya bears the physical pain to write young Alistair back.

Dear Alistair,

Thank you for your kind letter. I received it exactly when I needed it most, and I am pleased to hear that my books have brought you happiness.

To answer your first question, no, I do not currently intend to write more books about the place beyond the path, but I would not rule it out.

As for your second question, I am curious what kind of puzzle you believe you've found?

I eagerly await your response,
   Ilya

Ilya leaves the light at the end of the dock lit, and three days later, the young man is hunting in the woods and sees it. He retrieves Ilya's letter to Alistair.

Ilya wanders the house for weeks, thinking only of the boy and his letter. She reads it again and again, one day sure he somehow sees what she hid in the story, the next certain that she is wrong, and her hopes will be dashed when she receives his response.

Ilya hears a bell ring. The young man has returned in his boat. Ilya watches him drift back to the mainland before going to the dock.

She leaves the groceries, tearing through the bundle of mail to find Alistair's response.

Ms. Childress,

I am so happy to hear from you and hope you will write more books someday.

Thank you for asking about the puzzle. I have read the books over and over, which is why I found it. At first, I thought there was a puzzle to solve in one book, then every book, so my sister went online to see what people had found, but no one solved them or even found them.

I tried to solve them myself but didn't get anywhere.

Then I thought that maybe the puzzle was across all the books, or at least the first six. Then I found out that some pages fit better next to pages from other books instead of the page they are next to in their book.

My sister bought me paperback ones because I didn't want to rip my hardcover ones up even though they are not expensive or first edition or anything.

I switched out the wrong pages that I could find, and I think they tell a different story. Like there is another story in the books.

I don't know what to do next, but I will keep trying. I am not asking for a hint but is it a puzzle? Am I right?
> *Your reader,*
> *Alistair*

Ilya weeps over the letter. The boy can see what she hid in the stories. He only needs help to put it together, but Ilya fears telling him outright. Alistair may be her final chance, and if she interferes and the gate doesn't open—

She writes him back immediately.

Alistair,

Please call me Ilya.

You are right. There is a hidden story in the books, and you are the only one who has ever found it. A new story about the place beyond the path. I couldn't let everyone read it because it is a very special story.

Do you understand what I'm telling you?
    Ilya,

Ilya,

Yes, I think so. Is it a way to get to the little red house?

Is it magic?

Alistair

Yes, Alistair, it is.

It is magic, real magic. Everything in the books is true. I have been to the place beyond the path.

But to solve the puzzle and see it yourself, you must come here, to Neithernor.

And you mustn't tell anyone. Not your parents, nor your sister, nor your friends. If you tell, the spell won't work.

If you agree, I will send you money for the bus and food, and a map that shows you how to get here. You needn't bring anything else. I'll have a signed, first edition set of books waiting here for you.

Chapter 35

Alistair gasped for air, pulling her face away from the book in her lap as if she'd just narrowly saved herself from drowning. The breeze on the path chilled her sweat-sheened skin.

There was more in the book, but Alistair couldn't bear to keep reading. It wasn't just a book. Those weren't just words on the pages. The moment Alistair began to read them, her senses slipped into Ilya's lost memories. The deeper she went, the further into the story, the harder she'd found it was to pull away.

Ilya was gone. At some point, she'd left Alistair alone on the path, but Alistair could still *feel* her.

The light was still hovering somewhere between morning and midday. Alistair had no idea how long she'd been reading, how long she'd been lost in the book, but the light here meant nothing. Alistair knew where she was now. She was in the liminal world of the memento, the place where she'd last seen Ben alive. Alistair looked up to the blue sky. The zigzag cloud above her mirroring the crack in the glass of the pocket watch. How had she ended up here again?

Alistair winced. Her hands ached with residual memory of Ilya's arthritic pain. It felt like the hazy afternoons when Alistair would jump on the neighbors' trampoline until her parents called her home for dinner. Even when she stopped jumping, the tingling, weightless sensation remained in her legs, her mind tricking her until the memory finally faded.

Jumping on a trampoline. Fall leaves scatter with every bounce. The neighbor's dog racing circles around the yard. Her brother trying somersaults.

Alistair. He wrote to Ilya.

"I saw my way back through him," Alistair whispered to herself as a shadow passed over her. Ilya had returned, and Alistair had echoed the woman's thoughts, still connected to her mind and memories.

Ilya looked even younger now. The frailty that had bent her body before was gone.

"I called him to the island," Ilya said in a calm tone, her accent more pronounced now, "I had hoped I could pass through the gate when he opened it. He was just a child, and he believed me, what I promised, as only a child could believe."

"You stole him," Alistair sniped, still catching her breath, as she closed the book and shoved it onto the path in front of her. She felt her connection to Ilya guttering, replaced by an unbearable surge of sadness.

"Yes," Ilya said, her tone both consolatory and removed, "I have conflicting memories now. I stole him, and I didn't," she said as she looked at her own unwrinkled hands, her fingers moving in dexterous curls.

Alistair watched Ilya rediscover her hands, silent, wanting to hate her, but all of Alistair's energy was focused on the rawness of her grief.

"I began to remember the moment you opened the book," Ilya said. "It was all at once overwhelming and torturous, and like I had never forgotten in the first place. I found myself thinking about all those children, all the readers. And then— I was wandering the woods here. I read so many stories. I read for years without a moment passing. Countless memories of magic secreted away and stolen. All the pain and happiness, and the books. And I was a part of all of them. The joy and wonder, everything we lost, while still holding onto the echoes of our memories, sleep-walking through half-remembered dreams."

Ilya looked up into the sky and closed her eyes, the light shining on her unblemished face.

"Echoes of our memories. I didn't save Izaak, you know, not in this history, but I didn't abandon the red-haired boy for the path. I kept him close to me, and we survived, all the camps, and the war. When it was over, I brought him here instead, carried on the current of my brother's memory, to the island."

"The caretaker," Alistair muttered.

"The ghost of Izaak," Ilya replied.

"I need to find my brother's book," Alistair said as she scrambled to her feet, looking up and down both ends of the path.

"It isn't here," Ilya said as she bowed her head a little, almost in reverence. Her hair spilled over her shoulders, growing darker as Alistair watched, only a few streaks of gray remaining.

"It has to be." Alistair walked away from Ilya, dismissing her.

"I looked for it, for you," Ilya called out. "Penance, I suppose, a shadow of guilt left over from the woman I was, but his book isn't here."

"Then where is he?"

"Only altered memories live here," Ilya answered gently. "He wasn't in this world when the spell was cast. He has not been here in a very long time."

Alistair felt her legs give out from under her. She crumbled to one knee as the weight pressed on her, "I left him— I abandoned him."

"No," Ilya approached her, "I found *your* book. I felt how much you loved him, the love you knew he had for you. I saw your last days together."

"Don't."

"You both escaped the island. You found the place beyond the path, and the little red house. You spent years there. But something dangerous had been growing since my time there. You wanted to bring him home, to keep him safe. You didn't intend to leave him behind, but on the night the spell was cast, you were separated, and you came back alone, falling between worlds when the spell took hold. Half in one world, half in the other. It's how you remember."

"I *don't* remember! I can't even remember his face—" Alistair seethed, weeping.

"Memories are stories, not truth. What matters is not how a story is told, but what its telling means to you. You remember what's impossible to remember because you loved him. You didn't fail him. You tried with all your strength to hold on, to keep him with you, but he wanted to stay."

"Is he still there? Is he alive?" Alistair asked.

"I don't know. But you've seen in my memories that time moves very differently there."

"He's been there for hundreds of years, but he's still ..."

"Your little brother," Ilya answered.

Alistair rose to her feet. She turned to Ilya, who now looked as young as Alistair, "How do I get him back?"

"There is no way back," Ilya said, "the spell those children cast was irrevocable. The bridges have all been broken."

"But— the Six remember what happened. Their memories aren't here."

"That's right," Ilya confirmed.

"Then how do you know what they did?"

Ilya's face fell, "Because that terrible piece of magic would have remained lost, hidden, as it should have been, had I not sought it out and exhumed it from dark, forbidden places. Had I not sought the power to stay when my time beyond the path had passed," Ilya gave a sad half-smile and looked down at her hand as a shimmering, translucent sphere of purple energy coalesced in her palm. "I was going to break the bridges so that there would be no way back. Bridges, paths, conduits, they are called many things. They traverse the Fray, from our realm to the other, and they are built on belief, imagination, and memory. When I first found the path, centuries of conflict and conquest had corrupted the connection between the realms. The gates had been closed for a very long time. They did not know how I was able to cross the Fray and find the place beyond the path. I was unique. I was lauded, adored. The pathfinder. Centuries. But in time, even there, I grew older, my dreams calcifying, growing rigid with adulthood, longing less for what I could imagine and more for what I could possess. I pursued the oldest stories. Obregand and Ojorad and Vidivinty's Glade. I found the oldest magic. All I had to do was make our world fully and finally forget the place beyond the path existed, and all the bridges would crumble, all the gates would close. One word lost, and I could stay forever."

"What word?"

"The name of the place beyond the path."

"What is it called?"

"I just told you. It's called the place beyond the path."

"No— that's not it. I can almost remember it. It's one word. It's not called the place beyond the path."

"That not what I— Ah, the word is still stricken from your memory," Ilya thought for a moment, then, "Your mind is still bound to your body, your body to the world, and the world to the spell."

"Then how can *you* remember?" Alistair asked.

"I am no longer bound to our world," Ilya answered.

"What does that mean?"

Ilya was lost in thought, "I can see all histories now, real or conjured. I remember the place beyond the path. The source of wonder. A place that is impossible to resist, yet you broke its wondrous hold to try and take your brother home. That is a love more powerful than magic. A love I failed to honor time and time again."

The sphere of purple energy dipped back into Ilya's palm and rippled just below her skin, moving up her arm, then dissipating throughout her body.

"What's happening to you?" Alistair asked.

"Do I seem different?"

"You're young again."

"Old memories taking hold," Ilya answered as she walked to the nearest pedestal and touched the book atop it, "Remembering what I was. That's all magic is, really. Remembering in just the right way. I wish I could right all that I made wrong, but I'll have to settle for wandering these paths and bearing the pain of remembering for those who can't."

"You can't stay here," Alistair said.

"*You* can't stay here. I can't go back. Don't you remember? I went downstairs to get the key—"

"The caretaker," Alistair whispered, remembering.

"I kept him away as long as I could, but that frail body wasn't strong enough. I suppose whatever was left of me, my mind, my memory, would've drifted onto the aether had the watch not been close enough to catch me … but it doesn't matter. There's no Ilya left to return to now."

"I'm sorry," Alistair said.

"Penance, my dear, if nothing else. I was given a gift, fleeting and wondrous, and it wasn't enough for me."

"He pushed me," Alistair said, remembering, "He took the watch, and then he pushed me out the window. Then I woke up here. Am I dead too?"

Ilya craned her head to listen, as if the answer was a whisper on the breeze, "You are, yet again, between two worlds, still bound to your body for a few moments more, but also here, now, because you have already fallen."

Alistair nodded, "So I came all this way for nothing. I can't save him. I can't save myself. I don't even know my own name—"

"I do. You were named for your father's love of history and your mother's love of reading—"

Alistair laughed, wiping away fresh tears with the back of her sleeve, "All I ever wanted was to remember who I was, what I lost, and to have more books than I could ever read in a lifetime. And look where I ended up. It's perfect as far as dramatic irony goes. I wish Ben—" Alistair's face went slack at the utterance of his name.

The wind picked up and curled around them both. When it passed, another path was waiting a few yards away. Alistair rushed toward it. She turned the corner, but Ben wasn't there. Only an empty pedestal waited for her.

Alistair checked in both directions, her hand on the empty pedestal.

"He must have found his book," Alistair muttered.

Alistair looked back to Ilya, who had just made it to Ben's pedestal.

"Is he here?" Alistair asked.

Ilya's eyes narrowed, "Yes. But— he's wandered very far into the grove."

"Is he—"

"Alive?" Ilya looked up to the cloud that cracked the sky, "he's still bound to the world as well, but only by a thread."

"I can't stay here. I have to get him off the island," Alistair said.

"You can't go back, my dear," Ilya interjected. "You are already falling."

"But the lake is frozen over. I saw it. I remember now. I saw it through the window. If I make it, if I survive—"

"The tower is too tall."

"I know, but—"

"How would you survive—"

"I will," Alistair answered resolutely.

"My dear girl, you're safe here, how—"

"Because I will! Because I have to!" Alistair's voice quivered, "I don't know. But I can't leave him there. Not there. Not in that room. I'd rather die with him than leave him there to die alone."

It was a near-impossibility that she would survive going back, and even less likely she'd be able to help Ben if she did. But she couldn't think about that. He was running out of—

"Time," Alistair said aloud to herself, "Time moves differently here, just like— the place beyond the path," Alistair said, "I've been here before, with Ben. In a dream. He was unconscious for a couple of days, but to him, here, it was longer. A lot longer. He said he'd had all this time to think about the fox and me and who I really was. It might not be too late. I might have time to do— something before it's too late, a second to catch myself, or grab onto something."

Ilya tilted her head as if she'd had an idea, and the idea made her smile.

"How do I do it?" Alistair asked, "how do I go back?"

Ilya took both of Alistair's hands, "I'm going to show you something."

"I don't have time—"

"It won't be easy to see, but it may help you."

"Another memory?" Alistair asked.

"Another chance," Ilya answered.

And as the words left Ilya's lips, the grove was gone in a flash of white.

THE DOOR BACK HOME

Alexandria is ten. She is standing at the edge of a long, dark passage. She is scared. She looks behind her through a curved arch made of tree boughs.

Her brother Alistair is on the other side of the archway. He is smiling. He tells her that he loves her and that he will be okay.

She realizes he is not coming home with her.

She feels the passage pull at her, like a heartless tide dragging her away from land, and though her life is somewhere waiting beyond the black sea of the passage, she regrets ever leaving shore, where her brother is still standing.

She pulls against the tide, resisting with all her strength. She wrenches her hand free, lashing out, reaching for her brother—

Chapter 36

A nd Alistair's fist catches hold of the caretaker's collar just as he shoved her through the tower window.

The caretaker tried to pull her loose from his jacket, but Alistair's grip was too tight. With the watch still in his hand, he slung Alistair sideways to the floor of the writer's room. Alistair snapped several threads and landed on her knees, panting but poised to fight him.

"Don't get up," he growled at her as he turned his attention back to the pocket watch, flipping it over in his hands, "How does it work?"

"It only shows you what you lost," Alistair answered.

"How?"

A chill of sadness and sympathy momentarily cooled the angry fire in her.

"How!" He screamed at her, desperate to see.

"You— open it, and look through the glass," Alistair answered.

The caretaker found the button that released the lid, and when it was open, he peered through it—his expression transforming into a tragic mask of confusion and fear.

"How— It doesn't— what did you do? What did you do to it?"

"I didn't do anything," she answered.

"There's nothing in the glass!"

"Because your memories aren't in there."

"Yes, they are. They have to be. She said so. The book said so. Why doesn't it work for me?"

Alistair could still see the scared little red-haired boy looking up from Ilya's memory.

"Because you didn't survive."

The caretaker took a step away from her, "What? That's not true. I came here with her. I gave my life to her, to this place. There must be more. I—"

He looked into the watch again, his face contorting, a desperate howl rising from his belly as he pulled at the lid of the watch, trying to tear his memories from it.

"This, this, is the only life I was meant to know? This place? This hell! Please, please help me. It can't be true. There must something more than—"

A rotten floorboard snapped under the caretaker's boot, pitching him back toward the open window. Alistair gasped as he lost his balance, reaching for the threads of the web to stop his fall, catching them in his fists as he stumbled over the sill and fell through the tower window.

A hundred twanging threads snapped free from the walls. The writing table flipped as the typewriter and the contraption were yanked over, pulled by the cords the caretaker carried with him. They slammed into the floor with a rattling crash, skittered across the room, and smashed into the window frame before finally disappearing through it.

Alistair was frozen, in shock, her ears ringing so loudly she couldn't hear the caretaker or the contraption hit the ground.

It was as if the whole horrifying moment was frozen in time somewhere just outside the tower window.

※

Alistair descended the winding stairs back to the ground floor of the old house. Every ache and painful wound magnified by their momentary absence while she was lost in the watch.

Ilya's body was on the floor of the front hall, her head resting at an odd angle against the base of the stairs. Alistair wanted to carry her back to the parlor, to the fire, but she had to get to Ben.

Outside, morning had finally come. Beyond the porch, Alistair could see that the contraption was now nothing more than bits of broken junk littering the yard.

The Book of Briars forever unfinished.

The caretaker's body was folded over on itself on the stone path, and the web of threads spread all around him quivered in the wind like hands pleading to the heavens.

Alistair stepped off the porch, looking for the watch while trying not to look at the caretaker's open eyes.

The typewriter was still intact; the stone below it cracked, and the gold chain winding out from under it. She knelt, pushing the typewriter away, and found the pocket watch, shattered to pieces. Black swatches of soot marred the cracked stone around the broken watch like the stains left from a firework.

※

Alistair focused on her numb feet shuffling bit by bit across the slick white ice. The sun was high but hidden by endless winter clouds. Shearing, unimaginable pain shot down her back and shoulders, her hands raw and bleeding and her throat ragged from gulping hours of frigid air, but she wouldn't stop. She tightened her grip around the ropes slung over her shoulders, ropes hastily lashed around the shed door like a makeshift sled.

A sled that bore Ben's body across the lake.

***

Alistair couldn't lift him off the ice. Her back was too weak, her palms sliced open by the ropes. She would have to find the road she first stumbled across the night she was found. She would have to find help and bring it to him.

She knelt by Ben's unconscious body. His papery pallor was even more shocking in the last glow of daylight. She made sure her coat and layers of blankets were tucked tight around him. The more dangerous cold was creeping closer as the sunlight faded, and she wasn't sure how long it would take to get back to him.

Alistair looked across the lake to Neithernor. The island was nothing but a faint gray shape beyond the ice and fog. The briars would flourish, and the animals would have their feast of memories now that there was no one left to stop them.

She glanced up to the blue-gray sky to see if the crow was circling overhead, but he was gone. A stinging sadness surfaced at the sight of the island vanishing in the dark and the deepening fog. Not just for all the loss suffered there, but in Ilya's fading memories, Alistair could feel what the island once meant for the writer who lived there and for everyone who'd read her words.

It had been a place of wonder. A portal to a better world.

PART VI

The Book

OF ALEXANDRIA

I t was going to take some getting used to.

"Alex" was as close as she'd gotten to using her real name out loud, and only in settings where no one knew who she was otherwise. Like when the barista in the hospital cafe first asked what to yell when Alistair's Americano was ready.

Alistair always shuddered at the worn-out literary trope of "I'm a strong female character, so strong in fact, I might as well have a boy's name," but "Alex" felt and sounded like *Alis*, the name she'd imagined for herself with Bolden all those years ago. It felt like one safe step, one beam of light shining in the black void she'd been carrying with her all these years. She might not ever be *Alexandria* to anyone else, or even *Alex*, but just saying it out loud to a stranger felt like an accomplishment and made the ephemeral events of the past few months feel a little more real.

Alistair watched the meltwater curtain down the cafe window while she waited for her coffee. The window looked onto a little interior courtyard which was probably meant for smokers, but at the moment, it was covered in drifts of unsullied snow. New York City was a nightmare in winter. Well, New York City was stunningly beautiful a half-hour into the first snowfall of winter, and then it was five months of slush turning black from sucking up car exhaust and hiding mounds of rotting garbage until spring rolled around. But the little courtyard off the hospital cafe was still pristine white.

A shiver rattled through Alistair's body at the sight of the snow. The cold from Neithernor was still in her bones, even now, even when it was only days away from spring. It was a lingering reminder that the story wasn't over. Not until Ben woke up, not until she knew for sure whether his mind and memories had made it off the island.

Eighty-one days.

It had taken an hour to get from the frozen lake to the nearest road, where she flagged down a family in a minivan. She went back for Ben with paramedics, refusing to go on to the hospital herself until she knew he was okay, explaining that their situation had been the result of a hiking trip gone terribly, terribly wrong. At the nearest local hospital, Ben was given a breathing tube, put on a ventilator, and after hours of examination by the small-town staff, he was scheduled for a battery of MRIs and other tests at a larger hospital two counties over.

The first thing Alistair did after sitting begrudgingly through two IV bags of fluid herself was try and track down the closest person Ben had to a "next of kin." She knew about his parents from the pages she'd taken off the island, but they'd both died years prior. She eventually found the name of the man who owned the restaurant they'd holed up in after escaping the Silver, and hopped contact to contact until she got through to Ben's ex-girlfriend, Cor, sometime after midnight.

Cor drove through the night, arrived the following morning, and immediately took charge. She got a medivac ordered, her car picked up by the rental agency, and secured them both spots on the helicopter back with Ben. Alistair slept most of the flight, finally confident that Ben was in good hands, even though his prognosis was completely unknown.

Alistair's first memory of being back in Manhattan was Cor taking her hand as Ben's doctor said things like *secondary cerebral edema* and *vasospasm* and *spinal cord laceration* and *subarachnoid hemorrhage.* They were told the only chance Ben had of regaining consciousness was if they could get the swelling in his brain down as quickly and carefully as possible, and even then, it would just be the beginning of a road that might never end with Ben waking up again.

Before Ben could have visitors, Alistair went back to Ozone Park and spent two nights in her old room under the guise that her apartment was being painted. She felt like she'd been to the moon and back since that last dinner with Zev and Aunt Kath, but to her aunt and uncle, nothing had changed. The world was just the way it always was. Kath wanted her to stay longer, Gus didn't care one way or another in the nicest way possible, and Alistair woke up a few times a night thinking she'd heard Zev knocking on the wall behind her old headboard. She thought about dropping her real name into casual conversation with her aunt and uncle, but in the end, it was nice to just have a couple of days of *things just like they always were,* and that name would've changed everything.

When Alistair made it back to her apartment, she found Danny Chen had packed up her stuff and put it all in the restaurant's basement. She was surprised that he hadn't tossed it all to the curb. Alistair opened a couple of boxes, looking for anything worth taking with her, though she had no idea where she was going. She sifted through worthless books and clothes she never wore, and when she pulled out an undershirt Zev had left behind the night she called him, she realized she didn't want any of it anymore.

A week later, Cor found Alistair sleeping in the hospital lobby on a bench by the women's bathroom and forced her to take over the sunny little guest room in her apartment, claiming she didn't want to be alone after everything that happened. Alistair fought her until Cor played the ultimate guilt card— *Ben would want her there.* Within a month, they were bingeing true-crime documentaries together and debating where to order takeout.

Eighty-one days. That's how long they'd been back.

Alistair relished the stinging heat from the cardboard coffee cup. She wound through the hospital's labyrinthian halls to the neurocritical care unit. To Ben's room. She timed her arrival to the moment visiting hours began. A couple of nurses would sometimes let her stay the night, but otherwise, Alistair tried to be there until the moment they told her she had to leave.

When she *did* leave, whether for the night, for work, or just to stretch her legs, she always left something behind that Ben would immediately recognize as hers if he woke up. It might've been an old book she was reading or the journal she bought in a nearby stationery store because it had a fox on the cover. Now that they were on the cusp of spring, Alistair had been leaving her old, tattered coat on a hook across from his bed. She wanted to make sure he knew she never left him for long.

Cor was there too, once or twice a week, but the longer Ben's coma went on, the harder it was for Cor to see him there, his frail body, his sunken eyes, the vibrant heart of him now only beating because machines and spools of cords made it beat.

There wasn't much to do there but sit and listen to hissing pumps and beeping consoles and shuffling feet outside the door, so Alistair read to him, for hours at a time, sometimes until she lost her voice.

Alistair checked the calendar taped to Ben's door. The hospital-hired barber would be in later. Alistair made sure she was around when it was Ben's turn because they'd tried to clean-shave his face that first month and Cor wouldn't let them, saying Ben would be mortified if he woke up without the beard he'd worked so hard for.

So, Alistair was on whisker watch. She nudged the door open, sat her coffee on the small side table, and dragged the armchair over to Ben's bedside.

"Snow's finally melting," she said as she yanked her sweater off over her head.

Ben's room was always warm. She put the back of her hand to his forehead. She didn't know what she was checking for or what temperature would even be the right temperature to have given his condition. But it was more of a touchstone at this point. Maybe wherever he was, he could still hear or feel, so she would talk to him and touch him to let him know she was there even though there was no way of knowing if any of it got through or if Ben was even in his body. Alistair had no idea if his mind and memories had made it back to him after the watch shattered or if that's how magic even worked. The two people who *might* know, the Morrow sisters, were both missing. There was no mention of a body or an unconscious woman found in Central Park that night, and though the abandoned car Alistair left Marjory in had made the online version of that area's local paper, neither Marjory nor the driver the caretaker killed had been found.

Either one or both of the sisters survived, or whoever was leading the Silver now was still covering their tracks well enough to go unnoticed. Either way, Alistair wasn't getting answers. Alistair's mind drifted as she watched the gunmetal sky through Ben's window. Were all those memories destroyed, or were they drifting around out there in the gray mist, seeking out their owners, hoping to reunite somehow? Alistair couldn't trust her own memories to make that determination. She'd always remembered more than most people but hadn't remembered more since the island. Even if the memories survived and *could* be reclaimed somehow, most people would probably chalk them up to nostalgic neurons misfiring or repressed trauma or nut bag conspiracies like chemtrails. It's just the way the world worked. Magic was a harder pill to swallow than the Mandela Effect.

But if they weren't destroyed, if the memories escaped, did that mean Veronica's spell had been broken along with the watch? Was the name of the place beyond the path out there too? Could the broken bridges Ilya told her about be rebuilt with knowledge of that place? With memory and belief and imagination? Could she remember herself a way back to her brother?

Alistair wished more than ever that Ben was awake. She felt like she was living a book that had run out of pages before the story was finished. He'd help her dissect what happened, why it happened, and how to find the surprising yet inevitable conclusion. He'd be able to see the meta in the magic like he did on the island.

He'd like that turn of phrase, she thought. *See the meta in the magic.*

She reached over and took his hand. She brought Charlotte Brontë's *Shirley* to read to him, but she was too distracted. *Eighty-one days.*

She'd finally met someone she knew in her bones she could trust, someone who saw who she really was, both literally and literarily, and accepted her, not for what she could tell him, or find for him, or what clandestine secret society she could grant him access to, but just because he was a good man.

And he might never come home.

Pembrey.

Alistair was just distracted enough by her grieving rumination that she didn't realize for a few moments that a word she'd never spoken had just flickered across her consciousness.

Pembrey. Is that a last name or a place? Maybe a doctor's name?

Alistair pulled out her phone and searched the word, knowing how it was spelled despite its variations.

A village in Wales. A beach in the UK. An indie video game. A public park.

Alistair's thumbs hovered over the search bar before she added "New Jersey" to the end of the search.

Pembrey Lane.

A nothing street in a nowhere suburb in a forgotten corner of New Jersey. Alistair checked the street map images but knew before they loaded what Pembrey Lane was.

It was the street where she grew up, with her mother, father, a cat named Casper, and her little brother, Alistair.

❧❦❧

Alistair waited until she knew Ben's beard would remain unmolested, then set out for New Jersey. The train's last stop was almost four miles from Pembrey Lane. She planned to walk there and see if she remembered anything along the way, then cab it back if she got too tired or if the weather turned. The sun was beginning to set by mile two, and a drizzle light enough to be annoying without really soaking through her sweater had started.

Pembrey Lane wasn't some desperately held secret. She could've asked Kath and Gus at any time where she lived before they took her in. Honestly, she didn't know why she was going back. Her parents were dead, her brother wasn't even on this plane of existence even if he *was* alive, and unless Casper had been doing some dark magic of his own, Alistair was pretty sure all that would be left of her family would be cat bones in the back yard of a house that hadn't been theirs for over fifteen years.

Casper. Was that new? A new memory?

Alistair hoped she might recognize the house immediately, and she did. Three times. Because they all looked the same. She'd just reached the end of the street, which terminated at an open park so large that the wooded far end had already faded into the black of encroaching night. Dusk made it seem endless. Alistair turned and realized she'd come down the road the "wrong" way from her memories. This perspective, this view, felt far more familiar.

It was the view she'd seen from the shed window the last night she'd talked to Ben.

Her house was three doors down, on the left.

She couldn't tell if it looked bigger or smaller than she'd remembered. She wasn't sure she remembered it all, or if she just recalled what it looked like in her memento-made dream.

She thought about knocking, but there weren't any lights on, and the short driveway on the side of the house was empty. What would she even say to whoever lived there now?

She hiked up the raked driveway, glancing in the dark windows, trying to see if any of it sparked more old memories to life. A short gray, cedar-picketed fence separated the front yard from the back. Alistair walked to the gate and peered around the corner of the house; the backyard was illuminated by the light of taller houses looking down on it.

Though the house itself was modest, the yard was a pretty good size. Straight ahead, there was a rusted-out swing set with no swings, and there was a cracked concrete patio by the back wall of the house, outdoor furniture still flipped upside down to keep from accumulating snow. In the far corner of the yard was an old toolshed with a wheelbarrow leaning against its door. The shed was leaning a little to its right, and it looked like a few planks from its roof were scattered in the yard.

The paint was chipped and faded, and it was too dark to make out now, but Alistair knew what color it used to be because she'd helped her father paint it.

It hadn't always been a toolshed. It had once been her brother's little red house.

She unclasped the gate and walked across the soggy yard where she'd played countless hours of *the place beyond the path* with Alistair. *Alistair.*

It was the first time she'd heard the voice since the island, but it didn't scare her now. It was a warm and welcome reassurance. She hadn't left her brother on the island again. He was still with her.

Alistair pulled the wheelbarrow out of the way and turned the little wooden latch that kept the door of the shed closed.

Light from another house filtered through the broken roof where one of several fake chimneys used to be, and inside she found a lawnmower, garden tools, and faded outdoor kids' toys waiting patiently in the half-light. There had been a window on the back wall with a flower box, but it was boarded up now. The floor was made of planks from old wooden pallets, and Alistair remembered her dad pulling the nails out of them with his big brown hands. The moment when she'd learned what the claw end of a hammer was for. He was singing to himself while he worked.

Alistair ducked into the shed and closed the door behind her. She knelt on the floor, taking in the quiet, the memory of the small space. It was … safe. This shed was where she read to her brother. She could remember now. This is where they always wound up, panting, out of breath and laughing, pretending they found a secret path in the nearby park which led them here. Two names used to be etched on a board above the door.

Alis and Alex.

She was flooded with memory, memory that spilled over the edges and drowned her heart.

Maybe memories don't return to their owners, Alistair thought. *Maybe they belong to the places they were made.*

This was where her brother kept the books, in a hidden space their dad had made, lined with plastic bags to keep out rain and snow.

Alistair found a plank in the floor with a tiny knothole in it. Big enough for a child's finger to fit through. She put the tip of her index finger in the knothole.

What if the books were somehow still there? What if there was a way back? What if this little red house was a well, and a way to the other one?

She took a deep breath, sighed, then pulled up the plank

It was dark in the cubby hole, but Alistair could see well enough to know that it was empty.

No books about an impossible place, no covers emblazoned with a forbidden, forgotten word. No pages to pull apart and move around and make a door back to her brother.

Just memory and loneliness and creeping dark outside, and a slip of paper stuck between two planks.

Alistair reached down and pried at the yellow corner of paper until she could gently pull it out. She held it up in the single shaft of light and crumbled into tears as she realized what it was.

A little origami fox.

Alistair held it to her chest, leaning against the shed wall when she couldn't hold herself up any longer.

She was a paper box of pages, finally unfolding.

It hurt to let him go. Let him free. Some pains, like memory, fade with time. But the pain of loss never fully fades, because loss is built on love.

⚜

Alistair passed the last streetlight on Pembrey Lane and walked the four miles back to the train station in the rain.

Under the harsh fluorescent lights of the station platform, Alistair shivered and waited. According to the station clock, if the train arrived on time, she could maybe squeeze in an hour or so with Ben before visiting hours ended. She wanted to tell him what she found, what she remembered.

He might never wake up, she knew that. His condition might not have anything at all to do with magic, or lost memories.

The train whistle-hissed to a stop and Alistair and a half-dozen others boarded the empty train which was going against the nightly 9-to-5 exodus from Manhattan.

Alistair leaned back on the train bench and watched New Jersey roll away through the foggy window.

Ben had been there, in the memory grove, which is what Alistair had come to call it. He had read his book and wandered off, lost along the paths. She couldn't have stayed to look for him, to tell him to go back. He might not be alive at all if she had waited longer. She could still sometimes feel the breeze from the grove on her neck. Or rather, a gust of subway air or the exhaust of a passing bus *became* the wind from the grove, for a moment. Warm and sweet. Consoling. Memory transposed.

She couldn't remember the last thing she said to him, or he had said to her, in the shed, in their dream. Of all the things that were lost, for whatever reason, that was the memory she wanted back the most, though she couldn't explain why. It was something about the past. Inconsequential, most likely, but maybe somehow important.

This didn't feel like an ending. A surprising yet inevitable conclusion. It all felt unfinished, incomplete. This story, the books, the memories, the Mountaineers and the Silver and the Six, *The Little Red House* and *The Book of Briars*. It was all so much bigger than her and her brother. It couldn't just end with them, a train ride back from Jersey, and an origami fox.

She pulled the fox out of her pocket, looking him over in the light of the train car.

All at once Alistair just kind of *knew* why she had always remembered him the way she did. It was a spell. A spell he'd pretended to cast on himself when they found their way from the park to their backyard, to their own little red house. He would change himself into a little red fox, and he'd tell her she could always find him, no matter what, because he was the fox with the glasses.

Shapeshifting Arts. That's what he'd called it.

Alistair unbent the deckled corner of the paper fox's ear and found words printed on it. He wasn't made from origami paper. He was made from a page that had been torn from a book. The sight of the words wrapping around his pointed ear made her heart thunder.

She carefully uncreased the folded fox, his body unfurling, revealing what he really was. Alistair absorbed the printed words inside, one by one, knowing what she was reading and also what was waiting at the end of the page.

She couldn't bring herself to skip ahead and spoil the ending.

The surprising yet inevitable conclusion.

The fox was a poem. An epigraph from *The Little Red House* that she and her brother both knew by heart. A verse they'd used as a song, and a secret handshake, and a key that unlocked their hidden world.

She couldn't feel the train sway or see the lighting flicker overhead. It was only Alex and Ilya's writing now. The entire world stepped away, fading into humbled, reverent silence as she read the page, the last word waiting patiently at the bottom, like a spell aching to be cast.

The end of *The Book of Briars* was the beginning of *The Little Red House.*

Not a spell, but proof a spell was broken.

If you're walking in the wood one day
and feel a wind from far away
that carries scent of spice and dew
of memories you almost knew

Then look around, beyond the haze
to knotholes that go on for days
Or you might glimpse a wreath of thorns
and through it, things with crooked horns

Then rest assured, for without fail
You've found a path to Briarvale

Further Reading

AN EXCERPT FROM THE NEXT BOOK IN THE
BRIAR ARCHIVE:

THE BRIAR SOCIETY: CHAPTER ONE

Endri 1

꧁ꕥ꧂

When you get a random trove of hundreds of magically clandestine documents quite literally dumped into your inbox, there's only one logical response: organize.

Okay, fine, maybe I started reading a bit first, because who wouldn't? A secret society, hidden websites, and entire year's worth of events happening right under our noses . . . But I soon realized that without some sense of organization, nothing was going to make any sense.

I've done my best to group these materials in a way that makes narrative sense, falling roughly into three acts. From what I was able to gather in working backwards and reading everything through, most of these materials appeared to the Briars at random, with no warning or any kind of set schedule. Luckily for me, I also received the Briars' accompanying forum responses to each enigmatic post, or I don't think I'd have had any guiding sense as to where this story was going. But to know where this strange new story ends, you need to know where it starts.

Let's call this the beginning of Act One. A beginning born from a message written by a dear, and long-lost friend.

The_Well:

"Welcome to The Briar Society."

Like Jurassic Park, but not a disaster. I've rehearsed that line a hundred times. I'd never admit how excited I am because these are just my daydreams. Still, I do dream about a moment where I introduce dozens of people to a secret literary society that works in the shadows to fight for the light. For now, though, it's me, Bash, and Aether, working in a cold brownstone, fighting for the last crispy wonton. The total sum membership of the Briar Society since the manor fell, and we've been on the run.

How did we get here? The past 18 months have been a blur of panic, pain, and revelation.

It started with the box. That was the beginning. The locked coffin containing what the Monarchs dubbed the "Encyclopedia Magimystica." I'd just come to the manor, and Ascender wanted me to focus on the box. I was reluctant because, well, locked coffins, in my opinion, should mostly stay that way. The lock itself looked like a fancy skeleton key wrapped around a letter B. The teeth of the key kind of looked like two number 3s. Ascender said he'd half-remembered that symbol for decades, and it might've even been where he got the idea for Basecamp 33. "B33." I love a good lore reveal, but the coffin was magimystically sealed, the Monarchs had spent years trying to open it to no avail, and we eventually moved on to the rest of the manor's library and trying to repair the digital catalog that had been destroyed in the initial raid.

It was my idea to recruit Aether for that job, and I'm glad I did. We wouldn't have that database, or the well if it weren't for him.

Then things started crumbling, the Silver reared their heads again, and Ascender sacrificed himself to try and protect us all. The determiner spell didn't reach to the manor, so we were on borrowed time. We started offloading books and objects to secret locations while trying to figure out where we were going to go and what we were going to do when the Silver came back.

Then Bash and Aether found what was essentially the table of contents for the coffin. The "Encyclopedia Magimystica" was actually a collected history and knowledge of something called the Briar Society. A network of organizations, or "branches," that existed in the Book of the Wild for centuries, dedicated to the exploration, protection, and benevolent practice of magic.

In those last days at the manor, my sole focus turned to finding a way to open the coffin. Yes, it felt like hope, whatever was inside that box, but it was also Ascender's unfulfilled wish, and I owed him that much.

This first message, posted by a user called "The_Well" in a hidden area of the Ackerly Green forum called "The Briar Society," caught everyone who could see it quite off-guard. This area of the forum appeared to be restricted to about thirty-five Mountaineers, all of whom rapidly alternated between the shock of finding the message at all, and that of surmising the identity of the post's author.

Though they didn't explicitly identify themself in the post, there was only one person who could have written this message. One person close enough to Bash and Aether to recruit them to her cause, one person who we knew had been at Monarch's Manor with Ascender when he performed the Determiner-12 spell, a dangerously experimental protection spell which created a safeguarding veil around Ackerly Green and the Mountaineers but failed to protect the Manor, costing Ascender his life.

"Does this strike anyone else as funny?" Augustus_Octavian responded, via a comment on the forum thread that this post had created. "It's about Endri, but it doesn't seem to be posted by Endri. It references Bash and Aether in the third person, so I doubt it's by either of them."

Despite having been in regular contact with Eaves since the *Search for Magiq* events of the summer of 2019, no one had heard from Endri, or any of the other original Basecamp 33 leaders, since the Day of Change, 2017. Eaves had also not given any indication of having heard from them. So, it was more than a little strange to read what could only be Endri's words now, especially when they seemed less like a public-facing forum post and more like the private confessions of a personal journal.

This missive, wherever it came from, seemed to confirm that she had remained with Ascender since the Day of Change, as the Mountaineers had suspected after learning of his sacrifice during *The Search for Magiq*. But what *Bash and Aether* had been up to until now had remained a mystery, as was whoever had posted this indirect message to a hidden area of the forum, and why.

"Could it be that this is something that was written privately by Endri but then transmitted to us by "The Well", whatever that is?" wondered Wyvern. "Like a journal entry or something. It also seems like it's in a quote format, not written directly by the Well, if that makes sense, like it was taken from somewhere else and copied here." Neither Wyvern nor any of the other members of this new group had yet discovered the hidden application sharing this information with them, only the resulting posts on the forum. It wasn't until later that the Mountaineers would discover the forum posts were copies of content being shared from a central database hidden within Ackerly Green's own site.

Sorrel agreed that the message read most like a journal entry, which begged another question: "If the Well they found is

THE BOOK OF BRIARS

what/who sent this message, do our Three Musketeers know it was sent?"

The next message, which appeared a few days later, wouldn't answer Sorrel's question exactly, but it would provide more insight into the last days of the Manor, and all but confirm Endri as the proprietor of these thoughts.

Endri 2

The_Well:

Dreaming about fire. In the end, that's how the Manor fell, and I'm *still* getting my head around it. There's no way of knowing if the Silver caused it or if it was something as simple as faulty wiring. The place *was* old, but I wouldn't put the Silver above burning it down if they couldn't have its contents. The rest of the Monarchs had moved on. Knatz was in another country, and almost everything had been offloaded at that point anyway. Most everything except the coffin.

We'd tried everything to open it, but it seemed like it was a lock that had lost its key.

But—Aether and Bash were working on the genius idea of actually using the "aetherization" trap to gain access to the contents. It started when I found an entry in the Manor's database about research into the process of "aetherization." They posited that maybe that didn't mean destroyed at all and that the contents, the knowledge in the coffin whether material or not, could be somehow reconstituted by the safe keepers, instead of being utterly destroyed. They wondered why you would allow such precious contents to be destroyed without some way of safeguarding it.

Bash and Aether's Plan Z proposal was to break the coffin open and trigger the trap that would dissolve the "Encyclopedia Magimystica" while Aether's mind was "logged into" the Wi-Fi mesh we'd set up in the Manor. He would then try and capture the data of the aetherized books, effectively scanning them into a database. It was speculative, nothing more than theory, and none of us knew if the books would turn to magimystic data, some unscannable gibberish, or nothing at all—just dust.

We also didn't know if the Encyclopedia Magimystica was an actual book collection. What if the coffin held nothing but nebulous information? What if there was a real body in the coffin, and you could ask the corpse questions about anything? What if there *were* books inside but because they weren't supposed to be in this age, they would turn to nothing like *The Little Red House*?

So we sat on the idea and stewed (and had dreams/nightmares about corpses who were fathomless fonts of knowledge.)

But the fire made the choice for us. We were a skeleton crew at that point. Bash, Aether, Wilona, Marcus, and me. I saw flickering outside my bedroom window and thought it was fireworks. Silent fireworks. That image sticks with me even now.

But the light was the Manor going up in flames.

I woke everyone up, forcing them to the basement, to an old waterworks passage just in case the Silver was outside, but Aether and Bash refused because they knew the coffin was going to be destroyed. They knew how much it meant, to Ascender, to me, to the new age. They wanted to try their plan while the building was coming down.

Aether would log into the Wi-Fi magimystically, Bash would monitor the database Aether would attempt to scan the information into, and I would smash the coffin.

We tried. I still mull the sequence of events. I couldn't smash open the coffin; it was protected, so Bash and I dragged it out of the library, down the smoke-filled hall, and dumped it over the stair railing, down to the first-floor entryway. It cracked open, and I saw the books inside just before they vanished, just before a wall collapsed, and fire flooded the first floor. Then the power blew. We had to carry Aether's unconscious body out of a second-floor window, hoping he'd escaped the network before it went down.

We'd failed pretty spectacularly, but there were only so many variables we could account for. Fire hadn't been one of them. Bash and I hid in a motel outside of Philly with Aether's body. He was unconscious for nearly twelve hours when we finally got an alert on Bash's phone. He was alive, but we'd need fiber optic speed and clarity to get him back into his body. We couldn't go back to Philly. There were probably other options, but at the time there was only one person I could think of to help us.

Saberlane.

We were taking Aether to New York.

To Ackerly Green Publishing.

A t this point, it was clear that Endri was the only person who could be writing these messages. Nowhere in her messages did she mention any dates, times, or even seasons, so there was no way of knowing how long ago everything with the Manor happened, or when the trio had reached New York, if at all. If they had, this was certainly the first anyone had heard of their trip.

"Since these entries are clearly from the past, we can't know where they are at this moment," BrokenVoid observed, but even if the Mountaineers couldn't know where the trio currently were, wouldn't they have known if they had made it to Ackerly Green? If Endri, Bash, and Aether made it to Saberlane before his passing, was this information he would have withheld from them? And if so, why?

Both Nimueh and Augo realized, "Saberlane was on the same side of the Determiner spell as us. Maybe they never reached him."

With the Determiner spell still safeguarding the Mountaineers, the forum, and Ackerly Green from most of the outside world, Robert noted that it was entirely possible that Endri, Bash, and Aether had been physically unable to find Saberlane, much like when Saberlane had gone looking for Martin Rank.

For my part, if the trio had reached out to Saberlane before his passing or had attempted any other means of contact with Ackerly Green, I knew nothing of it. All I knew, I was learning belatedly, following the trail of Endri's messages along with everyone else.

Endri 3

The_Well:

We were pretty much lost once we got to NYC.

We'd had no contact from Marcus or Wil and no way to reach Knatz. Aether's souped-up wireless EEG was lost in the fire (he'd kept it with him ever since Kemetic Solutions, as a way of getting back to his body if this very thing were to happen again.) And it looked like the Determiner had worked, we were just on the wrong side of the wall.

Aether (or rather Aether's consciousness) messaged Bash (who was watching over his body in the van) with details about a package being held in a Hell's Kitchen post office (which he'd ordered the night of the fire while drifting around the internet like a self-aware Google search). I spent the better part of a day trying to contact or find Saberlane, his assistant Catherine, or Ackerly Green Publishing. All to no avail.

Luckily, I have a few librarian friends in the city, and one, a rocker Canadian ex-pat who works at an elementary school in the Village, was more than willing to help me with no questions asked. We needed ultra-high-speed internet, the new EEG and gigabit transceiver Bash had picked up from the post office, a quiet room, and several hours alone. She set us up in the school library (librarians rule), and by morning, Aether was back in his body.

And he had a plan.

Aether can sometimes see wells while he's out of his body. It's how he found the Oracular Eye and brought it to the Mountaineers. He thinks it's because wells are kind of—"digimystical." They, and some other elements of magic, sometimes blur the line between technological and magimystical. He supposed that wells were kind of like digimystical databases, where real and ephemeral things can be "stored."

While he was out of his body, and Bash was circling the AGP office, he could "see" the AGP well, even though I couldn't see the office or anyone inside it. He figured either the well was outside the Determiner wall, or it's bridging it.

His proposal—

What if we try and harness it, the AGP well, using his power and Bash's IT skills, and create a sort of user interface for it. A catalog UI that I could design from my reference experience and use to pick and choose what to pull in to the well. Like the aetherized Encyclopedia Magimystica, for example.

It sounded like an incredible game-changer. And we had absolutely no way of knowing if it would work or how the hell to do it. And more importantly, we needed a refuge, we needed money, and if we were going to attempt this, the well interface, we needed to try and get back the manor materials we'd squirreled away.

I wonder, Aether is your average but clever 20-year-old when he's . . . "corporeally intact," but when his mind is free of his body, he hatches plans like the Kemetic Solutions escape and the well UI. It's monumentally dangerous to leave him outside of his body, but who knows what things he could think up if he realized his full potential.

It was Bash's idea to use clues from TMP to find Deirdre's brownstone. Either to enlist her help if she was there or to hide out if she wasn't.

She wasn't.

A little breaking and entering later, and we had a temporary base of operations. From there, we set out to do everything else.

Almost nine difficult and uncertain months later, we retrieved less than half of what we hid.

Wil was lost, Marcus went into hiding, and we spent most of the year squatting in the brownstone, getting odd jobs in the city to survive, and using questionable methods and even more questionable magic to try and execute Aether's plan before the age ended and/or magic was completely gone.

We came to lovingly call Aether's plan *The W.E.L.L.*.

In our efforts to fight darkness from the shadows, exact a plan that seemed dangerous if not impossible, and retrieve the destroyed Encyclopedia Magimystica, we became closer than ever, the three of us. The merry band of orphans had become a family.

More than a family actually.

We'd become The Briar Society.

"Well, well, well . . ." Wyvern replied to the post. "It sounds like maybe their plan *kind* of worked? The W.E.L.L. might very well (oops, no pun intended) be a bridge, like they had discussed. If they were trying to connect to it digitally and put things in or out of it, it sounds possible that they accidentally put more in than they planned. I mean it's not like we know a whole lot about how digital data and magic interact, really, so something got dropped down the well that they hadn't intended. Maybe Endri's journal got pulled in and spit out here, on the 'other side' of the AGP well, like a wormhole."

Wyvern's reasoning was solid, but the question of intention was still in play. Was Endri writing these entries expecting someone would read them? Maybe, as BrokenVoid proposed, she was writing them in the hopes that she would be able to send them through the W.E.L.L. to reach the Mountaineers. It seemed increasingly likely, after all, that the W.E.L.L. was the processing power behind the forum account sending them this information in the first place. And if that were all true, would the Mountaineers be able to send a message back?

Another thing that struck everyone as odd were the italicized sections within the entry. Not only was the formatting different from the rest of the post, but as Augo noted, "It sounds like a different 'voice;' a different writing style than the rest we presume was written by Endri."

"It's definitely an odd part," Robert agreed. "We're almost hearing Endri's thoughts there. Like you said, if this was a journal, it wouldn't be in italics."

"Maybe we're getting two records jumbled together here?" Tinker suggested. "Like, a work notebook and a personal journal combo? Maybe Endri didn't choose to send us these entries herself but something else is distributing the information we need?"

"Has anyone tried messaging the W.E.L.L. forum account to see if they respond or if something goes through?" Eden asked. "A bridge could go both ways."

BrokenVoid volunteered to try and send a message but received no response. It was evident, though—and about to become more so —that even if the W.E.L.L. wasn't sentient, it was following some kind of internal logic. How else could anyone begin to explain the connection between Endri's apparently private thoughts and the documents that the W.E.L.L. was about to produce, which would appear to be from another time and place entirely?

The Story Continues:
The Briar Society: Chapter One

Available from:
www.AckerlyGreen.com
And other major booksellers

You Can Further Explore the World of Magiq By:

Discovering Your Magimystic Guild At:
www.magiq.guide

And Joining the Mountaineers in the Search for Magiq At:
forum.AckerlyGreen.com

Follow @AckerlyGreen on Instagram

About C.J. Bernstein

C.J. Bernstein is an author, maker, interactive storyteller, and proprietor of a magimystic publishing house.

He lives in the Pacific Northwest (as all good Ebenguards should) with his husband, kids, and dogs.

instagram.com/cjbofficially

Also by C.J. Bernstein

CPSIA information can be obtained
at www.ICGtesting.com
Printed in the USA
BVHW071318260421
605863BV00004B/784